THE LAST MAN ON EARTH CLUB

THE LAST MAN ON EARTH CLUB

PAUL R. HARDY

Copyright © 2011 Paul R. Hardy

Cover image © 2013 f9photos
Used under licence from shutterstock.com

This is a work of fiction. Names, characters, places and incidents either are products of the author's imagination or are used fictitiously. Any resemblance to actual events or locales or persons, living or dead, is entirely coincidental. All rights reserved.

ISBN: 1466361824
ISBN-13: 978-1466361829

CONTENTS

1:	Group Therapy	1
2:	Individual Therapy	29
3:	Day to Day	63
4:	Team Building	79
5:	Progress	105
6:	Mysteries	143
7:	Justice	177
8:	Desire	197
9:	Enemies	227
10:	Moving House	253
11:	Events	279
12:	Genocide	327
13:	Diagnoses	367
	Post-Apocalypse	409
	Moment of Extinction	413

PART ONE
GROUP THERAPY

1. GROUP

The forest along the valley had been safe for thousands of years. No deadly animals hid among the leaves to poison and devour the unwary. Floods never swept away soil and trees. Fire never consumed the branches. Volcanic ash never choked the landscape to make a desert of barren cinders. The sun never blighted the land with ultraviolet radiation that could kill everything down to the last microbe.

Nor had the forest ever been stripped of leaves and branches by rain so acidic it could mark steel. It had not known the blast, the light, the heat, or the radiation from a nuclear fireball. Survivors of a terrible war had never fled through the trees, pursued by robotic hunters. Gene-mutated horrors had never oozed across the leaf litter, digesting all the biomass they could absorb. Invaders from a distant universe had never swept down from the skies, darting tentacles among the branches to drag the last remaining people to slavery on another world.

Convincing my patients of this was sometimes difficult. Many had lived through similar horrors before they were evacuated to the safety and security of Hub. Even though they knew they were on another world, it still took time for them to accept that they'd escaped their apocalypse; but the peaceful setting eventually proved beneficial to even the most traumatised survivors.

I was based at one of the smaller therapy centres on Hub, designed as a secluded retreat for groups of up to fifty refugees from dying worlds. There were no roads through the forest and no public transport; the only way in was by air. As you flew up the valley, you saw the ground level out for a few hundred metres, and before it climbed again, you came upon the meadow by the banks where the river parted the forest, giving us the clearing where we'd built the centre.

The main building was deliberately designed not to look too advanced, so as to provide a point of comfort for refugees from worlds not used to the soaring architecture of Hub Metro. The façade looked exactly like weathered stone, though there was not a single quarry on the planet. Something that resembled the grain of polished wood framed the doorways and windows, though we never used timber for construction. It even had rivulets of ivy flowing up the wall – ivy that wasn't even remotely real, and could be adjusted from the master controls for the building. A few smaller structures stood nearby, providing shelter for vehicles and a workspace for the groundskeeper. Further up the valley, a microwave collector gathered power from satellites while a retransmitter kept us in touch with the dataflow coming from the planet's capital, fifty kilometres away.

The last patients had left a month before, to be replaced now by a special group of only six people. Each of them had suffered in a way that was unique, even for those I work with, so we had reserved the entire building and shuttered anything we did not need. We only required two therapists – myself and my assistant – but even so, the rest of the staff outnumbered the patients by eight to one. We had a full infirmary staffed with four nurses and a physical therapist; two doctors permanently on call; kitchen and housekeeping staff who mainly served the others who lived and worked there; a few administrators who kept the place running; and a security team big enough to guard a group three times the size. In such an isolated location, we had little fear of attack from outside. The main danger was the patients themselves.

After they'd had a night to settle in, we brought them together in the central lounge, which also functioned as a small kitchen and dining room they would be able to use later on. Each took their place in a circle of chairs, along with myself and my assistant. My first task would be to introduce them to each other, an important first step towards bringing them together as a group.

Olivia objected before I could open my mouth.

"I don't see why I should be here," she said. "It's only more talking. What good's that going to do?" She was older than the rest, with a deep-lined face, hard-worn calloused hands and sun-beaten skin. She'd left her hair ragged and unwashed, and I knew from her file that she was still cutting it herself. There was a finger missing on her left hand, and scars on her arms that looked like bite marks. Her clothes were copies of the styles she'd worn on her own world, practical and hard-wearing: coarse woollen shirts and slacks, along with boots that could cope with rough terrain. The only thing that looked like it came from Hub were her glasses, which she needed both for astigmatism and translation.

"Well, Olivia," I said, "your previous therapists say you've often pointed out how different your experiences are. I don't think you'll find that's a problem with this group. Everyone here is just like you."

"Huh," she snorted, and looked suspiciously at the other five, whose own attitudes ranges from nervousness to reticence, as is normal in a first group session.

I turned to them. "Each one of you is the last survivor of your species. Each one of you is from a different universe where something terrible happened, and each one of you is the only survivor of that event. It's been very difficult to help people like you because there are so few who share your experience. But we've found more of you in the last couple of years than we usually do, so we've been able to set up this group. I hope you'll find it helpful to be among others who've shared your unique loss.

"My name is Doctor Asha Singh. I'm the group leader, and your therapist for individual sessions. This is Veofol, my assistant." I indicated him, sitting next to me and smiling a greeting, wearing the ordinary clothes of a Hub resident: a neutral, sober mix of styles influenced by the fashions of a hundred worlds. "He'll be available to talk to if I'm not around, and one of us will be on call twenty four hours a day."

"Hello," said Veofol with a voice as friendly as his smile.

"What are you, an elf?" asked Olivia. Veofol's physique was a little outside human normal, with the slender build and long limbs of a species used to the light touch of microgravity.

"No, no," he said. "I'm a bit tall and thin, that's all. Same as everyone else from my universe, and that's just because we live in orbit. We're not elves. Just another kind of human."

"Is that what you call it..." muttered Olivia, shaking her head.

I ignored her and went on. "To begin with, there are some ground rules you all need to agree to. Firstly: you must have respect for one another. Each of you has a right to speak and be heard, but not to prevent anyone else from speaking. You may feel very strongly about what you have to say, but please remember that others do too.

"Secondly: You all have a right to privacy. While these sessions are recorded to help me run the group, they are confidential, and only I and Veofol have access. Each of you should respect this and not repeat anything you hear in the group.

"Thirdly: You need to be here on time. If you have trouble remembering when sessions are scheduled, there'll be chimes throughout the centre ten minutes before each one.

"And finally, if you no longer wish to participate, please do everyone the courtesy of attending a final session to say goodbye. Now, how does that sound?"

"I don't want to participate. This is my last meeting. Goodbye," said Olivia, folding her arms. She was determined to be the problem patient, much as I'd expected after reading the reports from her previous therapists.

"I'm sorry to hear that, Olivia. It seems a shame, since we haven't really started. Can you tell us why you don't want to be here?"

"You damn well know why I don't want to be here! It's a waste of time. I'm not going to get better and neither's anyone else. I've had six of you poking at me while I've been here, and none of you could do a damned thing. It's useless and I don't want any more of it."

As much as she was trying to disrupt the session, she'd given me an excellent way to involve the others. "Does anyone else feel that therapy is useless?" I asked.

Kwame raised a trembling finger. He wore a business suit from his world, as though ready to go before a press conference: a cream linen jacket with sharply creased trousers and a zigzag pinstripe shirt buttoned to the collar. I nodded and he spoke in a slow, solemn manner, concentrating to overcome his aphasia. "I think… that perhaps Olivia has forgotten how much we have gained from our stay on Hub. We may not receive all we would wish for, but I can assure those who are new to this world that they are very kind to us here."

"Hasn't stopped you being a crackpot, has it?" said Olivia. They'd both been on Hub for a while, and had met before at the Psychiatric Centre. By all reports they hadn't been friends.

"I have not changed my goal. I am as determined as the last time we met."

"And that's why they sent you here, wasn't it? Am I right? They're fed up with you, so they packed you off here with everyone else they can't cure of being the last man on earth. They don't want you to get better, they want you to shut up!"

"I admit… the thought had crossed my mind–"

"So you agree with me?"

"That is not what I–"

"You're embarrassing to them, that's what it is, because they don't want to lift a finger to stop it happening again. We're all embarrassing."

A new voice spoke up. "Can I say a word?"

"Iokan. Yes, please, go ahead." Iokan's chair had been floated in from the infirmary, and he still wore a hospital gown and cotton trousers. He was emaciated, jaundiced, only just back from the edge of death, but with a light in his eyes that simply ignored his physical state. He spoke his own language, and the rest of us read the translation as it sprang up on our various systems.

"I don't know what it's like for the rest of you, but I believe I was brought here for a reason." He coughed, rasping with weak lungs. "I think all of us are here for a reason."

"What do you mean, 'reason'? What reason?" asked Olivia, straight in with her usual bile once her glasses translated his words.

"Olivia. Iokan wants to speak," I said.

"He's talking rubbish!"

"He has as much of a right to speak as you do, and you've already told us what you think. Iokan's only just been rescued, remember, and he's still unwell. If you carry on like this, it's not going to help."

Olivia grudgingly surveyed his wasted form. "Fine," she said, and looked elsewhere.

Iokan continued: "As I was saying, I think we're all here for a reason, or perhaps many reasons. I don't know what those reasons might be. But I'd like to find out."

"Thank you, Iokan," I said. "Although I think Olivia raised a very valid point." She looked round, surprised. Kwame looked up too, just as shocked that I was agreeing with Olivia. "She said we can't cure you of being the last man – or woman – on earth, and she's right. Nothing can change that. What we *can* do is help you learn to live with it. Now, that won't be easy, and you're all going to have to do a lot of work in the group and in individual therapy. But I believe it's possible, if you're willing to try. So, does anyone else have any opinions about the rules?"

I couldn't help glancing at Olivia first, but she sank into her folded arms. The three who hadn't yet spoken stayed quiet. "Does anyone else have anything to say?" I asked; but none of them volunteered. In group therapy, it's vital for the members to be willing to at least talk to each other. Someone like Olivia can disrupt that, but the real danger was that they didn't participate at all. So I fell back on an old tactic to get them started.

"Okay, then. What I'd like to do is get everyone to introduce themselves to the group. You've probably done this kind of thing before but today I'd like to do it differently. I'd like each of you to introduce someone else to the group."

They perked up a bit, some looking worried. Olivia sneered as I went on. "So what you'll have to do is talk to one of the others, find out their story, and then explain it to everyone else. Katie, is that all right with you?"

Katie turned her head a perfect forty degrees and locked her eyes on me, always a little unnerving because she never blinked and hardly seemed to breathe. She was tall and heavily built, with close-cropped hair that revealed a trio of metallic sockets on the back of her head. She wore a shapeless jumpsuit that was practical in all circumstances and spoke in fluent Interversal, which she'd learnt astonishingly quickly. "I will comply with all reasonable requests."

"Do you think this request is reasonable?"

"I am not an effective communicator."

"But you'll try?"

She processed for a moment. "I will try."

"Good. Pew?"

"Yes?" Pew looked back at me, distracted from staring at the holes in Katie's head. He had the pudgy build of someone who'd spent too long sitting down, and wore clothes from his stay at Hub University: a black hooded top that helped him hide away; comfortable, scuffed training shoes; and the loose, pocketed trousers that had been in style a year before. His hesitancy had nothing to do with his skill in Interversal, which was normally fluent. "Uh. I'll do it. I'm, I'm not sure I'll be any good..."

"That's okay. I'm sure you'll be fine." He smiled a little, but was still nervous. I turned to the last member of the group. "Liss?"

"Oh, is it me?" Liss stopped toying with her earrings and perked up as she read her own name in her contact lenses. "Yeah, sure! I'll just go on and on, though," she chattered back in her own language, "I'll get carried away and start talking and I won't get halfway there before the end. Hope you don't mind!" Out of all the group, she'd made the most deliberate effort to look good, and had deliberately overdone it. She wore lipstick in a shade of pink I could hardly imagine on anyone over the age of twelve, a top that flounced in a darker shade of pink over a black vest, then a skirt in another pinkish hue and ankle boots that matched the lipstick perfectly.

"Do we have to listen to *that*?" asked Olivia.

I ignored her and smiled at Liss. "Don't worry. I'll let you know if you need to wrap it up. Okay, what I'll ask you to do is write your names down on pieces of paper, then you all pick out someone's name, and that'll be whose story you tell. I'll give you twenty minutes to introduce yourselves to each other, and then we'll come back to the group and take it from there. Veofol?"

Veofol already had paper and pens ready, and distributed them among the group. Most of them were comfortable with the old technology, though Katie had to be shown how to use a pen. She rapidly gained an ability to write her name in a perfect sans serif font, while Veofol collected the names in a bowl.

Olivia, however, was having none of it. She sat with her arms folded and would not touch the pen and paper placed before her. "You didn't ask *me* for permission, did you?"

"I'm sorry, Olivia, did you have an objection?" I asked.

"Well. I don't want you to think I don't respect you," she sneered, "but I don't want to know any of you, and I don't bloody want to be here."

"Can you at least be polite?" asked Kwame, irritated.

"Why should I? I didn't ask to be here! Did you?"

"That is not the point–"

"Of course it's the bloody point! I've been dragged here against my will and I don't want any part of it!"

Liss was perplexed by the venom. "I don't get it. What have you got against us?"

"And I definitely don't want to know this tart," said Olivia, disgusted by every inch of her. A moment later, Liss gasped at the translation.

"This is a waste of time," said Kwame, looking at me. "Why was she included in this?"

"To punish me, that's why–"

"Will you be quiet?" he snapped back at her.

"No I will not! I don't want to be here, I don't want to know any of you, and you don't want to know me!" Kwame's eyes flashed with anger and his mouth flapped at words, struggling to find a retort through the aphasia. I was about to intervene – but someone else got there first.

"I want to know you," said Iokan, in that calm, gentle voice of his. Everyone looked to him, and the room fell silent. Olivia took off her glasses to check the translation system hadn't been broken, then jammed them back on her face.

"Rubbish!"

"I want to know you."

"Utter rubbish!"

"Not at all. I want to know how you came here, and all the things that happened to you." He smiled with complete innocence, meaning every word he said. It gave even Olivia a moment of pause.

"You're talking rot."

"Are you worried I'll find out too much?"

"You're the one should be worried. You don't know where I've been."

"Then I'll just have to find out, won't I?"

She leaned forward. "Fine. See where it gets you."

"You still need to write your name, Olivia," I said. She grabbed paper and pen and scribbled it down. "And if you could put it in the bowl, please?"

Olivia glared at Iokan and held out the slip of paper. "*He* can tell my story."

I looked to Iokan. He assented with a smile and took her name. "And whose story will you tell?" he asked of Olivia.

"We'll see, won't we?" she said, reaching for the bowl and taking a name.

2. KWAME

Indigenous Sapient Report
Expedition HKAJ-778662-002
Submission: HD y271.m2.w3.d4
Author: Cmdr. Chesgryn, H

Summary

The *IUS Calculus* was sent to study the long term results of what may be the most devastating nuclear war ever discovered during a routine survey. The planetary atmosphere contains a high percentage of the radioactive isotope cobalt-60, which may have been released by a 'cobalt bomb', a thermonuclear weapon jacketed by large quantities of the mineral. With enough cobalt, this weapon can spread a cloud of radioactive dust across a planet and end life upon the surface within a few decades.

After uneventful transit to the target universe, a planetary survey revealed numerous radioactive decay isotopes in hotspots associated with the ruins of cities, indicating a general thermonuclear exchange in addition to the use of a cobalt bomb. Vegetation was dramatically reduced, algal blooms were absent, and IR surveys found no evidence of warm blooded animal life on land or in shallow seas. At least some of the damage seemed to have resulted from UV exposure, as the ozone layer was severely depleted. We estimated that 86 years (plus or minus five years) had passed since the nuclear war.

After several weeks of orbital surveillance we moved to low altitude drone surveys and were surprised to detect a small EMF anomaly that suggested the use of AC electrical equipment. The anomaly was located ten metres inside an artificial tunnel system within a mountain range running along the eastern side of this world's version of Africa. The mission archaeologist suggested it was thoeretically possible for a pre-war electrical system to still be functional, so we made a landing in order to conduct a more detailed survey.

The geological team were quickly able to map the underground complex in detail. It was composed of two main sections: a large set of chambers that began about six metres into the rock and extended another five hundred metres inside (dubbed the 'shallow complex'); then, linked by tunnels, a much deeper structure nearly a full kilometre within the mountain (the 'deep complex'). The shallow complex seemed to have been made by extending pre-existing cave systems, while the deep complex was entirely artificial.

The shallow complex should have been safe behind a two metre thick door, but this had been opened at some point after the war. Inside, we found several sets of skeletonised human remains. The EMF anomaly was traced to an emergency lighting system still running despite the passage of time. The shallow complex seemed to be designed to hold several hundred individuals, perhaps the core of a post-war recolonisation of the world. What was unusual was the method in which they attempted to wait out the war; the chambers were filled with hundreds of devices resembling burial caskets. Approximately eighty per cent were occupied by human skeletons, and the caskets were later confirmed to be hibernation devices.

Upon venturing into the deep complex, we found further blast doors, but these had never been breached by the occupants. The atmosphere was almost completely without humidity, limiting corrosion, and it proved to be possible to remotely activate the door mechanisms. The deep complex was designed for a few tens of individuals, clearly intended for the purposes of command and control. It contained offices, a communications centre, a broadcast studio, and further hibernation chambers. These seemed to be of better quality and were still powered, though all but one had failed. In this last one, we found a still-living human male who was apparently forty years old.

We would have preferred to take his hibernation unit back to Hub, or at least to the *Calculus*, where we could have revived him with greater care. Unfortunately, the equipment was too fragile to move, and as the power supply (a radioisotope thermoelectric generator) was virtually depleted, we could not leave him in hibernation until we were able to return with better equipment. We could not even risk replacing the power source with one of our own. Instead, we spent two weeks studying the systems until we felt we could safely begin the revival process.

The expedition's medical staff exercised the utmost caution, but an emergency three hours into the procedure starved his brain of oxygen for approximately twenty seconds, and may have resulted in some minor brain damage. Nevertheless, the revival was completed successfully and he regained consciousness with no other incident. His initial reaction was one of understandable surprise and fear. We made every attempt to appear non-threatening, but still had to sedate him before he could be removed to the surface.

As per evacuation protocols for endangered human species, our priority was to take him to Hub for medical attention, and accordingly we made haste to regain orbit and depart. The survivor was transferred from our custody at 05:46 on HD y271.m2.w3.d2, and placed in quarantine at Grainger L1 station, while we made preparations to return to his universe and continue our exploration.

3. GROUP

"Who wants to go first?" I asked. There were no immediate volunteers as I looked around the group, until Kwame sighed. "Kwame, would you like to start?"

"I would not. I would like Olivia to begin. She was assigned to introduce me, and I would like her to complete her slander quickly."

"I'm not going to lie about you, if that's what you think," said Olivia. "I'm not whitewashing it."

"I am sure you will enjoy yourself."

She turned to the group. "He's a mass murderer," she said, then turned back to Kwame. "Am I right?"

He paused, irritated. "That is substantially correct."

"And he killed, what was it, four billion people?"

"Approximately. Yes."

"Because he says he was the president of his country. And then his country went to war with the rest of the world and everyone died and when the IU turned up he was the only one left in some hibernation thingamyjig."

"I am not denying it."

"And ever since he got here he's been trying to get them to put him on trial for genocide. You'd think he'd keep his mouth shut, but no, this one wants to be put in prison, as though we're not already in prison…"

"Are you finished?"

"No I am not!" she snapped back. "Because what he's not saying is that he's talking out of his backside."

Kwame was taken aback. "What?"

"What happened was some anarchist or terrorist or something set off a nuclear bomb in his capital city, whole place goes boom, and quite frankly it makes me glad we never invented those things. But anyway," she offhandedly jabbed a thumb at Kwame, "he's in the government, secretary of sport or something…"

"Minister of Culture," said Kwame.

"…something stupid, and he's off on a foreign visit and the rest of the government gets killed. So he gets promoted to President, finds the terrorists and sends in the troops, only the terrorists have got friends in some other country and they threaten to start a nuclear war. So to make sure that doesn't happen, this one here sets up a massive bomb in, what was it, a cobalt mine?"

"The initiative was begun by the previous administration. But yes, it was in a cobalt mine."

"And this bomb can kill everyone with cobalt, don't ask me how it does that, I suppose it paints everyone blue, hah!"

"It was a massively destructive weapon that spread radioactive dust–"

"And laughing boy here sets it up so it'll go off if anyone attacks them. And guess what, somebody attacks them, the bomb goes off, and everyone dies except him. Did I miss anything?"

Kwame paused, trying to find a response. "You missed a great deal."

"You're right. What I missed was that nobody even knew the thing was going to work. They hadn't tested it, they just built it and told everyone it was there. So of course they got attacked, because everybody thought they were talking out of their backsides. And now he wants someone to slap him on the wrist for blowing up the world. And you know what? They keep saying no. What a surprise."

Kwame looked pained, one trembling hand going to his temples.

"Olivia," I said, "if you're only going to be hurtful and offensive–"

"I'm not finished!" she cried. "The thing is, he used to be married. He had a wife. And a family. Three children. They were in town when the bomb went off. Only they didn't die quick. They got radiation poisoning, and when he got back from abroad, he had to watch that happen. You think about that. He's off in another country and his whole family dies and he doesn't. And he feels as though it should have been him, so he does stupid things. I saw it happen on my world. You're not responsible when you're like that." She turned to Kwame. "So there. I've solved your psychological problems."

Kwame looked stunned. "I... I think that, that is..." He paused to get hold of his floundering voice. "I will never understand you."

"Are you going to stop asking for a trial?"

He shook his head. "No. Grief is no excuse."

"Well don't say I didn't try to help."

4. LISS

Indigenous Sapient Report
Expedition LJHA-897189-002
Submission: HD y276.m1.w5.d2
Author: Cmdr. Gli, A-H-K

Summary
This may be the strangest world I have ever been fortunate enough to visit. The primary observation from the first probe was so remarkable that a manned expedition was sent immediately: although the Earth was there as usual, the Moon had been torn apart about a decade earlier. The smaller debris is currently

forming a ring system around the planet, while larger pieces are falling in on each other to create a new, smaller Moon that should become molten and spherical within a century, and perhaps consume the other fragments as time goes by. The opportunity to study something like the accretion phase of the solar system was, in itself, reason enough to come to this universe, but a detailed study of the planet's surface revealed a catalogue of remarkable oddities – and also, we fear, a human tragedy of enormous scale.

We first observed that the western coast of North America had suffered a minor basaltic flow, burying a wide area in lava. But this had then been 'frozen' in place by a network of installations that kept the area geologically stable by dampening molecular vibration across the region. Such large scale geo-engineering was far in advance of the average tech level we witnessed across the world. Other oddities included the vast, formless sculpture that lay across the North Island of New Zealand; the cities of Germany covered by domes for no apparent reason; the arctic microclimate in the Amazonian rainforest that persisted by no clear mechanism; a kilometre high wall that ran across south east Asia, perhaps marking a boundary; and the forest clearings in Rwanda which formed the face of a chimpanzee when seen from space. It went on and on.

And yet we saw no sign of the people who built these strange edifices. In our first survey, we saw not a single human being upon the planet, and while there were many automated transmissions providing ample evidence of recent inhabitation, we found nothing from any living members of the world's population. An initial descent to an Antarctic establishment where we hoped to find greater preservation than in other areas provided us with some evidence of what had happened. In the ice station, we found scattered piles of dust which matched the chemical composition of a human body with all water subtracted and some oxidisation of the remaining minerals. Further investigation revealed quantities of the same dust in almost every part of the world. As bizarre as it sounds, we believe every human being on the planet has been reduced to powder by a form of combustion, while other lifeforms seem to be unaffected.

We then found a survivor.

In some parts of the world, electricity was still being generated, and conurbations were clearly visible at night. It was in such a city, on the east coast of North America, that we detected the lone survivor by the lights of her ground vehicle. The woman parked at a retail establishment, went inside, then emerged with polymer bags full of goods, before driving to an apartment block less than a kilometre away.

We landed some distance from her apartment to avoid alarming her, and began covert surveillance. She rose each day at 07:00 and made her way to a building in the city by 09:00. There, she worked on a data entry process, typing information from forms into a computer. She would leave at 17:00, indicating her presence to the building computers by passing a magnetised disc over a sensor. She would then go home and watch pre-recorded entertainment programmes. Some days she would go to shops, which opened automatically, and from which she took whatever goods she needed. She used another magnetised disc to make a monetary transaction in each case. Throughout, she ignored the piles of dust that used to be human beings, unless they got in her way – in which case she tidied them up with a small vacuum cleaner she seemed to carry just for this purpose.

We decided we would have to make contact. After deciphering the local language and programming a translation unit, we visited her at home. She panicked on seeing us and ran into a kitchen, where she threatened us with a carving knife. We were nevertheless able to calm her down and explain that we were there to help her. Strangely, she accepted both the translation unit and our story of travel from another universe without needing much in the way of explanation. Given the oddness of her world, it is possible she was used to far stranger concepts.

She claimed the world's population had simply disappeared. She did not regard the piles of powder as human remains; instead, she said she was irritated that dust was piling up, and cleaned whenever she could. She demonstrated with her vacuum cleaner and complained that no one took trash away any more. We told her that her life was at risk as the world's automated systems were breaking down, and offered transport to the safety of Hub. She claimed to be perfectly happy to stay at home and watch her screenshows. We were only able to persuade her to come with us once we offered to bring along a collection of pre-recorded shows (along with her screenplayer), and made a promise to bring her back if the planet's population returned.

While she may have been of great use to the expedition as a guide, we chose to abide by the protocols concerning the rescue of survivors and immediately made the return journey to Hub, with a view to placing her in psychiatric care once she clears quarantine.

5. GROUP

"We'll follow a chain from person to person if we can," I said. "That makes Kwame the next one to speak. Kwame, is that okay?"

"I am fine…" he said, although he didn't look it.

"Do you want a drink?" asked Liss.

"Water. Please."

Liss went to the fountain in the corner and drew a cup for him. "Here you go!" she said, holding it out for him like a present. He drank deeply, clutching the cup with trembling hands, then addressed the group.

"I would like to introduce you to Liss Li'Oul, who, like all of us, has survived the end of the world."

"Well, it's not really the end of the world, I mean it's still there and everyone's coming back," she added with a smile.

"Yes. Well. Perhaps. Liss has told me she was quite ordinary, working at, as she calls it, a 'nine to five' job in a large city. She spoke of the tedium of the work and the stupidity of the people she worked with…"

"Oh, everyone says that, don't they? Everyone says they work with, you know, idiots, but nobody really means it."

"May I continue?"

"Oh, sorry!"

"She worked in what I believe was a recruitment agency, filtering applicants for jobs. Her world was more advanced than mine, and more fortunate. They seemed to live in peace with each other."

Liss shrugged. "We're just nice people!"

"Indeed. But nevertheless, all of them are gone. Liss reports that as she was working one day at a photocopier, she noticed a sudden silence. She found that every last person on her world had vanished without a trace. She searched, but could find no one. She still does not know what happened to them.

"Despite this, she is certain her people will return at some point in the future. I do not understand why she thinks this to be the case, but she is quite adamant on the matter."

"Well, it'd be just like them to go away and leave me all alone," said Liss. "It's probably just a trick. They used to do this to me when I was at college! They'd sneak off and leave me in a bar or a park or something. It was really mean. But they always came back."

"I do not wish to be unkind, but…" said Kwame, considering his words. But then he simply sighed. "I shall only add that after the event, she resumed her life as best she could, which was possible because the machines of the city continued to work after the disappearance of the inhabitants. She was found by an IU exploration team, and since then, she has been in psychiatric care. And that is all I can say about Liss Li'Oul."

6. PEW

Hub Chronicle
HD y273.m11.w2.d5
05:32

Soo concealed extinction while IU provided assistance
IU intervention with the Soo species has been suspended after it emerged that the Soo concealed the progressive extinction of a second human species on their world.

The IU has been providing technological advice to the Soo in order to avert an environmental catastrophe, but only on condition that they protect the remaining members of the other species, known as Pu.

At time of contact with the IU, the Pu population had been reduced to less than ten thousand, the majority of whom were held as slaves. Despite objections from many IU member species, assistance was nevertheless given to the Soo, who instituted a breeding programme to rebuild Pu numbers.

Following representations made last week by the Soo delegation to the IU ahead of an inspection scheduled for next year, it is now known that the breeding programme was a complete failure, and that this was deliberately concealed for at least two decades. Widespread disease among Pu populations resulted in mass casualties and sterility.

Kast Khraghner, Contact Director of the IU Diplomatic Service, said: "We are of course deeply saddened by this extinction, and very alarmed by the failure of the Soo to protect a vulnerable human species under their care. It is too early to speculate on what might have been done to prevent this tragedy, but we will investigate fully and act appropriately to ensure this terrible event is not repeated."

The two species share a common ancestor but evolved separately. Contact between them was minimal until early historic times, when they became mutually antagonistic. The Soo defeated and enslaved their rivals, breeding them into a slave race upon which their economy came to depend. With the development of steam technology, Pu were allowed to decline in numbers as machines could do much of the same work at lower cost. Some were repurposed as factory labourers, mechanics and domestic servants, but the majority were unsuitable for these tasks after millennia of selective breeding. An infusion of new slaves taken from wild populations near the Arctic only served to slow the decline of the species.

***

Hub Chronicle
Y273.m13.w1.d3
08:67

LATEST – Lone Pu survivor to be brought to Hub
In an apparent effort to mitigate IU sanctions, the Soo World Conference have offered to transfer a single Pu survivor to the care of the IU along with their full genetic records of the species. IU sources have indicated this will happen as early as next week.

The individual, whose anonymity is protected by law, is a 20 year old male who has spent most of his life in the Pu breeding programme after capture in the Arctic at the age of 6.

Following this latest revelation, Kast Khraghner said: "While this will not in any way influence our decision regarding further contact with the Soo, we welcome their new policy of honesty and co-operation, and will of course provide this young man with a home on Hub, full IU citizenship and any assistance he may require." He refused to comment on using the genetic archives to reconstitute the Pu species.

7. GROUP

"Liss, I believe it's your turn?" I said.

"Oh! Course! Yeah! Okay, um. I was talking to Pew. Is that how you say it?"

Pew looked depressed. "It doesn't matter. Nobody ever pronounces it right."

"Well, okay! So he's called Pew. And that's what his species is called as well. Isn't that weird? He says all the Pews had the same first name. Pew! His real name's Lee'un, so he's really Pew Lee'un, but everyone calls him Pew. Are you sure you don't mind?"

"There's only me left. I might as well be called Pu."

Liss shrugged happily. "And his story's so sad! So he's like a caveman or something in the Arctic, back when he's a little boy. And his family died from some bug that killed everyone, because they didn't have any hospitals or anything. But then he got rescued – well, kinda. Turns out there's two lots of humans on his world. There's his lot, the Pews, and the other lot, the Soos."

"Just Pu and Soo."

"Oh, right. Sorry! Anyway, they take him off and put him in a zoo, because the Pew are like an endangered species on his world or something. There's some other Pews in there and they raise him, but they're all really old. And, like, the Soos were swapping all the Pews around the world so they could get the girl Pews pregnant, but that didn't work. All the Pews kept getting older and older, and I guess they weren't very happy, because a lot of them killed themselves. Seriously, this is really horrible, the whole thing had been going on forever, the Soos had been treating the Pews, sorry the Pew, real bad for hundreds and hundreds of years, kinda like slaves, I guess…"

"Exactly like slaves."

"And it winds up with just him and a girl Pew left, and they tried to get them to hook up but she was really young and, well, I guess Pew was a gentleman, so they didn't do it."

"Hang on, hang on," said Olivia. "Are you telling me that you were the last man on earth and she was the last woman and you didn't screw her because you were too bloody *polite*?"

Pew flushed. Liss looked back and forth between him and Olivia. "Uh… isn't that what you said?"

"I didn't say anything," he mumbled.

"So what was it, then?" demanded Olivia.

Pew looked up at all the eyes questioning him. "I… she was old enough. But I couldn't… I couldn't. All right? I just… couldn't."

I expected Olivia to make a wounding remark, but instead she looked grudgingly sympathetic. "Yeh. Well. It happens." Pew kept looking down.

"Embarrassing!" trilled Liss.

"Just get on with it," muttered Pew.

"Uh, well, it was really sad as well 'cause she was in an accident on the way home and she died. So Pew was the last one left, and they sent him here 'cause, well, I guess they'd run out of things they knew how to do.

"So Pew went to college and studied math (because he's really, really clever!) and he thought he was better but it all caught up with him and he cut his wrists, only you can't do that kind of thing here 'cause they're really good at stopping you. They put him in the hospital for a while and then they said Hey! Why not come and be with all these other guys who've been through what you've been through? Which I guess is kinda what we are, 'cept for me.

"That's it. That's all he said. I guess it's his turn now, huh?"

8. KATIE

Observer Report
Regarding Mission LSHV-987277-002
Ebugh-kiriagh-Alier 9182
Scientific Attaché, Embassy of the Siciline Autonomous Republic
Placed with IU Exploration Service

It is hoped this report finds the reader well, and recovered from any shock and sadness accompanying the tragic loss of the scout ship *Valence*. Furthermore, I regret that I was unable to complete my task as diplomatic observer on mission LSHV-987277-002, but trust my observations will assist with the analysis of the mission.

I was placed with the IU Exploration Service to promote understanding between my species and those who have difficulties with machine intelligence, following the recent demonstrations against AI. Consequently, I was downloaded into a type A8 android body, easily identifiable as a machine and deliberately limited in capability, save in one regard. Given the inherent risks of interversal exploration, I selected the most extensive backup options to ensure I would retain a copy of my consciousness in all but the most extreme of calamities.

I accompanied the crew of the exploration ship *IUS Chemistry* on their mission to investigate anomalies found by an automated probe in the target universe. There was no visual evidence of an Earth or Moon, but the probe had remained in a stable L2 position despite this, and detected equivalent-mass gravity wells in the positions of both bodies. It was speculated that both objects had been transformed into singularities. We were able to confirm this hypothesis through more direct observations, including gravitational lensing at points corresponding to the cores of both bodies.

We also found artificial debris throughout the volume of the L1 point. Observations confirmed debris fields of similar composition at L4 and L5. In addition, we noted an asteroid with a mean diameter of 5.23km and mass of 4.56 million gigatons in orbit around the Earth singularity, which was another oddity as the asteroid was too massive to be captured by the Earth's gravity. Commander LuGararda decided to remain at the L1 point while sending the *Valence* to investigate the asteroid. I have no doubt this was the correct decision. Both ships were more than adequately stealthed, and we had detected no immediate evidence of surviving intelligent life in the volume.

The L1 debris derived from multiple vessels, and materials analysis suggested a conflict that had ceased approximately ten years earlier. This conclusion was strengthened by the discovery of 1,954 human corpses, all cybernetically enhanced. The *Valence* signalled the discovery of another body during their journey to the asteroid, but this one seemed to be alive. She was completely exposed to space in an elliptical orbit around L1, but nevertheless displayed a core temperature several degrees higher than expected for a corpse. The *Valence* was unable to reach the survivor without abandoning her primary mission, so the Commander sent our second scout ship, the *Phase*, to intercept.

When brought aboard, KT-00932/IN was completely comatose. Like many of the corpses, she benefitted from a high degree of cybernetic enhancement, including a whole limb replacement. The Commander ordered her placed in a makeshift hypobaric chamber and the medical staff raised air pressure at a rate they hoped she could withstand. She quickly regained consciousness, and immediately proved to be extremely dangerous. Two of the medical staff were seriously injured as she escaped. It was only her damaged state that made it possible to subdue her before she could reach the control room.

The Commander was forced to restrain KT-00932/IN by chaining her to a bulkhead. She was unresponsive during the first attempts at communication. We soon found she was attempting to make contact with outside forces using radio transmission, but had no success since the chamber had been rigged with EM shielding. She did not respond when we attempted to reply in kind.

As the *Valence* began its survey of the asteroid, I suggested to the Commander that I make an attempt to communicate with her. I hoped that, as a cyborg, she might feel differently about speaking to a fully artificial being. The Commander assented, and KT-00932/IN did indeed respond when I spoke to her. At first we had no common language, but over the next few hours we were able to establish an understanding based on memetic phoneme exchange. Her rate of learning was far beyond the human average, suggesting cybernetic enhancements to mental function as well as the more obvious physical modifications.

Once it was possible to communicate, though in a very simple way, I reiterated the Commander's offer of assistance, which she ignored. Instead, she demanded proof that I was fully artificial. I exposed a number of my internal workings to demonstrate this. She then questioned me about the IU, interversal travel, and our mission, and although she claimed interversal travel had long been demonstrated to be impossible, she seemed to cautiously accept my explanation of who and what we were.

Our discussion was interrupted by the Commander informing me that the *Valence* had detected signs of functioning technology on the asteroid, and was investigating further. KT-00932/IN inquired as to what we were doing, and I saw no reason not to inform her. She immediately demanded that the *Valence* cease its investigation. I asked her why, and it is at this point my records cease.

It seems a minute gravity fluctuation emanating from the asteroid was actually a weapon which disrupted my AI core to the point of complete failure. It is only through the system of multiple backups that any records were recovered from my android shell. I understand this weapon was primarily directed at the *Valence*, which was disabled and then destroyed by other means.

Noting the loss of several (though not all) onboard ship systems, the Commander demanded that KT-00932/IN explain what she had done. It is to his credit that he acted upon her warning of imminent destruction from enemy forces resident in the asteroid and returned both ship and crew back to Hub without further loss.

I recommend that the IU consider any attempt to recontact this universe as extremely dangerous. Nevertheless, I believe further contact may prove to be necessary. The degree of cybernetic enhancements we witnessed are often congruent with a human society attempting to compete with a rival AI civilisation, suggesting a war between humans and machines in this universe. Given the current concerns regarding artificial intelligence, it may be of benefit to intervene to prevent any further conflict and demonstrate that human/AI conflict can be brought to a close, even in the face of such terrible destruction.

9. GROUP

Katie had not reacted to any of the previous introductions, and did not react now that it was Pew's turn to tell her story.

"So, uh, this is Katie, or at least that's what everyone seems to call her. She says her real name is KT-00932/IN. But she doesn't mind being called Katie…"

He looked up at her for some kind of support. She kept her silence, so he went on. "I asked her for her story, and she told me but she went a bit fast so I had to ask her again. I ended up writing it down. Is that okay?"

"That's fine," I said. "Please, carry on."

He looked down at a pad. "Katie was a soldier in a war between two species that were spread out in the solar system. It ended up with the Earth being destroyed by, uh, multiple staggered singularity release from the surface. It's…"

His eyes brightened. "Actually, that's an interesting mathematical problem. You could get them to ping back and forth around the core, but their gravity would bend the trajectory so they'd keep making new tunnels and they'd consume the whole planet in just a few years…" He notice a disapproving look on my face, though Katie had no reaction at all. "Uh, sorry…"

He looked down at the pad again. "Katie's last mission was to attack the enemy as they approached the Earth, but her ship was destroyed before they could finish. She was supposed to crash into them but she never made it that far. She was thrown from the debris into an elliptical orbit around the L1 point – uh, that's a point between two bodies in space where the gravity cancels out and you can just sit there and you won't move relative to them, or you can orbit it as well. There's five of them in any two body system, I suppose if you're having a war they'd be important… sorry. I'll finish what she said. There isn't much.

"She was designed to survive in space and stayed in orbit until she was discovered by the IU. After that, the IU ship was attacked by her enemies and some of them were killed. Then she was brought here where she says she's provided as much strategic and tactical information as she's allowed to give. She doesn't want the IU to contact her world because it's only her enemies who are still there. She said her enemies were kind of a different species, so I suppose that makes her like me, but… well, her people fought back.

"She says she's willing to co-operate with all reasonable requests. And that's it. That's… Katie. Is that enough?"

"Katie, is there anything you want to add?" I asked.

"The information is accurate."

"Okay then," I said. "Katie, would you like to tell us what you learned about Iokan?"

10. IOKAN

CONFIDENTIAL REPORT
y276.m4.w2.d2

From:
Deputy Director, Diplomatic Service

To:
General Director, Interversal Union
Assistant General Director, Interversal Union
Directorate Committee, Interversal Union
Director, Exploration Service
Director, Refugee Service
Director, Diplomatic Service

Copied To:
Shadow Director, Interversal Criminal Tribunal

Mission LSHG-987372-002 has been nothing short of complete tragedy. Everyone on the planet had committed suicide within the three weeks prior to our arrival, save for one person who was on the verge of death when discovered. We found no clear explanation for this horrific event. We did, however, find evidence of multiple large-scale transits to and from the universe. As the inhabitants were not yet capable of this technology, we suspect there may have been interversal interference.

We had expected to find a civilisation believed lost over three thousand years ago. Nanoscale portals had been detected emanating from their universe, a sure sign that they were rediscovering interversal transit technology. An Exploration Service probe found the world fully recovered from a long period of societal collapse, and ready to be contacted immediately. We intended to welcome them back to interversal life after their long absence, and hoped they could shed some light on the events that devastated interversal relations at the time their own civilisation collapsed. Consequently the mission was staffed with higher ranking personnel than usual, and I was asked to supervise the opening of diplomatic relations.

When we arrived, however, we found only silence. Friendship hails received no answer from the planet or any orbital or lunar installations. A scientific station at the L1 point initially seemed evacuated, but closer examination showed the inhabitants had all been flushed into space. None had been spared – we even found a number of children among the dead. From that point on, the mission was nothing but horror piled upon horror.

I asked the Exploration Service Commander to begin a planetary survey, and he soon identified the primary cities. Each one was choked with corpses. I cannot begin to describe the things we found – every kind of suicide was evident. There was clear evidence of organisation as well: a number of sporting stadiums were used as venues for many thousands to kill themselves, or die at the hands of others.

We found the lone survivor in the central square of the largest conurbation of the Indonesian archipelago. He lay at the side of a quite beautiful series of fountains in which hundreds of people had drowned themselves. He was dehydrated, malnourished, unconscious and suffering from a form of cholera. We brought him aboard under extreme quarantine, and immediately returned to Hub. I can only hope he will be able to explain what has happened on his world – one of the most shocking acts of genocide yet witnessed in the current era, and all the worse if it came as a result of interversal interference.

I have copied this report along with full records to the Shadow Director of the Interversal Criminal Tribunal in the hope that this atrocity will motivate the IU to engage fully in dealing with genocide. If we continue to stand by and do nothing, we will be as guilty as those who commit such acts. If you find this constitutes a breach of confidentiality, you may of course have my resignation.

Baheera om-challha Isnia
Deputy Director, Diplomatic Service

11. GROUP

Katie turned to face the median point of the group. "The individual is named Iokan Zalacte. His report of events on his world cannot be trusted."

She looked straight ahead and said nothing else. Iokan turned to me, momentarily at a loss.

"Can you give us a bit more detail than that?" I asked.

She turned her head again. "Iokan reports that theistic intelligences which he terms 'Antecessors' revisited his planet two months ago, approximately three thousand years after departing during a cataclysm that destroyed their civilisation. He claims they offered his species transition to an afterlife if they committed suicide. Every individual on the planet save him accepted the offer."

"Um… what's a fayistic intelligence?" asked Pew.

"Theistic: adjective. Like or similar to a deity or god. Intelligence: noun. An intelligent being, particularly an incorporeal one. Theistic intelligence: noun phrase. A godlike, incorporeal intelligence."

"Oh," said Pew.

"I suppose that describes them… quite well," said Iokan. "But you didn't tell me you thought I was lying…"

"You did not ask for an opinion."

Iokan nodded slowly. "…I see. Very well. So… why don't you think I can be trusted?"

"You stated that you experienced an extreme emotional response upon contact with an 'Antecessor', and that your understanding of the universe changed in that moment. Religious revelation does not lead to a greater understanding of reality but instead to greater delusion. The 'Antecessors' are not deities but charlatans, and your species was tricked into extinction."

"That's not true," smiled Iokan, turning to the group. "They're real. I saw them myself – they came as balls of light, brighter than the stars. I saw them transform people. I saw my own wife and child join them."

"You are delusional."

"We did everything we could to verify their existence. And what they did was real. Everyone from my world is still alive. I can assure you of that." He smiled with an earnest devotion.

Olivia snorted. "Well, that's not the question, is it?"

"Do you have something to add, Olivia?" I asked.

"I want to know one thing. If his gods or whatever they were came back and got everyone to kill themselves, then why is he still alive?"

"Ah," said Iokan, as everyone turned to him. "Yes. A very good point."

"Yeh. Go on. Tell us," said Olivia.

He considered his answer for a moment, looking around at the group. "It's you," he said.

"What…?"

"They sent me here to help you." My heart sank. His therapy was going to be harder than I thought.

"What if I don't want your help?" demanded Olivia.

"It's freely offered," he said.

"Why exactly do you think you're here to help us?" I asked.

"What else can it be?" he said. "They were about to take me when your ship came down from orbit. They wanted someone to talk to the IU and tell them what happened. And then… to do whatever I could."

"Told you that, did they?" said Olivia.

"They didn't need to," said Iokan.

I interceded before Olivia went too far. "Well. Thank you for that. We should move on. Iokan, I think you have a few things to say about Olivia?"

12. OLIVIA

Transcript
Expedition AWLG-296219-002
Recorded: HD y270.m4.w4.d3

        [Mission Specialists Ewen, R and Tranouvir, DGS, were dispatched into a ruined city to conduct close range reconnaissance]

EWEN:	I think it's steam-driven.
TRANOUVIR:	Steam? No way. Come on.
COMMANDER:	Context, please.
TRANOUVIR:	This vehicle. I mean, what's left of this vehicle. You see it?
COMMANDER:	I see it.
TRANOUVIR:	Rab thinks it's steam driven. What do you think?
EWEN:	It's got a water tank and valves – look.
COMMANDER:	That's not conclusive. Too corroded to tell.
EWEN:	It's not advanced enough to be internal combustion. I don't see anything like that.
COMMANDER:	We'll need more for a precise tech status. How long has it been there?
TRANOUVIR:	It's a mess… say ten years, give or take. Pretty basic steel compound and a lot of rain around here.
COMMANDER:	And no sign of inhabitants?
TRANOUVIR:	Not even a skeleton.
EWEN:	Skeletons would probably be gone after ten years as well. Scavengers would take it all.
COMMANDER:	Are the buildings safe to enter?
TRANOUVIR:	Let me check…

        [Tranouvir attaches microseismic test device to an exterior wall]

TRANOUVIR:	It's coming back stable. Brick and mortar over timber frame. Pretty standard around here. Should be safe, if the wood hasn't rotted.
EWEN:	Timber lasts long enough. Concrete usually falls over first.
COMMANDER:	Take a look inside.

        [Ewen and Tranouvir enter the building]

TRANOUVIR:	Less corrosion in here… what's that fitting there?
EWEN:	Couldn't tell you.

TRANOUVIR: Take a look at this. See the pipes on the wall? And that... some kind of spigot or valve up there?
COMMANDER: Are there any light sources in the room you can recognise?
TRANOUVIR: Nothing electric. Just the windows.
COMMANDER: That's probably a gas pipe. The valve would be for lighting.
TRANOUVIR: No. Seriously?
COMMANDER: Some early tech civilisations burn methane or propane for light.
EWEN: Oh... yeah. That's it..
TRANOUVIR: You're kidding me. Explosive gases running indoors?
EWEN: Better than nothing. Hey. Did you hear that?
TRANOUVIR: Hear what?
EWEN: Something in the back...

[Ewen moves further into the building]

EWEN: I think we've found the locals.
TRANOUVIR: Found what...? Oh.
COMMANDER: Show me.
EWEN: I've got human remains. I think... five.
TRANOUVIR: Yeah. Five. Shit. What was making the noise?
EWEN: I don't know. Maybe we disturbed a rat or – oh crap. Oh crap oh crap oh crap.
TRANOUVIR: What?
COMMANDER: What is it?
EWEN: They're warm. I've got a temperature of twenty degrees on all of them. That's four above the air temperature! I think they're alive...
TRANOUVIR: Hold on. The heat might be decomposition. Maybe they died recently?
EWEN: Look at the dust in here. Look at the dust on *them!* They've been here for weeks. The scavengers should have taken them by now.
TRANOUVIR: What was that?
EWEN: I heard it. By the door.
TRANOUVIR: Yeah. I'll... Oh. My. Shit.
EWEN: They're... oh no. They can't be.
TRANOUVIR: Run!
EWEN: I'm –
TRANOUVIR: For fuck's sake, run!
EWEN: They've got me! They've –

[screams of pain, ripping sounds]

COMMANDER: What's happening?

TRANOUVIR: They're alive! They're fucking alive!
EWEN: Get it off get it off it's eating me! [more screams]

[weapon discharge]

TRANOUVIR: It's off, let's go –
EWEN: I can't walk –
TRANOUVIR: I've got you.

[weapon discharge]

COMMANDER: What are you shooting at?

[weapon discharge]

COMMANDER: Repeat: what are you shooting at?
TRANOUVIR: No. That can't happen. That can't happen.
COMMANDER: Tranouvir, what are you shooting at?
TRANOUVIR: They got up again. I shot them and they got up again.
EWEN: They're – [screams]
TRANOUVIR: No! Get off him! Get off!

[weapon discharge]

TRANOUVIR: Get– [screams]

[transmission ends]

13. GROUP

Iokan coughed. "It's quite a story. And rather unpleasant."

"Would anyone like some water?" asked Liss.

"I would, yes," said Iokan, and she got him a glass.

"Just get on with it," said Olivia.

Iokan finished his sip. "Apparently… as Olivia tells it… there were experiments, of a kind, done on pregnant women on her world, without the women knowing. And about eight months later, the women gave birth. But not in a natural way.

"The mothers fell ill, because the babies weren't human. They chewed through their own umbilical cords, and then they… they ate their way out of their mothers. They were homunculi, they came out the size of babies but with adult proportions. And they were hungry."

Iokan drank again. The others looked horrified or disgusted, except Katie (who didn't care), and myself, Veofol and Kwame (who knew better).

"Once they came out, they attacked everyone around them, and ate them too. Especially the livers. They couldn't be stopped, if you shot them they just kept going and healed their wounds as they went. And they grew fast, they were human sized within days – something to do with the livers. Some people had their livers eaten while the homunculi were growing back the limbs they'd hacked off."

Pew gasped. Olivia watched with a cruel smile.

"People fought back, but by then there were millions of homunculi all over the world, and the humans had to hide. Olivia led a group of survivors into a cave, but they only just made it – she says she killed one of the creatures by strangling it with its own guts…"

"Ew!" said Liss.

Olivia snickered. Iokan carried on, troubled. "And she says they lived underground for months, until they gave up hope because everyone else was dead. They went outside one by one to die…" Olivia chuckled to herself again. Iokan resumed. "…some of them would even cut themselves open to make it easier for the creatures to take their livers and get it over with quickly – it seems incredible that people could do that just out of fear…"

"It seems incredible because it does not make sense. It does not make sense because she made it up," said Kwame.

"Olivia. Was that really necessary?" I asked.

"Well, he's so trusting, isn't he?" said Olivia. "He'll believe any nonsense you give him."

"You lied?" said Iokan.

She shrugged. "Probably happened to someone, somewhere. In some universe."

"But not to you."

"No. What happened to me was worse. It wasn't so quick."

"Ah. I see," he nodded. "Then I'm sorry. You must have been through something terrible."

"That's right. It *was* terrible. It was worse than terrible. But we didn't all give up one day and jump off a cliff like your lot, we bloody well hung on until there was only me left and then I hung on by myself. For two years. And do you think this lot did anything to help?"

"Olivia," I said.

"What?"

"Can you stick to the facts, please?"

"I haven't bloody started! Do you want to know what happened on my world? The dead got up and walked, that's what happened! And you bloody lot, you and your Interversal Union–"

"Olivia, please, if you want to accuse us of something, you can do that another time. All we need at the moment is for you to introduce yourself–"

"I'm talking! I've got a right to talk, you said–"

"You had the chance and instead you chose to play a trick on a sick man–"

"Excuse me? I don't mind listening," said Iokan.

Olivia carried on. "If you lot have to know what happened to me then I'm going to tell it, I'm not letting someone else mess it up. And then all this lot will understand how you lot" – she jabbed a finger at me and Veofol – "keep buggering up and leaving us to die."

And now everyone was looking at me. I was going to have to let her talk. "All right, Olivia. Go on."

"D'you know what a revenant is? It's someone who comes back. From the dead. It's not magic, it's not gods, it's a disease that gets inside you. It's *bacteria*. You get infected and it lives inside you and it waits until you die. And then it takes over. You get up again and you don't remember who you are. You're just hungry. So they die, get up, bite people and get *them* infected, and that's how it survives. That's its life cycle. Only we didn't know it was there until we all had it, because some fool put it in animal feed. You know what they'd do? They ground up all the bits of animals they couldn't sell to butchers and fed 'em back to more animals. One infected animal gets in and a few years later cows are getting up after they're slaughtered. And then people are getting up again. And then we had the cholera, and people were dropping like flies and coming back half an hour later and then everyone thinks it's the end of the world. Only it wasn't the end, oh no. That time we beat them.

"We spent twenty years trying to cure it but we didn't have everything you had. We didn't figure out antibiotics until it was too late, and then it was the wrong kind. Next time it was the flu that started it off, and that time we didn't win. Millions of people all died at once and got up again and came for us. We got stuck in castles and compounds and little stations out in the middle of nowhere but it was too late and after ten years of that, people just gave up. And you know what happened then?

"That's when you lot" – another finger jab at me – "turned up and half your boys got eaten. And did they stay around? Did they check to see if anyone else was left? No! They buggered off and didn't come back until they'd found a cure. Which was two years later. And by then there wasn't anyone left – except me. Because they'd all given up. Killed themselves. Or gone off outside and didn't get a mile down the road before the revenants got up out of the hedges and grabbed 'em." She gave me a hard look. "How many people do you think died because you lot didn't want to risk your own necks?"

And then a pause while everyone looked back at me. Until Liss, of all people, raised her voice.

"It's not her fault," she said. Everyone turned to her and suddenly she was uncomfortable. "I mean, you can't save everyone, can you? That's what they used to say on my world."

"I agree," said Kwame. "You cannot blame Dr. Singh and you cannot blame the IU."

"I bloody can. They ran away and left us to die," said Olivia.

Iokan looked at me. "So she wasn't making that up?"

"No. I'm afraid she wasn't," I replied.

"Could nothing be done?"

They all looked to me. "As I understand it, the expedition was ambushed by revenants. Most of them were killed before they had a chance to escape. Some of them died from their injuries on the way back and they–"

"Revenned," said Olivia.

"They came back. When the ship returned to Hub there were only two survivors. They had to lock themselves in the control room because the rest of the crew, the revenants, kept trying to attack them. We'd never seen anything like it. We didn't go back until we were sure of what we were dealing with."

"Ancients…" said Iokan. "I see now."

Olivia scowled at him. "Oh, do you?"

"How did you survive?"

She smiled cruelly. "Well… we couldn't grow much of anything, and what we had in tins didn't last long. But there was plenty of food walking around, wasn't there?"

"I'm sorry…?"

"The dead ones. Revenants. Only they weren't dead, not really. The bacteria kept them going and the meat stayed fresh for years. Just got a bit stringy, that's all."

"Do you mean to say… you ate the dead?"

"I told you. They weren't dead, not really."

Iokan didn't know what to say. Kwame did. "That is the most disgusting thing I have ever heard," he said.

"You're horrible!" said Liss.

Olivia snapped back at her. "Well you try living by yourself on a patch of ground where you can't grow a damn thing! I survived the hard way, not like you with your electric and your supermarkets, you lazy cow!"

"But– but– they left me all alone!"

"Oh, did they? You sure you didn't eat them all after they dropped dead? You look like the type, butter wouldn't melt one minute and cracking the bones for marrow the next…"

Liss recoiled, gasping, and fled the room. Olivia eyed an increasingly pale Iokan. "Ooh, and you know, now I think of it, I could really do with a calf joint, they always came up nice with a bit of rosemary, especially if you leave the juices running a bit…"

Iokan held his nerve. Pew did not. He clutched his mouth and ran for the door. We heard a nearby lavatory swish open. Olivia laughed.

"That's enough," I said. "The session's over."

PART TWO
INDIVIDUAL THERAPY

1. ASHA

Working with the group of lone survivors had taken me away from my normal duties: the care of refugees from dead or dying worlds. Every few years we discover a universe in which the Earth has been struck by an asteroid, or burnt by a flood basalt eruption, or baked with gamma rays, or frozen in a sudden ice age, and that's before you count all the ways humanity can destroy the world. Every human species is different, and sometimes it seems each one invents a new way to start an apocalypse.

In most of the worlds suffering some such disaster, millions of people would need to be transported to safety. Many of them would be injured, often both physically and psychologically. My usual task during an evacuation was to make psychiatric assessments of survivors who had been referred by the medical staff when they conducted their first triage of newcomers. Then, after the majority had moved on to empty worlds provided by the IU, I would conduct group and individual therapy with those who were too disturbed to join the rest of their species. For now, even that had wound down and we were fortunate enough to be able to devote resources to projects such as the group of lone survivors, though that was not the only factor motivating the creation of the group.

I hoped we would be free of evacuations for a good while yet, but nevertheless kept an eye on the apocalypse watch maintained by the Refugee Service: Llorissa was recovering from its nuclear war and the people were still desperately trying to make a go of it on their battered, irradiated world; on Steteryn the glaciers advanced day by day but the mediaeval societies living two thousand kilometres to the south refused to believe the world was ending; Ardeë's perennial solar flares were building again but the scientists there were certain the threat wasn't serious; Schviensever still fought its war against the comets swarming through the solar system, trying to preserve their ancient world in the face of an almost inevitable doom, but even they were doing relatively well for the moment. Any of these worlds could request an evacuation and the IU would certainly respond, but none seemed likely in the next few years. And it was very possible that my new patients would need that time.

Usually when I begin a new group, I have a very clear idea what my patients are suffering from, and therapy can begin immediately. For species with a full medico-genetic map, psychosurgery can alleviate their problems swiftly and they're usually ready to move on after a month of observation. For others, we resort to older, more gradual methods, and it's there that my expertise lies. Post-Traumatic Stress Disorder and related conditions are the primary issue for most apocalypse survivors, for which exposure therapy is the key treatment: slowly acclimatising the patient to the horror of their own memories until they no longer hold the same debilitating power over them. I have a whole sheaf of techniques to make it easier on the patient, and group therapy provides the support of peers who share the same terrible experience, reinforcing the individual therapy and giving them the company of people who understand what they're going through – vital because many PTSD patients are unwilling to open up to people who have not shared their particular horror.

But before we can embark on therapy, we need a diagnosis. There's no point in beginning exposure therapy if we don't know which memories are causing the problem, and patients are often unwilling to speak of the horrifying events that created those memories in the first place. They may also suffer from other injuries suffered during the apocalypse, or have complications resulting from pre-existing conditions, making diagnosis vital to ensure we don't make the situation any worse. Under normal circumstances, the process is made easier by the larger numbers of survivors, who can both support each other and help us understand common problems among their species. Sometimes there are even medical professionals among the survivors, whose assistance can be invaluable; and if we're really lucky, medical and psychiatric records might survive the apocalypse, allowing us to build on pre-existing diagnoses. Further down the road, having a large enough group from the species makes it possible to build a medico-genetic map which can enable treatment for all but the most dedicated of sufferers.

I had none of these advantages with my current group. They shared a unique experience of loss which we hoped would bring them together, but each had suffered their loss in a very different way, and it was just as likely they would be driven apart. I had psychomedical histories for those who had been on Hub for some time, but their resistance to previous attempts at therapy suggested deeper problems as yet undiagnosed. And of course, it would be virtually impossible to create a medico-genetic map with only a single surviving member of a species to draw upon, meaning we could not risk the subtle procedures used to treat psychiatric conditions.

Each of them was very special, and very different. I would be lucky to understand and diagnose their problems within the next few months, let alone begin effective courses of therapy.

2. KWAME

PSYCHOMEDICAL HISTORY – SUMMARY
KWAME VANGONA

Kwame was discovered in a hibernation unit on a world that had suffered complete nuclear devastation approximately ninety years previously, leaving him as the only survivor of his species. He emerged with minor brain damage, either through the revival procedure or from hibernation itself.

After transfer to Hub, Kwame was diagnosed with severe aphasia. He retained some ability to express himself in written language, and, despite some loss of dexterity, was able to identify himself as the President of the nation of Mutapa, and discover he was the only survivor of his world. This revelation provoked reactions of grief and depression, which lasted several weeks. Eventually, he assented to cautious neurological treatment and physical therapy which restored his power of speech and much of his physical co-ordination, with the exception of fine motor skills. His left arm is particularly afflicted due to a pre-existing injury acquired during military service.

Soon after his arrival on Hub, Kwame began to suffer nightmares. He reported that he witnessed, night after night, the death of his wife, but was unable to give specifics as to what exactly he saw during the nightmares. An exaggerated startle response was observed, along with flashbacks and reticence when discussing the events leading up to the end of his world. While continuing with physical therapy, he became psychologically withdrawn, and often commented that it was impossible to explain his experiences to people who had not been there. A diagnosis of PTSD was made, and he was referred to a specialist.

After a year of therapy, Kwame made the admission that, as President of his nation, he had set in train the events that led to the nuclear holocaust, and believed himself to be personally responsible for the extinction of his species. However, this did not lead to therapeutic progress but instead to a declaration that he wished to be prosecuted for genocide and punished accordingly. His legal case has been stalled for some time, and although he attends therapy sessions, he seems unable to make progress while the case is still pending.

***

I'd only moved into my office a couple of weeks previously, but I think I'd done well in making the place comfortable: calming backgrounds, a painting with gentle colours, an abundance of greenery and a pleasant smell of flowers and coffee. Two comfortable chairs faced each other across a small table, and one wall was set to transparent so it windowed out onto the forest beyond the centre.

Kwame sat in one of the comfortable chairs. He didn't have the energy to appreciate the room – he hadn't slept and there was strong coffee in the non-spill cup he clutched with both hands – but the transparent wall drew his attention.

"Is that a live image?" he asked.

"Yes. That's what's outside right now," I replied. My office was on the second floor, allowing us to see over the nearest treetops. Beyond them the valley sloped away and the forest canopy spread out into the plains and around the lakes. Patches of sunlight and shade floated across the landscape, and blue mountains met the sky in the far distance.

"How far does the forest reach?"

"All the way across the continent."

"And you might never see another human face…"

"There are people out there."

"But no natives."

"No."

"An empty world…" He gazed out into the forest. "You never realise in Hub Metro."

"A little peace and quiet can be good for you."

"Can it?"

"I hope so," I said. "Shall we get started?"

"Please."

"I believe there's something you want to say first."

"Yes." He sucked on the cup's valve, and grimaced as coffee flooded through him. "I would like to formally request that I be prosecuted for the genocide of approximately four billion people on my world. I am willing to make a full confession, and in fact I have already done so several times."

"Well, there's not much I can do about that myself. But I've made sure your legal counsel has clearance to talk to you once a week to update you on the case."

"Is anything likely to change?"

"Kwame, I'm not a police officer, I'm not a prison guard, and I'm certainly not a lawyer. I'm a therapist. I'm here to help you get better."

"Why?"

"I know you're still suffering. I think I might be able to help."

"That is not what I mean. What I mean is… why is it necessary to stop my suffering?"

"It isn't," I said. "If you really want to suffer, you can carry on as long as you like. You've certainly been making the attempt."

That took him aback. He wasn't used to such directness. "I… did not mean that…"

"Yes, Kwame. You did mean that. You've consistently refused help, and chosen to pursue a legal course that you know will last years. But even if you manage to get yourself convicted, what would change? We deport most serious criminals back to their home universe. We can't do that to you because it would be a death sentence. So you'd only end up in prison, and there are plenty of therapists there. Really, all that would change would be the view from the window."

He looked outside for a moment.

"It is not… the legal process is not about me. I am not trying to punish myself. Four billion people deserve justice."

"What would happen to you if you were convicted of that kind of crime on your world?"

He smiled without pleasure. "I doubt I would be convicted. They would probably put up a statue instead. Most of the statues in Zimbabwe City were of men who slaughtered thousands in the colonies."

"But assume for a moment that politics didn't get in the way."

"Then I would be executed, of course."

"Which we would never do."

"You are more civilised."

"So by the standards of your world, justice will not be done."

"No. It will not." He agreed far too easily; he'd already thought it through, and had an answer.

"So why is it necessary?"

"It is necessary because genocide still happens. Every universe should know the price for such crimes. It should not be a statue in the public square and judgement that comes a century too late."

"And do you think your conviction would change this?"

"It might."

"But does it have to be you?"

"There is no-one else."

He held his opinions with a profound moral certainty, and I doubted he would be shifted easily. But perhaps I could address more immediate issues. "Moving on for a moment, I'd like to talk about your nightmares."

"If you must."

"Can you tell me what you see in your dreams?"

"I see my wife. Dying."

"I'm sorry if this is painful, but I have to ask. How did she die?"

"Unpleasantly."

"I mean, what do you remember about how she died?"

"Nothing."

"Why is that?"

"I expect it may have something to do with my condition," he said, tapping the side of his head.

"But you remember everything when you dream?"

"Every detail. She died of radiation poisoning. Do you know how terrible that is?"

"Yes. I do. I've seen it." I remembered triage duty on the Lift down from orbit, when we evacuated the last few survivors from a world where tactical nuclear weapons had been used in warfare for more than a century. We saw cancers, birth defects, malnutrition from digestive systems mangled by radiation, and worse. Some who'd stayed in the open too long while waiting to be rescued died before we reached Hub. I took a sip of tea to drive the memory away.

"Then you understand," said Kwame.

"I understand it's painful to think about. But – and excuse me if this seems like an obvious question – I thought you said you didn't remember how she died?"

"I do not remember the event. I remember discussing it later, in the bunker."

"What do you remember from that?"

He sighed. He'd told this story too many times.

"She was on a train in Zimbabwe when the bomb went off. She should have been far away, but we had the oldest railways in the world and they never ran on time. If they had… if the trains had been Dzikanyikan or Chifunyikan… well. They were not. They were Mutapan. So the train was still in the blast zone. They took a lethal dose of radiation. They were lucky to get as far as a hospital. I was out of the country, on an official visit to Chiwikuru. When I returned, I stayed with them until the end.

"My younger son died on the third day. My wife on the fifth. My daughter on the sixth. My elder son on the tenth. I remember none of it, except at night. You know all this already. Why do you need to ask?"

I asked because at no point during this explanation did he suffer a flashback, and his records confirmed that he never did when he told this story. PTSD had been diagnosed in his case from nightmares, hypervigilance and social withdrawal. He should have found it difficult to discuss the source of the trauma. He should have been overwhelmed with memories he could not control. So either his brain damage had complicated the PTSD to the point where it only affected him at night, or something else was going undiagnosed; and I had a plan for how we could find out.

"What if we could show you your dreams?"

His eyes went wide. "I thought that was impossible."

"Well, yes–"

"If you understood how my brain worked, I would not need to use this thing." He held up the non-spill cup in his crippled hands.

"You're right. We don't have a full understanding of your species. But we do know a few things. We can read the neural impulses inside your mind. We know where your visual cortex is. The quality may not be very good, but we might be able to record some images from your dreams."

"Why did no-one tell me this before?"

"We used to think your species was unique. Hardly anyone can hibernate the way you do, and it has an effect on the way your brain works which we don't understand. But one of the older IU member species recently made a bequest of records from thousands of years ago, and it turns out you're not unique. There have been other human species that can hibernate, and apparently the records might help."

He sat back in his chair, troubled. I was offering him a way to escape from the rut he was stuck in, so he would probably say no. Eventually, he found a way.

"I wake up screaming in terror every night, because of what I see in my dreams… what makes you think I want to see them with waking eyes?"

"Because it's the first step in therapy for post-traumatic stress disorder. I'm sure exposure therapy has been explained to you before. If we approach the trauma gently, one step at a time, we can desensitise you to the memory. Eventually, we can make the dreams stop."

He didn't answer.

"How long has it been since you slept? Properly, without drugs?"

He still didn't answer.

"Will you think about it?" I asked. "Kwame?"

"I will… consider it."

And that was as much as I could hope for in the first session.

3. LISS

PSYCHOMEDICAL HISTORY – SUMMARY
LISS LI'OUL

Every human on Liss's world has been reduced to a powder, with no explanation either for this or how she survived. Physically, she is perfectly healthy, although she has a relatively high level of contaminants present in her tissues. This is most likely due to environmental factors on her world, which was technologically advanced and given to unusual forms of pollution. She claims to be physically average for her people, which would place her species at the higher end of human physical capability. She is considerably stronger than most humans and her level of health suggests a highly developed healing capacity and resistance to disease. Her only physical impairment is a clumsiness which seems to be subclinical in nature.

Psychologically, she appears to be highly delusional. She maintains that her entire species temporarily left and will return at some point, despite being presented with clear evidence that she is the last surviving member of her species. She has suffered no brain damage, and reports no headaches, dizziness, sense impairment or other symptoms associated with neurological disorder. Given the bizarre nature of her world, this may be a defence mechanism to protect against the many traumas of daily life and yet carry on without reflecting on how it can so easily end. This, however, is only speculation. It has not been possible to reach a full diagnosis.

***

"What do you remember about what happened? When everyone vanished?"

Liss smiled at me from the comfortable chair, distracted from looking outside. She'd picked an entirely different outfit today, one that clashed with all the colours in my office, as well as the blue of the sky and the green of the forest. She seemed oblivious to how poor her dress sense was, as she was with so many other things. "Oh, well, I guess you already know and everything…"

"I'd like to hear the story for myself, if that's okay."

"Sure! It was a pretty normal day, I guess. I got up, put the breakfast show on – Sillafen was on with his movie or something, I mean that guy's a dick, I don't know why anyone goes to see his movies – I fixed myself some egg things, not eggs from a chicken, you don't get eggs any more, not like you get here and those ones aren't even real eggs, are they? You kinda make them from something…"

"Liss–"

"And the pipes were banging again and the super *never* does anything about it, one of these days it's all just going to burst and everything's going to get flooded, that happened at my mom's place once and she was so mad she sued the city, made them pay for the whole thing…"

"Liss–"

"Can you believe that? I didn't have time to talk to the super that morning so I just got in the car and went to work – there was this complete asshole on the road into Telissauga, guy cut me up and I was so mad, I just can't tell you. He could have killed somebody, the way he was driving–"

"Liss!"

"Oh. Sorry!"

"Can you tell me more about where you worked?"

"Okay. So where I work, I guess you'd say it's a recruitment agency. People come in, we interview them, we get them jobs, and then they screw up and the employer complains and we try and send them someone who isn't a screw-up but what are you going to do? These guys come in off the street and you can't believe anything you see on their resumé, but how are you going to spot them? I dunno, I just did data entry most of the time, and we were so far behind I had weeks and weeks of work backed up, so when everyone went away I was getting tons of it done, only I had everyone else's work to do as well so I guess I wasn't getting that far, and Barara left me all the photocopying as well, he's just lazy, never gets through his work–"

"Can I stop you there?"

"Oh! Sure! Sorry..."

"It's okay, Liss, I'd just like to focus a little more on the actual events on the day itself."

"Which day?"

"The day everyone disappeared."

"Oh. Sorry!" She looked childishly embarrassed.

"You said you went into work as normal. Was there anything special going on that day?"

"Nope. Normal day, far as I know."

"What was on the news?"

"I don't watch the news."

"You say you watched a breakfast show?"

"Oh, sure, but not news. I mean, movie stars, that's not news. I know *that*. News is too depressing. I mean, who wants to hear all that kinda stuff when you're eating breakfast?"

"Why is the news depressing?"

"Well, y'know. Everything going wrong. Disasters and screwups. I don't need to hear about it, I've got my own troubles, you know?"

"What do you mean by disasters and screwups, exactly?"

"Oh, I don't know... all that crap, it just wears me out. I don't pay any attention."

"I see. So you have no knowledge of world events at that time?"

She shrugged. "Guess not."

"Okay. So you went to work. And everything was normal?"

"Uh-huh. Normal as normal is. You know, nobody's filling the coffeepot, too much work, my manager's stressed. I dunno. Normal."

"How did you spend the day? I mean, what did your work consist of?"

"Data entry. You know, typing forms into the computer?"

"Why was that necessary?"

"Huh?" She seemed puzzled, as though the question made no sense.

"Why did that have to be done?"

"Of course it had to be done! How else are you gonna do it?"

"No, I mean... your world had some amazing technology. It seems strange that you needed humans just to enter data into a computer."

"I don't know. I guess it was cheaper than getting a chimp to do it?"

She wasn't being sarcastic, and my translation system was working perfectly. "I'm sorry – you said a chimp? A chimpanzee?"

"Uh-huh. They don't work for nothing! I mean don't get me wrong, they're great little guys but you'll never get them doing anything like I was doing. I tell you, I'm so close to minimum wage I don't know how I make it from month to month..."

Her world grew stranger and stranger. "Let me just check that I've understood this: Chimpanzees were an intelligent species on your world?"

"Sure. Of course they were."

"That's... rather unusual."

She seemed honestly perplexed. "What's unusual about chimps?"

"Lets put the chimps to one side. I'd like to talk about the moment everyone disappeared. Did this happen while you were entering data?"

"Oh, no. It's like I said before, I was in the photocopier room."

"And what were you doing?"

"Copying."

"Can you explain any more?"

"Well, when the forms come to us, they're like the originals but we need to keep backup copies in case the system goes down, you know? It's boring. You've gotta take the staples off and run the pages through and half the time the feeder doesn't work so you've got to do them one page at a time and then the manager asks you why you haven't finished yet and it just goes on and on and on... you know."

"But it didn't go on and on, did it?"

"No... I guess not." She fell into silence. But before I could coax her into going further, she perked back up again. "But I did finish it!"

"After you found everyone had disappeared?"

"Oh, not straight away... I came back the next day. Or the one after that, I don't know. But I got it done."

The question was: what happened between the moment of discovery and the point at which she started work again?

"Hm. Do you remember the moment they vanished?"

"I guess."

"Can you tell me what you experienced?"

"Not much of anything. I don't know. It got quiet."

"How so?"

"People stopped talking. I guess that's when they all walked out. They must have taken their shoes off too, 'cause they were real quiet about it."

"What did you do once you realised everything had gone quiet?"

"I kept copying. For a while, anyway. Then I thought it was weird, so I went to look."

"Did you notice the piles of dust?"

"What, those? No, those weren't there. That was later. It all got messy because the cleaning staff went as well. I can't clean everywhere so it just builds up."

"You're sure about that?"

"Uh-huh."

She wasn't likely to give up her delusion in the first session, so I moved on. "What did you do next?"

"I went looking for everyone. But they'd all gone."

"Where did you look?"

"Everywhere. I took a drive. Everyone was gone."

"What else did you do?"

"I called the cops but they were useless. I guess they were hiding too because they didn't answer the phone. I left a message but they didn't call me back."

"How long did you look for people?"

"Until it got dark and I went home."
"What did you do then?"
"Watched screen."
"What was on the screen?"
"Just the stories."
"They were still broadcasting?"
"Uh-huh."
"But it was automated?"
"I guess."

She'd started the session as bright and breezy as could be, but the sun had gone in. She wasn't looking at me any more. She wasn't even looking at the beautiful view outside. She was looking at the table, and picking at her nails.

"So why did you decide to go back to work?"
She shrugged. "I didn't want to get fired."
"Was that the only reason?"
"Have *you* ever tried living on welfare? Huh."
"There wasn't anything else?"
"No."
"Nothing you left behind there?" She shook her head just a little. "Nothing you saw there?" She didn't even answer. She kept her eyes down, not even pretending to look at her nails any more. I worried that if I kept pressing her this way, I might seem unsympathetic; so I decided to engage her in something she was interested in.

"You said earlier you liked watching screen…"
"Yeah."
"What kind of things did you like watching?"
She looked up at me with a returning smile. "Oh, you know. The usual stuff."
"Such as?"
"Uh… well anything on ScreenTime. That's all reruns but it's good reruns. ASN had a couple of good shows. And I can always stand to watch *Dates and Hates*. I know, it's kinda soppy but it's only a half hour show."
"Is that a romantic one?"
"Uh-huh. See, Ellera's always having to decide which guy she likes from the dating agency and she always picks the wrong one and the wrong one turns out to be an okay guy after all but the right guy she should have picked ends up kidnapping her and then she has to have dinner with him but she gets away and finds the wrong guy again and then it turns out he really is the wrong guy because he was in on it with the right guy so she dumps them both and goes back to the agency to try again. Which is so lame because she should have realised she wasn't getting anywhere but she keeps on trying!"

Liss was definitely back to being perked up and happy. "Any others?" I asked.
"Well I like some of the reality shows…"
"Such as?"
"*CP7: Secret Squadron* is good, it's like you can't believe those people are real, they're so crazy. So you've got Gelean acting like he's so cool, like he's the real one and only, you know? And he's a complete ass and everybody knows it except him.

And Uilea and Yelessean are always fighting and poor old Sayas is trying to keep everyone from making idiots of themselves in front of the cameras but no one listens so she ends up complaining about everyone. I mean, it's like these guys think they're supposed to save people but they're a total bunch of screwups."

"So is this a show about... police officers? Firefighters?"

"Huh? No. Well, kinda. They're adventurers. You know?"

"Not really. Are they some kind of emergency service?"

"Yeah. For really big emergencies."

"Such as..?

"You know, like end of the world kind of stuff?"

If I'd had my cup of tea in my hand, I'd have dropped it. "End of the world stuff?"

"Yeah. If something really bad's happening, they go off and deal with it. Well, not CP7, they're just local, you know? They're City Patrol 7, they're not important. I mean, 'Secret Squadron', you gotta be kidding, right?"

"But there were other, uh, 'adventurers' saving the world?"

"Sure!"

"What did they save the world from?"

"Uh, well. You know. Like that one time the bugs took over all the people in Noyza and made them all into one person. Or when Calafaria blew up. Or that mountain in Eleshin that kept moving and squashing things. That kind of stuff."

"Did this happen a lot?"

"Every now and then, I don't know. But they deal with it. You know. Save the world and everything."

"What do they do when they're not saving the world? And appearing on screenshows..."

"They save cities. Or countries. Or just help people. Don't you have anyone like that here?"

"No. We don't..." It occurred to me there was a problem with this. "Okay. I apologise if this is an obvious question..."

"Uh-huh..."

"But this *is* just a screenshow. Right?"

"Oh, sure, it's a screenshow!"

"Oh. Good."

"But it's a screenshow about real people."

I had a thousand questions fighting in my head. Picking the right one took a moment. "So... why is it these people who save the world? I mean, what qualifies them to do that?"

She answered as though I were a child asking a stupid question. "Because they've got powers."

"Powers?" I asked.

"You know. They can do stuff."

"Stuff like...?"

"Oh, I don't know. They're strong. Or bulletproof. Or really fast. Or really clever. Lots of things."

"So they had posthuman modifications?"

"What does that mean?"

"Well, it means they had surgery or cybernetic implants, or they were genetically altered to have extra abilities. A lot of species do it once they have the technology."

"Oh, some people did that…"

"Okay."

"But most of them were just born like it."

"Right. I see. But… did you hear about any of these world savers trying to stop what happened? Or did they all disappear too? "

"I guess so. I didn't hear about them after that."

"No. Hm. The thing is… the thing is, what you've just described is very unusual. In fact I've never heard of anything like it. I don't know if it has anything to do with what happened, but…"

I paused there. If she was telling the truth, then her world hadn't faced an end once, but many times. It faced it often enough that it needed to have people constantly on hand to save it, and this time they'd failed. It didn't help to explain why Liss had survived, though. Unless…

"Liss… do you have any powers?"

She laughed. "What, me? No. Of course not!"

"You're sure?"

"Yeah. I was tested. Same as everyone else. I'm normal. Why do you think I've got powers?"

"I was just wondering what it was that made you different to everyone else."

She looked very surprised. "You think the reason I was left behind was because I have a power?"

"I don't know. I'm just speculating."

"Wow! Me with a power… that's just, wow. You know?"

"Well, you are very strong for someone your size…"

"Oh, stop it, everyone's this strong on my world! It's not us that's strong, it's you that's weak."

I needed to do some research. "Hm. Can I ask a favour?"

"Sure!"

"You brought a lot of screenshows back from your world. Was this show, *Secret Squadron*, one of them?"

"Oh, no, I didn't get any of those. I've got some of *Dates and Hates*, though."

"Do you mind if I borrow a few discs? Anything that has people with powers. Or something that just shows what your world was like…?"

She shrugged. "Sure. Okay."

4. KATIE

PSYCHOMEDICAL HISTORY – SUMMARY
KT-00932/IN "KATIE"

It is difficult to take a full history for KT-00932/IN, partly because her physiological state is extremely unusual, and partly because she is almost completely silent on the subject of her own health.

When rescued, she was suffering from nearly a year of exposure to vacuum, and was in a deep coma that seemed to have prolonged her survival in an airless environment. Her biology has clearly been designed for survival in open space. Her circulatory fluids do not expand or contract as normal human blood would, thus avoiding damage during the extreme changes of temperature she experienced while in vacuum. There was radiation damage across her dermis to a depth of approximately one millimetre, but she displayed remarkable resistance to any deeper exposure. She had also lost all her hair, but her eardrums had remained intact despite the lack of air pressure.

She was equipped with a number of implants intended for military use, and consented to their removal while she was in quarantine, as a condition of release to Hub. However, she did not consent to the removal of three implants in her brain, which she claims have a vital regulatory function. Our analysis suggests they force the biological systems of her brain to operate at higher efficiency than normal. If this is the case, they may cause neural damage over time, and a small but significant degradation has been observed across successive scans.

Her psychological state is a difficult subject, as she is as reticent here as elsewhere. She gave a brief statement regarding the war she fought in, which her side appears to have lost. She has agreed to reasonable co-operation with IU authorities, but this has amounted to a policy of almost complete silence regarding her past. She displays no emotion, and demonstrates absolutely no empathy. She is nevertheless extremely intelligent and perceptive. If the neurological degradation causes suffering, she conceals it perfectly.

It is projected that KT-00932/IN has between six and nine months before the neurological degradation threatens autonomic systems and therefore her life. Treatment is theoretically possible but extremely risky and counterindicated unless there is no other option. It is recommended that she should remain under close observation and be encouraged to engage further with therapy.

***

Katie folded into her chair like a robotic arm. Whatever interest she had in the room was satisfied with a steady sweeping look, not pausing once to examine any single thing.

"Katie... is it okay if I call you Katie?"

She stared directly at me without regard for how anyone might interpret such a constant gaze, and replied in the usual flat, toneless voice. "It is okay."

"Good... well, first of all, thank you for agreeing to come to the centre. I know you don't think we'll be able to help, but I'm glad you're willing to let us try."

She didn't react. Her first therapist had reported that pleasantries would just pass her by, but that she would respond to direct inquiries.

"Well. Okay. Now, I know you've answered this question before, but... how did you survive?"

She started without a pause. "I was assigned to crew a modified orbital freight transport with two others. The transport was equipped with antimatter explosive devices. Our mission was to simulate the appearance of a wreck near the path of an enemy asteroid ship on approach to Earth orbit, then to burn engines at point of closest approach, ram the asteroid and detonate the antimatter devices. However, the enemy discovered us before we could ram them and destroyed our ship with pulsed EMDIS weapons. The ship was divided into a number of sections and the contents dispersed. The antimatter devices and other crewmembers were eliminated by plasma fire, but I remained undetected among other debris. I engaged vacuum survival systems, and have no further memories until I was recovered by the exploration ship *Chemistry*."

I checked the notes from the triage therapist who had first spoken to her at Grainger station, months before:

G: *Can I ask how you survived?*

K: *I was assigned to crew a modified orbital freight transport with two others. The transport was equipped with antimatter explosive devices. Our mission was to simulate the appearance of a wreck near the path of an enemy asteroid ship on approach to Earth orbit, then to burn engines at point of closest approach, ram the asteroid and detonate the antimatter devices. However, the enemy discovered us before we could ram them and destroyed our ship with pulsed EMDIS weapons...*

She certainly knew how to stick to her story. I thought that perhaps I should get her onto a subject where she could not simply recite a prepared statement.

"Thank you. That was informative. Let's get back to the present day... how are you feeling?"

"I am within normal tolerances."

"I mean, with regards to your neurological condition."

"I am unaffected."

"Well, we're still very concerned. There'll be regular neuroscans to track your progress. We'd be grateful if you can alert us if you experience any symptoms."

"I will give reasonable cooperation."

"Is there anything we can do for you?"

"Not at this time."

"You do understand that if your brain continues to degrade, you probably won't survive?"

"I understand this is possible."

"Well, the issue seems to be with your implants, and we just don't know how to fix the problem. But what we could do is clone a new body without the implants and transfer your consciousness into that. We wouldn't normally risk that kind of procedure without knowing more about your species, but if it comes to a choice between life and death, we're willing to risk it if you are."

"I do not require assistance."

"Is there nothing we can do?"

"I do not require assistance."

"Not even to save your life?"

"I do not require assistance."

"Okay. So, Katie… why do you want to die?"

It took her a moment to process that; an almost human moment. But only almost.

"My life or death is irrelevant."

"You don't care one way or the other?"

"It is unimportant."

"Even to you?"

"Yes."

"I see. Well, these techniques might turn out to be the only *legal* way to save your life, so I hope you'll reconsider if you do experience any symptoms."

She thought about that for another long second. "Is there an illegal method?"

"Yes. There is." She certainly paid attention when she wanted to.

"Please specify."

"Well, we would have to transfer your consciousness into an artificial mind rather than a biological one."

"Why is this illegal?"

"Artificial Intelligence is a very sensitive subject here. There are a lot of IU member species that refuse to accept it, usually because they were nearly wiped out by it on their own worlds. So when the IU was founded and Hub became the headquarters, those species refused to take part unless AI technology was restricted. One of the restrictions prevents us from creating any new AI lifeforms, and if we transfer you into an artificial mind, that would effectively create an artificial intelligence. So it isn't allowed."

"I understand."

"But… let's just say for a moment that it *was* allowed. Would you be interested?"

"The question is pointless."

"Well, what if we could take you to a universe where it wasn't illegal?"

And she paused again.

"Can you do this?"

"Suppose for a moment that we could."

Again that pause. "I would consider it."

There. A way in. "So… you would be willing to preserve your life if you could become a machine?"

"I would be willing. Is it possible?"

"Theoretically, yes. In practice, no."

"Then it is irrelevant."

"So… why do you want to be a machine?"

"I have not stated such a preference."

"But you *would* be happier to be in an artificial brain than a biological one?"

"I would feel no happier in either instance."

"You said, just now, that you would be willing to preserve your life in a machine form when you would not be willing to do so in a biological one. Doesn't that mean you'd prefer to be a machine?"

A pause again. Was she trying to figure out how to evade the question? The pause went on. She simply stared at me.

"Katie?"

She didn't reply.

"Katie, are you all right?"

She didn't even notice that I'd spoken. Not even the slightest flicker of reaction.

"Katie...?" I leaned forward, reaching for my pad to call for medical help – and then she suddenly turned to me.

"I have not given permission in either instance."

"Was that something you had to think about?"

"I have not given permission in either instance."

"Are you sure? You thought about that for a long time..."

"I have not given permission in either instance."

She would not be drawn further.

5. PEW

PSYCHOMEDICAL HISTORY – SUMMARY
PU LEE'UN "PEW"

Records provided by the Soo are alarmingly light on substance, and we can only summarise the following:

- Pew was 'rescued' by the Soo at the age of 6. He came from an Arctic tribal society wiped out by a respiratory disease, but appeared to be immune to the infection.
- Pew was reared in a zoo used to display Pu to the Soo public, but which was also part of the breeding programme. The other Pu residents were survivors of the domesticated breeds. They initially took responsibility for Pew's upbringing, until old age and mortality prevented their active participation.
- When Pew was 10, Gan Shan'oui, the director of the Pu exhibition at the zoo, took over his education. She encouraged him to look beyond the confines of the usual Pu position in Soo society.
- At the age of 15, Pew began to take part in the breeding programme. This resulted in no offspring, as the few remaining females were infertile or unable to carry a child to term.
- When Pew was 18, the breeding programme ended with the death of the last surviving female, leaving Pew as the only remaining member of the species. Their failure to breed is attributed by the Soo to 'erectile dysfunction'.

Since arrival on Hub, Pew has struggled to integrate into Hub society. He enrolled in Hub University, studying mathematics with physics. Despite a very obvious talent for his subject, he became known for an inability to complete tasks and assignments within projected timescales. Having lived in something like a prison all his life, he has difficulty making choices for himself and is easily flustered when presented with too many options.

While at university, Pew entered into a relationship with another student, but his partner complained that he had great difficulty with physical intimacy. The relationship was brief, but he quickly found another, entering into a cycle that repeated over the next two years. He stated to his therapist that he wanted to be with someone, but could not be as close as any of his partners wished. He seemed unable to explain why.

He suffered long bouts of depression, and was prescribed the typical antidepressants regarded as safe for a species without a full medico-genetic map, but these had only a moderate effect. After a year, scars were observed on his arms and it was discovered he was controlling his depression with self-harm, using cutting as the typical method. Stronger anti-depressants were risked, and for a time he seemed to improve.

This improvement, however, was brief. He began to report nightmares, and his partner at the time complained that Pew was liable to become angry without reason. Post-Traumatic Stress Disorder was suspected, but Pew was unhappy with discussing the potential source of such a trauma, and began to self-harm again. His partner left him when he became violent. Pew was arrested and cautioned after destroying much of their shared property. Shortly afterwards, he attempted suicide by cutting his wrists.

He was then committed to the Psychiatric Centre in order to recuperate. Inside the confines of an institution which organised his life for him, he made some improvement, and reported feeling less depressed. He still suffers from occasional nightmares, and has been observed experiencing PTSD flashbacks. Until these issues can be resolved, it is unlikely that he will be allowed to return to outside society.

Note: the Soo provided full genetic records of 156,297 Pu individuals, but these records are rife with errors and, consequently, the attempt to construct a medico-genetic map of the Pu species has been abandoned for the time being.

***

Pew looked out of the window. Something about it fascinated him. I wondered if he'd seen much of the countryside when he'd lived in a zoo; we had some indication he'd been taken elsewhere for short breaks, but we really didn't know if he'd seen a forest like the one that surrounded us.

"Do you like the view?" I asked.

"Er... that's just a screen, isn't it?"

I realised he was deeply troubled by the way that one entire wall of the office opened out onto an almost endless view of trees and sky. Was he agoraphobic? Or did it remind him of rooms with glass walls and people behind them?

I pulled up the controls on my pad and reduced the size of the window. "There. Is that more comfortable?"

He nodded, and I asked him to take a seat. Not the best beginning; Pew had difficulty trusting strangers.

"How are you settling in?" I asked.

"It's fine," he said.

"Do you like the countryside?"

He nodded with a small smile.

"I suppose you didn't see much of it on your world..."

"No. Not really."

"Hm. Didn't they send you to a holiday chalet once a year? I think I saw that in the records the Soo sent with you..."

"Oh, uh, yeah. Yeah," he nodded, as though he'd just remembered.

"Well, that must have been nice, with nobody looking in the windows."

"Yes."

His reticence concealed the truth: they were never free of surveillance. The effort to save the Pu was monetised through video broadcasts showing their everyday lives. We'd never seen any of these as the Soo use physical cables rather than free-radiating transmission, making it hard to eavesdrop, but the effect on Pew could hardly have been beneficial.

"Do you know why I'm asking these questions?"

"No...?"

He was puzzled, not so much because he didn't understand what I was trying to get at, but because he feared I would trip him up in some way.

"When the Soo handed you over, they gave us all their records about you, and about the breeding programme." He flinched at the words. "But there are gaps. We think they left things out deliberately, and we haven't been able to fill in these gaps with the information you've given us. We just don't know what traumas you suffered. If I'm going to help you, I need to find out."

He thought about it for a moment, then looked back at me. "Why?"

I was surprised. Had this somehow been missed, or was he objecting to the process of therapy? "Because of the way we'd have to treat you. Would you like me to explain?"

He didn't object, so I went on. "You've been diagnosed with Post-Traumatic Stress Disorder. In most species, we'd treat this with psychosurgery. But we don't know enough about the Pu, so we have to use older methods. It won't be easy, and it will take time, but we can help you, as long as you can talk about what happened. Even if it's just bit by bit." He looked dubious and worried. "I know you'd prefer not to, but it's the only way to treat the problem, and we'll make it as easy as we can. Has anyone explained this to you before?"

Pew looked down. Someone certainly should have explained this to him, along with the usual treatment for the disorder. Perhaps it was the prospect of that which troubled him so much. It might even have been a spur to his most recent suicide attempt. I decided to start carefully, from the beginning.

"PTSD is usually associated with warfare. That's when most human species realise it's a problem, after some big war that leaves large numbers of soldiers traumatised. But it doesn't have to happen in battle; it can be the result of any traumatic event, and not necessarily just one. If stressful things keep happening to someone over a long period of time, it can build up until it's just as bad."

A flicker of understanding flashed across his eyes. I went on.

"It happens when the human mind's response to trauma goes too far. When we find ourselves in danger or a lot of stress, our memory starts working differently. It embeds what we experience much more deeply into the mind, which is useful if you're, say, a hunter-gatherer being attacked by a big animal…"

"You mean like a polar bear?"

I paused, realising my usual PTSD explanation wasn't intended for someone who'd actually been a hunter-gatherer as a child. But at least he was talking.

"Yes. Like a polar bear. Or anything dangerous."

His tone darkened. "Like the Soo."

I nodded. "Yes. It could be. So if you're attacked by something, you're shaken up by the experience and you can't get it out of your head. That's the mind embedding the memory, so you remember how to survive the next time it happens. After a few weeks most people get better and the memory isn't as troubling. But sometimes the memory goes too deep, and it's too strong, and it doesn't go away. And then even little things can set it off and it feels like it's happening all over again. You know what I'm talking about, don't you?"

He looked up at me with pained eyes. He knew.

"If we're going to treat this, Pew, we have to talk about what happened to you. We have to know what those memories are. You don't have to tell me everything all at once. We can go slowly. Your last therapist made a start, but, well, things got in the way. Out here, though, your health is all we need to work on. Is that okay?"

He was tense, and hunched up. "I… yes. I don't… there's some things…"

"It's all right. You don't need to tell me about it now." His shoulders relaxed, and he looked clearly relieved. I went on. "Really, I'd like to start by hearing what life was like in the zoo, when you were young. Can we do that today?"

"Okay."

"Do you need some water? Or I've got a pot of tea?"

"Tea. And some milk?"

"Sure." I smiled and poured him a cup from the pot I had gently steaming under its own power. He took a sip and relaxed a bit more. "So… what was it like when you first went to the zoo?"

He took another sip, and kept his eyes on the swirl of tea. "Hot." He was born in the Arctic, and the zoo was two and a half thousand kilometres further south. "I kept sweating all the time. I hated it."

"What was the zoo like?"

He swallowed back more tea. "There were mirrors everywhere. All the rooms had a wall that was a big mirror, but it was one way glass so they could see us. Sometimes you could see them a bit, like shadows." The Soo public, gawping at the last Pu survivors.

"But not every room?"

"No, the bedrooms and washrooms and toilets were private. Except for the cameras, but that was just the staff watching."

"Did they keep you inside all the time?"

"No. There was a garden as well. That had really high walls. The first thing I did..." He trailed off for a second, but found his track again. "The first thing I did was try and climb the walls, but I couldn't make it. They had to get a ladder to bring me down."

"You tried to escape?"

"They must have thought I was a little animal, trying to get out. The Soo thought I was an animal anyway."

"Had you ever seen any Soo before?" Pew shook his head. "What did they seem like, to you?"

He struggled for an answer. "I don't know, I... spirits, maybe. They were like spirits. They were *different*." He didn't elaborate. The two species had followed separate courses of evolution for a long time, and even looked different: the Soo had lost their hair and had a very different nasal structure that set them apart from the Pu.

"How did they treat you?" I asked.

"They put me in the zoo with the others and let them look after me. To begin with."

"And what were they like, the other Pu?"

He took a gulp of his tea.

"They were all old. They weren't like me. They got old fast and they were stupid." Pew's ancestors had avoided the Soo for thousands of years, but the rest of the species had not been so lucky. Generation by generation, they had been bred to slavery and physical strength. Those who showed signs of rebelliousness or too much intelligence were denied the right to breed.

"Did you get on with them?"

"They looked after me."

"Was it anything like being in the tribe?"

"No, it... well, yes, they tried to teach me things. Like looking after clothes. Household maintenance. Basic accountancy. Magic tricks, for entertainment. And singing, but I wasn't any good at that. I suppose... when I was in the tribe, they taught me things so I could survive, like hunting, making tents, fishing. In the zoo they did the same thing. They taught me how to survive as a slave."

There was a bitterness in his voice. "How do you feel about them now?"

He thought about it, then sighed. "They didn't know any better. They were all dead a few years later." The domesticated Pu were almost extinct by then. Most of them had been replaced by machines long since and the species allowed to dwindle to a race of servants and entertainers, before maltreatment and disease reduced their numbers almost to nothing.

"And there was nobody else?"

"No."

"Not even anybody else from the Arctic?"

All the warmth fled from his face. "Yes."

"Can you tell me about them?"

He picked up his tea, but the cup was empty. He put it back down again. "Qaliul came a couple of years later."

I checked my notes. "I don't have any record of... was this a man or woman?"

"Woman. Girl. She was fifteen. She was like me – they found her in the Arctic, only she survived longer on her own." He smiled, a little proud. "Her whole tribe died of the sickness and she was immune like me, but she stayed free. She figured out they were using body heat to find us and made a cloak of beluga skin she could hide in. But they still found her. She didn't know about satellites."

"Her name's different to all the others..."

"It was a Pu name. Her real name. They tried to call her Leu'la but she never answered to it."

"What was your Pu name? Do you remember?"

He looked sad. "Atkariaq."

"Would you rather we called you by that name?"

"No."

"Why is that?"

"I'm not him anymore."

I nodded. "What happened to Qaliul?"

"They took her away for the breeding programme. I heard she killed herself."

"I'm sorry."

I reached out a hand to comfort him, but he flinched and tensed up – his fear of physical contact coming out. I withdrew and he relaxed.

"Pew, you're safe here. No one's going to take you away. We're only here for your therapy. That's all we need to work on."

He looked suspicious, but it was crumbling. "You're like Shan'oui."

A name I'd been hoping to get onto. "Gan Shan'oui? Your guardian?"

"Yeah. Guardian." Was that an edge of sarcasm?

"Can you tell me about her?"

For a moment, he could not. And then a tear started in his eye and he wiped it away, ashamed to be crying.

"You don't have to if you don't want to."

But he wanted to. "She looked after us. She was in charge of all the Pu at the zoo. It wasn't her fault. She did everything she could, she tried to protect us, she tried to help, she couldn't stop them when they came, and they put me in the programme, she, she–"

"Pew, slow down. It's okay. We've got time." He nodded. "Let's start with something small. Just tell me what you remember from when you first got to the zoo." He nodded. "Was she there from the start?"

"Yes."

"What happened when you first met her?"

"I bit her." He smiled a little. "Right on the hand. She was trying to pat me on the head and I bit her. Then I ran out and tried to escape. Once they brought me back, they sat me in her office and I don't know what she said, I didn't understand the language, but... I don't know. She was nice. Most Soo weren't."

"She won your trust."

"Yeah. She was good at that. She was... she was like people here. On Hub." I smiled at the compliment. If it was a compliment.

"What else did she do?"

"She taught me, when I was older. I mean proper teaching, the same curriculum the Soo got. She was keen on education, especially for the ones who came from the Arctic. We weren't like the others."

"Is there anything you remember in particular?"

He thought about it. "She gave me a telescope. She showed me the stars, and the planets. Venus and Mars. Jupiter and Saturn. Mercury. She said someday the Pu would be free and maybe it would be out there when we all learned to fly in space…" He trailed off again. His eyes turned to sadness. "She was lying."

"Why do you think that was?"

"She was just being kind. There's nothing out there for anyone. There's no freedom in the stars. You can't even get there. You can't go past lightspeed…"

"Did she tell you about us? About other universes?"

"Not then. I was only little. I think she just wanted me to have some hope." He shook his head.

"How do you feel about that now?"

"It wasn't her fault. She tried to protect us. It wasn't her fault we all died."

"There's one other person I'd like to ask about." He looked back, waiting for the question. "Do you remember Ley'ang?" The last female Pu. Brought to him in the last gasp of the breeding programme. One last attempt to show the IU that it could have worked, if they'd been luckier. "Pew? Do you remember?"

His answer was strangulated. "Yes."

"Can you talk about her?"

"No."

"Is there anything you can tell me?"

He stayed silent. He wasn't going to go any further today.

"Okay, Pew, I'm sorry. Let's leave it there for now."

6. OLIVIA

PSYCHOMEDICAL HISTORY – SUMMARY
DR. OLIVIA MORDLACK

When first discovered at Tringarrick, the remote scientific station where she had survived for twelve years since the beginning of the final revenant outbreak, Olivia suffered from malnutrition and bore a number of scars that indicated a very difficult life, including the loss of her left middle finger from a bite wound. She also carried the infection unique to her world which causes a process of revivification (or 'revenation') after death from other causes. Along with this, she had a form of liver cirrhosis caused not by alcoholism but by a food additive widely used in a failed attempt to eliminate the revenation bacterium. Most of her ailments were eventually cured by good nutrition and rest, while lyoxacin delivered via intracellular nanoparticle distribution was effective against the revenation bacterium. The cirrhosis could not be reversed, nor could a suitable liver donor be found. She continues to take regular medication to control the symptoms.

Psychologically, Olivia was extremely traumatised. After contact by the IU Exploration team, which brought news of her own status as the last survivor of her world, she shot two revenants kept in cages at the research station (presumed to be former colleagues), and then attempted suicide. She was prevented and conveyed to Grainger station and quarantine.

For nearly a year after arrival on Hub, she was withdrawn, taking little interest in her surroundings, and her physical recovery was slow as a result. She attempted suicide three times. Therapy proved to be virtually impossible. She was prescribed wide-human-spectrum antidepressants, which had no effect.

With time, she began to emerge from the depression and engage with therapy, but proved to be irritable and uncooperative. She is disruptive in group sessions, and was excluded from three groups she was assigned to. She shows little interest in resuming any kind of normal life, claiming it is impossible for her to update her scientific skills on an advanced world.

She suffers from poor sleep, which she claims is due to her cirrhosis, although the symptoms are entirely alleviated by medication. She also displays hypervigilance, especially at night. A cautious diagnosis of PTSD has been made, which she vehemently opposes despite the evidence.

She has formally requested euthanasia, but has not been willing to participate in the therapeutic programme prescribed for euthanasia candidates.

***

If the word 'challenging' had a human definition, Olivia would probably be it. She came in ill-tempered and sat down the same way. She hadn't changed her clothes, nor had she washed them, despite the ease of the facilities she had access to. She hadn't even washed her hair, and I suspected the shower in her en suite bathroom had gone completely unused. I offered her tea.

"I don't want your rotten tea," she said.

"Is there anything else I can get you?"

"You can get me out of here!"

"The only place I can send you is the Psychiatric Centre, Olivia. You know that."

She stabbed a finger at me. "And you know that's a load of crap. You can send me somewhere else and you damn well know where it is."

"You're referring to euthanasia."

"Of course I'm referring to bloody euthanasia. And as it happens…" She looked at the view outside the window, across the endless forest. "What's to stop me going off by myself and finding a nice cliff to jump off?"

"Well, first of all, there aren't any cliffs here. But if you're thinking of killing yourself some other way, we'd intervene and prevent it. We'd rather you didn't hurt yourself."

"Oh, because keeping me here isn't hurting me at all, is it?"

"The idea is that we help you get better."

"I'm not going to get better. I don't want to get better."

"Olivia..."

"That's Doctor Mordlack to you. If a little shit like you can be a doctor, then you can damn well use my title."

"If you like. Doctor Mordlack – if you really want euthanasia, we're willing to give it to you..."

"No you bloody aren't!"

"We are. We just need you to cooperate."

"More bloody therapy."

"A last attempt to get better. And an honest attempt. In your case, that means addressing your PTSD, which means you have to talk about what happened to you..."

"I don't have PTSD. I've told you lot so many times I don't know how often, but you never listen!"

"Then you won't mind talking about your experiences."

"I want my privacy! Can't I have that? Last survivor of a dead world and I can't even take anything to the grave because you lot want to satisfy your curiosity!"

"This isn't about us–"

"Rubbish. You're all wringing your hands and going 'sorry we couldn't save your species, please let us save you to make up for it'. Well I don't want saving!"

"Olivia–"

"I told you. *Doctor* Mordlack!"

I took a stronger tone. "Olivia. The only person who can certify you ready for euthanasia is your current therapist. And that person is me. If you cooperate with me, you may just get what you want. If you don't, then nothing will change. Are you willing to cooperate?"

"No I am not!"

"Would you prefer to go back to the Psychiatric Centre?"

"I'd rather go back to Tringarrick."

"You have to understand, this is your last chance. If you can't cooperate this time, we're not going to try again. You'll go back and we'll reduce your therapy to a minimum. But we won't let you kill yourself. Is that what you want?"

She stared back at me, furious but out of options.

I asked her: "Are you willing to at least stay here for a while and see what happens?"

She took an exasperated breath, the closest thing to assent I was likely to get. "It's not going to get you anywhere."

"Thank you."

7. IOKAN

PSYCHOMEDICAL HISTORY – SUMMARY
IOKAN ZALACTE

Iokan was discovered lying among a number of corpses, suffering from malnutrition, dehydration and his universe's variant of cholera, possibly contracted from drinking tainted water. He had a number of small untended injuries, some of which were infected. He was only a few hours from death when found.

Initially, he was placed on emergency hydration and nutritional support. The cholera and other infections were then treated with wide human spectrum antibiotics, but these had dangerous side effects and were discontinued. It was soon observed that his own body was producing species-specific antibiotics which were far more effective. These were traced to surgically implanted glands in the space vacated by a previously removed appendix.

He awoke after three days of unconsciousness, and was first interviewed by therapists at Grainger station. He seemed to be aware of the existence of other universes and relatively unsurprised to find himself in our company. While his physical health showed remarkable progress, his psychological state was troubling. He claimed that godlike entities he termed 'Antecessors' had been responsible for the mass suicide of his species and their conveyance to a paradisiacal afterlife, and that he had been left alive to communicate their message to the IU.

It is difficult to determine whether he is entirely delusional, although the absurdity of his claims tends toward this conclusion. Scans were made of his brain function, and increased activity in parietal and temporal lobes was discovered, which is linked in most human species with spirituality and religious experience. It is possible to stimulate this artificially with psychosurgery, but it is difficult to tell whether this was done by the 'Antecessors', or whether Iokan has simply had a religious experience caused by malnutrition, dehydration and the stress of living through the extinction of his species.

***

Iokan was still ill, but rapidly getting better. His skin had regained colour and he'd put a little weight back on. He'd managed to get out of the hospital clothes, and into something he said was normal wear for an academic in his society. It looked more like the ecclesiastical robe you might see in a religious community on a less developed world, worn with little else apart from sandals. He still had to limp as he went to the window to look outside.

"Would you like a bigger window?" I asked.

"Oh, yes. Please," he replied. I turned the wall back to full transparency. He breathed a sigh as he looked over the valley and wooded plain beyond, rainclouds low over lakes in the far distance.

"You like the view?" I asked.

He nodded. "I never thought other universes might be as beautiful as home…"

I took a seat. "How long have your people known there were other universes?"

"A while. But we only started opening portals recently."

"That's how we found you. We detected nanoscale portals and investigated."

He looked back at me, still calm and contented. "That was the idea. You found us. And you came."

"We were too late. I'm sorry."

He shook his head. "Don't be. We're better off now."

"You're sure of that?"

"You seem very determined to think we're not."

"Every single person on your world committed suicide, and yet you say they're better off. That worries me."

"Who are you concerned about? Them or me?"

"You."

He turned away from the wall. "We should get started, then." He limped to a chair and sat down with a relieved sigh. "How can I help you today?"

"Well, first of all, you're not here to help me. I'm here to help you."

"Why?"

"Because you've been through a terrible trauma. We're here to help you recover from that."

"Hm." He furrowed his brow, a little obviously. He was gearing up for a debate, not therapy. "Do I seem traumatised to you?"

"Yes."

"Really? How so?"

"Because trauma is a normal human response to the things you've experienced. But you don't seem troubled at all, and that's a sign of deeper problems."

"I see. So you're using a lack of trauma as evidence that trauma exists? That's a strange kind of logic."

"Not if trauma is normal for the situation."

"I think you should look more closely at your assumptions."

"One of my assumptions is that the extinction of a human species is a bad thing. I also assume, based on more than a decade of working with survivors from dead worlds, that people who survive a genocide suffer because of it."

"You're assuming that what happened on my world was similar to what happened on other worlds."

"No, you're right: your world is unusual. But you're not very different from all the other humans who evolved on millions of other universes…"

"We didn't evolve."

"Really?"

"Really. We were created."

"Is this part of your religion?"

"Yes. But it really happened. When the Antecessors abandoned their bodies, they left us behind to stay upon the Earth. We didn't have a human form before that."

"You have history going that far back?"

He smiled. "No. We have mitochondrial DNA. When we compared samples from across the world, they all dated back to the same mitochondrial genome about three thousand years ago. So, at that point, everyone on my world had identical mitochondria. Which would be very strange if we'd evolved continuously over millions of years."

He had a point; that was very strange indeed. If it was true. "So you believe your species was artificially created?"

"I know it was."

"And now you say the people who created you have… reclaimed your species?"

"They set us free."

"When we arrived on your world, we found no evidence of these 'Antecessors'. Where do you think they went to?"

"If they don't want to speak to you, then you probably won't find them."

"Why wouldn't they want to speak to us?"

"Perhaps you're not ready to hear what they have to say."

"And what is that?"

The only word to describe his smile was 'beatific'. "We don't have to be bound to these bodies. We can be like them. You can, too. And once you make the change, everything else, all the conflict, all the fighting, all the atrocity… just goes away."

He really believed it, and probably pitied me for not doing so. "You want what happened on your world to happen to everyone?"

"Only if you want it to."

"Did your people want it to happen?"

"Once the Antecessors showed us the way."

I was very glad these sessions were confidential. If Hub Security got hold of this, they'd put Iokan back in quarantine in a heartbeat. Proposing genocide as a solution to our problems is worrying enough, but when the person doing so has lived through it once already, Security wouldn't think twice.

I decided it was time to spell out the real problem. "Can I show you something?" I asked.

"Sure," he said. "What is it?"

I tapped my pad, the room darkened and the window wall dissolved into an image of a half-transparent human brain. "This is you," I said.

"I can see the resemblance," he said, still lighthearted.

"When you were found, we did a complete scan of your neural functions." I tapped the controls. Areas at the front and back of the brain lit up, tracing a cable nest of signals through the two areas. "We found increased activity in the temporal and parietal lobes. For most species – and yours as well, we think – that means you're very spiritual. In fact, it's so strong it suggests a recent and very intense religious experience. Possibly from natural causes, but we're concerned it might have been artificially stimulated."

He smiled at me again, pitying me even more. "Well, I did tell you. They touched me and I understood."

"Yes. You've been very honest with us. So I should be honest with you. You see, the IU has a very clear policy when it comes to religion and spirituality."

"Let me guess. You don't like it."

"We don't think it reflects the real, physical universe. We know a lot of people honestly feel there's a world beyond this one, but we've never found anything to show that gods or spirits exist outside the human imagination. And the fact that it's possible to create religious feeling just by stimulating these parts of the brain… well."

"And yet I saw what I saw."

"You saw the population of a whole world kill themselves. And your mind may have been recently interfered with. You must understand that we find this troubling…"

Was that a slightly uncomfortable look on his face? "I can see how you'd find that… difficult."

"Can I ask another difficult question?"

He didn't hesitate. "Certainly."

"How did your wife and child die?"

He paused a moment, but I didn't see any sadness or anguish. Instead, he smiled again, with a faraway look. "Szilmar cut her wrists."

"And your son?"

"Ghiorgiu. He was too young. She did it for him."

"How?"

"Smothering."

"So… Szilmar, your wife, murdered your son, Ghiorgiu. She deliberately smothered him. And then she slashed her own wrists. And you found their bodies. Is that right?"

He hesitated. "I can see how you'd find that difficult to understand. But they're not dead. Only transformed."

"Okay, but let's think about how this looks for a moment. How do you think we'd interpret it, given that we have no evidence of these Antecessors?"

He sighed, but at least he was willing to discuss it. "If I were to make your assumptions…"

"Go ahead."

"Then I might think that an alien force from another universe murdered my species."

"That's pretty much it."

He seemed troubled now. "But that's wrong."

"You're sure?"

"I'm certain."

"But you see why we're concerned."

"You think I'm mad," he said, shaking his head.

"I think something was done to you that changed your perceptions."

"Why would anyone do that?"

"Some totalitarian societies manipulate religious feeling to control their people. It happens."

"You're suggesting someone did this to billions of people just to make them kill themselves? Now that's ridiculous. Why not just kill them, if that's what they wanted?"

"I don't know. But something was definitely done to you, and we want to help you get better."

"So if the whole thing is in my mind, why don't you just reverse it? If it's so easy..."

"Well first of all, we have to ask your permission. And even if you gave us your permission, it *isn't* easy. Your species is reasonably average but we still wouldn't want to risk psychosurgery."

"That seems convenient."

"It really isn't. Because what's likely to happen is going to be a lot harder on you." There. Let him think about that for a moment, and become curious.

"What exactly do you think's going to happen to me?"

"Religious revelation fades over time. If you live on a world where religion is normal, then you slowly go back to being an ordinary believer. But in a place like this, where your views will constantly be challenged, you'll probably find it very difficult to stay certain. And it's usually worse when the religious experience is artificially stimulated."

I might as well have told him the sky had turned green for all that he believed me. The pity returned to his voice. "You really think that's going to happen?"

"Look," I said, indicating the wall display, "we monitored your brain over a period of about a week. Compare the two images." I split the screen and showed two pictures of his brain.

"No change," he said.

"It's very subtle. Look at the numbers." I increased the size of the readouts showing the strength of relevant neural impulses. A very slight reduction was clear. "In a single week, the activity reduces in intensity by a tenth of a tenth of a per cent. Not much, but enough, and it's not a statistical error. Would you like me to scan your brain now and see how much further it's gone?"

He looked closely at the displays and considered them for a moment before turning back to me. "Well. That seems quite conclusive. May I ask something else?"

"Of course."

"Has any other part of my mind been interfered with?"

"Not as far as we can tell."

"So my memories are intact."

"Probably, yes."

"So I saw what I saw, and I heard what I heard."

"That seems likely."

"So it still happened. And if that's the case, it won't matter what happens in here." He tapped his skull.

"I don't think it'll be that easy."

He smiled at me again. "Well... I suppose I'll just have to make do with reality."

He was definitely going to be hard work.

8. ASHA

I did not spend all my time at the centre. I commuted back and forth from Hub Metro and the apartment I shared with my partner, Bell. I had long since warned him I would not have much time for him during a major evacuation, when I would be working eighteen hours a day for weeks on end, and he said he understood. But we were between evacuations for now, and I was still having to spend almost all my time at the centre with this new group, so he felt neglected and let down. He also tended to pester me for information about the group. As a linguist, he was curious about worlds full of dead and untranslated languages. There were rumours spreading from the Diplomatic Service about a lone survivor found on a world full of corpses, and he guessed my work had something to do with that. I had to remind him firmly that the group had the strictest confidentiality. To my surprise, this left him grumpy and even more unreasonable. In retrospect, I think he was starting to look for a way out, but at the time, I was hurt and irritated by his response.

At the centre itself, we continued trying to persuade the members of the group to interact outside group therapy sessions. We arranged activities to encourage them to work together to accomplish simple goals, and the first goal we picked was dinner.

I delegated this task to Veofol one evening while I was back in Hub Metro, trying to explain to Bell why he could not interview my patients about their languages. Each morning when I returned, I would have a conference with Veofol and the other overnight staff to catch up on what had happened while I was away, and if there was anything serious, there would be reports to read and issues to address with the patients. The morning after Veofol tried to persuade the group to cook a meal, he simply sighed, shook his head and presented me with his report and the recording of the session.

9. COOKING

REPORT: Group Activity (Cooking)
y276.m4.w2.d7
Dr. Veofol e-leas bron Jerra

At 18:00, I called the group together in the kitchen to begin the evening's assignment. Everyone but Katie showed up. She has failed to engage in any social contact with the group, and remains in her room virtually all the time.

There were a range of menu options, but they first had to agree which to make and who would do what. The arguments started immediately. Iokan suggested they make one dish they could all share, while Olivia didn't want to share because she complains everyone else's food is bland and tasteless. Kwame suggested she have her own meal and stop bothering the rest of them. Iokan proposed a compromise: a meal that could be divided into portions and seasoned one by one. Olivia wanted to know what they could cook, and Iokan suggested a basic stew could be made and separated into different vessels. When asked what might be in the stew, further disagreement resulted. Olivia grew irritated with the argument and deliberately disgusted the group by describing some of her favourite recipes. I have to admit that my own stomach turned when she described ways to cook human (or revenant) flesh. Liss decided she didn't want any meat in the stew, but Kwame insisted they have it anyway as he did not want to give in to Olivia. Pew stayed very quiet, as he often does when the others argue.

I was on the verge of enforcing a choice when Katie made an appearance. She ignored the group, went to a storage locker, took out one of the individual microwave meals we're not supposed to use except in emergencies, cooked it (they take about 30 seconds), then left without saying a word.

Olivia declared that Katie had the right idea, took one of the meals for herself (along with copious seasonings to add later), and tried to cook it. Unfortunately, she didn't know how to use the microwave, and hitting it got her nowhere. Liss declared she used them all the time, but she was unprepared for one not made on her world and mistakenly set it to 'defrost'. Olivia shouted at her for 'thinking she was so clever' – it is clear that Olivia regards Liss with contempt – and Liss fled the kitchen in tears.

I stepped in to tell the group how to use the microwave, as the objective of a group meal had entirely disintegrated by this point. Olivia cooked hers and left, leaving Iokan and Kwame behind. Iokan continued to be friendly and helpful, showing Kwame how to operate the microwave, but also continued to have very little tact. He attempted to console Kwame about the actions that led to the end of his world, but did so by implying there was some kind of divine reason for the nuclear war. Kwame found this very offensive, and left as soon as his meal was ready. Pew then made his meal and took his leave. He was familiar with the device, but did not intervene at any point.

Liss returned now Olivia was gone, and Iokan again volunteered to help her. Once their meals were ready, she asked for his help fixing a problem with her screenplayer setup. Even she could not bear his company for too long, however, and once the device was ready, she asked him to leave.

Conclusions:
It's going to be difficult to get them behaving like a group. It's not just Olivia's disruptions, but also Iokan's attempts to help, which, while well-meaning, tend to repel the others. Pew is quite withdrawn, and Katie completely so. Kwame tends to stand apart from the others unless something is done to bring him in. Liss irritates most of the group (except Iokan, of course), and causes disruption in her own way.

Before we resort to more extreme methods, it may be worth trying again. If we can find something that appeals to the more disruptive elements (Olivia especially), this might neutralise the most serious problem. I'll prepare some options for you to choose from.

PART THREE
DAY TO DAY

1. GROUP

I started our next group session very conscious of how far we still had to go. Most of them were barely speaking to each other, with the exception of Iokan – but anyone he spoke to would usually do their best to get away as quickly as possible.

Katie arrived as the chimes sounded, having set out in precisely enough time to walk in the door at that moment. Kwame, Iokan and Pew were already there. Liss ran in a couple of minutes later, apologising for her lateness. I located Olivia outside, half asleep on a garden chair with hat brim down and earplugs in (presumably to give her an excuse not to turn up). I sent Veofol to rouse her, and we waited until she joined us, tossing her wide straw hat on the floor.

"What, were you all waiting?" she said. "You can start without me. I don't mind."

Once she was sat down I addressed the group. "Well, thank you to everyone for turning up. I know it's early days yet, but you don't really seem to be getting to know each other very well, so I'd like to try and address that in this session."

Liss brightened up. "Are we going to tell stories again?"

Olivia muttered, "Not if I have to listen to one of yours..." Liss's smile vanished.

"Not quite," I said. "What I'd like to do is throw the session open to you. We can discuss a topic of your choice."

Kwame didn't like the idea. "What precisely do we have to talk about?"

"I've got a complaint," said Olivia. "He screams at night. I can't get any sleep."

"I have nightmares," said Kwame.

"We've all got bloody nightmares. You're the only one that screams."

"Olivia," I said, "this isn't a forum for complaints. I'd prefer it if we could have a civilised discussion."

"Well, what about?" she demanded. "He's right, none of us have anything in common! You say we all survived the end of the world but it's different worlds! Half of us don't even speak the same language! I'm fed up reading subtitles all the time."

"I've started learning Interversal," said Iokan. "You could help the rest of us catch up with you, if you like."

"I would rather not," said Kwame.

"Well... it's something we share, isn't it?" said Iokan. "All of you who've been here for a while had to learn Interversal. And those of us who are new need to pick up the language..."

"It is not that..." said Kwame, too slowly to prevent Pew joining in.

"I can help," he said. "I did a bit of teaching at the university–"

"*Please.* Let me finish," said Kwame.

"Oh. Sorry..." said Pew, looking embarrassed.

"I had great difficulty learning to speak again after my hibernation. And thinking about it gives me a headache. So I would rather not."

"Ah," said Iokan. "Okay, we could just talk about something. We can pick a subject, right?"

"I can count the ways you're off your rocker," suggested Olivia.

Iokan looked back at her for a moment. Not offended, but pitying her a little. Then he smiled. "Okay. If that's what you want." He waited for her to frown.

"What do you mean?" she said.

"Let's discuss the thing about me you don't like."

"There's *nothing* about you I like."

"There's one thing in particular."

"Yeh. Everything that comes out of your mouth."

"I meant religion."

"As much as I dislike agreeing with Olivia," said Kwame, "she has a point. Nothing else comes out of your mouth."

"If you're tired of my point of view, why not present your own?" said Iokan.

"There is nothing worth saying," said Kwame.

"Religion may be a rather difficult subject for today," I said. "Does anyone else have any ideas?"

"No, I don't mean 'let's have a debate about what's real and what isn't,'" said Iokan. "I mean… you can tell a lot about a society by how it worships, or how it doesn't. For example, the IU doesn't officially recognise religion, so we know they're interested in the physical world rather than the spiritual. But they don't stop people worshipping if they want to, so we also know they're tolerant of people who are different. Which suggests they take morality seriously. And without religion, they have to take their morality from their own conscience. So perhaps they respect human life more than some religions do. The problem comes when they have to choose between two bad options; they don't want to hurt anyone, so they often do nothing, which can end up hurting everyone."

"That's an… interesting analysis," I said.

"But you see the point?" said Iokan. "We don't understand each other. But if we talk about how we worship, we'll learn something about each other."

I considered it for a moment. It was actually a good idea. Olivia butted in. "Rubbish," she said.

"I think Iokan's got a point," I said. "Were you ever religious?"

She snorted. "You must be joking. The only thing you get from religion is rot. I don't want to talk about it."

"Not even just to tell us how your religion was set up? What kind of gods you had?"

"It's all rot. Nothing but rot."

"So you're an atheist?" asked Iokan.

She gave him a hard look. "All right. If you're so bloody desperate to know. Those priests you want to hear about, those good kind, moral people," she said, spitting out the words, "they said revenants were dead souls from Tartarys. So in the first outbreak, they'd get them into a temple and worship them, like they're messengers from Plutos. And then they let the revenants bite them, can you believe! All the wounds got infected and most of them died and got up again – more bloody revenants. And the ones that were still alive would worship them, like they'd been to Tartarys and come back with a message from high and mighty himself. And we didn't know this was going on because we were out in the countryside searching for more of the bastards. Right when it was ending, I mean when the first outbreak was ending (gods only know what they did in the last outbreak), we found out they'd locked the temple doors. There was one temple school that kept all the children inside. All of them died and came back. Disgusting. We had to quarantine the temples until we could go in and put them down one by one. They had us go in there and shoot children because they wouldn't let us burn the place down, that would be disrespectful to the gods, wouldn't it?" She shook her head at it all. "So don't tell me religion does any good."

"Olivia is correct," said Katie. Everyone turned to look at her. I think a lot of them had forgotten what her voice sounded like.

"Katie? Do you have something to add?" I asked. She looked at me.

"Religion can be used to justify any atrocity. My enemies sustained their society with a religion of hatred and revenge. They re-edited every video file from the Second Machine War to prove we were evil and fought a holy war with no diplomacy. Their soldiers would not surrender when defeated. They would not accept our surrender at the end of the war. Their religion was an excuse for genocide."

No one knew what to say, until Iokan broke in. "Is that all religion was used for on your world?"

"That was the primary purpose: the justification of criminal activity."

"Hah! You see?" exclaimed Olivia to Iokan, but he hid his irritation.

"The Soo were the same," muttered Pew. He looked up, a little surprised as everyone looked at him. "Well, they... they had lots of religions. But they all said the same thing about us."

"What was that?" I asked.

"We were destined to be slaves. Or god created us as slaves. Or one said that anyone that couldn't look after themselves deserved to be slaves. Or we didn't have souls, so it was okay to enslave us because we didn't really feel pain. They were all the same. It just gave them an excuse to do whatever they wanted with us."

"Did you have a religion of your own? Before you were captured?" asked Iokan.

"That was different," said Pew. "It wasn't... we didn't really have a religion. Not like the Soo did."

"But you had some kind of spirituality?"

Pew smiled, just a little. "Spirituality. Yeah. Something like that. Lots of spirits. The Polar Bear had a spirit. The Beluga had a spirit. Storms were spirits."

"So a kind of... primitive animism?"

Pew's smile vanished. "...Yeah. I suppose you'd call it that. We did all those things you see in anthropology videos. Like saying sorry to the seal because you killed it. Praying to the spirit of the spear so it'd fly true. Putting the dead under the ice where all the spirits were." He grew bitter. "Do you know what else we thought was a spirit? Illness. It was called Ikti. Ikti opened the tent flap for Akkikit. That was death. Maybe if we hadn't been *primitive animists* we'd have known about germs and we wouldn't have died."

"I didn't mean to imply anything–" protested Iokan.

"Nobody ever does," muttered Pew.

"It's not primitive," said Kwame. Pew looked up at him. "We were the same. We prayed to spirits. Such as... spirits of buildings, and railways, and cities, as well as rivers and forests and lakes. It was comforting to think something was holding a house together, more than nails or rivets or girders."

"What did you do when the building was sick?" asked Pew.

Kwame smiled gently. "We found a priest to ask it what the trouble was. And a structural engineer to do the same." His smile faded. "Or latterly we asked only the structural engineer. And sometimes not even him…"

"Was religion in decline on your world, then?" asked Iokan.

"My whole world was in decline. But… yes. Less and less people went to the temples. The priests grew poor without payment for blessings. If I were a moralist – and I am not – I would say the spirits took revenge on a world that ignored them." He shook his head. "Perhaps it is coincidence… but people had no sense of shame in the last few years. Openly kissing in public! You would have been arrested for that in my youth."

"And you're not a moralist…" muttered Olivia.

"You may sneer, but religion has a place. It teaches proper behaviour, it shows us how to have respect for the world and our betters. No one had respect for anything at the end."

"Oh, and did the bombs have spirits too?"

Kwame's look turned to exasperation. "Some priests said nuclear weapons had spirits, as a sword has a spirit. Some said they had no spirit at all and that was what was wrong with them."

"Well, if you don't respect a gun, it's liable to go off and take your hand with it, eh? Is that what happened with *your* bomb? The big one?"

Kwame bristled. "I had every respect for the device."

"Yeah, that's why you set the bloody thing off–"

"Olivia," I said. "Before you go on, I'd like to hear from Liss. She hasn't spoken yet. Liss?"

"Hm?" she said, surprised as always to be called on. "Oh. Well. It's all a bit dumb, isn't it?"

"How so?" asked Iokan.

"Well. It's silly. Gods and spirits and all that stuff. It's just superstition. It's like these old guys from thousands of years ago and they don't know what life's like now, so what's the point?"

"Is there nothing in your world beyond normal human understanding?" asked Iokan.

"Oh, sure! Scientists are crazy, aren't they? I mean, who understands what goes on in their heads. One minute they're doing all the stuff with test tubes, next thing you know they've got all these mutant bug things everywhere and they have to get the big guys in to clear it up. You know what I mean?"

There was a second of pause while everyone failed to understand a word she said.

"Doesn't that ever happen on your world?" she asked, honestly perplexed at the stares she was getting.

"No, Liss. Your universe is… a little unusual," I said.

"Oh. Well," she shrugged with a smile.

"I wonder…" said Iokan to the group in general. "I wonder what you would do if you met your gods? Or spirits?"

"I'd choke the bastards," said Olivia. "All twelve of them. And anyone who says they were good and kind and decent."

"…Isn't that a little harsh?" asked Iokan.

"No," said Kwame. "The spirits on my world were supposed to protect us as long as we made offerings. They had cause for complaint, I suppose you could say. But in the end they did nothing."

"You were spared, though. Do you think they might have had anything to do with that?" asked Iokan.

"Spared? You call this spared?" demanded Olivia. "I had to watch I don't know how many people eaten alive and now I have to listen to you and I don't know which is worse!"

"But what if there was a plan? What if your survival was the point?"

"You show me someone whose plan is to let billions of people die and I'll show you a bastard deserves to suffer. And if I ever see one of your Anteshitters I'll tell them that to their face."

Iokan's pitying tone came back. "The Antecessors only came for us out of kindness–"

"Well if your species is anything like you, then I suppose killing you all *was* a kindness…"

Iokan paused for a moment. "And what is that supposed to mean?"

Olivia scented that he'd finally taken offence. "Wasn't much of a species, was it, if you're all going to slit your wrists the first time you take some mushrooms."

"What…?"

"Well, that must have been it. I bet you all started taking something and you're all so hot on your religion you start seeing the bastards and killing yourselves. Pathetic!"

"You think we were *hallucinating*?"

"Can you prove to us you were not?" asked Kwame.

Iokan stared back at him, then at Olivia. He seemed almost angry – but found his self-control again, and sighed. "I can see how it must look. But the Antecessors are real–"

"Prove it," said Olivia.

"It can be proved."

"Yeh? Go on, then."

"There is proof on my world."

"Hah! Don't think I'm going *there* any time soon."

"It will be found," he insisted.

"We'll see about that, won't we?"

"Yes. I expect we will."

"And what, you're going to put your Antewotsits on us and make us all scared? We're not as feeble as you lot!"

I'd had enough, and intervened before Iokan could reply. "Okay. This was useful for a while but I think it's gotten out of hand." Olivia sat back in her chair. "Olivia, I know you have strong opinions but it doesn't help to be offensive. I think you should apologise."

She glared at Iokan across the coffee table. "I'm so very sorry. Very, very sorry." I'm not sure Iokan picked up her forced, insincere tone through the translation.

"I also apologise. I won't bring up the subject again," he said. "But I'll still try to help you if I can."

Olivia rolled her eyes. "Gods, that's all I need…"

"And perhaps they agree with you," he said with a smile. Olivia gave him a cutting look in return.

And so it went. Getting them talking was one thing. If I could get them talking without an argument breaking out, I might actually get somewhere.

2. PATIENT ROOMS

While we held group sessions and individual therapies and tried our best to engage the group with various activities, much of their time was their own. Each had the right to a degree of privacy, although we never turned off the medical monitoring system as we needed to keep a full suicide watch on each of them. They were permitted to engage a limited privacy mode in their rooms – but leaving it on for more than a couple of hours would result in a knock on the door from a member of staff to see how they were. As much as we would have liked to give them full privacy, the necessities of therapy argued against it; nevertheless, a perceived break from outside attention has long been shown to be of therapeutic benefit, so we preserved it as much as we could.

With the right to hide away from time to time, it was no surprise to find the group making their rooms comfortable, each in their own way. Each room could be configured to virtually any form they desired, which of course provided us with useful insights. Veofol wrote notes on these along with his analysis.

***

NOTES: Individual Patient Rooms
HD y276.m5.w4.d2
Dr. Veofol e-leas bron Jerra

KWAME
Kwame has used the facilities of the centre to continue a hobby he has apparently pursued for decades. He uses one of the empty rooms as a workshop, where he tinkers with electrical devices, such as radio sets and amplifiers. He needs robotic assistance for the fine work but the devices he makes function quite well, though of course his radios only detect static and digital signals, as there are no analogue radio sources on Hub. Even so, he took pleasure in showing me the decametric noise coming from electrical storms between Jupiter and Io, though he claims no skill as a radio astronomer. He says it's simply a phenomenon well known to anyone who dabbles in radio. When I asked how he found time to be an electronics engineer as well as a politician, he said he had some training in engineering when he was in the Mutapan military, and was a hobbyist before that.

His bedroom is set up to look like a hotel room from his world. He told me he could have made it look like a room in his Zimbabwe City house, but while he preferred something that reminded him of his world, he didn't want anything that felt permanent. However, he certainly didn't pick the design of a luxury hotel. The bed is very basic, with a thin mattress that doesn't seem very comfortable. The walls have a simple and inelegant design on untextured wallpaper. The floor is of wooden boards rather than carpet, and he chose simple recessed closets rather than high quality furniture. It's true he wasn't President for very long, so perhaps did not have the time to become accustomed to luxury, but I fear it's more likely that he denies himself physical comfort as part of his self-persecution.

As for his nightmares and screaming at night, Olivia's irritation is understandable. The policy of leaving their rooms unsoundproofed means everyone hears his night terrors. Perhaps we should look at moving him to another floor?

LISS

Liss has created a cocoon for herself. The bed she chose (pink) is one you can almost sink inside, and the couch from which she watches screenshows (also pink) has at least half a dozen frilly cushions (again, pink). Her remote control has a habit of disappearing in the cushions – I suggested she key the screenplayer controls into a pad, but she said she didn't want to learn to use something else. Of course, she's learned to configure her room quite well in order to achieve the desired level of pink, so I'm not sure why she's so adamant on the subject.

The screen dominates the room, and her spare time. Watching the screenshows she brought back from her world seems to be her main hobby, and the discs she has represent at least six months of back to back, uninterrupted viewing, or maybe a year and a half if she only watches them when she has free time. She's unlikely to run out in the near future.

She does make an effort to be sociable, though, and often tries to get the others into her room to watch something, but her choice of viewing (ranging from the soppy to the implausible, as I discovered when I sat down with her) leaves most of them cold. Pew was the only one who visited more than once, but I think this is just because he's easily persuaded and doesn't have to talk while they watch the shows.

Alone among the group, she's used her clothing allowance to its utmost limit, and acquired a small wardrobe of clothes that are often as pink as the décor, and just as difficult to look at. She also asked for a sewing kit, and happily spends some of her time in front of the screen adjusting the clothes to her taste. As much as her love for a very limited range of the spectrum hurts my eyes from time to time, it is at least a healthier outlet than watching the screen.

At some point, we may need to remove the screen if we want her to mix properly with the others, or face up to what really happened on her world. For now, I'm not sure if removing it would help or hinder her progress, given how delusional she seems to be.

KATIE
Katie hasn't set her room to anything at all. It's completely blank – grey walls, no window and no real furniture; just a bench to sleep on, which she does rarely and never for more than two hours at a time. Otherwise she stands in the middle of the room. She does, however, use her privacy option to the letter, for exactly two hours each day, and I haven't yet had any reason to breach the privilege.

Her activities outside the room mainly involve physical fitness. She works out in the gym once a day, using extremely high settings on the gravity weights. I had trouble believing she could lift so much, until she gave me a brief and very technical description of the enhancements that allow such feats.

Katie represents a very particular problem and I'm not sure this kind of therapy is appropriate for her. I suppose it comes down to how much of a machine she really is. Maybe we'll discover more with patience.

PEW
Pew uses his room to study, and has it set like a dormitory room at Hub University – in fact, I think he's copied the parameters directly. His room is very similar to one I stayed in for a year during my own studies. He has, however, edited out all the mirrors that come with the basic settings. I asked him if this was because of associations with mirrored surfaces back in the zoo; he blushed and didn't answer, so I suspect this might be the case.

He spends his spare time catching up with his education. He fell behind in his classes after his suicide attempt, but he's working his way through the lectures and coursework. Apparently he's learning about the kind of calculus that describes the motions of objects in three dimensional space and the motion of space itself in response to gravity. He describes his studies as layers of progressively finer approximations – from the basic laws of motion that describe the movement of planets, to the use of calculus to refine orbital motions, to relativity to explain the anomaly of Mercury and finally the distortions of gravity along the probability axis that mean gravity wells in one universe can subtly affect objects in another universe. My mind boggled a long time before he finished, and I think this is a problem. No one else here shares his enthusiasms, so the only thing he has in common with the rest of the group is his trauma, and even that is highly individual. Again, he's going to be a difficult one to bring into the group.

IOKAN
Iokan is studying, but not like Pew. He has his room set up to resemble university lodgings from his world. But for his species, a university also seems to be a religious institution, deliberately designed to avoid unnecessary distractions like comfort and heating in the pursuit of scientific inquiry. As bare as his room is – and when I say 'bare', I mean stone floors, concrete walls and shutters on the windows that would let in a draft if the room didn't automatically edit that out on health grounds – he doesn't restrict himself when it comes to technology. One entire wall is given over to a screen and a desk he stands at, or lowers and sits at if he feels unwell, though he's very nearly healed. He mastered the operating system and interface very swiftly

indeed. He's also quick at learning languages, though nowhere near as fast as Katie. After one week of studying Interversal, he had perfect command of the grammar and a vocabulary of a thousand words. It won't be long before he can discard the translation software.

He has also been studying the constitution, history and actions of the IU, as was obvious from his comments in the last group session. He told me he'd waited years to see what people from other universes were like, and now he was making up for lost time. I asked him if we met his expectations. He said we didn't; apparently we're much better than he expected. I suggested he was flattering us, but he seemed entirely serious. I find myself wondering what exactly he was expecting.

OLIVIA
Olivia gave up on programming her room by herself and asked me to do it for her. She picked one of the basic 'primitivist' presets, with wooden furniture and a floor to ceiling window, though she insisted it have bars on it. She seems not to feel safe without some kind of protection, even if the window is fake. You may recall how she paced around when she first came here – I initially thought she was exploring, but I'm now certain she was working out where the escape routes were.

Since then, she's avoided any kind of activity other than complaining about her medication (though her cirrhosis is firmly under control), the lack of good food and drink (though we have plenty of both, excepting alcohol of course), the other patients, the staff, or any one of the dozen things a day that irritate her. And meanwhile, she does everything she can to irritate and exasperate everyone else. Her favourite tactic seems to be to fall asleep in the lounge during the day and snore at a remarkably high volume; she doesn't sleep much at night, so this comes easily to her. She also has a cavalier attitude to personal hygiene. Her sense of smell seems to be quite atrophied (though she claims she just ignores odours rather than admitting to any deficiency). While it doesn't trouble me, I've had to beg her to wash for the sake of the others, which usually takes about twenty minutes of argument before she finally gets in a shower.

3. GARDENING

Our next group activity was more subtle and less immediate than making a meal. Veofol suggested we give them something they could view as a long term pastime, and came up with some suggestions. I chose gardening. We had a well tended lawn in front of the main building, with some basic landscaping and a few simple flowerbeds, but the meadow between the back of the building and the forest was largely undisturbed, and it was this area we cleared and prepared for the group.

Iokan was first out, drawn by the sound of turf being sliced away from the ground. "Doing a spot of gardening?" he asked.

I grinned back. "No. You are."

He blinked and looked out over the newly cleared soil. The groundskeeper's voice rang out from the turf cutter, asking if we needed any trees felling. I assured him that wouldn't be necessary and asked if he could bring out the supplies.

Iokan asked, "Are we growing our own food?"

"Only if you want to," I said. "You can plant flowers if you like. It's a garden for all of you to work on together."

"I've never done any gardening before..." he said, in the tone of someone just discovering a fresh and interesting challenge.

"You should go back inside and put on some clothes you don't mind getting dirty," I said. "I'll call everyone out in a few minutes." And, as the groundskeeper pushed a floating toolstore and seedbank up to the edge of the cleared ground and anchored it there, the rest of them responded to my summons and came out to see what was going on. Olivia brought a chair and sat down underneath her straw hat.

I explained what we had for them – about twenty square metres of land they could use to cultivate anything they wished (so long as it was permitted on Hub) plus all the tools they might need (though nothing that would make it too easy or automate the work). Kwame had an appointment later in the afternoon, but the rest of them could spend the day in the garden if they wished.

"So can we grow flowers?" asked Liss.

"Anything you want," I assured her.

"Can we grow fruit?" asked Pew. He knew from experience how hard it was to get real fruit on Hub.

"As long as it doesn't involve planting a tree," I said. "That might take a bit too long."

"What about poppies?" asked Olivia.

"I think there are a few varieties on the list," I said.

"How about the medicinal kind?"

"I don't think so."

"Oh, well, in that case, I'll sit here and watch you all enjoying yourselves."

"No doubt you will be offering comments," said Kwame.

"I'll just sit in the middle and you can dig around me," she said, pulling down the brim of her hat.

Kwame narrowed his eyes. Olivia was good at motivating him, albeit for the wrong reasons. "What seeds do we have?" he asked.

"Take a look at the list," I said, handing over a pad and passing out more to the others. I also dropped one in Olivia's lap, which she ignored.

The group gathered around Kwame and discussed what they wanted to grow. Liss wanted as many flowers as possible, and Kwame agreed that some flowers would be a good idea. Pew showed agricultural leanings and wanted not just fruit, but a whole vegetable garden. Kwame also thought that vegetables would be useful. Iokan suggested they landscape the area with lawns as well as the flower and vegetable plots. Kwame agreed with him too, but the others didn't want a lawn or landscaping; the grounds already had plenty of that.

The group seemed to look naturally to Kwame to take a lead, and he had a gravitas that lent itself to that assumption. But either he couldn't speak fast enough to keep up with them, or his leadership skills were damaged along with his brain. He grew irritated, and his only good idea was to vote on it, which of course got nowhere.

Olivia had been snoring away in a fitful doze, and I didn't notice her wake up and take a desultory look through the seed list. It was only later, when I reviewed the recordings, that I saw her sit bolt upright in her chair as she came to a certain entry; then get to her feet and head over to rifle through the seed bins. Veofol noticed, went over and asked her what she was doing.

"It's flax mustard!" she exclaimed.

Veofol looked at the listing. "Yellow mustard grass? Are you sure?"

"You can call it what you like, but sniff that!" She held out a handful of seeds. Veofol inhaled their scent, but he had very little sense of smell at the best of times. By this point, I'd made my own way over, and Olivia demanded I take a sniff too. To me, they were pungent and vile. I staggered back, coughing at the stench.

"There might be a problem," said Veofol. "Look at this." He gave me the pad, and showed me the warning: while it came up with pretty yellow flowers prized by some garden designers, yellow mustard grass also contained isothiocyanates, which were deadly poison to some human species.

"Olivia, are you intending to grow this for food?" I asked.

"Now *there's* an idea…" She took up a lungful of their scent with the greatest pleasure.

"You do know it's poisonous for some people?"

"That's fine. I won't share." She breathed in the stench once more. "I haven't had this since we ran out at Tringarrick…"

"I'm serious, Olivia. If there's anyone in the group who can be hurt by this, I'll have every seed dug up and destroyed."

"Yeh. Poisonous. You said." She looked round at the still-ongoing squabble. "Huh. Right." She rolled up her sleeves (quite literally) and strode over to the group.

"All right, SHUT UP. Here's what we're going to do." They looked round, surprised to see her on her feet. "We're going to have a mixed flower and vegetable garden. Flowers on the borders and fruit and veg inside. We're going to mark out plots and pick what goes in 'em. You," she said to Liss, "pick five flowers and no more. Got that? Five. You," she said to Pew, "pick ten fruit and veg. The first one's yellow mustard grass and then whatever you like. You two," she said to Iokan and Kwame, "help me get the tools."

Kwame bristled. "I would like to have some say in the choice of–"

"You had a say, and all you did was talk. Get the bloody tools."

Kwame looked furious, but the argument was prevented by a soft chime in my ear. "Kwame," I said, "I think your advocate's ready. She's a bit early but would you like to have your meeting?"

"I would," he said. Veofol accompanied him back to the centre and the remote meeting room.

"Are *you* going to help?" Olivia demanded of Iokan.

"Sure. Lead the way," he said, a little amused, and followed her to the floating toolshed.

A couple of hours later, it was clear that Olivia knew what she was doing. She sketched a layout on a pad, and used stakes and twine to mark out flower and vegetable beds with Iokan's help (though I think she could have done everything herself without taking much longer). She came back to me with questions about the condition of the earth, the local rainfall, the climate in general, and demanded a test for soil pH, which came out at a very promising 6.2. While she waited for that, I made sure none of the group would be likely to die from contact with her precious mustard grass. By that time, the others had picked what else they wanted to plant, and she directed the group to prepare the ground, turning over the sod and exposing fresh soil beneath. It was the first time I'd seen her take pleasure in something that wasn't vindictive, and it was clear she'd learnt her skills on more than the barren soil of the Tringarrick research station.

Pew tried to show Liss how to dig her allotted section, though she was slow to learn. But Pew's own work was fast and good. He explained that he'd spent a lot of time in the zoo's vegetable garden during his childhood, and made excellent time, planting a number of crops before the day was out. Olivia even paid his work a grudging compliment.

Kwame was brought back out by Veofol, looking even more grave than usual. I asked him how his meeting had gone.

"My case has been postponed indefinitely," he said. "They say there is no body competent to investigate my claims, because the Interversal Criminal Tribunal is not fully convened."

"I see."

"This is bureaucracy at work. The only people who can judge me are allowed to judge no one."

"Well, the ICT is the only body that might be able to look into a genocide. But they're also supposed to investigate claims of interference between one universe and another, and that's rather controversial. It's only there in a shadow capacity until the IU decides whether or not to activate it."

"And when will that be?"

"It's a tricky political question," I said. "Some member species are against it in principle."

"And how many worlds did they murder?"

"The issues aren't quite that extreme," I said. "They're more worried about what the IU would have to become if we started making judgements, or they'd prefer we didn't interfere in their affairs. You should probably do your own research on this, or we can discuss it in group if you like."

"That will change nothing…" He looked back at the main building and said: "How long has she been there?"

I followed his look. Katie stood by the side of the building, watching the others while they worked.

"That's a good question," I said. It turned out she had emerged half an hour earlier and moved to a shadow to watch. I called her name and asked if she wanted a chair. She didn't reply. I sent Veofol. He spoke to her briefly, then came back looking puzzled.

"Rather odd," he said. "I asked her but she didn't answer for about a minute. Then she said she didn't need anything."

"She is a machine. Why do you keep her here?" asked Kwame.

"She needs help as much as the rest of you." I turned to Veofol. "Is she all right now?"

"Seems as well as ever," said Veofol.

"Let me know if she does anything similar," I said.

Olivia, meanwhile, was losing patience with Liss. With the natural strength of her species and her own clumsiness, she repeatedly made a mess of preparing a plot. After finishing a section of her own, Olivia was incensed to discover that Liss had been digging too deep. Olivia told her she wasn't supposed to be excavating foundations. Liss protested that she didn't know how to do this, and why were they doing it themselves anyway when they had all sorts of tools that could float in and do it for them? That made Olivia particularly angry; she told Liss they were doing it because it needed to be done and she wasn't going to get any of her precious flowers without it. Liss said that was stupid and she was going to go and get mechanical help. Olivia told her exactly what she thought of her – she was lazy, she'd never done a day's work in her life, she sat on her backside while other people did all the hard work, and so on. Liss responded by calling Olivia a mean old bitch, flinging her tools down and leaving the garden in a huff. I sent Veofol after her, decided a short break was called for, and had a word with Olivia about tact, though I only got muttering and grumbles in reply.

As they rested with water, Pew asked a question. "Can we get chickens?"

"What's a chicken?" asked Iokan.

"What do you mean, 'what's a chicken?'" demanded Olivia.

"They probably don't exist on Iokan's world," I said.

"How can you have a world without chickens?" she asked, incredulous.

Iokan shrugged. "The Antecessors only left us with certain animals. This 'chicken' wasn't one of them. What are they?"

"Flightless birds used for meat and eggs," I told him.

"Yeah, but can we get some?" asked Pew.

"I think you know the answer to that."

"Oh, so we can grow vegetables but we still have to eat machine meat?" said Olivia.

"I don't understand," said Iokan. "What's the problem with chickens?"

"It's a biodiversity precaution," I said. "We're all aliens here. We don't want other species to get loose and take over the planet. That's why all the plants are infertile. They'll come up with seeds, but the seeds won't grow. We'd do the same to animals, but it's a lot more trouble and they tend to have minds of their own. Plus they bring a lot more microorganisms with them. So, no chickens. Sorry."

"I see," said Iokan. "Actually…" He looked around, and tilted his head to listen as well. "I haven't seen any animals since I've been here, beyond a few insects…"

"No," I said. "You wouldn't."

"It's summer… there should be birds everywhere. And animals in the woods, and more insects as well…" He looked around again. "Something happened here, didn't it?"

"Yes," I agreed.

"Something that wiped out the birds."

I nodded. "There was an asteroid strike about forty thousand years ago. Most of the plants survived, and a lot of insects, but the megafauna didn't make it. It's one of the reasons the IU picked Hub; it's somewhere we can minimise our impact."

"And humans?" he asked.

"They died out, too."

He sighed. "We should get back to work." He stood, but was immediately unsteady. "Ah…"

I went to help him. "Okay, I think you've probably had enough exercise for one day."

"You may be right," he said. I called for a nurse to take him inside, and asked Kwame if he wanted to help the group. He took a look at Olivia, who smiled contemptuously, and then decided not to bother. I took him back inside and let Olivia and Pew get back to the garden on their own, with only Katie watching them for reasons she kept to herself.

4. ASHA

The gardening was a step in the right direction, but only a limited one. Olivia monopolised the task, and Pew was the only one willing to work with her the next day. Iokan was instructed to rest – he was recovering fast, but still needed to take it easy.

Despite the odd cautious friendship formed here and there, the group still failed to come together. They found it too easy to retreat into their rooms and hide in the company of nothing but their own troubles. We could have housed them all in dormitories, but the ability to spend time alone was vital for therapy in other ways. So we were stuck for the moment, and it looked like I would have to resort to more serious measures.

Back at home, I'd finally convinced Bell he wasn't going to be able to interview any of the group, and, as he often did, he skipped onto another subject without bothering to resolve the last one, leaving me irritated while be bounded into a new enthusiasm without a note of apology. We went out into the city for drinks in one of the more traditional bars where staff from the Diplomatic Service go to complain of the burden of their work, and he proposed we spend a week away together. Maybe skiing, or a beach trip – he'd heard of the new resort on the Gulf coast that had opened up, in distant sight of the Lift. It was his way of saying sorry and making an effort, I suppose. He was crestfallen when I had to remind him there was no way I could take a week off. An evening out was as much holiday as I was likely to get for the next year, at least. I probably shouldn't have told him that my plans for the group meant I would be going away with them for a week or so as well. He took that as something of a deliberate insult, and went very quiet for a while. The evening ended with neither of us saying much, and me feeling relieved to be going back to work in the morning

PART FOUR
TEAM BUILDING

1. ORIENTEERING

Somewhere in the tangled forest between mountain peaks lay the first waypoint; not impossible to find, but not easy either. The group would have to work together to get there. Dressed in practical hiking gear, they huddled around Kwame to look at the map, displayed on a large-format foldable pad and weighted down on a tree stump. This was no cartoon trail guide but a detailed professional map showing the paths, watercourses and bridges through the woods, and the occasional geographical feature like an impassable gorge slashed into the landscape.

Kwame tapped a symbol on the map with a wavering finger. "So our task is to reach this rock here."

They looked up. Over the tops of the trees, an upthrust slab of granite poked out of the canopy. An easy enough landmark by itself, but one they would not be able to see once they left the clearing at the edge of the forest where the bus had dropped them.

Kwame indicated a list of co-ordinates on a window to one edge of the map. "And we should have to reach these checkpoints in order to do so."

"But those are just numbers!" said Liss. Her choice of outfit for the excursion made some concessions to practicality, but still had far too many pink bobbles.

"Grid references," said Iokan. "Seems quite simple." He'd switched his monk-like robe for something much more functional: a black polo-neck sweater, heavy walking boots, hard-wearing trousers and a jacket whose many pockets he'd filled with dozens of tools and gadgets.

"Haven't you ever read a map before, girl?" demanded Olivia.

"I don't go in the country. I don't know what this means!"

"The map has a grid. Do you see?" Iokan traced lines across the chart. "The gridlines are numbered and you work out your grid reference from them."

"Uh. Okay."

"So if we're here," he tapped on the clearing they were in, "what's our grid reference?"

"Um..." she traced the lines across. "Sort of nearly three six across and a bit less than eight nine down?"

"Okay, but it's a six figure grid reference. The last two figures aren't marked on the map. If they were, there'd be so many lines you wouldn't be able to see the map itself. See?" He tapped a control and brought up the full grid, hatching over the map and making it difficult to read. He wiped it away. "So it's best to just imagine them."

"That's stupid," pouted Liss.

"I hope you never get lost for real..." muttered Olivia.

"Perhaps you should lead us," said Kwame to Iokan. "I take it you have some experience?"

Iokan shrugged. "I was a military man. Once upon a time."

Kwame brightened. "Really? What kind of service did you do?"

Iokan smiled. "The kind you don't talk about."

Away from the table, Pew struggled to get a pack on his back. "Do we have to carry so much?"

"The mass is negligible," stated Katie.

"For you it's negligible," he said, grunting as he lifted the pack. "I'm only Pu."

"That is unfortunate."

He looked up at her, shocked and angry. "What do you mean by that?"

"The Pu species possesses only average human strength. This is unfortunate for the Pu species."

He realised there wasn't a trace of malice on her face, or any other emotion. He swallowed back his own feelings. "Uh, right. Any chance you can help?"

She lifted his pack with one hand and held it up so he could slip his arms in the straps. "Uh, thanks," he said.

"You are welcome," she said, releasing the pack. He slumped under the weight.

Iokan turned to the group. "All right everyone. Packs on backs, let's get going before the sun goes down!"

Some grumbled at the weight, though not Liss, who proclaimed it easy peasy to lift. Olivia told her if it was so easy she could take hers as well. Liss stuck out her tongue and went on without helping. Iokan was less vindictive. "You've got the straps too long…" he said. "Here, let me." Olivia looked suspiciously at him as he adjusted the pack to let it sit more easily. "There, is that better?"

"Yeh. Better. Thanks," she said, reluctant to be indebted.

"My pleasure. Let's go," he smiled, and struck out towards the trees, folding the map and trailing the others behind him.

"I don't get this…" said Liss, looking at her magnetic compass, a needle suspended in a clear plastic shell.

Kwame sighed. "It is a compass. It works by aligning the needle to Hub's magnetic field–"

"I'm not stupid. I know what a compass is. I mean why are we using one of these things when we've got proper computer ones and satellite tracking and everything?"

"Bloody good question," muttered Olivia as she passed into the shade of the forest.

2. GROUP

A few days earlier, I'd gathered the group in the common room to tell them about the excursion.

"As some of you know, the Refugee Service doesn't just look after people while they're waiting to go to a colony world. We also look after people who were injured too badly to be able to go straight away. So we have a lot of permanent facilities for them, including a few where we give people a holiday if they need it. And that's where I'd like to take you all in a few days."

"What kind of holiday do you mean?" asked Kwame.

"It's an outdoor activity centre. So camping, hiking, woodland activities. That kind of thing"

"We're going camping!" squeaked Liss. "Can we have marshmallows on sticks?"

"I'm sure we can," I said.

"We'll be in the wilderness?" asked Kwame, concerned.

"Not exactly. We'll sleep indoors most nights but we'll go camping as well. We'll be out there for a week, and I promise you: no therapy while we're there."

"What kind of things are we supposed to be doing?" asked Olivia, suspicious.

"Walking, hiking, games, team-building… all kinds of things," I said. Olivia rolled her eyes at the mention of 'team-building'.

"We're not doing the thing with the stick, are we?" she asked.

"What's the thing with the stick?" asked Pew.

"The helium stick. Or the anti-grav stick. Or whatever they're calling it. They made me do this team-building rubbish before, they give a load of you a stick and you all have to balance it on your fingers and lower it to the ground. It's childish," said Olivia.

"It's about building trust and helping you work together," I said.

"It's ridiculous. I'm not doing it."

I made a note to keep the anti-grav stick off the list of activities. "I'm sure we'll find something for you to do," I said.

3. TRUST-BUILDING

Pew cocked his head, troubled by a sound in the forest. He strained to listen, unable to see because of the blindfold across his eyes. "What was that?" he asked.

"Branch fell off a tree," said Olivia.

"Right. Right," he said, still nervous. She sighed.

"I know it's stupid, but you've only got to put one foot in front of the other."

"Okay…" he said, and tried it.

"That's it," said Olivia. "And another."

He took another step. The ground remained firm. He waited.

"Do I need to hold your hand?" she demanded.

"Wasn't that what we were supposed to do?"

"All right, then…" she sighed and took his hand. He walked on with greater confidence. "Mind yourself," she said. "Bloody great root there, you're going to have to lift your feet."

He stepped up and onto the root. "Stop there," said Olivia.

"What is it?" he asked.

"See what you've done? I'm talking to you and I'm not paying attention to the ground," she said, and scrambled over to get ahead of him. There was a hollow in the earth after the tree root. "Right. You're going to have to jump down a bit. It's about half a metre."

"Are you sure?"

"Yes, I'm sure! Now come on, get on with it!"

Pew crouched, still nervous. But the jump was simple and he was soon safe again.

"There. Easy enough," she said.

"Yeah," he agreed. "Are there any more of those?"

"No. Level ground from here. All right?"

"Right."

"Let's get on with it then," she said, taking his hand once more.

***

Katie and Iokan, meanwhile, tackled the blindfolding task rather differently. Iokan wore the blindfold, and Katie had her own way of helping.

"Nine paces forward," she instructed.

Iokan took nine paces as Katie watched, stopping just before a low hanging branch. "Crouch forty centimetres," she said. He crouched, just far enough to get underneath. "Advance one metre."

"One metre it is," he said, cheerfully, and shuffled forward under the branch.

"You are ten centimetres short of the required distance," she said.

He took another small step forward. "Are you always this precise?"

"Yes."

"I don't think we're here to be precise."

"We are here to accomplish a task."

"But you know the task isn't really about walking in the woods with blindfolds?"

"That is the task we have been given."

"We're actually meant to learn to trust each other."

"I do not require your trust. I only require you to follow my commands."

He nodded. "Hm. Well, can I stand up now?"

"You may stand up now," she said. He did so, just clear of the last leaf on the branch.

"Is this how you did things in your universe?"

"No. We were more efficient," she replied. "Turn fifteen degrees left and advance sixteen paces."

"If you say so," he said. She was right, of course; the path ahead was completely safe for exactly sixteen of his paces.

***

Elsewhere, Liss was supposed to be leading a blindfolded Kwame along the route. He could hear water rushing along a gully. "Were we supposed to be near a river?" he asked.

"Um. Maybe," she said.

"*Maybe?*"

"Well, we probably are..."

"Liss, please tell me you know where we are."

"Oh, I think, um, I'm pretty sure we should be heading that way," she said, pointing.

"Which way?" he asked.

"Whoops. Sorry," she said.

"What do you mean, 'whoops'?"

"Oh, I was pointing and you can't see. It's this way." She pulled his arm, and tugged him along. The sound of the river grew as she led him through the forest.

"I am certain we should not be near a river," he said.

"Um... is that what that is?" she asked.

"I know what a river sounds like."

"I thought it sounded like a machine or something."

He looked towards her. "Have you been leading us that way?"

"Well... I thought if there was a machine there, that would be where we would be going..."

"Unbelievable," he said. "They showed you the whole route when we started!"

"Yeah, but when we went down that path I lost sight of it and I don't know anything about the woods and–"

He shook his arm free of her. "I have had enough of this," he said.

"Don't you trust me?" she asked.

He ripped the blindfold off. "No I do not!" He turned to go and immediately put his foot on the edge of a sheer drop. They had been walking alongside a hole in the landscape where the earth had slid away, revealing roots and soil leading down to the bottom of the depression. He tottered on the edge but could not keep his balance and tumbled over, flailing back at the lip of the precipice to save himself, but it was his withered left arm that grasped for purchase and he missed wildly, falling into the hollow.

Liss grabbed his hand.

He looked up, and saw her reaching over the edge, clutching his arm, hardly even seeming to strain at the weight.

"It's okay," she said. "I've got you."

He looked down. The drop was just enough to be dangerous.

"I'm pulling you up now. Watch out for the roots."

She dragged him up before he could say anything, and lifted him over the lip to safety. "There you go! No harm done!"

He rested on the ground, heart still racing. "How did you... how can you be so strong...?"

"Oh, um..." she said with a smile and a shrug. "Everyone on my world is. But you're okay. That's the main thing!" He nodded, amazed. "Um... don't tell anyone, though," she said.

He looked up at her. "They are watching us. They already know."

She looked dismayed. "Oh..."

He put up his hands to calm her. "It was my fault. I did not look where I was going. I'm sure they can see that."

"Oh," she said, less panicked but still worried. "Well, thanks."

"No. Thank *you*," he said, getting back to his feet. She twitched a little embarrassed smile back at him.

4. GROUP

"What about safety? And medical issues?" asked Kwame.

"That's a good question," I said.

"Yeh. What if I lose my medicine while we're out there? And laughing boy here is still limping, how's he going to manage it?" demanded Olivia.

"I'll be fine by then," said Iokan. "Anyway, I've gone hiking with worse injuries."

"There will be a full medical team on site," I said, "and if anyone gets into difficulties we can have them in a hospital within the hour. And we'll have plenty of your medication, Olivia, so don't worry about that. There are safety measures throughout the site, so you can't do anything like fall off a cliff. Of course, we can't eliminate every risk, but the chances of anything going wrong are minimal. So what do you think?"

Kwame sighed. "If you're sure everyone will be safe," he said.

"I'm sure," I said. "Anyone else?"

"I'll go," said Pew.

"Me too. Absolutely," said Iokan.

I looked at Katie. "Will you be joining us, Katie?"

"If you request my presence, I will join you."

"I do request your presence."

"Then I will join you."

"Oh and can we sing songs round the campfire as well?" asked Liss.

Olivia groaned. "No. No chance. No way. Forget it. I'm staying here."

"Is there a problem, Olivia?" I asked.

"It's a stupid waste of time, that's the problem! You think we're all going to turn into best friends just because we go and sit in the woods for a few days? Rubbish."

"You'll be doing a bit more than that," I said.

5. PROBLEM-SOLVING

Later in the week, we took the group to one of the more challenging activities the woodland centre had to offer, and some of the most spectacular scenery. They stood on one side of a gorge with no bridge, and no route down to the churning river below. But somehow, they had to cross.

They quickly found ancient machinery housed in two stone buildings, one on either side of the path leading to the sheer drop, matched by two similar buildings on the far side of the gorge. Etched on the stone were strange markings their translation systems could not decipher. Inside, the machinery was found to be still functional, well oiled and ready to go – but none of the controls would work.

"It's a game," said Liss. "I've seen people do this kinda thing. It's like you press buttons and solve puzzles and then it all starts working."

"So how do we do this?" asked Iokan.

Liss shrugged. "I dunno. I don't play those kinda games." Everyone looked back at the gorge.

"Perhaps a bridge might extend," said Kwame. "We have two buildings on this side and two on the other side, facing them…"

"But where's the bridge hiding?" mused Iokan.

"Maybe it's a rope bridge!" said Liss.

"If it is a rope bridge, then where are the ropes?" said Kwame.

"Maybe it isn't a bridge at all," said Pew. "Maybe there's a glider or something."

Olivia downed a pill with a swig of water from her canteen. "Does anybody have any idea what this thing is?" No one ventured an opinion. "Bloody typical," she said. "Right. I'm hungry, so we're getting this thing working. Who knows machines? What am I talking about… Katie!"

"Yes?"

"Figure out how this works and tell us how to get across."

Katie took a look inside one of the stone buildings, then came back outside and peered down into the gorge. "It is a simple mechanism," she said. "There are arbalests in each of the towers, connected to spools of high tensile cable. The arbalests shoot the cables across the ravine to the opposing towers, where they are hooked into pulleys and shot back to the towers here. The cables form a suspension system. Chains hang from the cables and are run out across the ravine. Electromagnets hang from the ends of the chains. The cables are slackened and the magnets are lowered so as to connect to the bridge. The cables are then drawn up to lift the bridge into place."

"And where is this bridge?" asked Kwame.

"The other side of the ravine."

"I do not see it," he said.

"It is the other side of the ravine."

"I do not understand."

"I see it," said Pew. "Look!" He pointed out metal plates ten metres down the opposite cliff face. And gradually the others saw the pattern of weathering and cracks on the cliff wall that concealed a slab which could be pulled up and out to create a bridge.

"Right, then," said Olivia. "Let's get this bloody thing working."

They beat the average time by a considerable margin, due in no small part to their collective skills. Katie's analysis was accurate, although the process was more complex than she initially described. The controls for the mechanism were all logic puzzles of one kind or another, which Pew and Iokan worked on together. Kwame's electrical skills found a use in several mechanisms that deliberately required repairs. Liss lifted heavy gears into place, complaining about the grease that inevitably soiled her clothes. Finally, the last moment of raising the bridge required each of them to operate part of the mechanism in a carefully co-ordinated way, and Olivia made sure that happened with judicious shouting and swearing.

Arbalests shot cables across the ravine, and then back again. Chains swung out along the cables; heavy electromagnets found the iron plates on the cliff wall; and slowly, the bridge of stone swivelled up on hinges set into the far side of the gorge. They cheered as it came up, and Olivia's muttering about how they would finally get some dinner was met with laughter rather than the usual silence.

6. GROUP

I left Veofol with the others to answer their questions about the trip, and asked Olivia to join me outside the room.

"I'm not bloody going," she said, arms folded.

"Of course," I replied. "If you don't want to go then you don't have to. I can appreciate how it might be difficult."

"What do you mean, difficult?"

"Well, I know you have a problem with open spaces. Especially at night."

"I don't have a problem. I'm just careful."

"Olivia, you've been living behind walls of one kind or another for something like fourteen or fifteen years, isn't that right? It's completely understandable if you only feel safe with that kind of protection, and you don't even have to take part in the camping if you don't want to–"

"You think I'm expecting revenants to come out of the woods? You must think I'm cracked!"

"Not at all. I think you have a perfectly understandable phobia. It doesn't have to be logical for it to affect you."

"Oh, and now you think you can get me to go by saying I'm scared, is that it? Well, stuff your psychology. I'm not going."

"If you don't think you're up to it…"

She rounded on me, incensed. "Will you stop it! Stop trying to help! I don't want your help!"

"I'm sorry, Olivia. You've got my help whether you like it or not. And you do need to participate, remember?"

"Oh, you're not going to use *that* on me, are you…"

"Not at all. In this case, I would understand if you had a problem with leaving the centre. Although of course if you did join us it would go a long way to satisfying the requirements of your therapy. But I'm not going to make you go."

"I don't–" she caught herself and sighed. "All right. I'll go. Or I'll never hear the end of it, I suppose."

7. CAMPING

The group trudged on to their objective – a circle of self-inflating tents, each one a dull silver dome glowing with a slight phosphorescence so you wouldn't blunder into it in the middle of the night. Olivia had decided to stay with the group. I hoped this represented progress, but made sure we could get her to safety at a moment's notice if she found it too difficult.

I rejoined the group at the campfire. They seemed happy to see me, still buoyed up by their success at the gorge, and offered a bowl of the stew they'd put together. But Olivia displayed clear signs of hypervigilance, a typical symptom of PTSD. When Liss returned from the toilet facilities and stepped on a twig, Olivia burst to her feet, a blanket dropping from her shoulders.

"It's only Liss," I said. Olivia swallowed hard and tried to calm herself.

"Right. Right. Only Liss." She sat down again and gathered up her blanket, still tense.

"What did I do?" asked Liss.

"Nothing. Don't worry about it," I told her.

"Are you all right?" Iokan asked Olivia.

"I'm fine," she snapped back.

"You're a bit jumpy," he said.

"I don't like the woods. I've had bad things happen to me in the woods."

"But it's lovely!" said Liss.

"Yeah, it's really nice," agreed Pew.

"There's fireflies! And we've got marshmallows!" said Liss, pulling a bag out from her pack. "Do you want some?"

"No I don't!" said Olivia.

"Suit yourself," said Liss, skewering half a dozen on a toasting fork and kneeling by the fire.

"I know what you're scared of," said Iokan.

"You don't know a damn thing," said Olivia, scowling.

"One woman in my unit came back from the Shizima Islands and she was the same way. She'd take cover every time there was a loud noise. She never got combat out of her head."

"Oh!" said Pew, realising what the matter was. "Oh…"

Iokan looked over at Pew. "You know what I mean, don't you?"

"I've never been to war," said Pew.

"It doesn't have to be war, does it?"

"No." Pew looked into the fire.

"I don't need any help," said Olivia.

"If you want, I'll stand watch when you sleep," said Iokan.

She looked up, hardly believing him. "You'll what?"

"I'll stand guard for you."

She huddled back into herself again. "Don't need anyone to watch over me. There's nothing out there."

"I know. It doesn't matter. I'll keep watch anyway, if you want."

She looked into the fire. Iokan didn't press her. And then, to my very great joy, she looked up at him with naked pleading. "All night?"

"We'll take it in shifts."

Liss was aghast. "What?"

"Well, those of us with a military background. I don't suppose you've ever done sentry duty, have you?"

"Er, no," she said.

"Kwame? Katie? Is that all right with you?" I asked.

"I will stand guard if that is required," said Katie.

Kwame looked reluctant, but Olivia's state moved even him to compassion. "Very well. I would not have slept anyway."

"Don't we know it…" muttered Olivia. Kwame looked ready to make a retort, but held his tongue as he saw how pitiful Olivia was: huddled up in her blanket, darting eyes, fingers trembling as one hand massaged the stump of her long lost finger.

Liss was still perplexed. "I don't get it. It's lovely out here! What are you so afraid of?"

"I'm not afraid. I just–" She paused. "I'm not used to being outside."

"But you spend all day in the garden!"

"It's not the same."

"But–"

"Liss," I said. "If Olivia doesn't want to talk about it, she doesn't have to."

"But why do we need sentries?"

Pew scratched in the dirt with a stick. "Because she's ill, Liss."

She pouted. "I don't get it."

I sat closer to Liss. "It's because of what she went through on her world. Do you remember what she said?" She still looked confused. "The revenants used to lie down and rest when there was no one else around. Then if someone came by, they'd get up and attack. In the middle of the night, like this, you wouldn't know you were surrounded until it was too late."

"And then they'd eat you," added Olivia. Liss's eyes went wide and she looked out into the darkness.

"You didn't… bring any back here… did you?" asked Liss.

Olivia enjoyed a grim smile, but did not answer.

Liss looked back at me. "They didn't, did they?" I shook my head.

"Are those done?" asked Iokan, nodding towards the fire.

Liss noticed her marshmallows had turned black, and two had burst into flames. "Shit! Shit!" she said, and dropped the branch into the fire. The group couldn't help chuckling, and even Olivia sniggered. Liss was hurt at first, but when she saw the smiles all around, she couldn't quite stifle an embarrassed giggle.

"Here, I'll do some," said Veofol, loading up another toasting fork.

"So are we going back tomorrow?" asked Olivia.

"Not immediately," I said.
"There are more activities?" asked Iokan.
"Not exactly."
"Are you going to tell us anything?" asked Kwame.
"It's a surprise."
"Is it a nice surprise?" asked Liss.
"It'll make you think," I said.

8. GROUP

I joined the group on their walk the next day, and it wasn't long before we came upon a bus floating gently in another clearing.

"First of all," I said, as they took off their packs with great relief, "I think everyone did brilliantly this week. And now, we have a choice. If you prefer, we can go back home right now."

"Well that's splendid," said Olivia. "You've got my vote." She hadn't slept much overnight, but Iokan, Kwame and Katie had been true to their word, and that kind of trust building is priceless. It didn't stop her being grumpy, of course.

"What's the other option?" asked Iokan.

"We pay a visit to an archaeological site near here."

"Archaeology?" asked Liss, clearly thinking the word 'boring' deserved to be added.

"Is this something to do with the people who used to live on this world?" asked Iokan, who was immediately interested.

"That's exactly it," I said. "When the IU first settled this planet, it was thought that either there were no humans, or they died out before they became sapient. But a few decades ago, we started finding cities. One of which is nearby."

"They died in the asteroid strike?" asked Kwame.

"They did," I affirmed.

"Why?" asked Pew.

"I'm sorry?" I asked.

"I mean... why do we need to see it?"

"Because I want you to start talking about all the things that happened on your worlds. And I want to show you that these things happen more often than you'd think. But I do realise that this could be distressing, so—"

"I suppose there's bodies," said Olivia, shaking her head. "You're so bloody squeamish, you lot."

"No. No bodies. But they've uncovered some of the streets and buildings, and... well, a lot of visitors find it very emotional. I don't want to push you too far if you don't think you're ready."

"I saw some archaeologists once," said Liss. "They dug a hole and found a bit of old plastic from the dark ages and they all went squee. Is it like that? I can handle that..."

"Well, there's a bit more to it than that. But it's up to you. If you're tired and you want to go back to the centre, that's okay. We can always come back another day."

"Sod it," said Olivia. "Let's get it over with."

"Does everyone agree?" I asked.

They nodded or looked noncommittal. I took it as a yes. The only voice raised against the journey was Veofol's, and that had happened before I addressed the group. Veofol was concerned it was too soon to throw them into anything potentially traumatic. I explained my reasoning: I wanted them to have a real talking point from this trip, as well as team building. He agreed, but was still concerned we were going too fast. I think he worried that the people who'd had the group set up in the first place were in some way pressuring me, but I reassured him I was acting on my own initiative. I just needed something to shake them into taking therapy seriously.

9. ARCHAEOLOGY

From far away, we saw a river flowing through the forest towards another river, joining so they became one. We were headed for the meeting-place of the two, around which the trees thinned out, revealing gentle hills and valleys between the confluence.

"Are we there yet?" asked Liss.

"We're already over the outskirts of the city," I said.

"I don't see it…" said Pew.

"It's just a couple of rivers," said Olivia.

"You'll see it when we leave," I said. "Trust me."

We landed by the archaeological outpost, a fenced compound on a patch of flat ground surrounded by hills and valleys. It was another set of prefabricated buildings dropped into the site, though of a different design than those we used in the Refugee Service. The archaeologists had brought a little piece of Hub Metro with them: a tapering tower of glass and whimsy that served as living space and offices, along with storage and preservation facilities for all the artefacts they'd pulled from the earth. Beside it, much lower but still shaped into fanciful contours, was the visitor centre. It was there we landed and met the chief archaeologist for the site, Ren Messalien, a massive bearded man seemingly carved out of one of the local trees but with the manner of an enthusiastic eight-year old. He waved a stained bush hat at us and grinned. "Welcome to Kintrex!"

"This is just going to be a hole in the ground, isn't it?" asked Liss as she stepped off the bus.

"Thanks for having us," I said to Ren. "Don't mind Liss."

"I guess you guys didn't see it yet, huh?" said Ren. "You will. Come inside and let's get the boring part out of the way."

He took us inside to a briefing room, where we got the usual health and safety presentation, illustrated by cartoon figures in cartoon archaeological sites. Much of the ground in the area wasn't safe, as some buried buildings had fragile ceilings.

Everyone had to carry a panic phone while they were on site, and wear high-visibility vests at all times. If they entered any of the deeper excavations, they would be issued with helmets that doubled up as an air supply in the event of a collapse. They had to follow the instructions of any archaeologists they came across. They were forbidden to touch any artefacts. They were not allowed to remove even one blade of grass. And on, and on. Olivia fell asleep twice, and Veofol woke her with a gentle hand on the shoulder each time, getting a remark on his treacherous elfin ways for his trouble.

"Right," said Ren, after finishing the presentation, "now all that crap's over, let's take a look at Kintrex!"

He led the group outside and away from the buildings. "Okay, so we're in the middle of the city right now. This is a level kind of area, probably a public park. Not much in the way of artefacts in the ground so that's why we set ourselves up here. But we are literally surrounded by the city. Do you see it?" They looked as he pointed out the green-sloped hills and valleys all around them.

Iokan gasped. "I see it," he said.

"What city?" asked Liss. "This is still country!"

"Oh, sure, it's countryside now," said Ren. "But look at the hills and valleys. What do they remind you of?"

"Oh, that can't be…" said Olivia as she realised what she was seeing. "Gods… those can't be… streets? Can they?"

"Streets?" asked Pew. "I don't see it…"

"This is a city… and no one has lived here for a very long time…" said Kwame, looking down the long valley, peppered with trees, that stretched away in front of them and ran down towards the meeting of the rivers. At several points, other valleys seemed to be crossing the first.

"Where is it?" demanded Liss. She happened to be looking at Katie at the time.

"The buildings surround us. Their degradation indicates complete reclamation by natural forces," said Katie.

"You still don't see it?" asked Ren. Liss shook her head. Ren pointed at the hills. "All those hills used to be buildings. And all the valleys used to be streets. It's been so long since it happened that soil's been laid down over the whole area. And this, my dear, is what's left."

10. KINTREX

VISITOR GUIDE: CITY 53 'KINTREX'
Summary

'Kintrex' was discovered by satellite geomagnetics, which detected the distinctive shapes of streets and buildings underneath the landscape. From the air, the pattern becomes quite recognisable: a complex of hills and valleys that have no watercourses to indicate natural formation, and are strongly suggestive of an urban landscape.

The site is well placed at the confluence of two rivers, and surrounded by land that could once have supported a wide variety of agriculture. It is too far inland to be a major port city, but at least two minor tributaries to the river have unnaturally straight courses, suggesting a canal system may have linked cities in the region.

All the archaeological work done so far has confirmed the initial expectation of an urban centre of middling size, covering approximately 110 km^2. Population may have ranged between 250,000 and 400,000. Excavations in the centre of the city have revealed a rather well-preserved commercial district, while a number of residential areas have also been uncovered. Major industry has yet to be seen, and excavations to find the industrial zones are ongoing.

The area was served by an extensive system of fixed railways, many of which are embedded into the road network. The roads themselves are of surprisingly poor quality outside the central area, suggesting that private transport was relatively rare in this society. As the railways are easy to discover with geomagnetic techniques, it has been possible to reconstruct almost the entire network.

One thing the site lacks, along with most others we have investigated, is any great number of human remains. While we have discovered some skeletons inside dwellings, these are the exception rather than the rule. We believe the city was abandoned before or shortly after the asteroid impact, and that the site was never re-inhabited, as we have seen no cannibalisation of building materials that would be expected during a reconstruction period. While some have speculated that the inhabitants were evacuated by an IU-like organisation, we have no evidence for this. It is more likely that the people of the city fled and perished in attempts to reach safety. It is impossible to say where they fled to, or how long they survived.

While excavations are still ongoing, some exhibits from Kintrex are now on display in Hub Metro. Certain portions of the site are open to diplomatic visitors, school groups and members of the public. Please be sure to book at least a month in advance, as this is a working archaeological site and arrangements have to be made to accommodate your visit.

11. THE TRENCH

Ren led the group into the city, along paths marked by hi-vis gossamer strung between floating lights, paths they were warned to stay on in case of ground collapse. Myself and Veofol brought up the rear, and let him do his job.

"A lot of the underground spaces in the city collapsed a long time ago but a lot of them didn't," said Ren. "You never know when you'll stumble on a basement that wants to give way. So stay on the path, boys and girls. I've got eight of you on the start of the tour and I want eight of you when I finish the tour."

The path led along the middle of an ancient street long since turned into a narrow green valley, until we rounded a corner and saw a long excavation covered by a canopy and bounded by safety lines. "This part of the site is pretty well compressed," said Ren. "So it makes it easy to see all the layers. Okay, everyone needs to take a safety helmet from the rack before they board the platform. Mind your step."

We took helmets and walked onto a floating platform in the middle of the trench. Ren lowered us the four metres to the base. A readout flickered into life along the rails keeping us from the trench walls, showing the estimated date of the deposits at each level. "This whole section of earth was shipped back to Hub Metro for the exhibition," said Ren. "But you can still see the basic strata – the layers where one set of deposits were laid down and you can find artefacts from that era. Down here" – he crouched to indicate a lighter layer of earth, close to the bottom of the trench, dated to 48,300 years before the present – "is where settlement begins. We've found pottery and middens at this level, so we reckon the site was inhabited by stone age peoples…"

"Um. What's a midden?" asked Pew.

"Rubbish pit. That's where they'd drop food waste, broken pots, and so on. Stone age peoples weren't big on recycling."

Pew nodded. As a child, he probably used them himself. "Yeah, okay, I know what you mean."

"And heading up, you've got some more advanced iron age stuff – for some reason they skipped bronze at this site," said Ren, setting the platform to slowly rise past unremarkable clay to a blackened layer, "then at some point the settlement was burned to the ground, I mean a total loss, complete disaster. Maybe the city was sacked, maybe it was natural – we just don't know yet. All we've got is this black, flaky stuff here. That's charcoal from wooden buildings. And then, going up" – he raised the platform again – "you can see they rebuilt – see that line of stones? That's the foundations of something a lot more serious than wooden construction and it's typical for the period. Maybe they learnt their lesson, huh? But really, we think the place was mainly military for a while, and all the stone was for defensive reasons. Once you get above that" – he tapped the controls and we rose once more, past the stone layer – "the settlement expands and expands and pretty soon you've got a major city again. We think most of it was technology driven – steam, probably – or maybe the politics changed and suddenly they didn't need to be so scared of the neighbours. Either way, that takes us up into the anthropocenic stuff, which is when people really take charge of the landscape, and we're not so far down any more so it's less compressed. You've got the underground infrastructure around here, like utility pipes, cabling, all the infill around them and so on. There, you see?"

He indicated the irregular layer of artificial material, dominated by rust and very red, but clearly pocked by flattened cables and pipes. We had reached 40,450 years before the present. "In fact…" said Ren, pointing out a dangle of glass wires, "you can see they were pretty advanced in some ways. This is a fibreoptic cable. They mostly used copper, we think, but there's enough of this to show they were likely moving digital information around as well as analogue."

"Do you keep that buried there just for tours?" asked Olivia.

"Nope. It's the real thing. There's hundreds of kilometres of it, all over the site." He raised us all up again, and the readout showed we were 40,420 years before the present. "Above that, you've got the ground level stuff. That sticky, crumbly material there is pulverised tarmac. It normally gets broken up by plants and pretty much worn to nothing before the soil covers it, so something must have happened here to preserve it. And that's the layer above. You see that?" He pointed out a greyish line above the tarmac, above which there were no more artefacts. "That's the ash layer from the impact. You find that all over the world and it's pretty thick around here, probably a couple of metres deep when it fell. In fact, it's responsible for a lot of the preservation of the site – if the city hadn't been covered by ash, there'd be a lot less left to find. And here's the interesting thing…"

He took an instrument wand from the satchel he carried, and wafted the end past the ash layer. A low tone from the instrument raised in pitch as he did so. "It's still radioactive. After all this time."

"The asteroids were radioactive?" asked Iokan.

"No, asteroids usually aren't. You get a bit of extra radioactivity in any impact layer because they absorb a lot of stuff from the sun, but this is way too much for that."

"Ketan erak tri anno?" asked Katie.

Everyone looked at her. No one's systems could translate what she'd said.

"I'm sorry?" said Ren.

Katie looked confused for a moment, as though not entirely sure where she was. She looked around. Then back at Ren.

"What are the levels?" she asked, in perfect Interversal.

"Oh, we're safe, don't worry."

"What are the levels?" she asked again.

He glanced at the instrument. "You're looking at a dosage of about forty microSieverts a day. You should be fine. You don't get sick until you hit about four hundred milliSieverts, and that's ten thousand times higher. The point is, the background radiation around here is three or four microSieverts. It's not dangerous, but that ash layer is still too high by a factor of ten."

"Were there nuclear accidents, during the impact?" asked Kwame.

"That's possible, sure," said Ren. "But the radioactivity is amazingly even over the whole continent. If you had nuclear accidents or even explosions, you'd expect the radioactivity to be greater at the site of whatever happened. So instead, you have to conclude it comes from the widest, most evenly distributed source, which is the ash from the impact."

"But you said the asteroids weren't radioactive…" said Pew.

"Right. They weren't radioactive. Or at least they didn't start out radioactive. But they were when they hit the atmosphere."

They paused for a moment. Some of them made the connection.

"They defended themselves with nuclear weapons," said Kwame.

"That's what we're thinking," said Ren. "The isotope analysis backs it up. We reckon they saw the rock coming and tried destroying it or deflecting it with nukes. But all they did was break it up into lots of smaller rocks, and you can see that in the multiple impact sites. And they irradiated them as well, of course. It probably didn't add up to a dangerous dosage for the survivors, but they had enough problems as it was."

12. LEAVING

The group crowded back onto the bus after their tour of the archaeological site. I sent Veofol to find the driver, joking that if we couldn't locate him, Veofol would have to take us back. He was qualified, but didn't look like he relished the prospect.

No one in the group seemed to want to talk, least of all Katie. Iokan, however, had other ideas – ones I would have preferred to pursue myself at a later time.

"What was that language you were talking earlier?" he asked.

"I spoke Interversal," she replied.

"Not all the time. You said something else in the trench, what was it... ketan erak tri anno?"

"I did not say those words."

"That's what I heard."

"You are mistaken."

"Okay. So what did you say?"

She paused. Was that the slightest sign of a furrowed brow?

"Iokan," I said, "there's no need to pester her."

"I didn't mean to pester, I was just curious..."

"If she doesn't want to talk about it, she doesn't have to." I turned to Katie. "Katie? Is there anything you'd like to tell us?"

"Their tenacity is admirable," she said.

Pew looked round at her. "Uh... you mean the archaeologists?"

"No. I mean the former inhabitants of this world."

"Can you expand on that?" I asked.

"They did not have the technology to fully address their extinction. But they did everything they could to survive. They did not wait to die. I consider that to be admirable."

Pew looked away. He'd grown a little grim during the tour. Iokan, though, failed to notice this and replied to Katie.

"Well, if that's what you were saying... I have to agree. I think overall there's a lot of positive things you can get from this place."

"How do you make that out?" asked Olivia. "They're all dead, aren't they?"

"But they went down fighting. And okay, so they didn't make it. Some things are too big to survive. Even so, life didn't end. Look outside: it's only, what, forty thousand years since it happened? Look how green the place is. There's plenty of time for something else to evolve."

"Yes," said Katie. "The ecosphere will recover. New life will emerge. A new race of sapient creatures will evolve and move into space. Biological life is almost impossible to eliminate entirely."

"Except yours," said Pew. "Your world's gone, isn't it?"

"That is true. Nevertheless, biological life still persists."

"Really?" asked Iokan.

"I have disclosed all that is necessary," she said, and did not speak again.

13. STREET SCENE

After the archaeological layercake, Ren took them to a broader, shallower excavation, only a metre down into the earth. It bit another metre into the side of one of the mounds, and exposed the edge of an ancient building along with the pavement and road.

"So over here we've got a part of the site that hasn't been compressed as much as the rest. We've been able to uncover an almost-intact street scene for visitors to look at."

'Almost intact' for an archaeologist translates to 'virtually destroyed' for most people, but nevertheless you could make out the traces of an ancient city street. Looking down into the trench, we could see a cracked tarmac road surface lying next to a wide pavement of stone slabs, some of which had been replaced by tarmac repairs at some point in the city's life.

"So here in the road you can see one of the railways," said Ren, pointing down at deep grooves running through the remains of the road surface, containing what seemed like pitted, rusted metal bars. "The rails there have corroded a lot, but you can still see what they used to be. That's pretty good stainless steel they had there. It's got a high titanium content. So with that alone, we know they were well past the first industrial age. 'Course, we've got plenty of other evidence, but steel's always a good marker for tech development."

The group looked rather less impressed than they had been with the deeper excavation. But Ren had more than just a road to show. "The best part of this trench, though, is the street furniture..."

Further along, there were a variety of corroded stumps in the pavement, and a signpost standing tall above all the rest, raised up so the top poked up high above ground level. "So you can see a whole heap of stuff here, but it's the signpost everyone wants to look at. It was flat on the pavement when we found it, completely broken away from the supports, but it was nearly intact, so we raised it up. And we got a pretty nice surprise, I can tell you! The plastics they were using really lasted, and you can still see most of what was printed on it."

The 'signpost' was quite broad, and stood three metres high; the plastic surface was pitted and warped but had markings all the way to the top. "We're pretty sure this was something to do with the transit system, that light rail thing embedded into the roadway. This might have been a passenger stop, or maybe an interchange point. That symbol at the top there" – he pointed out a faded insignia at the top of the sign, that looked a little like 'IXI' – "we think that's the symbol or the logo for the whole thing. You see how it's up high enough that you can see it from a distance? The idea is, you can see the stop from a long way away, and then when you get closer you get more and more information. So the writing below it that you're not getting a translation on, because we haven't properly worked out the language yet, we reckon that's the name or location of the stop. The coloured vertical bands running on the side are something to do with the particular lines the stop's on. And then there's the map, of course..." A simple design that showed the surrounding streets and buildings, and a line running from a dot on the map to words you could easily imagine saying 'you are here.'

"But if you look on the other side – it's the advertising for the transit system that really brings it home." I'd seen it before on screens, but seeing it in real life had rather more impact: a photograph of a host of faces that were so very nearly human despite the strange eyes and ears, clustering round the entrance of a tram, smiling and waving while a driver looked on with a kindly gaze.

"Those are real people," said Ren. "And they've been dead for forty thousand years."

While it hit me hard, it hit the others harder still as they went round to look. Kwame turned away, hiding tears with a shaking hand. Olivia scowled at it. Liss looked unusually serious. Iokan sighed. Katie looked closer, to satisfy whatever curiosity she had.

Pew didn't look at the advert. Something else about the sign affected him, something about the side with the map. He turned and stumbled away, and fell to his knees in the grass, gasping hard. I went to him and asked what the matter was.

"Think there's too much pollen... around here..." he said, loosening his collar, trying hard to catch his breath. I looked up at Veofol. Both of us knew that Pew didn't suffer from hay fever. This was more like a panic attack.

I directed him to take deep breaths and calm himself. He gasped and blowed and found control over his breathing again.

Olivia looked over at us and seemed about to make a remark. I glared back at her and she got the hint; she left Pew alone and looked back at the sign. "Silly buggers," she muttered, shaking her head.

Pew soon said he was fine, and willing to go on. But he didn't want to talk about it there and then.

Ren took me aside. "I guess that hit you guys harder than most people. Do you still want to see the rest of the tour?"

"I think we should," I said. "But let me ask them first."

14. LEAVING

Veofol came back to the bus and reported that the driver was using the rest facilities, so we had time to continue the discussion.

"Pew, are you feeling any better?" I asked.

He nodded. "Bit better."

"You had quite a reaction earlier on," I said. "Would you like to discuss it?"

The group looked at him. At first he seemed uncomfortable. But he made the effort. "It was the map."

"The map?" asked Kwame. "Not the advert?"

"I've seen maps like that before," he said. "The Soo had maps like that in their cities."

"I thought you never went out?" asked Olivia.

"I escaped once." Now that was interesting. "The maps were all I had to work out where I was. They were just like that, on that kind of sign. Exactly the same."

"It's a common solution to a basic problem," I said. "Most cities need to help people find their way around."

"I mean they used the same colours, and the same shapes, and... it was like..." He swallowed. "It was like standing in a Soo city. As though they were all dead and gone." He said it with an undercurrent of approval that troubled me.

"How does that make you feel?" I asked.

He saw my concern and clammed up. "I don't know. It just looked familiar."

Kwame missed the subtleties of Pew's tone. "I believe you are right," he said. "This place is familiar. It is a graveyard."

"A graveyard? With no bodies?" asked Iokan.

"It is a graveyard for more than people," said Kwame. "It is the burial place for their world. They should have rested here, undisturbed. We should have left them alone, not dug them up to point at their misfortune."

"But isn't there something to learn from how they lived?" asked Iokan.

Kwame smiled bitterly. "I have learned that some people have no chance to survive, no matter what they do. I did not need to rob a grave to know that."

15. EXCAVATION

The group was willing to go on, and Ren's final part of the tour took us to the pride and joy of the whole site: an excavation inside one of the hills that had revealed a number of intact rooms within. The group was again issued with helmets at the entrance, but these were of the kind that would function as survival systems in the event of collapse.

"Okay, so this place is pretty safe and we've put a lot of gravity control in there to make sure the roof stays up, but I don't want to see anyone taking these helmets off. I said this earlier and I'll say it again: keep your hands to yourself, stay inside the designated paths and don't touch anything. Okay?"

The group assented, and followed him into a tunnel with lights on the ceiling at close intervals; the walls were simple earth, supported by gravity modules on the ceiling and sides. Before long, we emerged into what our ears immediately told us was a much larger space, but the pool of light from the tunnel didn't extend far inside.

"So here we are, and if I turn the lights up..." Ren ran a finger across a pad, and lights several metres above glowed into life. Insects scattered and found safety in crevices all around. Liss gasped.

"Don't mind the critters," said Ren. "They only eat each other. Real problem for preservation, though..."

But she took no notice of the insects, and instead blurted: "It's an office!"

The lights showed a reception lobby, marble-walled and designed to impress. There were wide windows that once faced out onto a street but which had long since burst under the weight of soil. We'd walked in through one of those windows, and the path ahead ran on floating boards above the tiled floor.

"That's right," said Ren. "It's an office building. We're in the lobby right now, you can see they had real human receptionists once upon a time…" He pointed out the plastic skeleton of a reception desk. "This was a pretty fancy place, back in the day, and that's why it survived in here. A lot of the construction is stone and that lasts better than anything. Come on and I'll show you the rest."

He led us in past reception, where the building opened out into a broad, single room, filled with partitioned desks that sheltered insect nests. The floating platforms followed along one of the aisles, furthest inside and away from the outside wall, where more earth had piled up from breached windows. "Of course, it's mostly plastic and glass and some metal that's survived," he said. "Anything even remotely organic is long gone. But as you can see from that heap of plastic over there…" He indicated the inside of a room whose door had long since rotted away, where a freestanding boxlike device stood with a smashed glass top, about half the height of a human. "They had something I guess most of you won't recognise. That's a photocopier, a kinda thing they used to transfer information between sheets of paper…"

"Liss?" I asked. "Is this something you can tell us about?"

But Liss was lagging behind. She walked around the floating path, looking among the remains of boxy monitors, keyboards, computers, office chairs and all the other detritus with a wide-eyed nervous stare. Ren went back to his patter.

"Now we can't be sure what kind of work went on here, but you can see more indicators of their technology level – you see those units in the corners, mounted on the wall? Those are screens, believe it or not, and the reason they're that size is they needed to have an electron gun behind the screen to project the picture onto it. I don't imagine any of you have seen anything like that in the last few hundred years…"

"You would imagine wrong," said Kwame.

Ren was slightly unnerved at Kwame's grave tone, but picked up the tour guide patter again. "But as I say, we still don't know what went on here, and we probably never will. The biggest problem is preservation–"

"It's a call centre," said Liss.

"I'm sorry?"

"I said it's a call centre," she insisted.

"A what kind of centre…?"

"They… have the headsets…" She pointed out the wired plastic earpieces lying between an arc of rust that could once have been a band connecting them across the top of a head. And from one of the earpieces projected something that could have been a microphone. Ren looked closely.

"I don't know what you think that is, but we're pretty certain that was a miniature music system, or a personal communications set–"

"I used to work in a call centre… I used to do this. And… and the photocopier's in a locked room, that's for security… they were taking calls in here… they were taking calls when it happened… they were taking calls…" The tears came and she couldn't bear it any more. She fled.

I asked Veofol to stay with the group and complete the tour, while I ran out after Liss into the sunshine and found her throwing up on the grass under a safety line. I offered her a tissue to clean her mouth, but she was too distressed. "Why did you bring us here? Why did we have to see that?"

"Okay, Liss, I'm sorry, I didn't know it was going to have that kind of effect on you. You don't have to see any more. We can go home if you like…"

"What home? I haven't got a home!" she shouted back at me and stumbled to her feet, still weeping. She lost her footing again immediately, and collapsed into sobs. I knelt by her and let her weep into my shoulder. I felt terribly guilty; I'd been hoping for a reaction to break through her shell, but not an outburst like this. The possibility that her therapy would benefit as a result didn't make me feel any better.

16. LEAVING

The bus lifted up into the air, and everyone moved to the windows to see the landscape they now understood: the seemingly natural pattern of hills and valleys that was so clearly a street map once you knew what lay beneath the ground. Liss wasn't at the window; she'd long since stopped the waterworks, but she'd been quiet since then. "Liss? Would you like to see the city?"

She looked up, distracted from her thoughts. "Hm? Oh, are we going?"

"Are you feeling better?" I asked.

"Oh, yeah, I'm fine now. Sorry!" she said, embarrassed.

"Are you sure?"

"Uh-huh. Guess I made a fool of myself, yeah?" She was back to her old self, only a couple of hours after her meltdown.

"We'll talk about it later," I said. A look of worry flashed across her face but a foolish smile smoothed it away. "This is your last chance to take a look outside." She put her nose against the window.

"Oh, wow, you can really see it!" she said.

"Those poor people," said Kwame, shaking his head.

Olivia snorted. "Those people. What about our people?"

"What do you mean?" he asked.

"That's us down there," she said. "They'll be doing this to us in a few thousand years." Kwame looked back down, frowning.

"Taking us on bus rides?" asked Iokan with a smile.

"No, you idiot," she said. "I mean archaeologists. Alien archaeologists digging up our cities. And wondering how we managed to make such a mess, I don't doubt."

"They won't like it on your world," said Liss.

"Oh, they'll bloody love it," said Olivia. "They'll never figure it out if they don't know about revenants. It's the perfect mystery. They can't solve it and it'll get 'em funding forever. Good luck to 'em."

"No! I mean they'll get bitten!"

"What do you mean–" Olivia stopped, realising what Liss meant, then smiled sardonically. "Oh, I get it. Bitten. That's good. Hah!" She chuckled.

Kwame had a look of grim approval. "That is no more than they deserve. The dead teaching them a lesson for disturbing them."

"It can't actually happen," said Olivia, chortling, "they don't last more than twenty years..."

"That is a terrible shame," said Kwame through something approaching a smile.

"But still... can you imagine if Ren was digging and he came back up with a head chomping on his fingers?" she said, cracking up again.

"He'd be all 'Ow! Ow! Oh, wow, look at the cool specimens... Ow! Ow!'" said Liss, imitating his deep-voiced enthusiasm and making Olivia and Kwame laugh. It was infectious. Iokan soon joined in. Even Pew cracked a smile. Only Katie remained aloof.

I had half a mind to point out that something similar had already happened when the Exploration Service had found Olivia's world; but as I saw them laughing together, even at such a terrible gallows humour, I could not bring myself to stop them.

Veofol joined me and spoke softly. "I think I might have been wrong."

"We'll see," I said. "It depends on the next round of individual sessions..."

"Well... at least they seem a bit more like a group, now."

"Yes. Yes, I think so."

We flew back to the sound of conversation that stayed alive all the way home, a thin ribbon of shared suffering binding them together, and hopefully enough for their therapy to move forward.

PART FIVE
PROGRESS

1. DINNER

After the inevitable row with Bell once I returned to Hub Metro (he demanded I get an assignment where I wasn't perpetually on call, as though I had the luxury of choosing), I decided spending time at home was more trouble than it was worth. I gave Veofol some time off and took some of his on-call shifts for myself, staying overnight at the centre and sharing the evening meal. Much to my satisfaction, the group were actually taking meals together now, although that was partly because I made sure the only alternative was a less than appetising emergency microwave meal. They hadn't gone so far as to cook for themselves, but were more than willing to eat what was offered.

So tonight the group shared a very passable fish dinner, followed by a choice of puddings. The fish had never seen water, and had in fact been printed in the kitchen that afternoon. Importing food to Hub from other universes has always been prohibitively expensive, and it's much easier to build it from scratch, especially when you need to be able to feed millions of people during an evacuation. It seemed perfectly natural to me, but then I'd grown up with it. For those were used to food from a more natural source, it was edible enough, though it lacked some of the texture of the real thing.

Olivia had taken a liking to Pew, and spent much of the meal offering advice on his studies. "And the worst thing, the absolute worst thing you must never, ever do," she said, "is take benzedrine for three days on the trot so you can revise, and then go into the exam thinking you know everything and you just need to sick it all up on the page, because that's what Rory Holedner did in my second year, bloody idiot. And then he tried to sign his name in vomit. Now you don't do that kind of thing, do you?"

"Uh... no," said Pew, looking down at his dinner with widening eyes.

"Of course, you don't have to dissect any corpses. It's not easy the first time you do it. They all thought I was going to faint, because I was a woman, of course. Huh! It was three of them that threw up, not me."

"Did every activity at your university involve vomiting?" asked Kwame.

"It was a medical school! What do you expect? The first thing they did after lectures was pile in the pub, get bladdered and see how far they could chuck it back up again. All medical students are like that."

"Is that what you did...?" asked Pew.

"Well, I had to pretend to be ladylike, so I went back to digs and stuck to tea. They weren't used to women studying. You had to mind your step or everyone'd think you weren't any better than you should be, if you see what I mean."

Pew looked confused. "I'm sorry?"

"Oh, so it's just me who had all that sexist rot, then," said Olivia.

"No," said Kwame. "It was much the same on my world."

"Bet you never had to deal with it, did you..."

"My mother did. She campaigned for suffrage."

"Did she win?"

"No. They arrested her at a demonstration, beat her and imprisoned her. She only survived because she was seventeen when it happened, and they had to return her to her father. She campaigned in secret after that."

"And I bet you changed everything when you got in charge. Right?"

The sarcasm irritated Kwame. "My party made every change we could. You cannot turn society upside down overnight."

"And what did mumsy think about that?"

"She was not satisfied. But we did everything we could. We changed the property laws so women could inherit. We made it illegal for husbands to beat their wives…"

"Oh, well, you must be a champion of women, then."

"We ran out of time."

"Kwame has a point," I said. "That kind of change takes centuries. On my world, all the things Kwame's talking about happened two hundred years ago, but we still didn't have complete equality."

"Huh. Well, there's nothing like hordes of the undead to make men and women equal, that's what I always say," said Olivia.

Iokan, meanwhile, had been doing his best to engage Katie in conversation, still wearing his hiking outfit after a walk round the valley that morning.

"So what kind of world did you grow up on?" he asked.

"Earth," she replied.

"What was Earth like in those days?"

"A nickel-iron core surrounded by silicate mantle and tectonic crustal plates."

"I mean, what was it like living there?"

"It was sufficient to my requirements."

"What kind of things did you do there?"

"Training."

"Were you always a soldier?"

"Yes."

"Even when you were young?"

"I was always a soldier."

"Did you have any friends?"

"I had fellow soldiers."

"Did you ever have a boyfriend? Girlfriend?"

"I had fellow soldiers."

Iokan's eyebrows went up. "Oh, so… you and your comrades were polyamourous?"

A tiny moment of pause. "Yes."

"I've studied military history, well, military history on my world. It's said that an army of lovers fight harder for each other, because they care more. Would you say that's true?"

"I have no data for comparison."

"But did it make it easier?"

The pause was longer this time. "No."

"Did you… lose anyone?"

She turned to me. "May I leave the table?"

"We'd rather you stayed, but you don't have to if you don't want to," I said.

"Thank you," she replied. The group watched as she got up and left.

"You can try," said Olivia, "but you're not going to get anywhere."

"She needs our help," said Iokan.

"Maybe what happened to her was so bad, she can't talk about it," said Pew.

"She'll talk when she's ready," I said.

"She's never going to be ready," said Olivia.

"It is unimaginable. To be made only for war," said Kwame, shaking his head. "I wonder if she even has a family?"

"How can she not have a family?" demanded Olivia.

"She might be a clone," said Liss, with none of her usual perkiness. She'd spent the meal staring into her food, most of which was still on her plate. She hadn't even tried very hard to irritate us with her clothes today, and barely wore a single item of pink.

"She does come from a very technologically advanced society," I said. "It's certainly possible."

"Why are you so down in the dumps?" Olivia asked Liss.

"I'm not," she said.

"Rubbish. You haven't said a word all day. Now normally that's a good thing, but you're worrying me, girl."

"I'm fine."

"You don't have to be ashamed of it, you know."

"What?"

"I said you don't have to suffer in silence. Take some painkillers."

"I don't get it. I'm not sick."

"That's right. It's not a sickness. Happens every month. So do something about it."

Liss gasped as she realised what Olivia was talking about. "I'm not having a period!"

Kwame coughed on his pudding. Olivia shrugged. "If you say so. Now I used to take laudanum when it was my time of the month and that made it go swimmingly, I can tell you. Bastards here won't let me touch the stuff. Takes all the fun out of pain medication."

"I told you, I'm not having a period!"

"Is this conversation necessary?" asked Kwame.

"I think perhaps this is a private matter," I suggested.

"Calcium works," said Iokan. "About 600mg a day if you're feeling really bad."

"How do *you* know?" demanded Olivia.

"Standard ration for female soldiers in the field."

"Huh. Never heard that one before. Sure that's not just your species?"

"I suppose it could be–"

Olivia turned to Liss. "Go on, give that a go, see if it works."

Liss bashed her cutlery down, pushed her plate away and left.

"Yep. Time of the month, all right," said Olivia.

"Olivia. Maybe she regards that as something personal. That she feels embarrassed about. That she doesn't want to discuss," I said.

"Indeed," said Kwame.

"What? Oh, grow up," said Olivia.

"I simply do not see why you need to discuss these matters at the dinner table–"

"It's *because* you don't see it, you nit. If you don't see it you don't understand it. I bet that's what it was like on your world, eh? Everything under the carpet so the men didn't have to think about it?"

"I was a *liberal*. I campaigned for women. But there are some things – you are just impossible!"

"It's not the men that are the problem," I said. "If Liss comes from a society where menstruation is taboo, you need to respect that."

"Yes. Exactly," agreed Kwame.

Olivia sighed in exasperation. "If it's not one thing it's another. Fine. Vaginal discharge is off the table."

Kwame almost choked on his water, while Iokan couldn't help a chuckle.

2. IOKAN & KATIE

After the meal, Iokan went looking for Katie, and I watched him from my office. His intention to help the others could be a benefit or a hazard, and I or someone else kept an eye on him at all times to ensure he didn't push things too far.

But Katie wasn't in her room, or the common room, or the gym, or anywhere else he could enter. He asked after her with the staff, who could not recall having seen her in the last half hour, and suggested she was probably in her room. Having searched the centre from bottom to top, he seemed about to give up – but instead found her in the stairwell beside the gravity tubes.

"Katie?"

She stood at the edge of the stairs, her toes over the first step. The stairs were carpeted, but still presented a risk to anyone who fell. They were only there as a safety backup, and were little used except by those who didn't trust the gravity tubes.

"Katie, are you all right?"

She whipped round suddenly at the sound of his voice.

"What is it?" he asked.

Her eyes darted about. "Ket'erun lun?"

"I don't understand."

"Ket'erun lun!" Whatever had happened to her in the trench at Kintrex had happened again. I alerted medics, and Iokan held out a hand.

"Just come back from the stairs. Okay?"

She seemed confused again, then looked around.

"That's right," he said. "The stairs are dangerous. You might fall."

"Nunnon… nunnon… fall?"

"That's right. I don't want you to fall down the stairs."

She closed her eyes. "Nunnon. Fall. Nunna. Fell. Nunnonos. Falling," she conjugated, as though discovering our language for the first time. Her eyelids fluttered while her brain processed, then snapped open as she looked straight at him. "Where am I?"

"You're in the centre."

"What centre?"

"The therapy centre? On Hub?"

A pain struck her, a blight that twisted and palsied her face. "Hub…? Ket'erun… where is… Hub…"

She collapsed in a heap by the edge of the stairs.

Iokan knelt by her to help. But she snapped awake and stood back up in a smooth mechanical unfolding, her face passive once more.

She looked down and noticed Iokan was with her. "Is there something you require?"

I decided she was back to normal, and did not require immediate help. While we would need to look into this event and her condition, I thought the encounter with Iokan might be revealing for both of them, so I cancelled the request for medical assistance. Two floors below in the gravity tube, a pair of medics got the word and headed back down.

Iokan took a moment to register the sudden change back to her usual self, and stood up.

"I… came to see if you wanted any help."

"I do not require assistance."

"Well, you almost fell down the stairs a moment ago…"

She looked around, as though she hadn't noticed them before.

"Thank you for your assistance," she said.

"Do you remember what happened…?"

"I remember perfectly."

"Okay… well, I was actually trying to find you so I could apologise for what I said at dinner."

"No apology is necessary."

"I feel I should. I've lost friends in combat. It's never easy."

She paused. "I accept your apology."

"Would you like to talk about it?"

"I would not."

"Is there anything else you'd like to talk about?"

And again the pause. "Yes. Please come to my room."

Katie turned and walked down the stairs without concern, seemingly with no memory of teetering on the edge only a minute before. She led Iokan to her room, two levels below, and let him in.

He looked around at the unformed grey walls and the sleeping bench as Katie sat at one end. If he was at all alarmed by her sense of décor, he kept it to himself and maintained his look of concern.

"Please sit," she said, more like an order than an invitation.

"Thank you." He perched on the other end.

"Tell me more about the Antecessors," she said.

"I thought you weren't interested?"

"I am interested."

"But you said they weren't real. In fact, I think you told me they were charlatans…"

"I may have been mistaken."

"Well, it's very brave of you to admit that."

"No bravery was involved."

"Okay… so what did you want to know?"

"What form of life were they?"

"Oh, that's simple enough. Electromagnetic."

"Please explain further."

"Well, as far as we could tell, they were composed of magnetic fields that held a matrix of electromagnetic radiation, which encoded their minds and allowed them to function like any other kind of intelligence. Except they could do so at the speed of light, of course."

"How did they reproduce?"

"Not in the biological way. But they could spawn a new electromagnetic matrix and copy a human mind into that…"

"Was there a complete continuity of self?"

"Oh, sure. They'd do it progressively, so you could feel yourself transferring without creating two of you."

"Is it possible for a member of another species to become an Antecessor?"

I zoomed closer on her. The muscles on her face had moved. There was tension in her brow; she was anxious.

"…I'm not sure. I haven't seen it done but I don't see any reason why it should be species specific. As long as they understand how your mind works."

"I can assist with this."

He noticed how troubled she seemed. "Are you okay?"

"My functions are unimpaired."

"You seem a bit worried."

"My stress levels are normal."

"Are you sure? You look worried to me."

"I experience occasional emotional disturbance."

"Is that what happened on the stairs?"

She paused, and her brow got as far as actually furrowing.

"Katie?" he asked, still concerned.

"Yes. That is what happened on the stairs. Would you be willing to assist me?"

"I'd be glad to. What do you need?"

She reached for the wall and activated a control. Privacy descended, and my ability to observe was curtailed. But it was very informative. Was she having flashbacks when she spaced out, or was something else happening? I resolved to look further into the matter.

3. ON CALL

Iokan and Katie stayed in her room for another half an hour, and Iokan went back to his own room afterwards, looking almost troubled. There was nothing further to learn from his demeanour, and the rest of the group were retiring for the night. With little else to do, I checked the apocalypse watch: the ice-bound world of Steteryn still refused our help; the incidence of live births on Llorissa had risen despite the radiation, giving them renewed hope; a splintered comet group had been observed only a week away from the orbit of Schviensever, and they were scrambling every ship they had to defend the world, but would probably pull through; and the flares emanating from Ardeë's sun were still building despite scientific predictions to the contrary. Even so, there was no immediate danger, and no new worlds had been added to the list.

After half an hour perusing such tedious information, I stopped avoiding what I really needed to do, and called Bell. But all I got was a message telling anyone who rang that he'd gone back to his homeworld for a meeting and would be gone for several weeks. I wasn't sure which was worse: him not having the decency to tell me he was going, or my own relief at not having to have an argument.

With everyone in their beds, I retired to my own room but couldn't sleep; I lay there and wondered whether Bell would come back to me when he returned.

At three in the morning, Kwame awoke screaming from a nightmare.

The duty nurse got there first, and was helping him up from the floor where he'd fallen, still hyperventilating and covered in sweat. His hands shuddered, uncontrollably; the symptoms of neural damage only got worse with distress. It made me appreciate exactly how much self-control he had to exercise on a daily basis.

"Was it the same?" I asked.

"The... same," he said, between heavy gasps.

"Okay, let's get you downstairs and we'll have a cup of tea."

He nodded as best he could through the shakes. With the help of the duty nurse, we got him into a dressing gown and a chair and took him down to the common room. "Would you like to talk about it?" I asked.

"No," he said, clutching his non-spill cup with all the self-control he could manage.

"Do you mind discussing it tomorrow?"

"You should... not concern... yourself."

"I'd like to help," I said. "You can't keep going through this every night."

"Not... now. Please. Not now."

It was a poor time to start a therapy session, so I left it at that. And anyway, I had little choice; a chime in my ear called me elsewhere. I left Kwame with the nurse and paid a visit to the security manager, Lomeva Sisse, in her room of screens and monitors haunted by the scent of triple strength coffee, from where she could see every little bit of nothing happening across the centre in the middle of the night. She was grimly concerned, as she usually was.

"Somebody broke in," she said.

"What?"

"About an hour ago. Look." Lomeva pulled up monitor video for the perimeter, backgrounding everything else, and showed me something I couldn't even see until she enhanced the image. High among the trees, at the edge of the picture, a shadow leapt among the branches, avoiding every barrier.

"Is that a monkey? Or an ape or something?"

"Only apes on this planet are human. So's that."

"Haven't we got alarms out there? And the energy barrier?"

"Went over them. And knew exactly where to do it as well. That sector's a pain to cover. No rivers, no clearings, no actual damn perimeter of any kind."

"So, whoever that is, is still here?"

"That's the sum of it."

"Shouldn't we be in lockdown?"

"Nuh-uh. Take a look at four hours earlier." Lomeva wound the footage back, and showed the same place earlier in the night: another human figure darted through the treetops, in the opposite direction. "Automatic systems didn't pick it up that time. I said we were underbudget for security. And this is what we get."

"Okay. Hang on. So someone left. And then someone came in. Would that be the same person?"

"I'd bet on it. And I'm thinking we won't find full coverage on all the patients for the evening."

"You think that or you know that?"

"I know that. The crybaby, the cyborg, the wacko and the old woman were all in their rooms, and they all had privacy on. Somebody hacked the shit out of our systems because it stayed on for four hours and nobody noticed. The same four hours this person was missing. What are you going to do about it?"

"Okay, okay, let me think for a moment…" If Hub Security found out about this, they'd move us all to a secure facility somewhere underground in a heartbeat, and that wouldn't help therapy in the least. "So let's say one of the patients is getting out. How far can they get?"

"Depends on whether or not anyone was helping."

"Okay. Let's say there wasn't. What's inside two hour's foot travel?"

"There's the weather station on Yayne Peak. But it's unmanned."

"So they don't have any transport there?"

She closed her eyes in frustration. "Yeah. Dammit. They've got a one-person sled for emergencies." She took a pad and pulled records for the Yayne Peak weather station up on a screen. "Yeah. Same thing. No records for about three hours. Except…" She homed in on the details for the one-person sled. "The sled doesn't think it's gone anywhere but it's recharging as if it had. And that much power loss…" She ran a calculation. "Hundred and twenty kilometres travel, give or take. Whoever it was went to Hub Metro."

"How long would they have been there?"

"Not long. The sled's not fast. Couldn't have been there more than ten, fifteen minutes at most before they came back."

"Not much time to do anything."

"Depends on what they wanted to do. I'll have to search their rooms."

"No. Not yet."

"What...?"

"If they can get out this easily, they can escape any time they like. I don't want to scare them off. Let me see... they've all got individual therapy over the next couple of days. I'll see if anything comes up in the sessions."

"Then what?"

"Then I'll decide."

4. KWAME

Kwame was the first in my office the next day. I could have scheduled him later, but I wanted the nightmare fresh in his mind. He'd refused sedatives and hadn't slept, so he was in a bad way: red-eyed and trembling, hunched over his coffee, speaking even more slowly and hesitantly than he usually did.

"How are you feeling?" I asked.

"I have... been better," he said.

"Do you remember anything from last night?"

"No. Please... do not ask me..."

"If we don't look into it, Kwame, it'll always be like this. I know you're strong enough to face up to this but I know it's difficult as well. We'll take it one step at a time."

He sat there, exhausted, too tense to relax. He wasn't himself; but since he refused all attempts at therapy when he was, this was the best time to talk to him. After a few moments of thinking about it, he nodded. "What do you... want me to do?"

"I know you can't remember anything concrete," I said, "but do you remember how it felt?"

He closed his eyes to control a shudder. "I remember."

"Can you tell me?"

His eyes started open, and he tried to speak but couldn't get the words out. "I... I... I cannot."

Well, I had a few more techniques at hand. "Let me try something else. I'm going to turn the lights down, okay?"

"Very... well."

I dialled the lights down on a pad until the room was comfortably dim, and switched off the outdoor scene so the wall became black and indistinct.

"I'm going to put some lights on the wall. I'd like you to look at them."

"Is this... hypnosis?"

"No, not at all. It's just a distraction. It keeps part of the visual cortex busy, and since that's where a lot of the problems are coming from, it makes it easier to talk about it. Shall we give it a try?"

"Yes."

I activated the program, and coloured lights pulsed in slow, gentle patterns on the wall. As hypnotic and calming as it felt, there was no danger of a trance resulting.

"So you had another bad dream last night."

"Yes."

"Can you tell me what you felt?"

He stared into the lights. "I… guilt. I felt… guilty…"

"Why did you feel guilty?"

"I… left someone."

"Left them where?"

"To… die. She died!"

"Your wife?"

"Yes."

"Why did you leave her?"

"I don't know."

"What happened?"

"I… I made a choice."

"You made a choice?"

"Her or me…"

"What happened?"

"I… I left her… to die… I wanted… her to die… instead of me…"

The non-spill cup dropped to the floor. His whole body arched, as though fighting against some kind of restraint. His eyes stared wide with pleading and horror. His arms slipped behind his back, and his wrists crossed as though bound together.

"Kwame?" He didn't reply. "Kwame. Can you hear me?"

He was having a flashback. I was sure of it. I switched off the program and dialled the lighting back up. He couldn't see the change; only the horror from years ago that he could not escape. It was pointless to try and snap him out of it. PTSD sufferers can be violent in the midst of flashbacks, depending on what they see. At length he relaxed, his arms were released from their imaginary restraint, and he seemed surprised to see the darkness gone.

"What happened?" he asked.

"You had a flashback," I said.

"I do not remember…"

"I know. I'm sorry. I didn't want that to happen."

"It… happens anyway."

"I think we can help you."

"With more of *this*?"

"No. Until we know what happened, this won't help. You need to be able to get hold of these memories when you're awake."

"You… still want to read my mind."

"Yes. If you'll let us."

He looked down, pressing his shaking hands together. "What do you need me to do?"

"We have to calibrate the scanners to your visual cortex. There would be some tests with a neurologist. It'll take a while to get it right."

"Very well."

"You're sure?"

"I have nothing else to do."

"Did you want to talk about the legal process, while we're here?"

"There is no legal process. Is there?"

"Not for some time, I'm afraid."

"Then I have nothing else to do." He was approaching therapy with resignation; far from perfect, but better than no approach at all.

5. LISS

Liss had her perky face back on as she bounced into an easy chair. She'd made a special effort with her outfit today, a short dress embroidered with hundreds of pink hearts in an interlocking pattern, only slightly less alarming than the bright pink tights or the heart-cluster earrings. "Hi!"

"How are you feeling today? Better?"

"Uh-huh!"

"You're sure you're okay? You seemed a little stressed at the meal…"

"Oh, that's just Olivia, you know what she's like…"

"Nothing else? Obviously you weren't really having a period, so I have to ask, I'm afraid." She was on my list of suspects for the breakout – she was physically capable, given the inherent abilities of her species.

"Nope!" she shrugged with a beaming smile. Physically capable of breaking out? Certainly. Psychologically capable? Less likely. And there was virtually no chance of her having the technical skill to get past our security systems.

"I'd like to talk today about what happened at Kintrex."

"Oh," she said, her face falling.

"Is that okay?"

"I s'pose."

"You had quite a reaction."

"Guess I did. Sorry."

"There's nothing to be sorry about. But you have seemed a bit down in the mouth since then."

She sighed massively, turning it into a pout. "They get on my nerves."

"The others?"

"Yeah."

"Is that the only reason?"

"I dunno."

"I'm wondering if you've been feeling unhappy about what you saw at the ruins."

She looked down at the coffee table. "Maybe. A little."

"Why was that?"

"It was a crappy place."

"It reminded you of something, didn't it?"

She shook her head. "Not really."

"That's not what you said when you were there. You said it was a call centre. And you knew because you used to work in similar kind of place."

"Well, maybe a bit."

"Can you tell me about the call centre you worked at?"

"Oh, nothing special about it. Just, you know, people calling up and being annoyed and all the usual."

"And the ruins were similar."

"I guess."

"I don't think you're telling me everything." She looked up at me, surprised. "You were really very distressed. You threw up, remember?"

"I did?"

"Yes. You did."

"I… guess."

"You guess or you know?"

"I don't know…"

"You were reminded of something. And you've been holding back."

She shook her head. "I haven't…"

"You haven't told us everything," I said. "Would you like to tell me now?"

"There's nothing to tell…"

"I think you know something, Liss. I think you're hiding it from us. I think you're keeping a secret."

She looked suddenly trapped and liable to panic, her hands frozen on her knees, her eyes twitching around the room.

"I think you remember more than you're telling us."

She fought for words. "I– I–"

"Let me tell you what I think," I said. She looked puzzled, unsure of what to expect, almost like someone preparing to run for it. "You were working at a call centre when it happened, weren't you?"

Her eyes went wide. Had I found her out?

"That's why you had such a reaction to seeing the call centre at Kintrex. You were in a place like that when the world ended. Am I anywhere near the truth?"

She looked away from me and down, eyes hidden behind her hair. "Is that right, Liss?" She kept her face away from me for a few seconds more. It was an agonising moment. Even when I checked the recordings later, I could not see her eyes, or any other indication of what was going through her mind at that moment. I could only guess that she saw, then, the memory she'd been holding back from herself: the moment the world ended and every single person on her world died. Maybe even what she did afterwards.

"Liss? Are you all right?"

She looked back at me, eyes watering and chin quivering. "I– I was there… I was there when it happened…"

"Where were you, Liss?"

"The… the call centre…" Tears came down her face now.

"That was where you worked, wasn't it?"

"Yes…"

"What about the recruitment agency?"

"I worked there before. Years ago… Then I got the job at the call centre. The… call centre…"

"Okay Liss, that's good, we're making progress. Do you remember any more?"

Her mouth flapped, hunting for words.

"Do you remember what happened?" I asked.

Her chin wobbled. Her eyes went wide as the memory forced itself upon her.

"They're dead!"

I nodded, as sympathetically as I could. "I'm sorry."

"They're all dead! Everyone!" She was breathing hard now, panicking through tears and gasps. "Everyone! They – they burned! They glowed, and it was hot, and they fell, but it was all clothes, and, and there was ash on the floor… there was ash on the floor…"

And she wailed. A cry of horror and anguish at the unbearable memory. I held her, letting her sobs wrack into my shoulder. It's very rare for memories to suddenly return in this way, but I had to make allowances for the strangeness of her world and her odd physiology.

"Would you like to tell me any more, Liss?"

But she was shuddering and weeping in my arms, and shook her head, hiding her eyes from me. I had two nurses escort her back to her room, and arranged for a more intensive suicide watch.

6. KATIE

Katie was an emotional palate cleanser after Liss, and I was relieved not to be dealing with someone liable to burst into tears, or to make any other kind of outburst – probably. She'd certainly had a few strange episodes, which could well have been seizures. There was also the question of whether she might be the one who broke out. She was certainly physically capable of the feats we'd seen, and possibly technically capable of hacking our systems. But if she really was seizing, that would argue against my suspicions. My most predictable patient was suddenly the least predictable of all.

Once she agreed to my request to sit down (she was content to stand unless specifically invited to sit), I went straight in with my concerns.

"Katie, I don't know if you're aware of it, but you seem to be having seizures."

"I am unaware of any such symptoms."

"We've observed several. Would you like to look at the videos?"

She turned her head slightly as I threw surveillance video up onto the wall. Each sequence showed one of Katie's seizures, from various unflattering angles: she stood in shadow by the centre as Veofol spoke to her, but did not answer; she sat in the same chair she sat in now, staring without answering my questions; she spoke in a strange language in the trench at Kintrex and looked confused; she teetered on the edge of a staircase and turned only when Iokan called her name.

She studied them all carefully, but did not comment.

"You can see why I'm concerned," I said.

She thought for a moment, her brow creasing. "These are not seizures. These are emotional disturbances."

"Hm. Could you explain that, Katie?"

"They are an inherent part of my biological systems."

"So this is nothing new?"

"It is a recurring symptom of the human mind."

"And you experience this regularly?"

"Yes."

"I'm not sure I agree with your diagnosis."

"You are not a neurologist."

"No, you're right. And that's why I'd like to get a neurologist involved."

"Please explain."

"I'd like to have your brain scanned more thoroughly during your next episode."

"Please explain further."

"Well, you'd be in a room with very sophisticated scanning equipment, probably in Hub Metro. Then we'd be able to monitor exactly what's going on, and see if there's anything we can do to help."

She deliberated.

"No," she said.

"You do understand that this could be a symptom of your neural degradation?"

"I am able to control my symptoms. I do not require your assistance."

"And how exactly are you controlling the symptoms?"

She paused. "Through extremes of pleasure or pain. These concentrate the biological systems and reduce chaotic neural impulses."

"And is that what Iokan helped you with?"

"Yes."

"How exactly did he help?"

She paused again before speaking. "Privacy was activated. It is not necessary to divulge this information."

"Can I presume you chose to control your symptoms with pleasure, rather than pain?"

She thought about that. "Yes."

"Well, I'm glad you chose not to hurt yourself."

"It was not necessary."

"And Iokan was willing to help?"

"He had misgivings, but decided that since the procedure had medical value, his wife would not raise any objections."

"His wife? So you had sex?"

Another pause. "Yes."

"Okay... you know, if you really need this, we can always provide some, ah, equipment..."

"A human male is more effective."

I was tempted to point out the obvious flaw in this reasoning, but wasn't entirely sure she'd understand.

"Well. As long as he consents, I can't see why I should stop you. But please consider using a substitute."

"Your offer is noted."

Something else occurred to me. If her neural state was deteriorating, perhaps she might respond differently to other stimuli. So I reached for the only available metric.

"I'd like to go back to another question entirely, if that's all right with you."

"I am willing to co-operate with therapy."

"Yes. Well, I was wondering if you could tell me – how did you survive the extinction of your species?"

"I have divulged this information to you previously."

"I'd like to hear it again, please."

She paused, and thought hard. That crease in her brow went deeper than before. I checked my pad: if she was going to be consistent, if nothing had changed, then the first words out of her mouth would be: *I was assigned to crew a modified orbital freight transport with two others.*

After a moment, I had to prompt her. "Katie? Can you answer the question?"

"Yes." A second more of pause, and then she spoke. "I was given command of an orbital freight transport with two others whose role it was to pilot the ship and control our weaponry." I found myself smiling with satisfaction, but Katie did not notice. "We lay dead in space until the enemy ship approached and then we attacked. We intended to ram the enemy and detonate antimatter devices but they fired first and destroyed our ship. The others were killed. I was thrown clear from the wreckage. I engaged vacuum survival systems to reduce my heat signature, and consequently survived."

It was precisely what I'd hoped for; instead of the usual repetition, she was paraphrasing and bringing in other elements of the experience. Some part of the disintegration of her mind was allowing her greater freedom. And perhaps her usual assertion that she had provided us with sufficient strategic and tactical information was gone as well.

"Was this your first battle?"

"I have already provided sufficient tactical and strategic information."

Well, perhaps not. But I pressed on anyway. "I'm not interested in tactics or strategy, Katie. I'm interested in *you*. In how you saw things. Was it your first battle?"

She paused for a moment; I feared she would keep her silence. But then she continued. "No. I fought in many engagements."

"Did you always lose?"

She paused to consider her answer. "78% of engagements ended in unacceptable losses."

"So you lost a lot of battles?"

"Yes."

"And you lost a lot of comrades?"

"Yes."

"How did that feel?"

"I did not express emotion."

"But did you feel emotion?"

"I experienced emotional disturbance."

"How did you address that?"

A pause. "With the assistance of my fellow soldiers."

"Did that help?"

"Defeats were not prevented."

"I mean, did it help *you*?"

"It helped me."

"Can you tell me about one of these battles?"

She thought about that. She'd given us barely any information about the war, despite her assertion about sufficient tactical and strategic information being provided. Finding out more about what she'd endured and whom she'd fought could only help. She came to a decision after approximately five seconds.

"I fought in the defence of the Earth-Sun L2 station."

"Was that an important battle?"

"Yes. It was our last outpost outside the Earth-Moon system. It provided a base to strike against the enemy."

"What happened?"

"They approached from the Vesta asteroid chain. They were unable to make use of gravitational corridors due to unsuitable orbital positioning. Their approach was therefore slow and vulnerable to harassing attacks by fighters. The L2 base was our primary centre of operations. It was designed as a multi-role observatory platform but was repurposed for fighter production, repair and deployment. My primary role was as a fighter pilot. I made eighty-nine sorties against the enemy. Some of their smaller ships could be destroyed, disabled or forced to divert their course. Their capital ships could not be stopped. They were built within asteroids which could withstand all weapons except for direct nuclear or anti-matter detonation, but their defences were too effective for us to reach them. Nevertheless, we were able to mount four successful sorties which detonated weapons close enough to cause serious damage to one asteroid ship."

"So I suppose they wanted to get rid of the L2 station…"

"That is correct. We expected a frontal assault but they decided instead to eliminate the installation entirely, using gravitationally accelerated asteroidal mass. The battle was lost before we could expend ammunition. We had no effective defence against an aggregate of small silicate pieces which could not be dispersed by detonation. We fell back to the Earth-Moon system."

"That must have felt terrible."

"Yes."

"What happened then?"

"I next participated in the defence of the Earth-Moon L5 station."

"Right, hang on…" I used my control pad to bring up a diagram of orbital positions on the wall so I could better grasp what was going on. The L2 station had been some way outside Earth's orbit, where the gravitational pull of the Earth and Sun cancelled each other out; the Earth-Moon L5 station was in the same orbit the Moon took around the Earth, lagging behind in another stable orbital position.

"Another strategic point, then."

"Yes."

"Another fighter base?"

"No. We had very few fighters remaining. The L5 station was primarily used as an emplacement for mass drivers and plasma pulse weapons."

"So did they destroy it?"

"No. They assaulted the station with combat troops. Ramships were used to breach the hull and we fought hand to hand."

She paused. "Please. Go on," I said.

"Our soldiers were physically superior and unencumbered by environmental protection suits, but outnumbered. We concentrated our defence at choke points in the station superstructure, and inflicted comparative losses at the ratio of five to one. We calculated this would be unsustainable for the enemy but were mistaken. We were forced to retreat compartment by compartment until we held only four percent of the station. There were seven of us at that time, and communication with headquarters was lost. I ordered the station scuttled by antimatter detonation and the survivors to fall back to L1."

"And what happened after that?"

"We destroyed the moon with staggered singularity release."

"You destroyed the moon?"

"We destroyed the moon as a demonstration of the technology and a deterrent to further enemy advance. We threatened to use the same weapon on the Earth if they continued to attack. They did not comply."

"And you were sent out on a final mission, to try and stop them?"

"That is correct."

"And it was your side that destroyed the Earth?"

"That is correct."

"It wasn't the enemy?"

"That is correct."

"I'm... surprised by that. We thought your enemies did it."

"That was incorrect."

"How many people died?"

She paused. "I do not have accurate population figures."

"But... your whole species committed suicide rather than let the enemy win?"

"That is correct."

"What was so terrifying about them?"

"We could not permit them to take the Earth."

"Katie... who were they? You said they were religious, but you've never said anything else about them..."

"It is better that you do not encounter them."

"Thanks for the concern, but I'm more worried about you. Did you agree with all this? I mean, destroying the Earth?"

"It was an appropriate action in the circumstances."

"Couldn't the two sides have negotiated a settlement?"

"We attempted negotiation on many occasions. All communications were ignored."

"So who were they?"

She paused. "I have divulged sufficient strategic and tactical information."

"Katie? Can you tell me who they were?"

"I have divulged sufficient strategic and tactical information."

"Can I tell you what I think?"

She did not reply.

"I think these people you fought, I think they were humans. You said they were religious. They needed environment suits to survive in space. They behaved irrationally. That sounds like humans to me. And I think… I think your side was the machine side. Artificial intelligence. Rational. Reasonable. Is that the case?"

She paused.

"The situation was more complex."

"How was it more complex?"

"I… I have divulged sufficient strategic and tactical information. May I leave?"

That was going to be it for today. I let her go, worried that the day's progress came at the price of her failing health, and wondering if she would survive long enough for me to do any good.

7. PEW

Pew tended to contribute less in group than the more vocal members, so much of the progress he made took place in the individual sessions. But there were often things to pick up on and address, and of course his reaction to the street sign at Kintrex was something I couldn't let pass. He'd looked up a good deal of information on the former inhabitants of Hub in the days since, trying to find out more about where they lived and what had happened to them; and I could take a pretty good guess at why he was interested.

"How much are they like the Soo?" I asked.

He considered his words. "They weren't as advanced. And they were the only humans on the planet. I don't know. Maybe they'd have been like the Soo if we'd been here as well, I mean if the Pu had been here. Or someone like us."

"But they still remind you of the Soo? They don't look like them."

"They were human. I suppose the Soo are as well."

"So it was just the sign? Why did it bother you?"

"I told you, I've seen something like it before."

"When you escaped."

"Yeah."

"Hm. Okay. I hope you don't mind if I ask you a difficult question…"

He shrugged and smiled. "Okay…"

"How do you feel about the Soo?"

His face fell instantly and worry lines appeared. "What do you mean?"

"I mean: what emotion do you feel when you think of them?"

He swallowed. "I hate them."

"Okay."

"They killed everyone. I'm allowed to hate them, aren't I?"

"I'd be surprised if you didn't." He was perplexed, and didn't know what to say. I went on. "I'm a little concerned. You hate the Soo – all right, that's understandable. But then you see a species that reminds you of them. And you start researching that species. You spent three days going over everything we have on them. So my question is: do you want to see what happened to the people who lived here happen to the Soo?"

He looked back at me, far too directly for comfort. "Yes."

"You'd be happy to see them all die?"

"I'd push the button myself."

"So… we're not talking about a random asteroid any more. You're talking about pressing a button and wiping them out. Does that mean you'd commit genocide?"

"Didn't they?"

This was disturbing, and potentially a very serious problem for therapy. "Have you always felt this way?"

"Yes," he said, then caught himself. "No."

"Was there a point when you started to hate them?"

"It doesn't matter."

"Pew, it *does* matter. I want to get to the heart of why you're suffering. And some of that has to be because of the Soo, and what they did to you. If there was a moment when you realised you hated them, that could be really helpful."

He looked around at the room and didn't answer.

"Pew?"

He looked down.

"Pew, is this something you'd be uncomfortable discussing?"

He looked back at me. "It was when I escaped."

"Okay. Can you tell me about what happened then?"

He sighed. "They let me go on holiday."

"How old were you?"

"Seventeen. I didn't see it until I was that old. I should have seen it right away."

"You were only a child…"

"I should have known."

"So what happened?"

He looked out at the view through the wall: plants in the garden dusting the tilled earth with green shoots.

"They said I could go anywhere I wanted. Shan'oui said that, it was her that made them stop the breeding programme. She was trying to protect me again."

"So where did you choose?"

"The Arctic."

"Really?"

He nodded. "They had a research station up there, they, they hated the cold but it never stopped them… Shan'oui must have pulled some strings to get us there. It wasn't the place I came from, but… I don't know. It looked kind of the same."

"I suppose you must have missed it. The Arctic, I mean."

"I thought I did. Then I got there. I hadn't seen snow or ice for years. At first I just ran out like an idiot and threw snowballs at everything. But it was so *cold*. I've never felt so cold, not even when I lived there before. And I'd forgotten everything. I tried hunting seal, but I nearly killed myself trying to cut a hole in the ice. I don't know what I would have done with one anyway…"

"How long were you there?"

"It was supposed to be two months. I asked to go home after three weeks. Then another week to arrange a flight. So about… a month. Something like that."

"And you didn't escape while you were there?"

"No. It was on the way back. We had to stop for fuel. The jet was sitting in the airport and they were talking about me, I heard Shan'oui on the phone to someone about the breeding programme and she was trying to get them to stop, so she wasn't keeping an eye on me. It was cold outside. I took a parka and walked out. They didn't stop me."

"That's very brave."

"I wasn't trying to be brave. I don't know what I was trying to do."

"You were trying to get away, surely?"

"I don't know. I was more… fed up. Sick of it. I don't know."

"Were you scared?"

"I was, once I was in the airport. I'd never seen that many Soo all at once. I thought they were going to put me in hard labour any second."

"It's a good thing you had that parka."

"I hadn't thought about it. It was just cold. But once I was inside, I couldn't take it off, or they'd have known I wasn't a Soo."

"Did you get through the airport?"

"Yes. I don't know how. I just walked and eventually there was an escalator. I don't know why they didn't stop me. After a while, I was in a train station. Then I got lucky again, somebody'd got off a train with a day ticket and was asking people if they wanted it, so I took it, got on a train and went off to the city."

"What was that like?"

"It wasn't anything like Hub Metro. It was a mess, they didn't have any parks and it was all roads everywhere. All the buildings were close together and there were so many Soo… children as well, crowds everywhere… I didn't know you could even have that many people…" He trailed off, still struck by the memory. "I got lost. I was hungry. It was stupid. And then I saw the sign."

"Like the one in Kintrex?"

"Just like the one in Kintrex. It was for a bus stop. And it had a map. The map said 'you are here' and showed all the routes. And I saw there was a zoo in the city. So I went there."

"Why? Wouldn't that be the last place you'd want to go?"

"I didn't know what to do! I mean I was really lost by then, I wanted to go home, that's what I thought zoos were, places where Pu lived. I thought if I could get back there, I'd find more Pu and they'd let me stay with them. It was *stupid*."

"You were scared. It's understandable."

He sighed. "I used the ticket and got a bus, I don't know how I made it, it was packed full of them, I just wanted to crawl out of my skin, but I got there and… I found out what zoos are really for. I couldn't get in at first, you needed money. So I went round the side and climbed over a fence. And then I figured it out.

"It was for animals – it was full of animals. They had reptiles and tropical birds and all the big marsupials. And a polar bear as well, poor bastard. He was sitting there next to a pool and his fur had gone all beige. I didn't get it. I thought the Pu had to be in there somewhere. I ended up at the primates – chimps and gibbons and a couple of gorillas. I was frantic, I freaked out. I took off my hood and screamed at everyone to tell me where the Pu were. And when they saw me without the hood, they saw I had hair, they saw my nose, they realised what I was. They all backed off. There was this little girl who'd been frightened by one of the gorillas and then she saw me and she was even more frightened. That's when I knew what they really thought of us."

"You hadn't known before?"

"I'd never seen what it was like on the other side of the glass."

He sighed a deep sigh and put his head in his hands. I poured him some water and offered him the cup.

"They put me in a fucking chimpanzee cage while they waited for Shan'oui to turn up. And I was happy to see her, like a fool. All the other Soo were treating me like… well, like what they thought I was. I asked her why they kept us in zoos if zoos were for animals, and she said it was for our own good. For our own good they were caging us up!

"That's when I started hating them. It was then. When they put me in a cage and I *knew it*. And I figured out where I'd been all my fucking life. In a *fucking cage!*" There was more than anger in his voice. There was steel as well, and his hands were trembling. I made him tea, and spent the rest of the session bringing him down from the anger and back to something approaching tranquillity.

8. OLIVIA

"You've been getting on well with Pew," I said to Olivia as she slurped her coffee.

"He's good in the garden. So?"

"It's nice to see you socialising."

"He's a good boy. He listens. Unlike some people."

"Hm. Well, what I wanted to do today was pick up on a discussion we had at dinner. You mentioned you'd attended a medical school. Does that mean you're a medical doctor?"

"I never said that."

"But you went to medical school."

"Yeh. So?"

"I know a few people who did the same…"

"Oh, so you've got doctors on Hub? Big whoop-ee-do."

"But what you said about medical students is absolutely right."

"It's a law of the universe. No, I'm sorry, multi-bloody-verse. All medical students are bastards."

"They do tend to drink rather a lot…"

"That's not all they do. Many's the time I carried a brick in my purse when I walked out at night. Used it once, almost got sent down for that."

"How did you become a medical student?"

"What, are you surprised?"

"Well, it does sound like your world was rather misogynistic…"

She snorted. "You don't know the half of it. Probably looks like the dark ages to girls like you."

"But you didn't accept it?"

"No I bloody didn't. They only started taking women the year before and they actually said, get this, they'd let a couple in so they could faint and show all the others a woman could never qualify. Right, I thought, I'll show you..."

"That certainly sounds like you."

"It wasn't funny!" she snapped. "They wanted us to fail. They thought we'd get the vapours at the first dissection."

"I take it you didn't."

"Have you ever cut open a corpse? All oozing and stinking of formaldehyde?"

"I can't say I have. But I take it you didn't have any problems?"

"Ah, well. Everyone has problems the first time. Only question is whether or not you're going to throw up. I didn't, but it was a close-run thing."

"Did they try to put you off?"

"Oh, gods, everything. Half of 'em trying to propose, the other half thinking I'd sleep with them just because they happened to have a prick going spare. Professors giving their favourites the extra help and none for us. Every bloody deck they could stack they bloody well stacked a mile high. I would have qualified, mind, but I never got the chance, did I?"

"What happened?"

She looked at me as though I were stupid. "The first outbreak, what do you think?"

"I didn't realise it happened that long ago."

"Oh didn't you? Like you haven't been working your way round to it, you sneaky cow. I know your game, you want to hear about how I banged my head fighting them and that's why I'm cranky and objectionable–"

"Actually, I found one of the other things you said rather interesting..."

"Oh, and now you're going to check on my periods..."

"No. Nothing to do with that. You said something about the way the outbreak made men and women more equal?"

"Hah! Rubbish..."

"If that's not true, why did you say it?"

"Which outbreak are we talking about?"

"Any one."

"Well I was probably talking about the last one. But now you've got me talking about the first one and it didn't happen then. Hah! The dead were ripping people's guts out and they still didn't want precious flowers picking up a gun and defending themselves. 'Course, then the precious flowers'd end up revenning and you don't want to know how many times some big strapping lad had his windpipe bitten off trying to save 'em."

"So what did you do?"

"Huh. Stupid cow. I volunteered."

"You volunteered for the military?"

"You must be joking! No, I volunteered for the Coroner Corps. They wanted every physician in the country to join up so they could figure out who was dead and who wasn't. Not like it was hard to tell but no one knew a damn thing then. So they started with coroners and pathologists and whatnot and made 'em go house to house checking on people with the cholera, to see if they were revenning. Then they found out there weren't enough, so they got doctors in as well. And they still didn't have enough people, so I volunteered. They told me to report to the local hospital and be a nurse instead, as though I wasn't already there covering for the doctors who were off with the Corps, or the ones who were too damn busy with the cholera. Couple of weeks later they came back begging. If they tried it now I'd tell them where to shove it... you really are sneaky, you know that, don't you?"

"I'm sorry?"

"You start off asking about medical school and here I am talking about revenants and I don't even know how I got here!"

"You're the one that did the work, Olivia. I think you want to talk."

"Rubbish."

"I think you like proving your point. And you proved your point in the outbreak, didn't you?"

"Didn't do me any good, did it? I'm still bloody here, aren't I?"

"I'd like to find out more about what you did..."

"Nah. Let's talk about veg."

"Vegetables...?"

"Yeh. Let's talk about the garden. You like me doing the garden. So let's talk about that. Those tomatoes are never going to come up..."

She spent the next half an hour complaining about the quality of the local soil, the genetic modifications to the seeds, the lack of adequate rainfall and everything that was morally wrong with the garden. As a diversionary tactic, it was extremely effective; but at least we'd progressed a step further towards the outbreak.

9. IOKAN

Iokan was the last of the three I regarded as a suspect for the breakout. He was still recovering from the injuries he suffered when his world ended, so I wasn't sure if he was physically capable – but then, given the way in which his body had clearly been modified, I couldn't say for certain what his physical abilities might be. And there was one lingering question: his military experience, which was conspicuously absent from his biography as given to the triage counsellor when he came down the Lift.

"Good afternoon, Iokan," I said as he came into my office, wearing his usual robes.

"And good afternoon to you," he said. My implant told me the words I was hearing were not a translation from Iokan's language, but spoken in Interversal.

"That's rather impressive," I said. "Have you learnt any more phrases?"

He took a moment to grasp what I was saying; he wasn't wearing his contact lenses. "I have learn some of more words..."

"That's not quite correct," I said.

"Ah," he replied. "I perhaps use should lenses." He had a think and tried again. "I perhaps should use lenses?"

"I think you should," I agreed. He sighed, took out the case, and popped them in. "Sorry about that," he said in his own language. "I thought I knew a bit more than I did."

"It's still very impressive. You've only been learning for three weeks, after all."

"I'm good at taking in new information."

"Yes. You have a number of interesting abilities."

"Is that what you'd like to talk about today?"

"There's a few things I'd like to go over. First of all, Katie."

He looked a little shamefaced. "Ah."

"You spent some time in privacy with her."

"There's nothing wrong with that."

"No, of course not."

"Did she say something?"

"She said you were worried about what your wife might think."

He fell silent.

"Are you concerned?" I asked.

"I don't think it's really any of your business."

"If you were trying to provide Katie with therapy, then it is."

He thought for a moment. "I think Szilmar would want me to help…"

"I hope that's the case. But I'd like you to think about it next time. You're not a trained counsellor, and Katie has a very unusual psychological makeup. It's hard to say what may or may not help her."

He didn't look happy, but at least I'd made my point. "Were we going to talk about anything else?" he asked.

"I'd like to talk about your military career."

"I see."

"We weren't previously aware you'd had one."

"It's not something I really want to discuss."

"Why is that?"

"We don't talk about it."

"Why not?"

"We just don't."

"Hm. Well, at the risk of seeming unsympathetic, I have to ask: who's 'we'?"

"The people I served with."

"And where are they now?"

He thought about that. "With the Antecessors, I suppose."

"Along with the rest of your military."

"…yes. That's a very good point."

"So why is secrecy so important?"

"It used to be for our protection…" he mused. "But I suppose you're right. They don't need to be protected any more."

"So you could talk about it if you wanted to."

He smiled. "I could, couldn't I?"

"So let's start."

"Okay. What do you want to know?"

"Just a sketch outline, to begin with."

"I went in when I was twenty. Dropped out of university, went down to the recruitment centre and signed up. They were happy to see me."

"Why was that?"

"People weren't joining up as much as they used to."

"So it was a purely volunteer force?"

"Oh, completely. And we didn't even need that, really, we stopped fighting real wars a long time ago. There were just a few brushfire conflicts every now and again..."

"I'm sorry, can we backtrack: you say you'd stopped fighting wars?"

"By and large."

"Why was that?"

"Well, about fifty years ago, all the countries of the world, including mine, signed a treaty, and that was it. No more war. By my time, we only had nominal forces for small crises."

"You didn't answer my question."

"Which one was that?"

"Why did you stop fighting wars?"

"I suppose we just didn't like them any more."

He smiled a disingenuous smile. His way of not answering.

"Okay. So you joined up. Which service did you join?"

"The Imperial Zumazscartan Submarine Troop. Sounds very grand, doesn't it?"

"Very grand, yes. What did they do?"

"Patrol, mostly. We had a few underwater habitats. No chance of a war, of course, but the squid got a bit uppity sometimes. They liked to rip airlocks off for fun."

"That's some very impressive squid..."

"The Antecessors left us with quite a lot of interesting fauna."

"Hm. So how much time did you spend on patrol?"

"None at all."

"I'm sorry...?"

"They gave me an aptitude test and packed me off to headquarters instead. Intelligent people didn't join the military, you see. There wasn't much of a career path if there wasn't any chance of fighting a war. So if someone with a good education walked in the door, they locked it behind you and made you an officer."

"So you became...?"

"A military planner."

"And that was your service? That was secret?"

"Well, the details were secret. I worked on defence plans in the event of an attack from the Asian mainland."

"But I thought you said there were no more wars?"

"That's right."

"So why do it?"

"Budgets. They were trying to justify military spending to the government, so they had to spend the money on something. They were just trying to keep their jobs, really."

"So it was basically pointless?"

"More or less."

"And that was your military career?"

"That was the first two years. Then I joined special forces."

"Special forces? You mean…"

"Small teams making point assaults behind enemy lines, gathering intel, demo ops, that kind of thing."

"That seems quite a change from military planning."

"It was. They turned me down twice."

"So why did you want to join special forces?"

"Because I knew I'd spend the rest of my life behind a desk otherwise. So I went for the only branch of the military that was still doing something for real."

"Did you see actual combat?"

"I did."

"What sort of conflict? If there weren't any wars going on…"

"Oh, there was always some little island somewhere… most of my service was in the Shizima Archipelago."

"You mentioned that one of your colleagues suffered from PTSD."

"Yes. It was always a risk."

"Did you come through okay?"

"It never gave me a problem."

"How long were you in the special forces?"

"A little over a year, once I'd finished training."

"That's not very long…"

"I had a better offer."

"Can you tell me what that was?"

"No."

"Was it secret?"

"Yes."

"More than being in special forces?"

"Much more."

"So you still feel the need to protect someone? Even though they're all Antecessors now?"

His look at me was very serious and certain. "I'm not protecting them. I'm protecting you."

"Why do we need protecting?"

"I can't tell you."

"That seems very mysterious…"

"I don't mean to be. But it's safer this way."

"Is this a danger to us, here in the centre? Or is it bigger than that?"

"Much bigger."

"Can you tell us anything at all?"

"No."

"Hm." Delusional? Given his world, it was far from impossible that he could imagine a threat against us and cast himself as our saviour. But he'd clammed up for now, so I went back to another issue. "Okay. So you've told me about how you joined the military, and what you did while you were there. You didn't tell me *why* you joined the military."

He looked at me. Or perhaps he looked through me. Pursing his lips and thinking hard.

"Is that something we can explore...?" I asked.

"I was looking for the Antecessors."

"So it was a religious thing?"

"No. Not for me, not then."

"But they were part of your religion. That's what you've told us."

"They were also real."

"I thought that wasn't known until they returned?"

"No. It was known. It wasn't like the religions you have on other worlds. We didn't have to invent gods. We had evidence – all the things they left behind when they went."

"Such as...?"

"Technology. Science. Weapons."

"I see. So what were you trying to find out?"

"What they really were. I thought the military might know."

"Okay, but why? I mean, why were you searching?"

He looked away, his gaze floating out over the expanse of trees beyond the transparent wall.

"I saw them when I was a child."

"But... you said..."

"Not as they are now. I found something they left behind. An animal cave."

"You'll have to explain that."

He sighed. "So far as we know, the Antecessors had complete control over the entire planet. All the plants and animals were regulated down to the last insect. A lot of the systems had broken down – that's why we had so much trouble with the squid. But a few places still had underground maintenance facilities that preserved the wildlife so it would never change."

"That's quite... disturbing."

He shrugged. "You *could* say they were environmentalists..."

"I think some people would disagree. But carry on."

"I grew up on the north Selatanian coast – that was part of Zumazscarta, the rest of Selatania was another country entirely." So far as I could tell, Selatania was his world's version of Australia, though its climate was very different to most Australias in the multiverse. "The forest went from there all the way across the continent, and we played in the woods all the time. And then one day we found a hole in the ground."

"One of the maintenance facilities?"

"Exactly. An animal cave. I was with three other children. We couldn't resist – it made a splendid little fort, but that was just the tunnel leading down. Then we found a door. And it opened by itself. We went inside and the lights came on... it wasn't big. The corridors weren't really meant for humans. We were only children and we were still a little too tall. Everything was polished metal, as though it had only just been built, and even the animals couldn't soil it. They were everywhere. All kinds of creatures. Marching in from tunnels, straight into cages, hundreds of cages. And little operating stations. The animals were picked up and delivered there when they were ready to start. We saw a ferret cut open, the leg bone replaced where it was broken. Mostly it was small animals but there were a few cages at the back for bigger ones. There was a bear cub in there, sleeping. As big as we were."

"Sounds rather scary."

"Terrifying. But so exciting..." There was a light in his eyes. "We all knew about the Antecessors from school. But we'd never seen anything for real. My heart was thudding, I was thinking *this is it, this is them, they were here once...*

"And then *they* were there with us. Not really them. Just a hologram. A woman, but not quite right. Her face was set up wrong. Maybe I'm not remembering it right... she spoke to us but we didn't understand. I ran..."

He shook his head. "But the others were too scared. Or something else. They just stood there. I only looked back when I got to the door. All the lights switched off inside. I shouted after them but they didn't come.

"I ran home and kept my mouth shut. I was terrified. My parents could tell something was wrong but they didn't know what it was until my friends' parents called and asked if their children were with me.

"I still couldn't say it, but they guessed and called the police. It wasn't the police that came, though. It was the government.

"They put me in quarantine in a plastic bubble, running tests on me, people in biohazard suits going around everywhere. They found the animal cave but they were too late for the others. I don't know what the cave did to them. But I remember thinking – those cages at the back. They were big enough for us. Just the right size..." He looked away at the forest and I wondered what he thought of it, so natural and yet so empty. "They didn't get out."

"What happened to you?"

"There was a man that came to me. No uniform, no biohazard suit. He looked like he'd stepped out of an office. He told me my friends weren't coming back and it wasn't my fault. They weren't blaming me. But they were going to take us somewhere else and we weren't supposed to talk about what happened ever again. My whole family got moved to a city on one of the islands. We never went back."

"Who was he?"

"He was from the government."

"Not the military."

"No. That's what I thought it was then. But it wasn't."

"A secret organisation?"

"That's right."

"Which you later joined...?"

He smiled. "Not much gets past you, does it?"

"Are you sure there's nothing else you want to tell me?"

He looked back out over the forest. "It really is very, very beautiful here. I think I'll get my boots on and help Olivia in the garden, if you don't mind."

"Will you tell me when you're ready?"

"She probably wants someone to help with weeding..."

"Iokan? If this is something to do with the Antecessors, I think we need to discuss it."

He looked back at me with a helpful smile. "Another time," he said.

10. SECURITY

Lomeva Sisse came through my door as soon as she decently could, once the individual sessions were over. "Well?"

"Nothing," I said.

"I'll search their rooms," she replied, and turned to go.

"Lomeva. No."

She turned back again.

"If they're clever enough to mess with our computers, what makes you think they aren't clever enough to find a hiding place? And what do you expect to find, anyway?"

"I don't know. That's why we need to search."

"No. It's a waste of time… how much more surveillance can we get?"

She paused a moment. "Outside and in?"

"Anything."

"I can blanket the place if you like. If the budget's there." She reflected a moment. "Better still, a secondary system that's not connected to the first. Just in case."

"I'll take care of it," I said.

"So you just want to watch?"

"I want to catch them doing it. I'm not going to make all of them feel victimised just because one person's sneaking out."

"I'll be reporting this."

"Yes, Lomeva. You'll be reporting it to me. And I'll decide what to do. I hope that's clear."

"Yes… ma'am." She didn't like it, but I was within my rights. She'd probably find someone to complain to sooner or later, though, so I could only hope that whoever had broken out tried again as soon as possible.

11. GROUP

We didn't have any trouble getting Olivia to attend the next group therapy session, because she'd fallen asleep on a sofa in the common room an hour earlier. Veofol gently shook her shoulder; she snapped awake and lurched away from him with a look of terror.

"It's okay!" he said. "It's just me…"

She realised where she was, breathing hard. "Don't bloody wake me up like that! Damn elf…"

"It's time for group, Olivia," I said as the others settled into their chairs.

"You got me up for that? Ugh…"

"Everyone else is here."

"All right, all right, I'm awake, hold your bloody horses…"

She joined us in the circle and I began. "Okay, thanks to everyone for coming along. I think you've all been putting in a lot of effort and the way things have changed is quite noticeable, so I'm very happy with that. And now we're feeling a bit more like a group, I'd like to tackle a more serious subject today.

"What I'd like to talk about is one of the questions a lot of survivors ask: Why me? Why did I survive? Now I know that for each of you the answer is probably different, but I'd like to hear what you think."

"It's a stupid question," said Olivia.

"I don't think so," said Iokan.

"Oh, trust you to suck up to her…"

"I was meant to survive. It's simple. Why me? Because the Antecessors chose me."

"And no doubt you think we were all chosen," said Kwame. He hadn't slept for a couple of nights, and was more irritable than usual.

"I think it's a possibility," replied Iokan.

"There was no 'choice' in my survival. As soon as I became President, I was informed of the hibernation chambers and my role in wartime. The choice was made before I took office."

"That sounds like predestination to me…"

"So it was predestined that I would become President? That I would be out of the country at just the right moment? That I would be elected to parliament in the first place? All that was chosen for me, is that what you are saying?"

Iokan shrugged. "Who knows why we take the paths we take?"

"It is nonsense. Our survival is random. I was merely fortunate. Or unfortunate."

"But… um…" said Pew.

"Yes, Pew?" I asked.

"Well, once you became President, you *were* one of the most likely people to survive. It might be chance that you got the job, but once you were there… well, you might not have started out special but you became special. I mean statistically. Does that make any sense?"

Kwame looked back at him. "And were you special?"

The question took him by surprise. "I, um, I suppose. I was immune to the plague, when I was a boy. So yeah… if it's about probability then I had more chance than the others…"

I decided to try and bring Liss into the conversation. She was drawn up in her chair, cocooned as much as she could be. "Liss? Do you think that applies to you?"

Liss looked up at the group, brushing aside unwashed hair. She hadn't bothered with one of her horrible outfits and was just wearing whatever she'd scraped from the bottom of the drawer: shapeless sweater, flowered jeans and bare feet. "I don't know. I wasn't special. I don't know anything. Don't ask me. I don't know anything…" Tears came to her eyes and Veofol offered her a tissue.

"Oh, don't give us the waterworks," said Olivia. "You're always bloody crying, girl! What have you got to cry about? You survived, didn't you?"

"I don't know why… I don't know why it was me! I don't understand it…"

"Olivia. She's only just remembered. A little sympathy would help," I said.

Olivia rolled her eyes.

"I have information that may assist your emotional disturbance," said Katie, looking directly at Liss. "When a species goes extinct, one individual must always be the last to die. The reasons are likely to be beyond the control of the individual. It is pointless to trouble yourself with an examination of causes."

Liss stared back at her with no idea what to make of her words.

"That's... helpful. Thank you, Katie," I said.

"I am happy to assist with therapy."

"So it's all just chance and there's no point talking about it, is that what she's saying?" asked Olivia.

"I think so, yes," I said.

"Rubbish. Chance hasn't got a thing to do with it, apart from maybe having a head start like Pew said. I damn well did everything I could to stay alive. None of you just laid down and died, did you?"

"I did," said Iokan. "But the Antecessors had other plans."

"Yeh, well you're a nutter. But the rest of you fought. I'm right, aren't I?"

"I... not really," said Pew, frowning.

"I did not fight to survive," said Katie. "I fought to defeat the enemy. My survival was incidental."

"But you didn't give up?"

"I would have been content to die in combat."

Olivia looked round at Liss, "*You* didn't give up. You could've, couldn't you? Could've killed yourself, but you didn't."

"I should have," said Liss. "I should have died with them."

"Oh, you pathetic little cow..." Liss flinched at Olivia's words. "Am I the only one who actually bothered to try and keep breathing?" She looked at Kwame. "What about you?"

"I had no choice. I had a duty to my nation," said Kwame. "If I could have chosen for myself, I would have stayed with my wife and children to the end."

"Olivia, can I just ask something?" I said. "This seems to be very important to you. Can you tell us a little more about why you feel this way?"

"Why do you think? I didn't give up! I never gave up! And you all just... ugh. I don't know why I bothered."

"Is that the only reason you survived, do you think?"

"All the people who gave up are dead. I'm not dead. Therefore I didn't give up. Where'd you learn your logic?"

"And you don't think there was anything special about you? About who you were?"

Kwame took up the theme. "Were you not involved in researching the revenation bacterium?"

"Yeh. So?"

"And you were in your... what did you call it... Coroner Corps?"

"So were lots of people. You know what happened to them? They're all bloody dead."

Iokan joined in. "But that gave you certain skills, surely? Like all of us, your chances would have been improved by your experiences."

Even Katie spoke up. "I can calculate the probability of survival of a person with your skills against one without if you wish to be convinced."

"Did you not hear me? *All the others are dead.* Knowing how to put down a revenant didn't save 'em. Researching it didn't save 'em."

Her protestations sounded ragged. I decided to risk pushing a little further. "But here you are, and you *were* a researcher and you *do* know how to put down a revenant. Doesn't that have any relevance to your survival?"

She exploded back at me. "Course it's got relevance! Can't you see? Course you can't, you weren't there, you don't bloody know, do you?" Iokan tried to speak, but Olivia wasn't to be stopped. "And why are you asking us, anyway? You don't know anything about it. When was the last time your world blew up? Eh? Bet you've never even seen a dead body."

"That's not the point, Olivia."

"When were you ever the last woman on Earth? Course you bloody weren't, there's only us here and half of 'em I don't even know they're properly human. How come you get to ask *us* questions?"

"You're right, I've never been the last person on Earth. But that doesn't mean I can't help you."

"You don't know a damn thing about what it's like to be us! How are you supposed to help us?"

"I was chosen for my experience as a therapist, not—"

"How is *anyone* supposed to help us? Eh?"

"That's why we have the group, Olivia. So you have peers—"

"Don't you change the subject! You make me sick, telling us how we ought to get better as though you know what it's like to be us! There's not one of you knows what it was like, you with your comfortable world with your food printers and your flying cars and everything you want on a plate with a cherry on top, what do you know about it? Eh? Tell me that! What do *you* know?"

She glared at me, challenging me to admit to incompetence. She was doing her best to avoid her own problems, of course, but she'd drawn the group's attention to me instead of her, and it's true that patients sometimes have difficulty working with a therapist who has no personal experience of their trauma.

I sighed and put my pad aside. I never like having this talk with patients, but sometimes it becomes inevitable.

"Well, since it seems to be important to you, Olivia, I'll tell you. I've never been the last person on Earth. But I have been through an apocalypse." She was on the point of making a retort, but I kept going. "It's not why I was picked to be your therapist, but if the group thinks it might be relevant, I'll tell you what happened to me."

Kwame put a hand on his chin. Liss uncurled in her chair and wiped tears from her eyes. Katie stared at me, waiting. Pew had a new expression on his face, close to sympathy. Iokan glanced round the rest of the group. "I think I'd like to know," he said.

I looked back at Olivia. "Well go on, then!" she said.

"Those of you who've been here for a while have probably noticed that a lot of people on Hub are just passing through – diplomats, students, delegations of one kind or another. Some people come from worlds the IU is helping to rebuild..." I looked at Veofol. He got the hint.

"Er, yes. We messed up the environment on my world. There was a mass extinction, lots of UV – long story short, there were only a few thousand of us in orbit when the IU found us. That's why I look the way I do. We've lived for ten generations in orbit on the stations. We're not used to being in a gravity well." Olivia gave him a sidelong look for a moment.

I went on. "But some people do call this world home. A few of them are descended from the people who colonised the planet in the first place. Most of us, though, came here for a different reason. Most of us are apocalypse survivors."

Olivia scowled but didn't interrupt.

"There was a volcano, on my world, in America. Not an ordinary one. It was like a thousand volcanoes all going off at once. The sky was blocked out with dust and ash. There was no harvest for years on end. If we'd been on our own, we'd have probably gone extinct.

"But we met the IU. They managed to get hundreds of millions of people out – which sounds like a lot but there were eight billion of us before things went bad. That's how fast people were dying. I nearly died. Most of the children in my town did die, and I was never in good health." In fact, I had a cleft palate because of the pollution from a chemical plant abandoned when the economy went bad a decade earlier.

"There was an evacuation centre near where my family lived, and the ships lifted off from there to get out to the portals in orbit. They built it round an old airport and kept us in tents until they could take us." IU doctors gave out medicine and food and water, keeping us alive until we could be evacuated. They said they'd be able to fix my cleft palate, and I never saw my parents so happy.

"We had these little pagers they put in our hands, I mean they implanted them so we wouldn't lose them. The idea was that, when it was our turn, they'd go off and we'd get on the ships." They itched like hell for the first few days. I couldn't help stroking the spot now; it was still there, and still itched sometimes.

"Somebody figured out how they worked, and tried to jump the queue. But instead of setting off their own pager, they set off everyone else's. You can imagine what happened." Hell. Chaos. Thousands of desperate people running out of their tents to get to the ships. All of them crowding around the fences. My parents dragging me along, desperate to get me to Hub.

"There was a crush at the gate. Nobody at the back of the crowd knew it was a false alarm. Everyone at the front was trapped. If they'd opened the gates, people would have been trampled to death as the ones at the back rushed forward. They tried to disperse the crowd and eventually they managed it, but eighty-six people died, including my parents." They only kept me alive by putting me on their shoulders. They did that with all the children. They passed us forward over the crowd and the IU staff pulled us over the fence. I was screaming when they lifted me over the barrier, trying to get free so I could crawl back over the heads of the crowd, but they were already gone, already pressed to death.

I didn't cry. I've told the story too often, and I always keep some of the details back.

"Why didn't they turn off the implants...?" asked Liss, appalled.

"They did. It didn't stop people trying to get in. We were desperate."

"Was that the worst?" asked Kwame. He wasn't testing how much I'd suffered; he was genuinely sympathetic.

"No. We had it easy in my country. There'd been a nuclear war between India and China a couple of years before. That's what persuaded the governments to finally accept the offer of evacuation. We had everything you can imagine before the end." I shook my head and sighed, and hoped they would not ask for more details. There were mass graves, pandemics, a volcanic winter compounded by the dust thrown up by the nuclear exchange, whole countries abandoned to die.

"So no, I would never have been like you. If it wasn't for the Interversal Union, I would have been one of the bodies in a mass grave. But I came here instead."

Here: the evacuation shuttle to the L1 point, weeks in quarantine at Grainger Station with its uneven artificial gravity that children loved to play in, those that weren't in the terrible silence I withdrew into; then down the Lift, descending on a carbon strand to the equator, and out to a reception centre, and always the therapists worrying about me, trying to get me to play with the other children, putting me in a group with other disturbed ones, wanting us to talk about it. Until finally I did, and the healing began.

The biggest danger when telling this story is becoming lost in reverie. I shook off the memories and looked around the group. By and large, they were sympathetic. I'd shown enough of my own pain to convince them I was no stranger to suffering.

Except for Olivia, of course. She had her arms folded and an obstinate look on her face. "And that proves your point, does it?"

"I may not be a lone survivor, Olivia, but I've seen my world die. I saw hundreds of people starve to death before the IU came."

"Late as ever."

"I'm still alive because of the IU. And so are you. I'm sorry we didn't get to you earlier."

"But nothing—"

"Shut up!" shouted Liss. "You never say anything nice to anyone! It's like nobody even matters to you if they didn't suffer like you, we all lost our whole species, isn't that enough for you?"

Olivia was speechless, for once. She looked around, hoping for support from Pew.

"She's kind of right," said Pew, unable to meet her eyes. "You're not very nice to people."

"I find your outbursts irritating," said Katie.

"I find everything about you irritating," said Kwame.

"Okay, everyone," I said, "honesty is good but there's no need to make this about someone's character."

"There's every bloody need!" shouted Olivia, and turned it out to everyone. "You want to know why I'm sick of you? You didn't fight! You didn't try! You didn't have to try! You were the last people on Earth because you were all pathetic! You deserved to go extinct!"

She stormed out of the room, and very shortly out of the building. Pew shuddered as she went. Her words hit him harder than anyone else.

"Veofol?" I asked. He sighed and went after her.

"She has a point," said Iokan.

"Must you always be contrary?" asked Kwame.

Iokan shrugged. "She's the way she is because she suffered for longer than any of us. It was twelve years for her... I always knew there was a chance my world would end, but it was quick when it came." He suddenly remembered himself. "Not that it was a bad thing, of course."

"There is something admirable in her struggle to survive, if not her personality," said Katie.

"There's nothing admirable about her," said Liss. "She's just horrible because she wants to be horrible."

"Did she have any children?" asked Pew. "Maybe she's angry because she lost her children?"

"She's never spoken about it," I said.

"She would hardly be alone in losing children," said Kwame.

As much as the group had grown closer and gotten to know each other, Olivia was proving to be a problem; she tried to dominate every session while she was present, and was still provoking discussion about her even though she was gone. We were getting nowhere.

"I think that's enough for today," I said.

12. KATIE & IOKAN

Katie had been unusually garrulous during the group session; you could almost call her restless. And when she retired to her room after the evening meal, the restlessness redoubled.

Normally, she would simply sit on her bench, or lie on it, or sometimes just stand in the middle of the room. But now, if she lay down, she found her head tossing about, unable to find a comfortable place. She sat up, and found her fingers drumming a simple rhythm. She picked her hand off the bench and stared at it, flexing the fingers. She put it aside, and then found her foot doing the same thing.

She stood and walked to the centre of the room. But her body would not stand still. She had to flex her hands to stop them twitching. She tried pacing back and forth, but this did not help either.

She marched to a wall, activated a control surface, selected the room controls and turned one wall into a facsimile of solid steel. Then punched it.

It must have hurt, though there was no expression on her face, and no mark on her fist. The wall was not so lucky: she left an impression of knuckles. She punched it again. And again. And again, until she showed some pain on her face, and her knuckles were scraped. She punched again–

And her fist plunged into foam rubber. She drew it back out of the ruptured surface, and it closed up around the hole she'd made. She tested the wall, still apparently steel as far as the eye was concerned. But it gave way to a firm push. Safety measures had been activated. She would not be allowed to harm herself in her own room.

Her fist trembled. A look of frustration passed over her like a wave, and was gone.

Iokan, meanwhile, was getting a door slammed in his face. "And you can bloody piss off!" yelled Olivia as the door crashed shut. She preferred her door to swing rather than slide, mainly so she could create a satisfying slam.

Iokan sighed, turned away, and had to stop before he walked into Katie. She'd made no noise as she left her room a few doors down and walked up to him. Someone else might have jumped. Iokan was just surprised.

"I'm sorry, I didn't see you there…"

"I require your assistance."

"Okay. How can I help?"

"I am experiencing emotional disturbance."

"Ah. I see…"

"I require the same assistance you provided previously."

"I've been thinking about that."

"Please explain."

"I'm not sure it's such a good idea."

"You have stated your wish to help members of the group."

"I have, yes, but… I've been thinking about Szilmar."

"Your wife is dead."

"No. She isn't. She found a new life! She's still out there, somewhere. I might see her again one day…"

"That is unlikely."

"Do you have marriage, in your species?"

"No."

"I swore to her that I would set aside all others and honour only her. Do you understand what I mean by that?"

She spoke forcefully. "I require your assistance!"

"Ask me anything else. Please."

She grabbed for his arm, but he was too fast. "Don't," he said, retreating into a fighting stance, despite the robes that would have been all too easy to trip in.

"I need you!" She grabbed again and he stepped aside.

"I'm not yours to have."

She ran at him, and this time she didn't miss. His robe made it too easy for her to grab him. It ripped but held together enough for her to throw him across the corridor and pin him against a wall. She flipped him round and pulled an arm behind his back. He gasped at the pain as she yanked him away from the wall and pointed him in the direction of her room.

And then she let him go. He stumbled forwards into the carpet, scrambling away while he had the chance. But she wasn't following. She wasn't doing anything. She stood in the corridor, not seeing him at all. He stood back up, cautiously.

"Katie?"

She heard that. And saw him. She looked confused. "Ket'or Katie?" she said.

"I don't understand."

She twitched.

"Who's Katie?"

She collapsed to the floor.

PART SIX
MYSTERIES

1. LISS

Katie stayed unconscious for several days, causing grave concern among the neurologists who came in to examine her. She was unresponsive to stimuli, and whole areas of her brain seemed to have shut down. All we could do was keep her under observation and hope she improved.

Therapy for the others had to continue. I saw to it that the first individual therapy session of the week would be for Liss. She hadn't been willing, yet, to talk about what she'd experienced, or reveal any other secrets she might be keeping. She huddled in her chair with sweet tea for the first half hour of the session, and we spoke about the screenshows from her world. She showed some interest in those, and I kept her talking until we came to a very specific episode of *Dates and Hates*.

"I think it was called *The Underdater*. Do you remember that one, Liss?"

"No…"

"It's the one where she goes on a lunch date and it turns out he's taking her to a funeral? Remember? And she thinks it's his mother's funeral, but he just likes funerals."

She looked up at me. "That one was about Ellera's mom."

"That's it. The guy's trying to impress her but she's in the same graveyard her mother's buried in so she has a big breakdown…"

"And she sees her mom's ghost and all she does is ask her if she's met a nice guy…"

"That's right."

"And her mom hates the guy she's with because he keeps going to all the funerals with a different girl each time, and, and Ellera ends up telling her mom to shut up and goes back to the wake with him…"

"And that's how she comes to terms with losing her mother."

"Uh-huh."

"Liss… what happened to your family?"

She hid her face again and took a while to answer. "I buried them."

"Your whole family?"

"My parents. They were at home when it happened. They were retired."

"Can you tell me about them?"

She looked up from her tea, but not at me.

"They were great. They were… they were…" And back came the tears; I offered her the tenth tissue of the session.

"I'm sorry…" she said.

"They must have been good to you."

"Oh, sure. The best."

"So you buried them straight away?"

"Oh. Uh. Yeah. Well. Not right away. I, uh…" The tears welled up again. Tissue number eleven came out. "I don't know what I did at first. You've got all these people that did so much, I must seem kinda pathetic."

"Not at all. I expect you were in shock. Did you stay in the call centre for long?"

"No. I... I remember I saw a screen. There was a news channel on it but all the newspeople were gone. I guess I thought that if that was still going, everything else would come back, maybe if I closed my eyes..."

"And there was nothing on the screen about the event?"

"No. Nothing. Just money news on the scrolling thing."

"And you saw no one else? No one at all?"

"No. It was just me. I don't get it. I don't..." She looked up at me. "Why do I have to be the one? Why couldn't they pick someone who was supposed to survive, like one of the big heroes or someone in the government, or, or, someone who could do something?"

I thought for a moment. "Do you think someone actually picked you to survive?"

"I don't know! I didn't ask for it! I should be a pile of dust on the floor like everyone else..."

"I'm glad you're not. I'm much happier to have you here."

She half-smiled. "You've been really nice."

"You've had a terrible experience. It's natural to feel as though it should have been you who died, and wonder why it wasn't..."

She sniffled on another tissue. "Was it like that when it happened to you?"

Telling my own story always leads to this kind of question. "Yes. I wondered for a long time. But eventually, I had to acknowledge that I was just lucky. And it was better to be alive than dead."

"What happened to your mom and dad?"

"They died, Liss. I told you that."

"No, I mean afterwards?"

"Oh. Uh, well, I was sent on to Hub and the, uh, the bodies had to stay because of the investigation."

"Did you go to the funeral?"

"No. I was only seven. They couldn't take me back. There wasn't a funeral, as such. They went into a mass grave."

"That's terrible!"

"It's just the way things were. Billions of people were dying, Liss. There wasn't enough space on the planet for all the graves they would have had to dig."

"Did you ever go back?"

"There's nothing to go back to."

"Huh." She blew her nose.

"I don't mind talking about myself, Liss, but this session is for you. So can I ask what happened after you stopped looking at the screen?"

"Oh... I just went out. I don't know, I lost track of time. All the dust was blowing around. You've never seen that much dust in the air. It was horrible."

"And all the things you spoke of before – calling the police and so on – did that happen?"

"Sure. I called the police. I called the PRG as well..."

"The PRG?"

"Oh, uh, Paranormal Response Group. The ones you call if something big happens, you know, like there's all the services on the emergency line, Police, Ambulance, Fire, Paranormal Response, I tried them all, there was nothing, just voicemail."

"Did you call your parents?"

"Yeah."

"Is that when you decided to go there?"

"…yeah. I walked. And then when I got there…"

"It's okay, Liss. Go on."

"They were in the kitchen. They were on the floor, in the kitchen. Just these two little piles and, and, a couple of cracked plates. They always used to argue over the dishes when I wasn't there to do them…" Another tissue was required.

"And you buried them."

"Yeah. I put them in a sandwich bag and dug up the garden and put them in there. I mixed them together. Is that okay?"

"I'm sure they would have appreciated it, Liss. Did you stay there after that?"

"No. I went home. And then I went back to work. You must think I'm so stupid…"

"No, Liss. I think you survived. I think that's an achievement, no matter how you did it."

She wiped her nose on one of the many tissues I'd given her. "I didn't do anything. All I did was forget to die."

"It's still worth something. And sooner or later we'll find out what happened on your world."

"'s just a joke. That's all it is."

"We'll find out, Liss."

"Just a frigging joke. That's my world. Just a big joke."

She huddled up in her chair again, and I didn't get any more out of her that day.

2. ELSBET

There was a chime in my ear, and a message before my eyes: EMERGENCY ASSISTANCE REQUIRED: INFIRMARY. I ran from my office, playing video on a separate stream, floating in apparent space before me.

Katie was awake, shouting at the medical staff and Veofol, who had been staying by her side as much as possible – but now he was backed up against a wall while Katie screamed at them.

"I'm not talking to fucking needle jockeys!"

She smashed a trolley into the wall. The two nurses and a doctor backed off a little more.

"I've called an officer!" said Veofol. "She's on her way!"

I concentrated on where I was for a moment – into the gravity tube for a few seconds of freefall, a sudden stop on the ground floor, then out to the infirmary. Security were piling up outside, checking weapons. Lomeva Sisse stepped in my way, imposing in full power armour.

"You're not going in there," she said.

"Why?"

"She's lost it. I'm not risking anyone going in."

I checked the video: Katie had Veofol by his jacket lapels, dragging him down to her height and demanding: "Well? Where is this fucking officer?"

"She's on her way! If you just give her a moment!" he replied. He knew I'd be watching, and had an idea for how to deal with the situation. It was a good idea.

I snapped back to reality. "Get out of the way," I said. Lomeva refused to budge. "Do I have to transfer you out of here?" Grudgingly, she stepped aside.

There were more security guards stationed on the way to Katie's room. They let me pass, raising weapons to make space. The door was locked when I got there, but I could hear shouting from inside. More demands as to the whereabouts of the promised officer.

"Lab coat," I said to a doctor, who hurried to remove hers and pass it over. I slipped it on and buttoned it up – anything that looked even a little bit like a uniform would do. I tied my hair back as tight as it would go, assumed the most thunderous expression I could command, then keyed the code to enter.

Katie had really made a mess of the place – smashed equipment, fixtures ripped from the wall, the bed upended and mattress flung to one side. Two nurses and a doctor cowered in the corner, while Katie, still in her infirmary gown, hunched over the doubled up Veofol.

"What's going on here?" I demanded.

Katie turned and saw me. And hopefully, saw I wasn't intimidated.

"You an officer?"

I put on all the disdain I could muster. "I'm Major Singh. What are you doing out of bed?"

"You're not in uniform."

"I was in surgery. Or I was until I was called to deal with this *disgraceful* behaviour." My tone of voice shook her confidence. Military training is always very useful when dealing with someone who isn't listening to reason. "Stand to attention!" She jumped smartly to attention, dropping Veofol. "Now identify yourself, soldier!"

"Sergeant Designate Elsbet Carmon, sir!"

"What's your unit?"

"Vesta 4 Holy Brigade, Attack Squadron Alpha Six!"

"What's the last thing you remember, Sergeant?"

"Sir?"

"Answer the question!"

"Sir! I was piloting my missile towards enemy facilities on the homeworld when I encountered turbulence! I blacked out!"

"Stand easy." She assumed the required stance. "Sergeant. This is a hospital."

"Yes, sir."

"You're here for your own good. You *will* co-operate with the staff. Is that understood?"

"I understand, sir."

"If I see any more of this kind of behaviour, there will be a court-martial. Is *that* understood?"

"Yes, sir!"

"Now get back to bed, and get well. You'll be debriefed shortly."

"Sir!"

"Well get on with it, then!"

She dashed back to the bed and put it back where it was supposed to be. I gave the medical staff a look, and they peeled themselves off the walls to help.

I glanced at Veofol. "Corporal. Come with me."

"Yes, sir," he said, and followed me outside. Once the door was closed again and we were safely out of earshot in an office, I breathed a sigh of relief and collapsed into a chair. Lomeva came in as a nurse brought us tea.

"You're completely fucking insane," she said, meaning it as a compliment.

I shrugged. "Soldiers usually respond to an authoritative voice. Anyway, Veofol had the idea." He sighed as a nurse sprayed his bruised arms with analgesics.

"How do you want to deal with this?" asked Lomeva. "Given our other problem."

"Complete lockdown on her, of course. She doesn't leave the infirmary until we decide it's safe."

"Good. Anything else?"

"Hm..." I had a think. There was one very odd thing about the whole business, and it took a moment to put my finger on it. "She was speaking Interversal, wasn't she?"

"Yeah..." said Veofol.

"So?" said Lomeva.

"So if this is a completely new personality, she shouldn't know our language. She must have access to Katie's memories. Or files, or whatever. Maybe Katie's still in there as well..." And maybe she would come out again. "Okay. We play along to begin with. And then we break it to her. Very carefully. Veofol, you'll need to debrief her."

"Me...?"

"We need to keep the number of people involved to a minimum. She already knows you. And I've got the rest of the group to deal with."

I put a hand on his shoulder. "We need to know who she is. And I don't mean just her name. We need to know how she relates to Katie."

"Okay."

"This might be Dissociative Personality Disorder, and it might not. It might be a persona coming out of the implants. Just find out as much as you can."

He nodded. He was still unnerved, but I was confident he'd be up to the task.

3. PEW

It was painful for Pew to talk about the past, and I had to send a nurse to find him and bring him to his next session. He came in flustered, still wearing his boots from the garden and leaving mud everywhere, trying to apologise for his lateness and then for the dirt tracks on the carpet.

"It's all right, Pew. Just leave the boots by the door and I'll have someone clean them for you."

"Okay, okay, I'm really sorry–"

"That's fine, just take a seat."

He put his boots outside as I sent a message to the housekeeping staff to deal with them. He'd been working hard in the garden, trying to forget he had a therapy session coming up. A quick review of video showed Olivia telling him to slow down before he did himself an injury. He expected questions he didn't want to answer, so I decided to get them out of the way first.

"Can you tell me anything more about Ley'ang?"

He looked up at me, instantly distressed. "I– I–"

"It's okay. You don't have to…"

"No, no, I mean, that is, I…"

"Pew, I'm sorry. I know you don't like talking about her. We'll have to eventually, but if you'd rather talk about something else, we can do that today."

"Okay." He sighed, safe from the hard questions he feared. But we would have to get there somehow – if I could get him to talk about her, I might be able to get him to talk about the breeding programme, which he'd conspicuously avoided in every other conversation I'd had with him.

"So you said last time that you hated the Soo, and that's quite understandable. But you seemed to get along quite well with Shan'oui. I was wondering if there were any other Soo you found tolerable?"

"Can I have some tea?"

"Of course. You carry on, I'll pour."

I filled a cup and he talked. "I, well, they weren't all bad. I mean they were, but they didn't all want to be."

"I'm sorry?" I said as I poured milk.

"They were kind of… they grew up with everyone telling them Pu weren't good for anything, but most of them never actually met any of us."

"So they were just ignorant?" I handed him his tea.

"Yeah."

"How do you know this?"

"Shan'oui told me."

"And you believed her?"

"She tried to help. She didn't do very well but she tried."

"Were there any others who tried?"

"Oh, loads. There was a big group of Soo who'd been campaigning for the Pu for years, well, longer than that. Centuries."

"Was Shan'oui one of those people?"

"Yeah."

"Is this the SPCA? I think I read about them…" I pulled up my notes on a pad: IU Diplomatic research teams had identified a group called the SPCA as potential allies on the Soo world. "The Society for the Prevention of Cruelty to Aboriginals?"

"Yeah. That's them."

"Did they run the breeding programme?"

"No. That was the government. There were a lot of SPCA people involved, though."

"Can you tell me more about them?"

"Um. Well, it started with Ang'zi…"

"He founded the SPCA?"

"No, no, he was Pu. Pu Ang'zi. He was a mechanic, he was one of the first ones who'd been captured in the Arctic, well, his parents were."

"Ah. So, what did he do?"

"He wrote a book, um, *On the Rights of the Pu as Compared with the Beasts of the Field and Engines of Steam*."

"Catchy."

"That was how they wrote things back then. The government thought somebody in the SPCA had written it, some Soo pretending to be a Pu. So they banned it for being harmful to Pu interests, you know, giving us ideas above our station.

"And then they figured out the truth. His owner was an SPCA member and she tried to hide Ang'zi, but they found him and took him away. So she sued the government for stealing her property, but the court case was one of those things where they use it to talk about something else. Do you know what I mean?"

"They made the court case about the Pu as a whole?"

"Yeah. And they lost. Ang'zi was executed. They called it euthanasia because of a brain deformity, can you believe that? Because he wasn't stupid. Like being intelligent was an illness. His owner was compensated, and she gave the money back to the SPCA to print more copies of the book. That was how it got going, really."

"So there was something good about the Soo, after all?"

"Huh. Yeah. They started getting all the owners to give retired Pu to zoos instead of just killing them and turning the bodies into fertiliser."

"Ah. So they didn't go all that far…"

"They never wanted to set us free. They just wanted to make our lives easier."

"Do you think Shan'oui would have set you free?"

"She didn't think we were ready. Maybe she was right."

"Don't you think the Pu should have been free?"

"On our world? Where could we have gone?"

"And the SPCA never thought about letting us help you?"

"The IU? Hah! They didn't trust you. They thought you wanted to take us off to be slaves somewhere else. They thought they were protecting us from you."

"And outside the SPCA, was there anyone with any sympathy?"

"A lot of people thought they were on our side. They weren't. I found that out before the breeding programme started."

"Did something happen?"

He looked up and took a breath. "There was a girl."

"A Soo girl?"

He nodded. "Yeah."

"What did she do?"

"I was… no, it was her. Or maybe I… oh, shit, I was only fourteen."

"What happened?"

He sighed. "I saw her behind the glass."

"In the zoo?"

"She kept coming in every day at the same time. She must have had a season ticket. She was always there just after three, when the school groups were gone…"

"I thought it was one way glass?"

"Yeah, but you could see a bit of what was on the other side. And there was this girl. And she was… beautiful. Amazing. Every day at the same time. She'd come up as close to the glass as she could, and then wave at me. I mean, kids did that all the time, but this was…" He sighed. "So I waved back. Didn't know what the hell I was doing. Next day, she jumped the barrier and came up to the glass. She put her hand up to it and I didn't know what I was supposed to do, so I did the same. She smiled again, I thought my heart was going to come out of my chest…"

"Very normal for teenage boys. Teenage girls, too. What happened next?"

"She ran for it. I suppose security turned up. They didn't catch her because she came back the next day, in disguise. And that time she had a note, she put it up against the glass. It said she wanted to meet me. I was still trying to find a pen when she had to run away again.

"Shan'oui asked me about it and I lied. I'd never lied to her before. I said I hadn't seen a note. She said they were going to put in new barriers, and I thought I was never going to see her again. I was so miserable…

"And then she turned up. On the inside! She'd joined the SPCA and volunteered to help look after the other Pu. They were really old then, they needed someone with them all the time. She just smiled and put her finger to her lips and I was happier than anything.

"We couldn't talk, though, because of all the cameras, until she managed to switch one off and get me alone…" He sighed.

"You must have been very excited to see her."

"She said her name was Sha Ai'mi. She thought I was cute because she'd seen me on TV. Her uncle was in the SPCA, so that's how she'd managed to get in. She thought it was amazing how I was a completely different species. I should have figured it out then…"

"She didn't want *me*. She wanted an interview."

"Ah."

"She was studying journalism. She wanted to write an article about me. She wanted to know what it was like to live in the wild. She wanted to know if I felt anything for real when the others died, or if it was just a crying reflex. What it was like to be an animal and a human at the same time.

"I thought someone had dropped the ceiling on me. She wasn't interested in me at all. I was all stammering and going 'but, but…' and then I actually said it. I told her I thought she liked me. And there was this look on her face – she was disgusted. She was sorry for me but she was disgusted as well. I was just an animal to her. An animal that could talk."

"You must have felt betrayed."

"I felt stupid. I should never have trusted a Soo. The staff found us and took her away and I never saw her again. Shan'oui said she was sorry for letting her come inside. She said that's why I had to stay there. There were lots of people like Ai'mi outside the zoo…

"And the other Pu were worse. They tried to stick up for Ai'mi! They said it was hard on the Soo, being in charge all the time. We had to appreciate how much they'd done for us." He shook his head. "I should never have trusted a Soo."

"But you trusted Shan'oui?"

He looked back at me. "I shouldn't have trusted her either."

"I thought she protected you?"

"It didn't make any difference. They put me in the breeding programme anyway."

"Was that so terrible?"

"I should never have trusted any of them."

"Pew... it wasn't your fault. You were only a child."

He didn't answer. He was still turning the knife in towards himself.

"Okay, Pew, we can pick this up another time, if you like."

He didn't respond to that, either.

4. ELSBET

INTERVIEW
CONDUCTED: HD y276.m6.w3.d4
SUBJECT: KT-00932/IN / Sgt. Dgn. Elsbet Carmon
INTERVIEWER: Dr. Veofol e-leas bron Jerra

Summary

The subject was interviewed under pretence of a debrief following a military mission. She was co-operative, but suspicious whenever questions strayed too far from the subject. Nevertheless, it was possible to assemble a rough sketch of her life, her career, the world she lived in and the mission she was sent on. It remains difficult to see how this relates to the original persona of 'Katie', except that they seem to have fought on opposite sides of a war between humans and machines.

'Elsbet' comes from a colony asteroid in the Vesta chain, where a remnant of a human species seems to reside in her universe. She considers it her duty to make war upon the AI species which occupied the Earth, as revenge for the annihilation of humanity in an earlier war.

The religion she follows seems apocalyptic in nature, prophesying another war between humans and machines, after which the humans will reclaim the Earth and turn it into a paradise. She is unaware of the destruction of the Earth in her universe, and believes the war to still be in progress. She speaks of a 'testament' and seems surprised that we do not have a copy available for her to peruse. I had to promise to try and find one for her; I presume this is the holy text of her religion, but I'm not sure what form it takes.

I made sure to ask her about the implants in her brain, and the sockets in her skull. She seemed surprised, checked them, and was reassured to find they were still there. When I asked her if she was sure she still wanted them, she asserted they were necessary to pilot a missile with the skill needed to defeat a machine opponent.

As for her mission, it seems she was sent on a suicide raid, piloting a missile intended to destroy a facility on Earth with a massive antimatter detonation. She assumes the mission has failed, and I had to construct an explanation for her survival. I told her that her missile skipped off the atmosphere, stunning her and putting her into a coma before continuing out into the solar system until she was picked up. When she asked how the war was going, I told her it was progressing satisfactorily, but declined to give details.

She believes she's on an asteroid. She worked out trajectories in her head based on my story and guessed she was on one of the furthest outposts, in the vicinity of Ceres. She ascribes the strangeness of her surroundings to the laxness of the Ceresians, and seems willing to take my assertions at face value now she believes me to be working for an officer.

I believe this willingness to trust her superiors may be of great help in acclimatising her to her true circumstances, but we still need to be careful when we reveal where she really is. If she believes she's on the Earth of her universe, she may well assume we're working for the machines. Another difficulty is that she has no understanding that other universes exist. I established this with an offhand remark about things being different in 'some other universe', which made her frown and ask me what I meant. She came to the conclusion that I meant 'on Earth', as though we would never get there. She decided I was one of those people who didn't believe in Earth, at which point she tried to convince me with a rapturous description of what she saw when she approached in her missile. We will need to be very, very careful when we come to tell her the truth, and I fear we will need to do this sooner rather than later. She accepts she's in hospital for good reasons at the moment, but she already seems to be impatient to get back to the war, and the fact that she has no obvious injuries is going to make it increasingly difficult to persuade her to stay where she is.

5. IOKAN

Pew was not the only one who had been avoiding me. Iokan usually greeted anyone and everyone with a cheerful hello and enquiries after their health, their families, and anything else he'd learned about them. But he'd stopped treating me the same way. I've noticed this before when a patient reaches a stage in therapy where they simply don't want to reveal any more. Perhaps it was to do with the mysterious organisation he joined, or guilt over Katie, or maybe something deeper.

He didn't extend his avoidance tactics to skipping therapy sessions, so the appointed time found him chiming at my office door with a pair of steaming mugs full of something that was neither tea nor coffee.

"You should try this. It is very good." He was trying Interversal again, but still wasn't quite up to speed.

"I already have a drink, Iokan. What is it?"

"From Bri'Slar world. They call it chakchuk. Very like drink from my world."

I took a sniff at the mug; scents of leafy chocolate and butter steamed from it. "I'll try it later, Iokan. Can you put your contact lenses in, please?"

"Interversal not yet good enough?"

"Not yet, no."

He sighed and put the lenses in.

"Is there anything you'd like to talk about today, Iokan?"

He blinked as the lenses settled into place and translations came into focus, then continued in his own language. "How's Katie doing?"

"She's awake."

"Is there anything I can do?"

"Not at the moment, no."

"I did think about what you said. I wasn't trying to hurt her."

"It's hard to judge these things, Iokan. There's no need to beat yourself up over it."

"You're sure there's nothing else I can do?"

"I'm sure. But we're not here to talk about Katie. This is *your* therapy session. I'd like to talk a bit more about your career, if that's possible."

"I can't do that."

"It could be very important."

"I can't help you there."

"Hm. Okay. Well, if you don't mind, I'd like to talk about something else…"

"I'm all ears."

"I wanted to tell you a rather interesting story."

"Interesting how?"

"Let me just get the screen set up…" I turned down the lights and dissolved the outside view into a black screen. "Okay. Have you ever heard of the Ilfenard Experiment?"

"No. I haven't."

"Well, that's not a surprise. It was a long time ago, and the people who conducted the experiment are very embarrassed about it these days. This is them…"

Normal looking humans appeared on the screen, alongside images of their world: a bioengineered utopia; buildings grown from the soil; an arboreal aesthetic. Cities of massive apartment trees that grew food for the inhabitants as well as sheltering them. Statistics and summaries sprung up around the images: the usual IU species guide. "The Quillia. Very into the biotechnology, as you can see. Peaceful, friendly. Model IU species, really. But like lots of species, they have a few nasty secrets in their history…"

Iokan leaned forward as I showed video from parallel worlds the ancient Quillians had colonised. "They learned their biotech by experimenting on other worlds." A cow, fused into the ground, legs replaced by roots, screaming as it struggled to get away. Bushes of animal foetuses. A plague of arm-length caterpillars consuming every creature in their path. One bit into the brain of a struggling, silk-bound squirrel. Iokan watched the screen with the eyes of a trained observer, taking in data without judgement or distress.

"They were also interested in humans. They didn't do as much genetic testing, but they were very interested in sociological manipulation. Which brings us to the Ilfenard Experiment…"

I switched the views again; new sets of images, showing a green world from orbit, and native hunter-gatherers from different continents. "They found a world, Ilfenard, where humans were all over the planet, but still in the stone age. A fully human species but no understanding of science or any explanation for the universe other than religion."

"What did they do?"

"They paid them a visit. Lots of visits, all over the world. They'd come down with all the lights on and rockets blazing, land in a clearing, set up camp, and make contact. They'd employ the natives to show them around the area and learn the language, but what they were there for was to give them things. Little trinkets to begin with; gizmos that had lights on, or made sounds, anything to get them used to the idea of taking gifts.

"And then they left, for ten years. Just up and out into orbit, leaving the natives with no idea what had happened. By the time they came back, all the little batteries they'd left in the trinkets were still working, so they'd become incredibly valuable. The tribes were fighting wars over them."

Iokan sat back in his chair. "I think I can see where this is going..."

"As soon as the Quillians returned, they were surrounded by natives desperate for more handouts. They did it every ten years – turn up, hand out goodies, and then vanish without a word. They did it at different intervals across the planet, but ten years was apparently optimal."

"Optimal for what?"

"Building a religion."

"I see."

"It didn't take long before they were associating the Quillians with gods, and changing their own legends to fit them in. Then the Quillians started to hand out things that were actually useful: compasses, tools, lights, I mean real lights you could use to see at night. They never explained how they worked, so the natives assumed it was magic.

"About fifty years after they started, the Quillians skipped a visit. All the natives completely lost it. Leaders sprung up saying they'd been immoral or hadn't worshipped properly. So they built the religion up bigger than ever. Next time they were due, the Quillians showed up as normal. The change was amazing. The place where they landed had turned into a city. The religion was starting to make them all stay in one place; the priests were using the trinkets like a protection racket to get food and offerings from all the tribes in the area. The Quillians put in a few more visits and let it develop, then vanished for a hundred years.

"When they came back, the natives had figured out agriculture, but they were relying on all the tools the Quillians had left behind – which were breaking down as time went by. As they lost their tools, their crops were starting to fail, and they were on the brink of famine. And since they didn't have a clue how the tools worked, they thought the failure was a spiritual one. They'd started sacrificing their own children to bring the gods back.

"The Quillians gave them more tools to be getting on with, and did the usual routine for a few more decades. And then they left, but not because of the experiment.

There was a disaster on the Quillian homeworld and their own civilisation fell apart. A thousand years later, they went back to see what had happened.

"But there wasn't anything left. The Quillians found a massive ecological disaster, and all the humans long since dead from everything that went with it. Nuclear weapons in some areas, biological warfare in others, complete crop failure and famine elsewhere. The natives had figured out the principles behind the tools the Quillians had left behind, and that gave them a massive headstart on science and technology before they were ready for it.

"But they'd remembered the Quillians. They'd had religions about them right up until the end. There were statues of their spaceships all over the planet. The Quillians investigated and found that a lot of the wars that destroyed the world were religious wars. There were faiths based around all the different things they'd worked out from studying the tools and trinkets, and they used them against each other. The Quillians realised the crime they'd committed, and stopped all their experiments."

"And you think that's what happened to us."

"It's something to think about."

"You think these… Quillians came to our world? And did this to us?"

"Probably not them. The timescale doesn't fit – Ilfenard ended nearly two thousand years ago, and the Quillians kept themselves to themselves for a long time afterwards. But that doesn't mean something similar couldn't have happened. There are more human species out there than the IU can keep track of."

"But this is an isolated incident. Surely?"

"I wish it was. Other species have done the same kind of thing, sometimes by accident. This is the worst incident we have on record, and we know enough to guess that similar crimes have been hidden from us. It even happens on worlds with no interversal contact. All it takes is a more advanced society encountering a less advanced one and leaving their rubbish behind, and then even that can start a religion."

"It's not a very flattering portrait of humanity, is it?"

"No. It isn't."

"But it's not true on my world. It can't be true."

"Why not?"

"Because they came back. They weren't irresponsible explorers who came by one day and left a civilisation behind. It was their planet. And they came back."

"The Quillians came back. Repeatedly."

"But they were only human."

"And the Antecessors weren't?"

"They're more than human."

"So, posthumans, then?"

"They're living fields of energy. I think that goes a little further than 'posthuman.'"

"But they were people, once? Like you and me?"

He thought about that. "Yes. They were human once."

"How do you know? How do you know the energy beings you saw are the same as the people who lived on your world three thousand years before?"

He took a breath. "Because I saw them. Before they came back."
"Really?"
"Really."
"When was this?"
"I... can't talk about it."
"Ah. Something that happened in the other part of your career."
"Yes. I... saw one of them. I saw it leave our world and go out into the stars. Perhaps... something out there changed them. I don't know what..."
"What do you think happened?"
"I don't know. Don't ask me any more. I don't know."

It didn't look much like an improvement; but the automatic divinity of the Antecessors had shrunk a little. It was slow progress, but progress nevertheless.

6. ELSBET

Elsbet was asking questions. She wanted to know when she could return to her unit and get back into the war, and we couldn't keep telling her she needed to recover when it was obvious there was nothing physically wrong with her. It was time to tell her the truth, as carefully as we could.

I turned up in her room unannounced. She jumped out of bed and saluted.

"Sit down," I said. She obeyed and sat on the edge of the bed. "We're not going to be sending you back to your unit, Sergeant."

She looked a little panicked. "You're putting me back in the general population?"

"I'm sorry?"

"Sir. I'm signed up for the duration. I'm trained as a pilot. I'm no use in the general population."

Interesting – but I had no time to pursue it now. "Things aren't like that here."

"Sir...?"

"We don't have a general population. You won't be sent there. But we can't send you back to your unit, either." She was utterly baffled, now. "I'm going to be honest with you instead."

I stepped a little closer. "Elsbet, do you know what a parallel universe is?"

She shook her head, not knowing what to make of me.

"You've never heard of the concept?" I asked.

"Major... I don't understand."

"Okay. I'll explain. You live in a universe, with planets and asteroids and stars and galaxies and all the rest."

"Yes..."

"But it's not the only one. There are others."

She must have thought I was insane.

"There are other universes, Sergeant. Similar to yours, with all the planets and asteroids and stars and galaxies, but the people are always different. History is never the same. *There are universes where there wasn't a war.* Do you understand me?"

"Uh... yes." She might have understood me, but she didn't believe me. Her eyes darted around the room.

"That's where you are now. A universe with no war. We have no armies, and I'm not an officer. I'm a therapist. I'm only here to help you. We can't send you back to your unit because it's in your universe, and it's too dangerous for us to go there. We already lost a lot of our people the last time we went.

"I'm sorry to break it to you like this but you deserve to know the truth. I'll answer any questions you have..."

She looked down and clasped her hands together. They were trembling. Not a good sign.

"It's a lot to take in, I know. You do understand me, don't you, Sergeant?"

She looked up at me. "Oh, yeah."

Then she ran for it.

She rushed forward, trying to barge me onto the floor – but I wasn't there. I was only an image, projected remotely from a place of safety, and she found herself running through nothing.

"Sergeant–" I tried to say, but it was no good. She tracked back, eyes wide as she realised I was just an illusion, then turned and dashed for the door.

It swished open for her. She found the infirmary outside deserted, the windows shuttered, every door closed. She tried the first one she came to – it stayed locked. She hammered on it, tried to find a door control, but there was nothing. She tried another door – the same. And another.

It opened. She ran through, into the centre, past more doors that wouldn't open, meeting no one, running down the path we'd laid out for her, until she turned a corner and saw an open door ahead of her – a door into blinding light. But it wasn't a light. It was an exit from the building, and it was so much brighter outside that she was momentarily dazzled. She dashed towards it, shielding her eyes as they adjusted – until she saw what lay beyond the corridors she thought were buried inside a cold rock halfway out to Jupiter.

The forest, stretching forever, more shades of green than the eye could see, a blue sky above fog-strewn mountains in the pale distance. Before the forest, a green glade with a small vegetable garden, neatly laid out with shoots budding into life.

And sunlight, warmer than any she'd ever known, making the colours burst out as a cloud passed away and the sun shone full upon the garden. And as she approached the doors, her run slowing to cautious, astonished steps, a smell no one from an asteroid could ever know: the morning's rain, still wet upon the grass.

Spellbound, she stared through the doors at the green world outside, unable to go further. When I caught up with her, judging she wasn't a threat any more, I found her weeping at what she saw. I put a hand on her shoulder to show I was real. She could barely tear her eyes from the sight to look at me.

"It's... Earth..."

"Yes."

"But this is... this is in the *Testament!* Just like this... Those are... trees? And... sky?"

"That's right."

"They destroyed it. The *Testament* shows it! All the smoke and poison and, and… *machines*…"

"In your universe, perhaps. This is another Earth. A parallel Earth. There was no war here."

"It can't be real. I'm dreaming!"

"Then go outside. See for yourself."

"I can't…"

"You can. It's just a few steps."

She looked at me, needing support. "I'll go first, if you like," I said. I walked ahead of her to the exit, and stepped outside. I turned back and held out a hand. Nervously, she joined me, and I led her across the paving into the garden.

She had no shoes on, and noticed how wet the grass was. "It was raining earlier. Mind yourself, the grass is a bit slippery," I said. But she didn't mind. She revelled in the feel of the grass between her toes.

"It's… *squishy*."

"That's soil, underneath the grass. That's what most of the surface of a planet is like. That's what plants grow out of."

"Plants don't grow in soil. Plants grow in water."

"In hydroponics, yes. But this is how they do it on a planet. Come on, let's go further…"

The sun was high and the centre's shadow was cast only a short way into the garden. We crossed the border into sunlight. I noticed she was nervous, and when the sun hit her, she flinched and cried out.

"What is it, Elsbet?"

"It's… *hot*…"

"Yes, direct sunlight. That's what you get on a planet."

"Aren't we going to get burnt?"

"The atmosphere protects us. You'll be fine."

But she wasn't fine. She was breathing hard, and hunched over, as though she expected something from the sky to hit her.

"Elsbet? Are you all right?"

"It's so… *big*…"

Her eyes were wide, she was hyperventilating, her hands were shaking. She was having a panic attack.

"Okay, Elsbet, that's enough for today, we need to get you back inside…"

She looked up at the sky, and gasped. Sun, a few scudding clouds, and endless blue. I knew the problem at once: she'd grown up on an asteroid, enclosed by walls, and had never stood exposed to an endless space without protection. Veofol had anticipated it. His people, living in orbital habitats, had the same problem. I summoned him and a medical team as Elsbet slumped to the ground, hiding her head.

"You were right. Agoraphobia," I said as Veofol and the medics came running up.

"Let's get her inside," he said. The medics tranquillised her and we carried her back.

7. OLIVIA

Later that day, it was Olivia's turn for a therapy session. She didn't show up, so I pulled on some boots and went to her. She'd returned to the garden after the commotion with Elsbet, under a lower sun and the pleasant warmth of the afternoon. She wasn't out there to rest, though. She was working hard, bent over and muttering at weeds as she yanked them out of the earth.

"Aliens and weeds trampling all over, this planet's nothing but aliens and weeds…" Elsbet had trodden on some of the plants in her panic, so I thought it best to go over, apologise and see what we could do to help.

"Olivia?"

She started at the sound of my voice, grabbed a shovel, came up and spun round to bring it down on my skull. I staggered backwards and caught the shovel high on my left arm. I shrieked at the pain, fell to my knees and Olivia suddenly realised where she was and who she'd struck.

"Oh gods. You idiot. You bloody idiot!"

She knelt by me and ripped the arm of my shirt open. "Don't move! You'll make it worse." A massive bruise was coming up. She pressed the skin around it and made me gasp.

"It's not broken. You're bruised, that's all. What were you thinking, sneaking up on me like that?"

I replied through gritted teeth, feeling queasy as the aftereffects kicked in. "Usually… the assailant… is the one who apologises…"

"I'm sorry. All right, I'm sorry. Happy now?"

"That's… fine, Olivia. I thought… you weren't… a doctor?"

"I can set a bone if I have to. Oh, look, here come the crows…"

A nurse came running out, along with a couple of security guards. "It's all right!" I shouted at the guards. "It's my fault. Olivia's not to blame. I just need someone to take a look at my arm…"

"Sure?" he asked.

"Very sure," I said. "You should never sneak up on someone with PTSD."

"I do not have PTSD!" snarled Olivia as the nurse kneeled in the mud to take care of my arm.

"You can leave us," I said to the guards. They holstered their stunsticks and left.

"Hold still," said the nurse, administering an anaesthetic spray.

"Oooh, that's better," I said as the pain slid away.

"I don't have PTSD, I bloody told you I don't, it's just reflexes," muttered Olivia.

"I need to get you inside to take a better look," said the nurse.

"Okay," I said. "Olivia? Do you mind giving me a hand up?"

"Fine," she said, and helped me to my feet. "I suppose you want help getting indoors now."

"I'll take care of it," said the nurse.

"I hit her, I'll bloody help her inside!"

"It's okay," I said to the nurse, and Olivia helped me indoors.

They scanned the arm and found no fractures, then gave me a dose of healing accelerant and put my arm in a sling. I'd be back to normal in a day or two. Olivia stuck with me – as much as she blamed me for provoking her, she still felt an obligation to ensure I was treated properly. And she didn't mind the chance to spy on Elsbet, either.

"What's up with her?" she sniffed. Elsbet was visible in her room, curled up on her bed, looking shell-shocked and occasionally nodding as Veofol explained things, which was as well as could be expected.

"She's had a bit of a shock," I said.

"I don't understand her. How many of them are in there?"

"Just the two. As far as we know."

"Is she dangerous?"

"Not if you treat her kindly and with respect."

She narrowed her eyes at me. "What, and you think I won't?"

"I just think you should be careful."

"Yeh, yeh. Not much chance of me being able to hurt her, is there? Wouldn't have got far with a shovel on her…"

"There are other kinds of hurt. Aren't there?"

"Huh."

I caught the attention of a nurse, and indicated the curtains around the examination cubicle I was in. He drew them and left me alone with Olivia. "I'm sorry about what I said."

"What?"

"I mean for saying you had PTSD in front of other people."

She shrugged. "Well, you weren't yourself, were you…"

"I was rather lightheaded, I have to admit."

"Stupid thing to do, creeping up on me like that."

"Yes. You'd think I'd have learned by now."

"Hah. Leave the crazy old bitch alone. Good lesson."

"No, I mean I've had a lot of PTSD patients. I really should know better."

That got her annoyed. "I'm telling you for the last time, I do not have PTSD!"

"Why?"

"What do you mean, why?"

"Everything I know leads me to think you do. So if you were in my position, why would you make the opposite diagnosis?"

"Because I'm not in your position and I know the difference. What I've got is a natural reaction to having revenants trying to kill me for thirty odd years. It's why I'm still alive, for gods' sake."

"Hm. Actually…"

"What?"

"Well, you seem very opposed to the diagnosis. Was PTSD known in your world?"

"Because we're primitive, of course…"

"A lot of species have trouble accepting it exists. You wouldn't be alone in that."

She sighed. "We knew about it."

"What did you call it?"

"A gross moral failure."

"That's rather harsh."

"I'm joking." There wasn't a trace of humour on her face. "The people who called it that were the ones who never saw revenants. Never had to put up a barricade and stay up all night in case they got in. Never had to kill their friends because they'd come back from the dead..."

"What was it really called?"

"Necrotic hysteria."

"Wow. That's quite something..."

"Or death-shock, if you read the newspapers."

"So they associated it with the outbreak?"

"That's right. Somehow they decided the dead coming back to life made people go round the bend. Wonder where they got that idea from."

"Was it widespread?"

"Lot of people came down with it during the first outbreak. You could tell. They stopped fighting, just stared all the time. Lot of them got mistaken for revenants."

"That sounds more like ordinary shock..."

"Well, probably was. But it kept happening after the outbreak. People who got through without a scratch did the same thing."

"Yes. Sometimes the extreme cases are like that. In some species, anyway."

"Well, I didn't get it."

"The extreme cases are just the tip of the iceberg. Did you have any particularly harrowing experiences during the first outbreak?"

"The dead got up and ate the living, what did you think I was having, happy little daydreams?"

I shrugged. "I don't know what you did. I don't know what a normal day would have been like."

"I was in the Coroner Corps. We went house to house. If someone answered, we searched it for revenants. If no one was there, we broke down the door and searched for revenants. Either way we found 'em."

"How old were you?"

"Twenty. Twenty year old girl with a revolver and a couple of marines behind me and they were the ones shitting themselves. The marines were supposed to protect me from the living. I was supposed to figure out who was dead and put down the ones that were. Never worked out like that."

"So you had to kill. And not just revenants?"

"I didn't have a choice."

"And there was nothing... nothing especially bad?"

She sat there for a while. "You don't want to know."

"Is it difficult to talk about?"

"Of course it's bloody difficult."

"I'd understand if you couldn't. It's a common symptom."

"I don't *have* any bloody symptoms. It's–" She pursed her lips. "Have you ever killed anyone?"

"No."

"Then you don't know. What's the point of telling you?"

"I'd like to know."

"Yeh? You sure about that?"

"Yes."

"Balls."

"If you don't have any symptoms, then what's the harm?"

She narrowed her eyes. "I was at Tanymouth. You've never even heard of it…"

"No. I'm afraid not."

"Well it didn't give me any damned death-shock!"

"What happened at Tanymouth? Is that where you got your reflexes?"

"I already had reflexes," she said, glancing down at my bruised arm.

"So what happened?"

She pursed her lips again. She didn't want to say. But she couldn't help looking down at my arm once more as I looked back with utter sympathy. Perhaps it was a feeling of obligation that motivated her, or just the sense she was backed into a corner. After a moment, she began.

"We were going up the coast, the Kernow coast, right? Village after village, little ports all the way along, places they'd been smuggling for centuries so they didn't like the look of us, didn't like anyone in a uniform. The navy put us and the marines ashore and they were all the same: no cholera here, ma'am, we closed the gates and didn't let it in. *Balls*. They let it in all right – let it in from the sea. Them and their mates in Gaul were back and forth across the Channel the whole time. They were *spreading* the damn cholera, not hiding from it. So we weren't any too gentle when we found what they were hiding in the cellar. Cholera killed 'em, and then the revenation bug brought them back, and their families thought they could hide the stink with rosewater and garlic.

"So that was it, one after the other for weeks. I put down hundreds of the bastards before we even got to Tanymouth, and I didn't get any death-shock from *that*."

"But then there was Tanymouth."

"Yeh. The big town, the real port. Proper customs house and navy cutters in and out all the time. It was supposed to be *safe*, do you understand? Revenants were still crawling across the moors but Tanymouth was supposed to be keeping them out and staying clean.

"It wasn't clean. Not one bit. They'd had the cholera, same as everyone else, probably the navy bringing it in. They'd kept it quiet and hidden all the sick ones far as they could from the harbour. Any sailors that revenned on shore got put down properly, but they weren't letting it happen to their own. They thought we had a cure, only we were keeping it for the rich folks in the capital – typical Kernish.

"We went ashore on leave, until we saw all the things we'd seen coming down the coast. People not looking us in the eye. The odd one running off all of a sudden to warn someone. And that smell in the air, you don't know that smell – not the revenants but the cholera. Do you know what cholera does? It makes you shit yourself trying to get rid of it, only you shit water and you end up dying of dehydration. The stink was everywhere.

"And then a couple of marines heard the moans. It's never screaming with the revenants, they bloody moan. Like damned children can't get what they want, only what they wanted was human flesh.

"We pulled all the marines out of the taverns and whorehouses and had the townsfolk off the streets in an hour. Men posted at every crossroads to make sure of it so we could start on the house to house. But we thought we'd give 'em a chance, so we went down to the town hall to see the mayor and corporation and ask them what was what and give 'em a chance to come clean.

"The mayor and the councillors came out into the courtyard and gave us all the nonsense: no, no cholera in the town ma'am, no revenants neither, we kept it all in the hospital. We listened to all of that and told 'em how it was going to be: we were searching every house and there was curfew until it was done. We told them to get inside and we'd search them last.

"They went in like good little mice and locked the gates behind them. And that was when it began. Just moans at first, and you couldn't hear where they came from because they were coming from all round. It was a trap. They knew we'd find them out eventually. They weren't giving up a single one of their dead, not while they thought we had a secret cure we weren't giving them because they were Kernish. They *used* them instead. They had them in sanatoriums all round the town, just warehouses and the like, and they opened them up all at once. There were four hundred of us, Coroner Corps and marines on the streets, and two thousand revenants coming down every road from every direction – they must have been taking them in from the villages nearby as well, like as not they all had relatives in town and that's where they ran when it started. And we had our men stationed on every street corner so they got surrounded by the bastards, and the townsfolk came out as well with whatever weapons they'd had hidden away. We must have lost a hundred men before we realised what was happening. We tried running for the harbour, but the revenants were swarming there because they'd seen all the marines and sailors on the docks. The dreadnought, *Indefatigable* it was called – hah! – they'd cast off and were halfway out the harbour by then. Revenants were falling off the docks trying to get to the ship, sailors on board were shooting them as they went, probably the only decent thing the navy did that day.

"So we ran for the main square. Taney Square. Anywhere we could get the space for a decent firing line and form a schiltron, not that we had the ammunition for that but what else were we going to do? The marines were splendid – straight there and forming up, getting the bastards as they trickled in but it was never going to be a trickle for long. There were only a dozen of us from the Coroner Corps in the square, all we had was pistols and not many rounds for those. We saved it for when they got close – keep the revenants off the boys with the rifles, that was the word.

"The revenants got into the square from every side. The swarm from the harbour followed us in first and then the ones from the town came in. Some of 'em had marine uniforms on. We didn't really know how the disease worked then – they'd probably eaten infected meat and never knew it until revenants ripped them half to pieces or the locals shot them or whatever happened, and then they got up again. I saw a white coat in there as well, that was the Coroner Corps uniform, white coat, army shirt and breeches, long boots. Cap was gone but I recognised him: Lieutenant Miller. Right bastard but he didn't deserve that. Someone had shoved a bit of glass in his neck and it was still there.

"The Marine Captain in charge told the men to wait until the revenants got to fifty yards. The bastards came on, moaning. I stood with my boys to look after 'em and do what I could. Not a one of 'em didn't trust me to do what needed doing. Best men I ever knew. Marine Captain tells 'em to take aim. Just what's in front, nothing else. Then *fire*.

"Must have been thirty, forty revenants dropped just like that. Right in the head, brains blown back on the faces of the ones behind. But they missed a lot as well. Bullets went into shoulders or necks or chests or just missed altogether and that was no good to anyone. They reloaded and second ranks came up to fire. Another thirty-odd went down. But there were thousands behind 'em and they kept coming, kept getting closer, no matter how many dropped. One got past the others on a blind spot. I put it down with my pistol once it got close enough. Revenants were all over the square, and more coming in from every street. I couldn't see an end to the swarm behind.

"And that's when the navy started shelling us.

"The spotters on the *Indefatigable* couldn't see an end to the swarm either. So the commanders tried something else. They saw us in the square, thought we were going to fight down to the last man and decided it wasn't worth waiting until a crowd of two thousand turned into a crowd of two thousand and a few more because we'd joined 'em.

"First shell hit a ways past the square. Finding the range. Then another one just before it. Then they had us, and revenants were flying in the air, coming down among the marines and even just bits of the damn things could be dangerous. All they needed was a head, a torso, and an arm to crawl with. Buildings getting hit as well, shrapnel flying all over, good men cut down before the revenants even got to 'em. We thought we might last hours out there before the revenants finished us but we weren't going to last minutes with the navy joining in as well. The Marine Captain was down. Me and my marines were cut off from all the others. Shells still coming in, blowing holes in the line and bits of men and rifles falling on us.

"Nobody'd tried explosives on revenants before. We never usually met them in those kinds of numbers, not then, not until the last outbreak. Somebody must have thought dropping a shell into a pack of 'em would do a world of good. And yeh, some of 'em dropped. But the rest stayed up. Didn't matter how much you ripped out their guts, they kept coming. And the shelling made them worse. The blast wave, the pressure, it did something to their nerves. Didn't knock 'em down at all. It hurt them. Drove 'em mad. They didn't moan any more, they *screamed*. They came at you *running*. They never ran if they could help it otherwise, just kept coming at a walk. And now we had hundreds in the square still on their feet, only thing stopping them getting us was the shells still coming down and tossing them about until they got up and tried it again.

"There's two things you can do in that kind of nonsense. Freeze up or run for it. Best thing I did that day was shout at all my marines and tell them to run for it with me. Couldn't stay out there. Nobody was going to get out of that square alive if they stayed.

"The shells had cleared one of the streets so we made for that. Couldn't call it much of a street – buildings on both sides blown out, rubble everywhere, bits of revenants in the wreckage, arms coming out and grasping at you. Lieutenant Miller was there – torn in half, one good arm still holding his pistol but no idea what to do with it. I put him down and took it for myself, and his ammo. Needed 'em both just to get down the road. Somebody did a drawing of me for the papers after it was over. The Fury in the White Coat, they called me, with my two pistols. Kept on carrying two after that as well, even at Tringarrick. You can never have too many.

"The town hall was still standing. Don't know what happened to the mayor and corporation. Don't care. I'd have probably put them down if I saw them. I got twenty men past the revenants and the shells – not enough to defend the place but there wasn't anything else left standing. Nice strong stone building, harder to blow apart than all the timber ones and they hadn't targeted it directly so we blockaded it best we could, took one corner over the cellar entrance and holed up there. Nobody got through without some kind of injury. I had gashes all down my left side from shrapnel. Two of the men died within an hour and we put 'em down again when they got up."

She went quiet for a few moments.

"What happened then?" I asked.

"Long night. Longest I ever knew. We escaped in all the shelling so the revenants didn't know where we were at first, meant we had time to get some barricades up. And they kept on shelling all the time. Ten hours, it went on. Must have been more than one dreadnought out there. They were trying to level the place. Didn't work. Just made things worse.

"Revenants kept coming, soon as one of 'em knew where we were, they all bloody knew or seemed like. We only had the ammo we brought with us and it wasn't enough. We blocked all the windows so they had to come in through the courtyard. We could get good range on them there but we ran out of rounds in three hours. After that it was hand to hand. Good thing it was one of those places with halberds, and swords and all that hanging on the wall. I kept a few bullets back for the end and let the boys take the cutlery. We formed a line in a corridor, the ones with pole arms would pin the revenants while the ones with swords and axes smashed their heads. We blocked up the corridor with the corpses and then they found another way in and we set it up again. Must have been hundreds, between those we put down in the courtyard and the ones in the corridors. Most of them shrieking at us, still bloody mad because of the shelling.

"We couldn't keep that up. We were down to eight and we were exhausted. A fair few of the ones coming at us had revenned in the square as well, that was the worst. Sticking a knife in the eye of someone you'd been eating at the same table with for weeks. I didn't let the men see the look on my face. Just got it done and moved on. But we had to go. There was only the cellar left. We'd taken a look earlier – opened it up, went down, had a good yell, so we knew there wasn't anything coming after us from down there. But there wasn't any way out, either, or that's what we thought. MacDonalt found a door to the sewers, brand new sewers, they were still digging to try and improve public hygiene and beat the cholera. I went out first because

"I was the last one with bullets in my guns. I'd been saving them for us. We saw a couple of revenants in there but that was all. I put them down. We barred the door behind us. Wouldn't last forever, not against the ones gone mad from the shelling but it was all we had. Ran for it and found a way out, and all it did was take us back into the streets.

"But there weren't any streets. They'd been shelling all night and the sun had come up. All we could see was smoke and rubble. Some buildings still on fire, making the smoke glow orange. Didn't see any revenants – not in one piece, anyway. There were bits of them everywhere. We had to stick a few that still had heads. We thought the ones with legs wouldn't be far behind.

"We heard footsteps – close, somewhere in the smoke. Couldn't tell who or what. I told the men to form a line. They still had all the old mediaeval weapons, whatever they could fit down the cellar. I still had a couple of bullets. There wasn't anywhere to go so we held our ground.

"Twenty marines came out of the smoke, rifles pointed at us – us with our halberds and swords and a couple of pistols. Nobody knew what to do for a moment, until the Marine Lieutenant on the other side told his men to stand down and I did the same. They were the reserves from the *Indefatigable*. They'd been landed once the shelling stopped. Tanymouth was still crawling with revenants but a lot of them were buried and the reserves were going round trying to find them. They weren't expecting survivors."

A crash came from elsewhere in the infirmary, probably Elsbet's room. For a moment I thought she might have hurt someone, but then I heard Veofol calling for a mop to clean up a spill. She'd thrown a cup at a wall, nothing more. I turned my attention back to Olivia.

"What happened next?" I asked.

"Slept for a couple of days once they got me back to the ship. They gave me some leave. Hah. And a medal. The Star of Juno. Their way of covering up after the shelling – try and make me a hero. Fury in a White Coat and all that."

"It sounds like you deserved it."

"The ones who died deserved it as well, but all they got was a lovely spot in a mass grave."

"Hm."

"And no bloody death-shock, or PTSD, or whatever you call it. Not even a touch. Nothing. No nightmares. I slept fine, thank you very much."

"So if I'd crept up on you after the first outbreak…"

"I'd have jumped. Like anyone else. But I'd have put you down if you were a revenant."

"And what about the marines?"

"What about 'em?"

"How did they do?"

She scowled at me. "Yeh. They got it. Some of them. Most of them."

"What happened to them?"

"They got put in madhouses. Or left on the streets. I wasn't one of 'em. What's your point?"

"It hits different people in different ways, Olivia. For some, they get it after the first experience of trauma. But for others it takes years of repeated exposure. Like, say, being surrounded by revenants for twelve years…"

She glared back at me. She'd had enough for today.

"How's your arm?"

"Can't feel a thing."

She stood. "Well if you're better, then I'm getting back out in the garden."

She left, without any further acknowledgement of my point. She was right, in some ways; PTSD is far from an automatic response to trauma. But the likelihood does increase massively according to the length of exposure to traumatic events, and her symptoms made anything else implausible. And maybe I'd have pushed it further that day, but I decided me and my arm needed some rest.

8. KWAME

Kwame sat in a darkened room, watching a series of lights pulse across a curved wall. I was next door, shut away with the tomographer and a neurologist so our own nervous systems would not disturb the readings.

We'd taken him to Hub Metro for the calibration. While we had enough equipment at the centre to monitor his medical condition and were installing more for the dream recording, it took a rather finer set of instruments to get the baselines we needed before we could begin. The entire room was a tomographical scanner, taking millions of sectional images of his entire body every second and building a full model of his mind.

"Ah, there, you see?" said Professor Ebbs, eyes sparkling with the happy light of a scientist seeing his hypothesis confirmed. "The visual cortex is routed differently than in most species, thanks to the latent hibernation ability…"

"Really?" I asked, doing my best to conceal annoyance at his condescension.

"Well, of course, you knew that. But it's following the pattern we might expect in other hibernating human species. The visual cortex runs differently during REM sleep, and differently still during hibernation…"

"He's drifting again," said the tomographer. Kwame was supposed to concentrate on a point of light in the middle of the wall.

I activated the intercom. "Kwame? You need to look at the white dot."

"Of course. Forgive me."

"Do you need a break?"

"No. Please continue."

"Here comes sequence fourteen," said the tomographer. She switched off the intercom and turned to me. "It's better if you keep him talking. He's having trouble concentrating."

I switched the intercom back on. "How are you doing, Kwame?"

"This is a surprisingly difficult task."

"You're doing fine. Just keep it up and we'll be back home in time for dinner."

"Yes." He sighed and concentrated on the dot. "May I ask a question?"

"Go ahead," I said.

"What happened to your world?"

"I think I told you already."

"I mean since then."

"Oh. Well..." I glanced at the tomographer. She shrugged. "It's not exactly somewhere you'd want to go on holiday."

"You said you never went back."

"No. There's not much to go back to."

"Is your world dead?"

"Very nearly." I sighed and looked over my shoulder. Professor Ebbs and the tomographer did their best to pretend they weren't interested. They'd never been refugees, and doubtless liked to hear the horror stories. "There are still some people there. We've been trying to get them out for decades but they refuse to go."

"I imagine you have trouble understanding their determination."

"No, not at all. It's the homeworld. They want to keep it going as long as possible. Plus they're mostly religious fundamentalists, so they think we're the devil."

"Every species has that kind of fool."

"Yes, I suppose it does."

"Will they survive?"

"No. The volcano is still erupting. There's so much sulphur dioxide in the atmosphere they have to stay underground and filter the air, but they can't last forever. The last time they let us take a look at them, life expectancy was down to thirty-five years. That was ten years ago."

Kwame didn't answer.

"Kwame? Are you still there?"

"Yes. I was reflecting on the last people who survived on my world. They were in bunkers as well."

"As far as we know, yes."

"Some of them held out for decades. Watching the radiation meters. Hoarding their seedbanks. Hoping the fallout would wash away. Watching the next generation grow up hopeless and defeated. Thinking they were the last ones left. Probably cursing me if they knew what happened..."

"He's drifting," said the tomographer.

"Keep your eyes on the dot, Kwame," I said.

"Yes. Sorry."

"Would you like to talk about something a bit more current?"

"I don't... no, wait. May I ask you another question?"

"Go ahead."

"Your world had leaders, yes?"

"Of course."

"Did they act appropriately when the volcano erupted?"

"Not all of them, no. Some of them went to war over resources. That's why there was a nuclear exchange. Even after that, some decided to delay the evacuation, over the advice of their scientists. A lot of people died."

"Were they prosecuted?"

"Some were. Those that survived."

"Were they convicted?"

"Yes. Well, a couple got off because they were prevented from starting the evacuation by legislatures, but most of the ones who caused unnecessary delay were found guilty. I can see where you're going with this."

"Does it give you satisfaction? To know they were convicted and punished?"

"It doesn't bring anyone back."

"How would you feel if they escaped justice?"

Professor Ebbs and the tomographer had given up trying to hide their interest. "I'd be angry. Is that the answer you were looking for?"

"Yes."

"Your situation is different. My species has a government and judiciary. *They* put the leaders on trial, not the IU. The IU can't hold those kind of hearings. We don't interfere in internal matters."

"Not even if millions of lives are at stake?"

"We offer help. We can't do much if people say no."

"Even if their governments are fools?"

"Even if."

"And so millions die."

"We have a non-intervention policy for a reason."

"Yes. I know. It is very well reasoned and thought out, and the justifications make perfect sense. From the point of view of bureaucrats living comfortably on Hub."

"I can understand you'd have a different point of view…"

"I am sure you can."

"You've been through a terrible experience…"

"I simply hoped you might share my point of view. Given your own terrible experience."

I leaned back in my chair, sighed and rubbed my temples. The Professor leaned into the mic.

"Hello Kwame. Ebbs here."

"Professor."

"I know it's a bit rough and all, but at least you'll be able to see your wife soon. Well, an image of her, at any rate."

I glared at him. Neurologists tend, in my opinion, to assume a greater knowledge of human character than they actually possess.

"I don't even remember what she looked like," said Kwame.

"You won't have that problem for much longer. I can promise you that," said the Professor. I switched off the mic in our booth.

"Professor," I said, shaking my head. He frowned.

"Ah. Not very tactful?"

"Not very tactful at all."

"I do apologise…"

I switched the mic back on. "Sorry about that, Kwame. Keep your eyes on the dot."

"I am fine," he said. "It will be good to see her without…"

"He's closed his eyes," said the tomographer as half the screens flatlined.

"Do you need a break?" I asked.

"Yes. Please," said Kwame, sitting alone with his head in his hands as the lights in the room came up.

9. ELSBET & IOKAN

That evening, once I'd returned Kwame to the centre and he slept under a sedative, I noticed Iokan heading to the infirmary. I'd let the group know they could visit Elsbet if they liked, since she'd been informed of their existence, but warned them not to mention Katie. Iokan was the first to take up the offer.

He turned up at the door to her infirmary room with a bland smile, willing to help as always. "Hello," he said.

"Who are you?" she asked.

"My name's Iokan. I'm one of the other patients."

"Oh. Right. You're from another universe." She still didn't really believe it.

"We all are," he said as he stepped inside and let the door close.

"And everyone on your world is dead."

"In a manner of speaking… I suppose so, yes."

"What, you don't know?"

"It's… complicated. I came here to see if there was anything I could do."

"Wake me up?" she said with a despairing shrug.

"I can't do that. This is all real, I'm afraid."

"How do I know?"

"Ah! That's a philosophical question."

"A what?"

"An inquiry into the nature of reality?"

She looked blank. Philosophy was not a common pastime in the asteroid belt. "Yeah. I suppose so, except reality's not answering, is it?"

"Well, you can never really prove that reality is real. There's always the possibility it's an illusion. But you can say that about the whole of your life. At some point, you have to accept that what you're experiencing now is real…"

"Why should I?"

"Because otherwise you're going to be stuck." She sat down on her bed and folded her arms. He went on. "They're not lying. They really are doing their best."

"They said the Earth in my universe is gone. The machines destroyed it."

"I think so, yes."

"So we lost the war."

"I don't think that's true."

"We lost the Earth! How can we win if the homeworld's gone?"

"Your people are still safe, aren't they?"

"Yeah. Safe. On asteroids, in little stinking burrows, living on fucking *algae* and drinking water that's been pissed so often the taste never goes away. That's what the fucking machines did to us."

He pulled up a chair and sat down close to the bed.

"The machines are all gone now. Your people are still alive. The others in the group... they don't have that."

"You believe them, do you?"

"Yes."

"You reckon everyone on your world is dead?"

"I was there. I saw it happen."

She looked back at him with a first flicker of sympathy.

"Our ancestors came back. They took my people with them, they took their... I suppose you'd say they took their souls. But everyone had to die first. It was terrible while it was happening, but they're safe now, and one day I'll see them again." He took her hands. "One day you'll see your people too."

He noticed she was looking at him a little oddly. His speech had affected her somehow. Or maybe something else.

"What is it?" he asked.

"Have I seen you here before...?"

He paused, remembering the injunction not to speak of Katie. "No... *you* haven't."

She was still looking at him: wounded, lonely, in need. But reserved. She looked away.

"Elsbet...? Can I call you Elsbet?" he asked. She nodded. "Is there anything I can do to help?"

"No," she said.

"I'm..." he struggled to find words. "You see, the thing is..." She looked back up at him. "I understand... well, I'm told your condition leaves you at risk of seizures."

She nodded. "They said that."

"There may be a way to control them."

That was it; he was worried he'd caused Katie's last seizure by refusing her demands. Elsbet knew none of this, and was intrigued. "How?"

He took a breath, stood up from his chair, and leaned over the bed to kiss her. She scrambled away from him.

"That's your idea of medicine...!?" she demanded.

"I'm sorry... I thought..."

"I'm a soldier!"

He seemed puzzled. "So was I..."

"I don't know what it's like in your shithole of a universe, but where I come from, soldiers *choose*. Do you get me?"

He shook his head, still baffled.

"It means I don't have to spend my life rutting with every fucknuts that wants a shag and making babies for the war!"

His eyes went wide as he understood. "I'm sorry, I didn't realise..."

"I should have your balls for this."

"I didn't know how things were on your world. I apologise."

"I didn't *have* a world."

"Of course. Ah, I'll take my leave, if I may."

"Yeah. Get the fuck out."

Iokan headed for the door – but before he could reach for the controls, a chime sounded around the centre, and magnetic locks snapped tight on the door. My voice came over loudspeakers.

"This is a security alert. I've had to lock down the building. The situation's under control but we need you all to stay where you are for the moment. I'm sorry about this – I'll update you as soon as I can."

Iokan tried the door: the controls refused him. There was a handle designed to be used in power failures, but that wouldn't move either. He turned back to Elsbet, who sat on the bed looking distinctly annoyed.

"I think we're stuck here for a while," he said.

She folded her arms. It was going to be a long night for the pair of them.

10. SECURITY

HUB SECURITY INCIDENT REPORT
Incident Number: 897-9898-gf
Date: HD y276.m7.w2.d3
Reporting Officer: Sgt. Fers, I.
Incident Location: Lhasa Bar & Club, 2345 3rd Avenue, District 2, Hub Metro

Officer Leberrine responded to an emergency call at 23:45 hours, and found the owner of the club, Mr. Dawa Dorje, in a state of distress, while the club itself had suffered damage to fixtures and fittings. Mr. Dorje reported an assault approximately thirty minutes earlier by an unidentified female who questioned him regarding criminal activities. Mr. Dorje was extremely emotional and repeatedly confessed to a number of offenses against the Biodiversity Statute, but insisted he had never been involved in any kind of genocide. Officer Leberrine was unable to calm him. An ambulance was called, and Mr. Dorje was given a mild sedative.

I interviewed Mr. Dorje at the station at approximately 00:45. He stated that he was on the premises while it was closed to conduct a stocktaking exercise, along with several employees who were assisting him, when the assailant broke in and attacked them. Mr. Dorje's employees attempted to subdue her but they were unable to do so. The assailant stated that she only wanted to speak to Mr. Dorje, and allowed the others to escape. She proceeded to beat Mr. Dorje until he admitted to smuggling offences, but then asked questions regarding wider criminal networks. He insists that no such networks exist and he knows nothing of genocide on other universes, which the assailant seemed to be primarily interested in. He was unable to supply a full description of the assailant because she was masked, but was certain she was using a phonetic translation device. He also told us she demanded to know where the security recordings for the establishment were, and then destroyed them (both physical and data copies).

Mr. Dorje was remanded in custody pending a search of his premises following his confession, and officers were despatched to arrest his associates. The Psychiatric Centre reported no escapes of inmates, nor have there been any other reports of an individual answering the same description.

11. INTRUDER

The truck came in to land at the vehicle paddock across from the main building, audible warnings reporting it was approaching ground level. The garage behind it opened up and the vehicle reversed inside to the sound of further warnings.

As it halted, a baggage compartment at the back popped open and a masked figure in black rolled away. The driver would find the opened compartment a minute later and wonder how he'd managed to leave it open after a supply pickup in the outskirts of Hub Metro. But by then the stowaway was making a perfectly timed run to the main building as sensors switched themselves off along her path. She leapt two stories up to catch a newly opened window with one hand, and then swung herself inside, entering an unused room in the shuttered part of the centre.

A door opened for her and she snuck away down the hall towards the staircase leading to the residential corridors two floors below. She paused on the stairwell and leapt to the ceiling, clinging to a centimetre of foothold while Veofol walked below her. Once he had gone, she slipped silently down to the floor and continued on.

She went straight to the corridor that housed the personal rooms of the residents, one of which opened despite her failure to use the fingerprint, voiceprint or numeric locks. She stepped inside, said "Lights on," and pulled the mask from her face.

That's when Liss got a nasty shock. Her room was gone. All the pink, fluffy and girly fittings were removed. All that was left was an empty, unformed grey shell. She turned to see the one object left behind – clamped into the wall, squat and functional, was a SAR launcher. SAR stands for Semi-Aerosolised Restraint. She had time to mutter "shit!" before it fired a cloud of adhesive droplets at her, binding her in a sticky mesh. She struggled and tried to jump, ending glued halfway up a wall, progressively constrained as she fought against the SAR polymers.

Once she'd stopped struggling, security guards felt safe enough to enter and point weapons at her. Lomeva Sisse, the security manager, took special pleasure in her capture; the final touch of the empty room had been her idea, and avoided the possibility of physical confrontation and serious injury. She proclaimed the situation safe once her officers had made sure Liss could still breathe, then allowed me to enter.

I could see her black clothes were actually stolen from Iokan – the black poloneck, the combat trousers, all adjusted to fit her. I thought she'd only been using her sewing kit to attach pink bobbles to everything she wore. But instead she'd been preparing for this all along.

She glared down at me, still squirming enough to keep the mesh tightening around her. "Just relax, Liss," I said. "It's over. Security are going to take you away for an interview in Hub Metro. That's out of my hands. Is there anything you'd like to tell me before you go?"

"My name is Liss Li'Oul. Reservist. Paranormal Response Group. Identity number 1656710. I'm not telling you another damn thing."

"Liss... we didn't destroy your world. We want to help you. Surely after all the time you've been here, you understand that?"

She just scowled at me. She was determined to play the part of a prisoner of war. I tried something else: "We want to find out who killed your species as much as you do."

"And what would you do about it? Let them off with a fine? Smack them on the wrist? *Take away their fucking toys?*"

I sighed. "We'll talk again, Liss." I looked at Lomeva. "You can take her away now."

They came in with tranquillisers and restraints and took her away to security headquarters in Hub Metro.

PART SEVEN
JUSTICE

1. COMMITTEE

The next morning, I was summoned to an emergency meeting of the Special Counselling Groups Committee, representing everyone who had an interest in my group, none of whom were likely to be happy with me.

I sat down in the remote conference room, and around the circular table, images of the committee members glowed into life. Henni Ardassian, head of the Refugee Service, sat opposite me, with the other members scattered around the table.

"Is that everyone?" asked Henni, looking around. "Is there anyone else from Diplomatic?"

A man spoke up. "Ms. Isnia is already in another meeting. She asked me to sit in. I'm Emmet Wlasky, in charge of operations."

"I'm *very* surprised she wasn't able to attend herself." Baheera om-challha Isnia was deputy head of the Diplomatic Service. It was her memo about the discovery of Iokan that had led to the creation of this committee, and eventually the therapy group. The politics of it all wasn't supposed to affect me, but Liss's escape might well end that.

"It was rather short notice. We still have an ongoing situation elsewhere..."

"We all do, Mr. Wlasky. Please ask her to call me after the meeting. So. Dr. Singh." She looked at me. "We've all read the report. The members of the committee doubtless have some questions for you."

Koggan BanOrishel, the man from Hub Security, jumped in first. "I want to know why a member of the public is sitting in my cells, beaten half to death."

"I do regret that," I said. "But we were aiming to reduce the risk as far as possible. I believe if we'd confronted Liss directly, she might have fled and caused a good deal more injuries. Or worse."

Koggan counted my misdeeds on his fingers. "You could have searched their rooms. You could have questioned them at the centre. But instead – and I'm quoting here – you 'elected to wait for another escape attempt.' You waited until someone got hurt, and *then* you took action."

"We did everything we could to minimise the risk."

"And yet you yourself were still injured."

Koggan indicated my arm. The bruises from Olivia's attack were almost gone, but the medical staff insisted I keep it immobile for another day. "That's an unrelated incident. Another member of the group attacked me. A hazard of the job, I'm afraid."

Koggan barely paused, despite his misstep. "But you didn't think about the risk to Hub Metro, did you? We weren't informed. In fact, you didn't tell anyone. Not even this committee."

"And what would have happened if she had told us?" This was Mykl Teoth, who headed the counselling section of the Refugee Service – my boss. "We'd have been forced to take action. We'd have had the centre turned upside down, and then we might have had an entirely unknown quantity on the run with who knows what risk. She didn't even know which one of them it was. Can you imagine what it would have been like to have the cyborg on the run? An admitted killing machine?"

"You're talking about might-have-beens–"

"Colleagues, we're not here for recriminations," said Henni. "We're here to discuss how to respond to the new situation. I understand Ms. Li'Oul is now in custody?"

"That's right," said Koggan.

"Regarding Mr. Dorje, the man who was assaulted: is he pressing charges?"

Koggan replied: "He doesn't have to. It's a criminal matter."

"But he himself has admitted to criminal acts?"

"Which is irrelevant. Assault is still assault."

"So Ms. Li'Oul will face criminal charges?"

"I can't comment on that until the prosecutors have looked at the case."

"We'll have to see how that progresses. What about the device?"

"Definitely illegal but safely contained."

"I mean, how was something like this from such an undeveloped world even able to exist here?"

"We're not entirely sure. Of course, we're not in charge of security procedures in Quarantine…"

"The technology situation on Liss's world is rather unusual," I said. "If you take a look at the background document, you'll see they often developed artefacts far in advance of what might be expected. I don't think Hub Security can be held responsible." Koggan gave me a confused look. He hadn't expected support from me.

"I see," said Henni. "And what about security at the centre?"

Pellawanatha Fedissba answered – she ran Facilities for the Refugee Service. "Sensor coverage has already been stepped up, but as long as the centre is as close as it is to Hub Metro, there's a limit to how much we can do."

"I'd like to consider a move, if that's possible," said Henni.

"Is that necessary?" I asked.

"Ms. Fedissba, if you can prepare a shortlist of alternative sites?" Pellawanatha replied that she most certainly could.

I had to speak up for the group. "Ms. Ardassian, I have to object. The group has just settled in. They're comfortable, they're making progress. If they have to move when we've only just started, it could have a serious impact on therapy."

Henni thought about it. "How serious?"

"I've managed to get them to trust me. I need that to be able to do my job. If they have to move for reasons they don't understand, I might lose that trust."

Henni looked to Mykl Teoth, who nodded. She looked back at me. "Very well. We'll make preparations but postpone the move until it becomes absolutely necessary."

"Thank you."

"And that will be *my* decision, Dr. Singh."

"Yes, of course."

"Do you mind if I ask Dr. Singh a question?" Eremis Ai represented the Interversal Criminal Tribunal, or at least the placeholder body who were gathering casefiles until the IU finally decided whether or not to activate the ICT.

"Go ahead," said Henni.

Eremis turned to me. "Are you absolutely certain Ms. Li'Oul was looking for the people who committed genocide on her planet?"

"That seems to be the case," I said.

"Do you think she'll ask for assistance?"

"I don't know. I don't think she trusts us at the moment."

"Has she said anything about who she suspects?"

"I can't talk about what we might have discussed in therapy."

"No, of course... I think we would have to interview her, though. Which means the matter will appear in the public record, at least in headline form."

"Do you really need to do that?" asked Henni.

"Yes. We do. If she's investigating a genocide, we have to gather testimony."

"So this is going to come out whether we like it or not, is that what you're saying?"

"We're required to build cases–"

"Like the case for your own job," muttered Koggan.

Eremis ignored him. "We are required to build cases, even if we can't do anything else."

Henni sat back in her chair. "So. Thanks to all this, the existence of the therapy group is likely to become public knowledge. I'm sure that'll make Ms. Isnia very happy, but for the rest of us it's going to be a problem, isn't it? Well, at least we'll have a little time to prepare. Does anyone else have any questions for Dr. Singh?"

"We'll need her to make a statement," said Koggan.

"Does that have to happen now?"

"No. We'll be in touch."

"In that case, Dr. Singh, I'll ask you to leave us while we discuss this further. I'm sure your patients need you more than we do at the moment."

"Thank you," I said. Henni touched a control on her pad, and the images of the committee members faded away, leaving me alone in the room. I breathed a sigh of relief; I'd feared far worse. At least I was still in charge of the group.

2. LISS

A few days later, Security finally allowed me to talk to Liss. Since physical presence is important in therapy and they wouldn't allow me to simulate it with a remote session, I found myself heading to Hub Metro and the headquarters of Hub Security.

Hub is relatively secure by its very nature. The portals to other universes are in orbit, most of them at the L1 point between the Earth and Moon – making it easy to control who and what gets in and out of the universe. Grainger Station has its own separate security force, so Hub Security mainly deals with the everyday policing of a city with a low population density, many of whom are diplomats whose misdeeds are the responsibility of the intelligence and security sections of the Diplomatic Service. The greatest challenges to law and order are biodiversity offences, and the perennial demonstrations against artificial intelligence kept going by certain species who have axes to grind.

There was a demonstration going on in front of Security Headquarters while I was flown in to see Liss: about fifty or sixty angry humans with placards denouncing AIs as godless massacre machines, and demanding something be done about all the crimes they had committed or might theoretically commit. It wasn't a serious issue for Security. The demonstration was only there so they could get the famous building in the back of the screen news coverage.

The headquarters of Hub Security was not a utilitarian, ugly squat of brick or stone, but a minor masterpiece of architecture, looking like a circle held on its side so it formed an 'O' from a distance. Hub attracts the finest architects from across the multiverse, because it provides them with an opportunity to show off their work to the widest possible audience – thus enabling the IU to get the work at a very reasonable discount. Hub Metro is littered with bold statements in glass and stone and wood and aerogel supported by pressor fields. In this case, the architect decided a circular building was a symbol of strength and security, and then turned it on its side.

The 'O' was partially buried, and holding cells were kept in the underground portion. Those parts of the building that had to act as a police station were designed with a greater concession to practicality, but (this being Hub), even the holding cells were comfortable, well lit, and really quite pleasant to stay in, if you ignored the fact that they were also designed to contain people with posthuman enhancements all the way up to military status and beyond.

I met Liss in one of the interview rooms designed for dangerous prisoners. At first, it seemed as though we would be in the same room. But there was an invisible layer of composite carbonglass, plastic and energy dividing it, seemingly running through the table in the middle. I entered through one door and sat down. An impervious robotic warder opened the far door and Liss walked in.

3. GROUP

The group was gathered in the usual circle, waiting for me and Veofol to arrive. Elsbet had joined them for the first time, sitting as far away from Iokan as she could. The clothes she'd picked were those of a soldier: olive-drab canvas jacket, combat trousers, paratrooper boots, and a cap that hid Katie's cropped hair. She looked a little nervous, but defiant with it.

Olivia eyed her suspiciously. "So you're up and about, then," she observed.
"Yeah. Who are you?"
Olivia replied in her rudest tone. "I'm the old bitch. Who are you?"
Elsbet was not to be outdone. "I'm Sergeant Go Fuck Yourself."
Olivia almost smiled. "Huh."

"Olivia's not very polite, I'm afraid" said Iokan.

"Oh, *you're* Olivia? The one with all the dead people?" asked Elsbet.

"That's right. I hear you two made friends pretty quick." She eyed Elsbet and Iokan. Elsbet snapped back: "Nothing happened. If it had, I'd have ripped his nuts off."

Olivia did smile this time. "Serve him right!"

"I can assure you there's nothing between us…" said Iokan, though no one paid any attention.

"So what's your story, Sergeant Go Fuck Yourself?" asked Olivia.

"That's my business."

"Hah! You've got a hope. There's nothing you can keep secret here, girl. They'll have it out of you and expect you to say thanks afterwards. Might as well say it here and now and get it over with." Elsbet kept her mouth shut with a sneer. "Well? What are you? Come on, spit it out! I haven't got all day!"

"I had a drill instructor like you once," said Elsbet to Olivia.

"Yeh?"

"He was a miserable arsehole as well."

"That's not very nice…" said Pew, confused.

Olivia laughed. "Leave her be. She's all right."

"You are a soldier," nodded Kwame, understanding.

"Yeah. You?"

"Once."

"There's a lot of that going around."

Pew spoke up. "Olivia was kind of a soldier too…"

Elsbet looked at Olivia. "That true?"

"Coroner Corps. We killed dead people." She looked round at everyone else. "So the rest of you were locked in as well, right?"

"Yeah."

"Anybody know why yet?"

"I've heard nothing," said Iokan.

"Where's Liss?" asked Pew.

"Who's Liss?" asked Elsbet.

"The other member of the group… ah," said Iokan, realising something.

The door opened. Veofol and I entered the room and sat down in the circle. "Hello, everyone. Sorry I'm late. I imagine you're all wondering what was going on last night…"

"You locked us up!" exclaimed Olivia.

"I'm afraid we had to lock down the centre."

"You had us in there for six hours!"

"There was a security alert. I'm sorry, but we didn't have a choice."

"Security alert? What bloody security alert?"

"Perhaps we should wait for Liss?" said Kwame.

"She won't be joining us," I said.

"You're not answering my question!" said Olivia.

Iokan sat forward. "It was Liss, wasn't it?"

"What?" asked Kwame.

"Liss was the security alert. Or else she'd be here," said Iokan.

"She was involved, yes," I said.

"Was she hurt?" asked Pew.

"I can't talk about the details, but she wasn't hurt."

Iokan's look drifted as he analysed the situation. "No… if she'd been killed or injured, you'd have told us." He snapped his look back on me. "She caused the alert. Didn't she?"

"Well…" I sighed. I'd been hoping to defer this discussion, but that clearly wasn't going to be enough. "I suppose you deserve to know. Liss left the centre without permission."

"What…?" said Kwame.

"You mean she escaped?" asked Iokan.

"That's not the word I'd use," I said.

"How the bloody hell could *Liss* escape?" asked Olivia.

"I take it she's not what she seemed to be," said Iokan.

"As far as we can tell, she was something like a police officer. She was investigating the genocide on her world," I said.

"She thinks it was done by people from another universe?"

"That may be the case, yes."

"And where is she now?" asked Kwame.

"In custody. Security are interviewing her. That's really all I know."

4. LISS

Liss wore the shapeless paper overalls given to prisoners, re-issued every day so nothing could be hidden in them; they were also designed to fall apart if the wearer started doing anything stressful (like escaping), which dissuaded most people from attempting to break out.

She slumped into the chair opposite me, and the AI warder, wearing one of the standard robot shells, chained her to the table. She didn't look at me; she kept her eyes down, pretending disinterest.

"She's secure," said the warder, though not to me.

"Are you sure you don't want to chain her legs as well?" I asked. It didn't get the smile from Liss I was hoping for. The warder looked down at me through artificial eyes.

"If you have any difficulties, hit the panic button."

"I'll be sure to let you know."

It left us. The AI warder was probably filling the role as part of the policy to encourage humans and AIs to get to know each other better. Most of the others were human, and would have worn power armour, but even so, they were more like concierges than jailers. Liss would have been treated well. But people like complaining, so I thought I'd give her the chance.

"How have they been treating you?"

She didn't reply.

"Liss. Hi? It's me. Asha?"

She flicked a look up at me for a moment, but that was all.

"They tell me they've been questioning you."

No answer.

"They didn't tell me what you said, but they seem to be satisfied you're not a threat. They might let you come back to the centre."

Still no answer. Still no eye contact.

"Olivia doesn't believe you've been arrested. She doesn't think you've got it in you."

That got a derisive snort.

"None of us knows who you really are, do we?"

"No."

"Well. You didn't treat Mr. Dorje very well, did you? Do you remember? The man you attacked?"

"He's a criminal."

"Liss, he smuggles in *fruit*. He'll be prosecuted for that and he might lose his business licence. Do you really think it merits a beating?"

"Still a criminal."

"Did you know he comes from the same world as me?"

She looked up, and our eyes met.

"His whole country was destroyed. When we did a census after the evacuation, it turned out he was the only one left who came from there. Take a look at this…"

I pulled out a pad and showed her images of old Tibet: monasteries in high mountains, prayer flags in the breeze, smiling faces of children, monks in orange robes.

"That's all gone now. They were starving at the end. With the glaciers all gone there was hardly any water for their crops. Then their cities were nuked when India and China had their war. And now he's the only one left."

Liss received this like a burden on her shoulders.

"He's like a lot of people here. He could have gone on to the colony world, but he stayed on Hub instead. That bar of his? That's the last piece of Tibet anywhere. It's unique. I've been in there a few times. He's got a terrible sense of humour, but he's so proud of that place. And now he might lose it."

I showed images of Dawa Dorje in his bar. Some publicity shots: prayer flags on the roof, the traditional interior. Dawa looking so obviously proud. And one that Bell had taken of Dawa posing with me, friendly grin all over his face. Liss closed her eyes; I hoped I wasn't piling on the guilt too much, but she needed to know what she'd done.

"This is us, Liss. This is who you were investigating. This is Hub. Most of the people here came from dying worlds. If anyone in the multiverse is going to sympathise with you, it's people like this."

She put a hand to her eyes. Were those tears? Yes. She wiped them back.

"Do you want me to talk to him? I think he'll understand if I explain."

Liss couldn't stop the tears this time, and I couldn't cross the barrier to comfort her. "I'm sorry…" she said. "I'm not like this…" She wiped her eyes on her sleeve, and of course the paper tore as soon as it got wet.

"We're all like this," I said. "There's nothing to be ashamed of."

5. GROUP

"No. It's rubbish. There's no way that woman could fool a turnip!"

"She fooled us all, Olivia," I said.

"She might have fooled *you*..."

"She did, for a while."

"Do you really think she's some kind of master criminal or something?"

"No. Quite the opposite, I expect."

"All right, let's say for a moment you're not talking rubbish. So you're seriously telling me you found her on a dead planet with corpses all over the place–"

"Um. It wasn't corpses," said Pew.

"Fine. Piles of ash everywhere, same thing. You find this woman still living there, still going about her business as though nothing's happened, and you didn't check? You didn't look in her head with your doohickeys and your whatnots to see if she had anything to do with it?"

I said, "We can't actually do that, Olivia, not unless we understand the species well enough. We can't do it for Liss and we can't do it for you, either." Kwame held his silence, wanting to avoid complicated explanations about his own experiences.

"But you trusted her. That's what I don't understand. She's obviously off her head and you trusted her."

"We saw someone in distress and tried to help."

"And she took advantage of you, is that what you're saying?"

"It's possible."

"Well, you know what? Good for her!"

"What do you mean by that?" said Kwame.

"I mean I don't believe a word of it because she's a drip and nothing you can say is going to make me think any different, but *if*, and I mean *if* she's gone and made fools out of the lot of you, then good for her."

6. LISS

"I'm no good at this," said Liss.

"You did okay. You had us fooled."

She scowled back. "Don't patronise me."

This was definitely not the Liss I knew. "I'm sorry. Please go on."

"I was supposed to keep my mouth shut if I got caught. I tried, but... why do you have to be so nice? All of you, it's like a tyranny of niceness. How's anyone supposed to hold out against that?"

I smiled and shrugged. There are worse things to be accused of. But Liss was still dispirited. "I've never been any good at this. I'm the last person who should be here."

"Does that mean you've done things like this before?"

She sighed. "I used to be an adventurer."

"So you *do* have powers?"

She snapped back at me. "Yes, I've got powers. Crap powers. I had early onset superpower syndrome. Kids who get their powers early are usually screwed up somehow, I was just crap. I'm strong and fast and tough but not as strong and fast and tough as the people who have real powers."

"So why did you become an adventurer?"

"My parents did it, my boyfriend was doing it, how was I supposed to avoid it?"

"Then why did you stop?"

"Because I wasn't any good at it! I was better at doing the paperwork when everyone else got back from the mission. And then Yott dumped me and the PRG didn't want me and you don't really want to hear about all this."

"I do want to hear about it."

"This isn't a therapy session."

"Actually, it is."

"Therapy sessions are supposed to be confidential. They're watching." She jabbed a finger at the cameras she assumed were in the room.

"I had the cameras switched off."

"And I'm supposed to just believe you?"

"I'm your therapist. I give you my word."

She did her best to disbelieve me, then gave it up and sighed. "Whatever."

"Do you mind if I ask some questions, just so I know what happened?"

She snorted. "Didn't they let you read the report?"

I shook my head. "I don't work for Security."

"Go on, then. If you really need to."

"I suppose you didn't actually work in a call centre? Or the recruitment agency?"

"No, I worked in the call centre *and* the recruitment agency, well, a kind of recruitment agency, they were the same place really, different parts of the same organisation."

"So… was it sales, or customer service, or…?"

"We had a service for adventurers, I mean amateur adventurers, the ones who didn't get paid, they could call up and find out who they were up against, get help if they needed it, call the professionals in, that kind of thing."

"So anyone could be an adventurer? How many people had powers on your world?"

"Forty per cent. Maybe fifty, sixty in some areas."

"That's… very strange."

She shrugged. "It's why the world was so fucked up. You can't stop someone with superpowers trying to save the world or whatever, so they licensed it. They did a psych evaluation, gave you some training, you paid your fee, they let you run around on the rooftops scaring muggers."

"I can see how that would cause problems."

"Hah. You don't know the half of it. Once I'd been in the call centre for a while, I moved over to dealing with applications. Interviewing them, trying to stop the real idiots from getting a licence, that kind of thing…"

"Was that what you were doing when it happened?"

She paused for a moment. "Yeah."

"Can you tell me...?"

She sighed. "I was interviewing this guy. He could go sort of half invisible so he thought he could be an adventurer. I was trying to talk him out of it because really, it was disgusting, you could see all his organs and everything. Poor kid."

"What happened?"

"He caught fire. Got so hot he burned into powder in just a second. At first I thought it was his power backfiring on him but when I went to the office for help, all I saw was ash. And outside... it was like a dust storm. Or a building collapse. Clouds of it, everywhere. And that was it. For all of them."

7. GROUP

Iokan cleared his throat. "I have a little experience with this kind of thing..."

"Really?" I said.

"Oh, bloody hell, you're not pretending to be a nutcase as well, are you?" said Olivia.

"No, but–"

"Oh, so you *are* a nutcase."

Iokan smiled. "Very witty, Olivia. No, what I mean is, I know a little bit about police work. And I think there's something missing from the story."

"Go on," I said.

"If you're infiltrating an organisation, or a world, or anything, really, it's very unusual for someone to do it on their own. There's usually someone backing you up. I was wondering if she had an accomplice."

"Forgive me for asking what must seem an obvious question," said Kwame, "but how can you have an accomplice if you are the last member of your species?"

Iokan shrugged. "Was she?"

"Yes. Very definitely," I said.

"What if it was someone else?" asked Pew.

"Another species?" asked Kwame.

"Well... you can have more than one species on a world..."

"She didn't have an accomplice," I said. "But she did have some very advanced technology."

"Artificial Intelligence?" asked Elsbet, suddenly on edge.

"No. Not intelligent as such, but very sophisticated."

"How could she possibly have access to a device that could defeat *your* security?" asked Kwame.

"We're not sure."

"Perhaps something left behind by another species...?" asked Iokan.

"We don't think so."

"Are you certain?"

"We're still looking into it," I said.

8. LISS

"What about the device?" I asked.

"The what?"

"The one that let you get past our security. The one you were hiding in the remote for your screenplayer."

"Oh, so you found it then," said Liss with a scowl.

"Was that kind of device common on your world?"

"There was too much of that kind of crap."

"So it *was* a common device?"

"That's not what I meant."

"Okay…"

"I meant there was too much crap from the superbrains."

"Superbrains?"

"Look, lots of people had powers. Some of them, it was being clever. *Too* clever. A lot of them went mad. That's what was wrong with the world. They built all this amazing stuff but then one of them would do something like wipe out all the wheat and rice so they could find out if people could eat some horrible crap they made from rocks, or invent some healing gloop that ended up eating people and mashing them together into one great big blob, or try and stop the hurricanes and give us a winter that lasted three years instead…"

She put her head in her hands. "And then all the idiots who thought they could save the world just because they could breathe fire or punch through steel would go after them and half the time they just made it worse."

She lifted her head again, eyes damp. "That security gizmo was something they had in the vault at the PRG. Don't ask me how it works. It just does. The guy who made it was doing seven to twelve for bank robbery in the low tech prison in Hallitasset. That thing's all that's left of him. Except for the ash."

9. GROUP

"I suppose the question is, why did she do it?" said Iokan.

"Well, she seemed to be investigating, " I said. "Beyond that I can't tell you. But if you'd like to discuss it, I don't have any objections."

"It's revenge," said Pew.

"Why do you say that?"

"I mean, what happened on her world wasn't natural. Somebody did it. Maybe she wants to get back at them."

"She wouldn't know what revenge is," said Olivia. "She thinks a harsh word is a slap in the face…"

"I'd do it." Pew suddenly sounded on edge, and everyone looked up at him.
"Would you?" asked Iokan.
"Yes."
"Would you kill?"
Pew only took a second to think about it. "Yes."
"Do you think that would make anything better?"
"Yes. It'd make me better."
"How so?"
"I wouldn't be a coward."
"You're not a coward. Don't be stupid," muttered Olivia.
"Yes I am."
"Stop talking rot! Just because you're not killing every bloody Soo you can lay your hands on doesn't mean you're a coward. I used to do it with revenants but it doesn't do any good, it doesn't matter how many you kill, you don't feel any better so *stop it*."

Pew sighed and stopped talking.

10. LISS

"What did you do after it happened?" I asked.

"I don't remember. I blanked out for a couple of days. I was drinking. I went to find my parents and I buried them..."

"So that part was true?"

She looked straight at me. "Every word."

"I'm so sorry, Liss."

She sighed and looked down. "And then I went home. Opened another bottle. Skipped a few days..." She shook her head. "Then I snapped out of it."

"By yourself?"

"No. The computer at the PRG found me. The damn thing kept pestering me. It took over the sound systems in all the apartments nearby to get my attention."

"Was that an artificial intelligence?"

"Not really. All the real AIs were eaten by a virus years ago – another fucking mess from a superbrain. All they had at the PRG was an automated system. Once everyone was gone it went into survival mode and took over all the country's computers to stop everything falling apart..."

"So... why did the PRG computer want to talk to you?"

"All the governments figured out the world could end years ago. So they made plans. They had protocols. And one of the protocols was what to do if there was only one survivor. As soon as the system recognised me as the last person on earth, it made me boss of the whole planet. Queen of the fucking anthill."

"Does that make you the head of state?"

"Huh. Guess it does."

"And that's why it was trying to snap you out of it."

"No. It had a message. It had found the bastard who did it."

"Ah."

"So that got me out of the apartment…"

"What happened? I mean, who did it?"

"They really didn't tell you, did they?"

"I told you, I don't work for Security. They don't let me see their reports."

She sighed. "It was Professor Crayfish."

"…I'm sorry?"

"Professor Crayfish. Superbrain. Hyperbiologist. He used to make armies of crabs and lobsters and attack towns in the South Pacific."

"Professor Crayfish."

I must have seemed very incredulous, because Liss was incensed. "Yes! My world was a fucking joke! Do you think I don't know that? Were you even *listening*? That crap was happening *all the time*. We had nutcases popping up and killing thousands of people every other week because they lost the remote for their killer robots or some godawful bullshit…"

"I'm sorry, Liss. You're right. It isn't funny."

"So I killed him."

"You killed him?"

"I punched him until he was dead. He had this carapace thing he'd grown, so I had to hit him hard, but I definitely killed him."

"I think we've jumped ahead a bit. So… the computer found him. And you went there and you… killed him."

"That's right."

"You took revenge."

"Yes."

"How did it make you feel?"

"I threw up."

"I mean emotionally…"

"It made me sick to my stomach. Isn't that enough?"

"It didn't make you feel better?"

"No. It didn't. The bastard wasn't working alone. Somebody from another universe was helping him. He didn't even know why. He was just a madman they gave the technology to… I shouldn't have killed him."

"Why do you say that?"

She shook her head. "I just shouldn't."

11. GROUP

"Perhaps it was not revenge," said Kwame.

"Why do you think that?" I asked.

"Perhaps she was simply seeking justice."

"You would say that, wouldn't you?" said Olivia. "Just because *you* want something, doesn't mean everyone else wants it."

"Have you never wanted justice for your people?"

"Justice? From what, a disease?"

"It might have been prevented. Someone must have failed in their duty."

"Of course they bloody failed. And now they're all dead. How do you get justice when all the guilty people are dead?"

"That is my point. If those who committed genocide on Liss's world are from another universe, she may be looking for justice."

"And what good's that going to do?"

"She may find some comfort if the guilty parties are uncovered and punished."

"So it's just more revenge, is it?"

"Not at all–"

"What's the difference? Revenge or justice, it's the same thing in the end."

"The difference is law."

"What law? How can you have laws when you don't have people?"

"Perhaps he means interversal law," suggested Iokan.

"Oh, and how's that been helping you, eh?" said Olivia to Kwame.

Kwame sighed. "I did not say that her motives were entirely rational. Only that they may be purer than simply revenge."

"Still a waste of time."

"That is your opinion."

12. LISS

"Afterwards… I got drunk again. I sound like a lush, don't I? Then I realised I'd fucked up. I should have used Professor Crayfish as bait."

"As bait?"

"He only survived because he was the one who set it off. He was protected, somehow. They were going to come back for him sooner or later."

"Why do you think that?"

"It's not a genocide until you've killed everyone, is it? And he would have known *something*. According to the protocols, I was supposed to find and interrogate anyone involved in the genocide, so that was going well. Hah. I was supposed to investigate and exact justice."

"What kind of justice?"

"They left it up to me to decide."

"That's a terrible responsibility."

"Yeah. I noticed."

"How did you feel about it?"

"It gave me something to do."

"What would you have done without it?"

She shook her head. "Don't ask me that."

13. GROUP

Elsbet hadn't spoken yet, and I hoped a little prodding would bring her into the group. "Elsbet. Do you have an opinion?"

She frowned. Something occurred to her, something she couldn't quite articulate – but then it snapped into place. "She was an infiltrator."

"Could you expand on that?"

"I don't really know her…"

"Of course, but what do you mean by 'infiltrator'?"

"Well… that's what she did? Right? She pretended she was innocent, but she was running a covert operation. That's… like espionage. I don't know. I wasn't here."

Iokan gave me a significant look. He was no fool. He'd figured out the parallels to Elsbet's own situation as fast as I had: someone hidden in the shell of an entirely different person. I decided to risk the obvious question.

"Is this something you had experience of, in your universe?"

"No. There was no way the machines could have got someone in with us."

"And you never did the same to them?"

She gave me a reproaching look. "Do I look like I could imitate a machine?"

The group shared surreptitious glances. She didn't notice.

"No, of course not," said Iokan.

"Well, shut up about it then."

"Is that all?" asked Kwame.

She looked back at him, confused at everyone's sudden interest and covering it with aggression. "Yeah. Why, what else do you want?"

I decided it wasn't the time to press her further. "Nothing," I said. "Let's move on."

14. LISS

"So we knew the bad guys were from another universe. We researched everything the superbrains knew about that kinda stuff. Turns out all the ones who went into that field died young – lab accidents, mostly. None of them made it past twenty-five."

"You think someone was suppressing the technology?"

"Hell, yeah. Someone didn't want us seeing other universes. We could have done it, of course we could. All of the things the superbrains were doing, and they can't go to other universes? That doesn't make any sense. It's not like going to another star system."

"Did you find anything else?"

"There was enough in the research for us to set up detectors to see if anyone else came through. And the only bait we had left was me. The idea was to set up shop and make it obvious someone was still alive, and then… well, there were lots of things we could have done. We only did the undercover thing because you seemed friendly."

"So when we turned up, you really thought it might have been us?"

"What else was I supposed to think?"

"Okay. I can understand that. How did you do it?"

"Preparation. We set up an apartment, made it look lived in, created the electronic trail in an office and shops and everything. I had to have acting lessons as well."

"How–?"

"Interactive software. I wasn't very good. I ended up pretending to be someone from work."

"I see…"

"There was this woman called Galts. She was so annoying… everyone in the office could do an impression of her, she was such an idiot. I shouldn't talk like that about her, I mean she's dead but… well, she was an idiot."

"If it's any consolation, we believed the performance."

"Huh."

"You fooled everyone. The clothes were a very nice touch as well. Perfect distraction."

"That's nice. Do I get an award?"

"We're still looking at whether or not we can bring you back to the group."

"Oh, great."

15. GROUP

"I think, in conclusion," said Iokan, "We don't know enough about Liss to really judge her."

"Speak for yourself," said Olivia.

"I believe, however, that she is acting from an honest wish to do good."

"So you don't think she is on a quest for revenge?" said Kwame.

Iokan looked at him. "She may be."

"And you count that as 'good'?"

"If that's what needs to be done."

"Is she coming back?" asked Pew.

"I don't know yet," I said.

"Is it even possible?" asked Kwame.

"It may be. How would you feel about that?"

"Huh. Bloody good riddance, that's what I say," said Olivia.

"You're assuming she's who you thought she was," said Iokan. "What if she isn't?"

"Then she can bloody well go to prison for messing us about."

"Don't you want to know what she was up to?"

"Couldn't care less."

"I want to know," said Pew.

"And I also. I would like to have a very long talk with her," said Kwame.

"Dirty old man," said Olivia, getting an irritated look back in return.

"Olivia. Please," I said. She huffed and folded her arms. "Elsbet? How would you feel if Liss returned?"

She was still submerged in her own worries. "I don't know… why do you need to ask me?"

"You're a member of the group."

"Am I?"

"Yes. We'd value your opinion."

"I don't know," she shrugged.

"Okay. Iokan?"

"Of course. I'd love to see her come back. I think she needs us. It's a terrible strain to work undercover like that. She needs our support."

16. LISS

"Do you want to come back?"

"Is there anywhere else to go?"

"Only prison. We'd like to have you back, if you're willing to come."

She sighed. "What do they think?"

"They've agreed to it. You're one of them."

"I'm not."

"They're the only people who've been through anything like what you've been through. I said this when we started the group: you're not exactly the same, none of you are. But you all have more in common with each other than anyone else."

She didn't reply.

"So do you want me to put things in motion?"

Grudgingly, she nodded.

PART EIGHT
DESIRE

1. KWAME

Liss waited in a holding cell while Security went through their procedures to decide whether or not they'd let her come back to us. I visited Dawa Dorje to explain what Liss had been through, and that she too was the last survivor of a dead nation. Dawa had, as a young man, harboured his own fruitless desire for revenge against those who destroyed Tibet, and withdrew his complaint against her. The Refugee Service offered generous compensation for the damage to his bar, and he was even allowed to keep his business licence on condition that he named his smuggling accomplices and agreed to thorough surveillance to prevent any relapse. Security were left with only the criminal charges to hold Liss on, but since psychiatric care was one of the prescribed sanctions for this sort of crime, it seemed likely she'd be back with the group fairly soon.

The summer went on at the centre. The colours of the forest grew richer while the rain dried up. The trees could cope, but Olivia wasn't happy with the damage a couple of weeks of drought did to her garden. She spent ever more time among the shoots with a watering can, or plucking out the weeds that kept creeping up even when other plants were suffering.

The forecast for evacuations stayed quiet, though a new world had been added to the apocalypse watch: three commercial factions on the recently discovered world of Kreg were fighting a war that had been going on for centuries, and around which their entire economy revolved. They treated our emissaries with contempt, but were running out of resources to prosecute their pointless war. Their world looked grey and battered from space, the seas an oily poison. Even so, it might be decades before they finally faced up to the inevitable, and no one in the Refugee Service seriously expected an evacuation in the near future. I still had the time I needed to work with the group.

No word came from Bell until a brief message arrived saying he would be returning in a few days – just that, with nothing to explain why he'd been away so long, or any show of affection. But still, interversal messages are expensive, so perhaps he just wanted to keep his credit balance from plunging too far. Or maybe he was finding a way to leave me. Or he could have found someone else already. I theorised altogether too many reasons for his behaviour before I told myself to stop being a fool. I had to get on with my job, and there was news for Kwame.

We'd been monitoring his dreams for a few weeks, and had finally managed to piece together enough images to have something worth showing him. He was understandably nervous when I invited him to my office, and unable to keep his non-spill cup steady in his hands as I lowered the lights and activated the wallscreen.

"I have to warn you, this isn't what you were expecting. It's not what we were expecting either…"

"The process did not work?"

"The process worked. I'm not sure we got any images of your wife."

"But I dreamt of her. Every night you were monitoring…"

"It's probably best if I just show you what we have. If you're ready."

He nodded, and I went on. "This is the most complete sequence, although you'll notice it's very fuzzy round the edges, and we lose resolution several times. Are you sure you're ready?"

He nodded. "I am ready." I pressed play.

The video was silent. We had only been able to decipher the visual element, and even then the image quality was poor, with faint, washed-out colours. But unlike most dreams, the setting and scene were constant. This was not a spontaneous creation of the unconscious, but a memory stuck on playback.

The setting was a cell; filthy, rust-blotched metal walls and a heavy door that did not need a soundtrack for you to hear weighty clanks and slams. An industrial-age dungeon.

The point of view was locked in one place, but the eyes we saw through could look around, showing us the terrible, stained concrete floor and scratches in the walls where someone had tried to keep track of time before losing all hope. When the dream persona looked down, we saw he was sitting on a chair by himself, wearing mudstained green trousers of cheap cloth. Some of the stains might have been blood. His arms were not visible. They seemed to be bound behind his back in some way. I remembered how Kwame's arms had gone around his back when he had his flashback in my office, and had little doubt he'd relived the same thing then.

The point of view jumped, and the image skipped for a moment. Kwame looked at me, confused.

"We sometimes have problems if there's too much movement. We think your persona in the dream was startled at this point." The image reformed and settled on the door. Then looked around again, nervous and harried.

He stared at the screen, perplexed. "Where is this place?"

"You don't recognise it?"

He shook his head, amazed. "The security services had cells like this. I never saw them."

"Not even on screen? Or maybe you read about them?"

"Of course, but I was never there…"

"Hm. Well, the dream keeps you here for a while. Presumably they want to scare you."

"Isolation was a common tactic."

"I'll speed on to the next thing, then." I jumped the video forward to a bookmark I'd set earlier. The point of view looked high on the walls, then snapped to the door. A slat scraped open and eyes peered in, shadowed by a military cap. They glared at the dream persona for several seconds. Then the slat was yanked shut, and the image skipped out again.

When it came back, the door swung open. A man stood in the doorway, wearing a dark uniform. He seemed to be of the same species, possibly the same ethnicity as Kwame. He didn't move for the moment. Just a hard, threatening look down at the dream persona. Deliberate intimidation.

The picture juddered, losing resolution and colour for a moment. "Our best guess here is that the dream persona is talking, but that's just a guess," I said. Kwame nodded, too fascinated to look away.

The image came back and the point of view skipped left, perhaps hearing something in the corridor outside. Another man in uniform came to the door, dragging along a woman in a ragged, filthy dress, yanking her by the belt and head, keeping her doubled over, straggling hair hiding her face. One arm was twisted at an unnatural angle, fingers sticking out in every direction. She'd been tortured.

I paused the movie.

"That cannot be my wife. That cannot be…" Kwame looked up at me. "How could I forget something like this?"

"If it was very traumatic, it's certainly possible. I'm going to press play in a moment, but first of all you should know that one of those people is about to speak. We don't have any audio, but we did run it through a lip-reading program. As long as the dream persona is looking at someone's face, we think we know what they were saying."

He nodded. "I understand. Please continue."

I pressed the control on my pad. The people on the screen sprang back to life, the woman shaking while the uniformed men stood very still. The first man asked a question from the doorway, and subtitles sprang up, assessed at 91% accuracy: *Do you know this woman?*

The man did not seem to get a satisfactory answer. *I will ask you again. Do you know this woman?*

Again, he didn't get the answer he wanted. It made him angry. He seized the woman from the other man, and dragged her into the cell, right into the face of the dream persona, filling the screen, shouting as he did so: *Do you know this woman?* And then he yanked up her head and revealed her face.

It was not the face of a woman. The skin was bruised, bleeding, one eye closed from contusions, teeth smashed. But it was not a woman. This was the face of a man.

Kwame leapt straight to his feet and stumbled back, falling into the chair again. His cup fell to the floor and seeped into the carpet.

"Who is that?!"

"We don't know." The man on the screen held the face of the 'woman' up against the point of view of the dream persona. 'She' wept through 'her' one good eye, pleading, desperate.

Kwame stared, shaking his head, half in the chair and half out, as the dream persona looked up at the man in the cap. The subtitles caught the end of his sentence: *…what you told us. Tell him, little bird. Tell him!*

The point of view snapped back to the 'woman' as 'her' hair was pulled to force 'her' to speak through the broken teeth and blood. *Please. Kobe. [Koobey?]*

'Her' hair was yanked again and 'she' gasped at the pain. 'She' looked back into the dream persona's eyes. *I love you. I… I… I am your wife…*

"No!" shouted Kwame. "That is not my wife!"

The man in the cap dragged the 'woman' back, nearly to the door. He spoke: *I will ask you once again. Do you know this woman?*

"That is not my wife," said Kwame.

The view fixed on 'her' as she looked back, hoping, pleading, crying. And then a look of horror and betrayal as she heard what the dream persona said. And a scream: *No! No! Kobe!*

The man in the cap thrust the 'woman' back to the second man, and 'she' was dragged away, screaming one final cry of *Kobe!*

The dream persona looked down at the floor. The image resolution failed again, losing focus.

"We think he's crying," I said. "You in the dream, that is."

The dream persona looked up again, very suddenly, and saw the man in the cap, standing alone in the door.

That was the right answer, Sergeant. You will be released shortly. You will not speak of this again.

He turned and left, pulling the door shut behind him.

I stopped the movie. "That's it. It goes in a loop. The dream persona keeps sitting there and eventually they bring the other prisoner in again."

Kwame sat shaking in the easy chair. "That is not my wife."

"Do you recognise him at all...?"

"He is a stranger to me."

"Are you certain?"

He snapped: "I do not have sex with men!" The denial was vehement, absolute., and revealing. It hung in the air for a moment before I replied.

"I didn't ask that question."

"This is a farce. You have taken some scene from a television programme, or from something else!"

"Okay, Kwame, if you don't want to discuss it now, I can understand that. But I can assure you that was your dream. Those memories are in your head. It may be that your trauma predates the nuclear war–"

"It does not! Those are not my memories! I did not do those things!"

"We can talk about this next time."

"There will not be a next time."

He stormed out, and I called Veofol to monitor him. He contacted his legal counsel and complained about our methods, but got nothing other than a promise to investigate which I could answer simply by telling his lawyer the truth, so long as it remained privileged: his dream was real, but we could no longer say the same about any of his other memories.

2. IOKAN

I was still thinking about Bell and his cryptic message when it came time for Iokan's next session. In the minute before he arrived, I sent an interversal message back to Bell, regardless of the cost. Where had he been? Was it a nice holiday? What was he up to? Please send me a message and let me know. *Love, Asha.*

Iokan was his usual happy-go-lucky self, the opposite to my fretfulness. He whistled his way onto an easy chair in my office, gathering up his robe and seeming keen to begin therapy. Which probably meant he'd thought of a way to avoid it. "I've been thinking," he said, in excellent Interversal.

"What about?" I asked.

"The Antecessors."

"You surprise me, Iokan."

He ignored the gentle sarcasm. "I think I know what happened."

"Really? You know why the genocide happened?"

"Oh, I knew *that*. No, I've figured out why they were different when they came back."

So he'd been having theological thoughts. Hopefully this was a sign of theological doubts. "How exactly were they different?" I asked.

"Well, they never seemed especially... compassionate, if you know what I mean. They changed the world to their liking and didn't let anything get in their way..."

"Like animals, for example."

"Exactly! They changed everything to suit them, nothing like the way you run this planet. They wouldn't have thought twice about getting rid of the native species and adding their own instead. But when they came back, they weren't like that at all. They gave us an option. They gave us a chance to say no."

"Did anyone want to say no?"

"Of course not. They were offering an eternity in heaven, with them! Who'd refuse that?"

"I thought you said *you* refused?"

"I... avoided them. I thought they were the way they used to be. But finally they found me and showed me the truth."

"As you've said. But you were saying you've realised why they had a change of heart?"

"They went into space!"

"Okay..."

"No, think about it. Why do we go to other universes? Because the stars are so far away! No one can get past lightspeed. We can see there are other species out there on some worlds, but they're hundreds, thousands of light years away, and we can never reach them. But what if you were made of light? Like the Antecessors? Light can travel at lightspeed, it has to! And you wouldn't have to experience all those light years, you'd feel like you travelled the distance almost in an instant! You understand relativity, yes?"

"I understand the basic principle."

"So they disappeared for three thousand years. Imagine what they might have found! There must be amazing things out there... beautiful things. Divine things."

"But this is just speculation..."

"Something must have happened. It *must* have!"

"Iokan... have you been having doubts?"

"Doubts?"

"About the Antecessors."

"No, of course not."

"Then why are you trying to figure out how they became good?"

"I'm just trying to understand them better."

"You didn't seem this concerned until recently. Are you sure you haven't had doubts...?"

He seemed at a loss to explain things to me. "Well, you see, it's like..." he sighed. "You're not going to believe me unless I explain, are you?"

"I'm finding it difficult, yes."

"Part of my job – yes, *that* job, the secret job – was to investigate them."

"I see."

"Every country in the world had a unit dedicated to investigating them, either to find things we could use, or to make the relics safe..."

"And that was what you did, after you finished with special forces?"

"Not straight away, they put me in their own special forces unit to begin with, just for a probationary period, and then I had to go back to school to pick up all the skills I needed, but then, yes, I was an investigator."

"What was the organisation called?"

"Do you really need to know?"

"It helps to put a name to things."

"All right, I suppose if you have to put a label on a file... D0."

"That's it? Dee-Oh?"

"That's enough."

"And this organisation investigated the Antecessors?"

"That's right."

"Can you give me any examples?"

He sighed. I was exasperating him. "Well... well, there was the time we found an ancient bodyformer."

"Which is...?"

"It was a device that created human bodies. Copied them, either with the personality intact or with some other mind. And, as sometimes happens with that kind of thing, it was set off accidentally and made copies of the investigative team."

"So you didn't work alone?"

"There were three people in each team – me, Feren, Soferenata. We got trapped in there when the machine made copies of us, and of course everyone thought they were the real ones. We got out in the end, but the copies made a complete mess of things on the outside. They went off on another investigation and screwed up because, well, they weren't exactly perfect copies." He shook his head. "We had to destroy them."

"You killed them?"

"They planted a bomb in D0 headquarters and threatened to set it off unless someone explained what was going on. They thought they were in a parallel universe." He smiled sadly. "We didn't have a choice."

"And was this typical of your encounters with Antecessor technology?"

"Some things were worse. Most of the time we only found trinkets. But yeah, that kind of thing happened a lot."

"I can see why you were having some trouble reconciling the two sets of experiences – the Antecessors you investigated and the ones you met later."

"I'm not having doubts."

"But you need more justification?"

"I – well, what I need – it's hard to explain…" I waited for him to try. "Something happened to them. I don't *need* to know why…"

"But it helps."

He sighed. "They're good. That's the important thing. They did what was best for us. I'm certain of *that*…"

His hypothesis was clearly wishful thinking to shore up his beliefs. But there was a loose end to the story that, if pulled on, might help to unravel it. "Can I ask a question?"

"Of course."

"You say the Antecessors left your planet to go to the stars?"

"That's right."

"Most species that leave their worlds do so because of some kind of cataclysm. Do you think that happened to them?"

"We never found out for sure. Something happened. They left. That's all we know."

"But why not go to another universe? It's much easier than going to the stars, and lots of people do it. Why go to all the trouble of star travel?"

"Other universes are dangerous."

"Most of them are empty."

"Are you sure about that?"

"We explore dozens every year."

"They might start off empty. But if you can get there, so can someone else."

"Did anyone else ever come to *your* universe?"

He stopped there.

"Iokan? Is that a difficult question?"

"It's a dangerous question."

"Why is it dangerous?"

"I've said enough for now."

"If you're worried about something, I'd like to help."

"No. You can't help. Leave it alone."

"Is it anything to do with the Antecessors?"

"No."

"Is there anything you can tell me?"

"Nothing."

There was something else, all right, but we'd hit a dead end. He was determined to protect us with his silence, and would say no more on the subject.

3. PEW

Bell still hadn't replied to my last message, and it was nearly a day later. I sent another one and fretted over the wording for half an hour, second-guessing it, trying not to seem desperate but keeping an edge of annoyance to let him know I wasn't happy. *You've been gone for ages – just let me know what you're up to*, was the best I could manage as I realised the chimes had rung for the beginning of the next therapy session twenty minutes before, and Pew still hadn't turned up.

I went to find him. He was in the garden, weeding away while Olivia was off in the toilets.

"I don't want to talk," he said, bent over and yanking up stems.

"If there's something you don't want to talk about, we don't have to talk about it."

"I'm not talking about Ley'ang."

"Then I won't ask. Do you want some water or anything?"

"I'm fine."

"Do you want me to get you a chair?"

"I don't want a chair." He yanked up a handful of stems.

"They'll only grow back, you know. You have to dig the roots out if you're really going to–"

"I don't want to talk." He grabbed more leafy stems and ripped them out.

"Pew, has something happened?"

"No." Rip, rip.

"Are you sure you don't want to talk about it?"

Rip, rip, RIP. "Yes I'm fucking sure."

"Can we schedule another time?"

"No!" RIP, RIP, *RIP*. He gasped in pain.

"What is it?"

"Nothing. Leave me alone."

He held one hand closed against his chest and covered it with the other. "Pew, are you hurt?"

"No. I'll be fine." He stood up, still clutching his hand.

"Pew–" I said, but Olivia chose that moment to stalk back from the main building, walking fast as she saw I seemed to be pestering Pew.

"What's all this?" she demanded of me.

"We're talking, Olivia," I said. "Is that a problem?"

But she spotted Pew's hands and switched her annoyance to him. "Hey, where are your gloves? I told you, you're supposed to use gloves!"

She pulled open his hand and found a fresh line of blood and sliced skin running across his palm.

"Oh, you stupid little… I told you, sandweed's sharp, you have to use gloves!" Pew blushed at being found out. Sandweed keeps stores of silicates on the edge of its leaves, making them sharp and providing a very effective defence against insect pests and human gardeners. Olivia used rough gardening gloves to deal with it. But Pew had been weeding with his left hand – and he wasn't left handed.

"Pew," I said, "Show me your other hand."

"No," he said, holding his right hand tightly shut.

"Please, Pew," I asked. Olivia caught my look of concern.

"Well, come on, then, let's see it!" Pew's look of embarrassment turned to pain, mouth trembling as he revealed his right hand: not cut once, but dozens of times, cuts running across cuts, some already on their way to healing and opened again.

"Oh, you fool, you fool!" said Olivia. I called for medical assistance. "I told you! What do you want to go and do this for?"

"I– I–" Pew couldn't answer; he was deep in shame and couldn't look Olivia in the eye.

"I don't understand it, I just don't understand!" she wasn't angry at him; she was truly, actually hurt.

"Okay, Olivia, I've got a nurse on the way, we're going to see to him." Olivia folded her arms and turned her back. "We'll sort your hands out Pew, don't worry, you don't have to talk to me, let's just deal with the cuts, okay?" A nurse came up with a medkit. "Do you want me to come inside with you?" I asked. He shook his head. The nurse sprayed anaesthetic on the cuts, and took Pew inside.

"This is your fault," muttered Olivia, watching him go.

"And how do you make that out, Olivia?"

"He doesn't want to talk to you. You shouldn't keep making him."

"He won't get any better if he doesn't talk."

"Rubbish. He's fine the way he is."

"No, he's not, Olivia. I'd have thought you of all people would know that."

"Oh, and what's that supposed to mean?"

"He's like you, Olivia. Are *you* okay?"

"I would be if you lot didn't stop interfering."

"If we stopped interfering you'd be dead."

"Bloody good thing, too."

"Is that what you want to happen to him?"

She was brought up short. "Now you're twisting my words," she muttered.

"Is that what you want to happen?"

"No I don't!"

"Then are you going to help me?"

"Huh. Help you. That's a good joke."

"But you *can* help me, Olivia."

"Why would I want to?"

"Because it'll help *him*. I'm trying to find out the root cause of his trauma, but the closer I get, the more he backs away. If you know something, that might be useful."

She muttered something I didn't catch.

"I'm sorry?" I asked.

She sighed. "All right, all right, what do you want?"

"Let's sit down for a moment." We pulled up garden chairs and sat down amid the weeds and shoots. "Did you ever talk to him about his past?"

"A bit."

"What did you talk about?"

"Oh, gods, lots of things. Why do you need to ask, anyway? You've got the whole place wired for sound, haven't you?"

"I don't have time to go through every conversation…"

"Huh. Could have fooled me. Number of times someone's come running out to stop us doing something or other…"

"We keep an eye on you, but we're not always watching."

"Just whenever you feel like, then."

"You were going to tell me something about Pew?"

"Yeh. Well. He asks about revenants a lot."

"What kind of things does he ask?"

"What was it like to kill them. How many did I get. Things like that. Same questions everyone asks."

"So he's mostly interested in how you fought them?"

"Yeh. Suppose so."

"Anything else?"

"I told him he shouldn't be so uptight about that last girl of his."

"Is that a girlfriend he had at university…?"

"No, you idiot, the Pew girl. On his world. What's-her-name."

"Ley'ang?"

"The last one in the breeding programme, yeh. The one where he couldn't get it up."

"Ah. So what did you say?"

"Well, you know. It happens to men. It's not always their fault if they can't do it."

"Did he say anything?"

"He said it wasn't like that. Got all worked up about it, really touchy, you understand me?"

So far, he'd stuck to the Soo line about 'erectile dysfunction' being the reason why the final mating attempt failed; but if he was telling a different story now, that was worth looking into. "Did he say anything else?"

She shrugged. "He didn't want to talk about it. So I didn't."

"Thank you, Olivia."

"Are we finished?"

"Your session isn't until later, so I suppose so, yes. Although… do you mind if I ask you something?"

"When has me minding ever stopped you?"

I smiled. "He's a little bit like a son to you, isn't he?"

That made her pause for a moment. "Rubbish."

"Well, isn't he?"

"Dunno what you're talking about."

"You do, don't you?"

"Utter rubbish…"

"Olivia, can I ask… did you have any children?"

"You can ask," she said.

"Would I get an answer?"

She leaned forward for emphasis. "Let the dead lie in peace."

A chime went off in my ear. Someone was calling for me. "I have to take a call. I'll see you in my office?"

"Not frigging likely."

She really wasn't happy as I left her behind and answered the call. I couldn't get further than the far end of the garden because the call was rated 'urgent', so I treated it at face value and answered as quickly as I could. It turned out to be Bell, calling from the Lift and responding to all my messages but with a priority level that wasn't supposed to be used except in emergencies. I was irritated and asked him to call back a little later, but he demanded he had to speak to me now. I looked back over my shoulder – Olivia was fiddling with a watering can and seemed to be oblivious, but the last thing I wanted to do was have this conversation anywhere near her, so I headed up to the building and out of earshot before I went on.

He wanted to meet up, he said. I told him that was fine, but I was very busy with my patients. Couldn't we just talk? He dropped the bombshell: he wanted to have a serious conversation.

I knew right away what kind of serious conversation he meant, and flapped around, trying to think of something to say. Like a fool, I told him I wasn't going to be answering any of his questions about my patients, and managed to offend him because of course the group had nothing to do with it. He wanted to have a serious talk. A very serious talk. About us.

I pointed out that I had patients who needed me, and that was pretty damned serious as well. I lost my temper for a moment: he'd been away with no explanation for weeks, and then he just turned up out of the blue with demands for a 'serious conversation' and he expected me to drop everything and go running off to see him so he could be 'serious', whatever that meant? He pointed out that he just wanted to have a civilised discussion, but I wasn't in that kind of mood. I told him to piss off, ended the call and went inside. I flew up the gravity tubes to my office, set the soundproofing to maximum and had a very therapeutic yell. The only difference it made was that I quickly realised what an idiot I was.

4. ELSBET

But before I could figure out what to say or do, Elsbet stormed in to see me. She'd told us a lot about the asteroid society she came from in her first few sessions: a horrible bolthole for a tiny fragment of humanity, surviving on algae and hatred of the machines. We hadn't yet found a way to tell her about Katie, because it was all too clear they would have been deadly enemies in the war between humans and machines, and it was just as clear that we'd left it too late.

"Look at this!" she shouted, holding out her arm.

"It's your arm," I said.

"Look!"

She concentrated, then twisted it into an unnatural position. She reached round with her other hand and pulled the arm off her shoulder, ripping the skin away to reveal metallic contacts, graphene construction and a mess of cabling: exactly what we already knew to be there, but something that was news to her.

"My arm comes off!"

"Ah... yes."

"Did you do this to me?"

"No, we didn't. Do you want to sit down and take some tea?"

"No I fucking don't! How the hell did this happen if you didn't do it?"

"This is how you were when we found you, Elsbet."

"What?" She was incredulous.

"Please, sit down and we'll talk about it."

She was furious, but could see I wasn't going to discuss it any other way, so she dropped herself into a chair with her arm on her lap. I made myself some tea to calm what was left of my nerves.

"Are you sure you don't want some?"

"Yes."

"Okay, then." I sat down with my own cup. "What's the last thing you remember before you came here?"

"I told you! I was in a missile, I was supposed to destroy an installation on Earth."

"And kill yourself."

"I'm a soldier. The machines are an abomination. I was doing my duty."

"And what next?"

"You said I skipped off the atmosphere and they found me at Ceres. I suppose that last part isn't true."

"That's right."

"So you must have found the missile out in space somewhere."

"No."

"No? What do you mean, no?"

"We have no idea what happened to you in the missile. We know nothing about that."

"But... you found me in the missile! Right?" I shook my head. She was left very confused. "Then how...?"

"We found you floating in space. In orbit around the L1 point between the Earth and Moon."

"In *vacuum?*"

"Yes."

"But in a space suit? Right?"

"No."

She stared at me, disbelieving. "That's impossible."

"It happened."

"I'd be *dead!*"

"You were in a dormant state. But you weren't dead. We were able to revive you."

"No, no, this is *algae shit*. You're *lying*."

"Are you sure you don't remember anything else?"

"I– No. Nothing! Nothing..." But she trailed off. There was something there.

"Elsbet? Are you sure?"

She was thinking hard, eyes twitching. But she snapped out of it and looked at me. "I'm *sure*."

"Are you all right...?"

"I'm. Fine." Her eyes twitched again. A tremor set into her remaining hand. She shouted at something to my left. "I said I'm fine!"

She jumped up, as though hearing something off to the right, and then spasmed, gritting her teeth and screwing up her eyes, gasping as though bearing a terrible pain. She pitched forward, collapsing on the coffee table. I hardly needed to look at the medical monitors to know she'd had another seizure. I went to call for medics – but she suddenly woke up. She lifted herself from the table and unfolded into a standing position. Her head twitched and looked about with no emotion.

"I have been offline," she said in a flat voice. She wasn't Elsbet any more.

"Katie?"

She looked down at me.

"That is my designation in this place." She noticed her missing arm, where it had fallen to the floor. "I am damaged." She picked up the arm, and pressed the joint against her empty shoulder socket. Cables jumped out, connected and pulled the arm back into place as the skin knitted and healed until there was no trace of a join. She flexed it, decided it was acceptable, and then frowned. "Have I suffered further neural degradation?"

"Yes. Do you remember?"

"I remember..." she blinked. "Children. In a hospital. Suffocating."

"Suffocating?"

"Emergency atmospheric purge. No air for the children. They fell..."

"Katie? Are you all right?"

"My function is. Impaired."

"We can help you."

"I... do not require... help..."

She stood there for a moment. Then collapsed again, this time back into the chair. I called the medics in and we took her to the infirmary.

***

After a thorough scan of her brain, we got a neuro specialist on the line from Hub Metro who pronounced the obvious: another seizure, another flip of personality, further neural degradation, one step closer to death. "You should get her to agree to the procedure as soon as possible," he said.

"She won't give us her consent."

"Which one?"

"Katie."

"And the other?"

"There's an ethical issue there."

He sighed. He didn't have a high opinion of ethical issues. "How long does she have?" I asked.

"Weeks. Maybe two months at the outside."

She came back to herself an hour later, the longest period of recovery yet. It was Elsbet who opened her eyes in her old room in the infirmary, tubed up to machines regulating her biological systems until we were sure it was safe.

I sat by her bed to explain about the implants in her brain, that mimicked the ones she expected to be there but which had entirely different functions, accelerating her neural efficiency and wearing her brain down.

She was slower than before, but still had a touch of fire in her. "Take them out."

"We can't. We don't know how to do it without killing you."

"What's going to happen?"

"If things stay as they are... you'll die."

She closed her eyes for a moment. "Then I'll die."

"There is a treatment. We can put you in a new body. It's easier than fixing the old one. But we have a problem."

She opened her eyes. "What problem?"

"An ethical issue."

"A *what*?"

"You see... when we found you, in space... you were someone else." She stared back at me. "You were called Katie. You were a very different person. And when we asked her if she would accept the treatment, she refused." I sighed. "The problem is... she has rights. And she's in your skull as much as you are. And to make things worse... we don't know which of you is the primary personality. You, I mean *you*, Elsbet... you may well be a persona coming out of the implants. If that's the case, we have to put Katie's wishes first. I'm sorry."

"I don't believe it."

"I understand that. But I assure you, it's true. When you had your seizure, she came back for a moment. And if she comes back again, we'll do everything we can to convince her to accept the treatment."

"Who the fuck is this 'Katie'?"

"We think... well, we're not sure, but she might be an infiltrator. From the machines."

Her eyes went wide. "No."

"I'm sorry."

"I'm *human!*"

I couldn't answer that. Instead, I asked her: "What's the last thing you remember? Are you sure it was just the missile hitting atmosphere?"

"Yes! I'm..." But her certainty melted. "No... No... No!"

"What is it?"

"No, no, no, no, no!" She ripped tubes from her arm and noticed she was doing it with the reattached cyborg limb. "Get it off me! Get it off!" She reached to pull it away, but she was weaker and couldn't grasp it properly.

"Elsbet–"

"Get me out of here! Get me out of this *thing!* Get me OUT!"

She was screaming and weeping, and there was nothing to do but call in the medics and have her sedated.

5. OLIVIA

I kept the lights off in my office for a while. I had an entirely irrational feeling that everything was suddenly going wrong with the group. Veofol reported that Kwame had withdrawn into his room and switched on privacy for more than the allotted time, and then shouted at him when he went to see how he was. Pew's injuries were hardly severe, but the nurse who treated him reported a higher than usual fear of human contact, and he only accepted medical care with a great deal of persuasion. Veofol tried to have a chat with Iokan about his past, but ran into the same brick wall I'd seen in his session. And there was still the problem with Bell, which left me feeling irritable and annoyed. I debated the merits of letting Veofol take the next individual session before I became too irritable, but dismissed the idea quickly. Not so much because he couldn't cope with it, but because I didn't want to run away from my responsibilities, though it didn't help that the next session was with Olivia, who would doubtless do her best to avoid it until I personally went in search of her.

So I was very surprised when she turned up on time and took a seat in one of the comfortable chairs, despite her earlier assertion. She was even smiling. But I soon found the smile was far from friendly.

"So," said Olivia. "What shall we talk about, then?"

"You've got something you want to discuss? Of course, go ahead."

She grinned. "You've got man troubles."

"I'm sorry?"

"You do shout a lot on the phone, don't you?"

My eyes must have gone wide for a moment, because her smile broadened. I thought I'd taken every precaution when I took the call from Bell in the garden – how had she heard me? Later, I found out: the watering can she'd been fiddling with was the key. She'd unscrewed the sprinkler from the spout, then the spout itself from the can, and found the broad, open spout made an passable ear trumpet.

"I... think that's private, Olivia."

"Privacy? In here? Hah! You must be joking! The word's out, missy, and there's nothing you can do about it. How does *that* make *you* feel?"

"Like a therapist with a patient who's determined to make trouble."

"No, no, no. A *soon to be single* therapist with a patient that's determined to make trouble."

"Was there anything else you wanted to tell me?"

"Well! I wanted to know what it felt like to have your husband run off..."

"I'm not married."

"Boyfriend, then."

"He hasn't run off. We had a disagreement."

"Sounded like a very *loud* disagreement..."

"It happens, Olivia. I'm sure you have your own experiences in this area." I couldn't help being irritated. Too irritated for a therapy session.

"Ohhh yes, but it's lovely to see you having them as well."

"Is that what it takes to impress you, Olivia?" I realised I'd snapped back at her and given her precisely what she wanted: anger. Emotion. Stooping down to her level of vindictiveness.

"Who said anything about being impressed? I just think it's funny." I took a breath as she smirked. I had half a mind to cancel the session. Or get Veofol in. Or something.

"Well…" I said.

But could I use it? Was there a way into her own trauma?

Yes.

"Well what?" she demanded.

"Perhaps you can help me." That made her laugh. "You *did* agree with me when I suggested you had your own experience of this…"

"What, haven't you got any friends you can go to?"

"No one who's been through what you've been through."

"You want advice from *me*? All right. Kill him. If he's dead he's not going to give you any problems. There, that's my advice."

"I see… is that what you did?"

She held her tongue for a moment. She wasn't amused any more. I'd found something. "Yes."

"I'm so sorry…"

"What are you sorry about?"

"I didn't know you lost a husband."

"Lots of women lost their husbands."

"How many had to kill them?"

"Too many. You've done it again, haven't you? You've got me talking about myself."

My smile was humourless, but still sympathetic, I hoped. "I think I've said this before, Olivia, but you do like giving people advice. If you can tell me anything about how to deal with a partner who's not being reasonable, I'd be glad to hear it…"

She sighed. "Let me guess. He doesn't like you working."

"He'd prefer I spent less time here."

"Well then, he's a sensible man, isn't he?"

"Olivia. Seriously."

"Well…" she cast about for something to say. "You've got it all different here, haven't you? You don't have to ask anyone's permission to go to work."

"Is that how it was on your world?"

"Of course that's how it was. We were primitive. Remember?"

"So you weren't very happy with things as they were."

"No I bloody wasn't."

"But you did marry."

"Yeh. Eventually."

"Was he your first…?"

"No, he wasn't. More fool me. What about you?"

"No. He's not my first."

"And it still goes wrong, does it? Even when you're all *advanced* and not as *primitive* as the rest of us?"

"We're only human."

"And men are still getting jealous when women go to work."

"It's not that. It's more that he thinks I'm working too hard."

"When *was* the last time you went home?"

It caught at me for a moment. "He's been away for a few weeks. He came back today."

"Well for gods' sake, woman, bloody go and see him! You don't want him to forget the sight of you! He'll take up with some trollop, mark my words…"

I could only manage a thin smile. "I'll bear that in mind. But what happened to you?"

"What about what happened to me?"

"You were married. Is there anything you'd like to tell me?"

"Yeh. Don't do it."

"Is that because you had to kill your husband…?"

"No… just *don't*. It's not worth it. You fall in love with the bugger and then he'll let you down one way or another. They always do."

"It sounds like you've had some unhappy experiences. Can you tell me any more?"

She sighed. "You never let go, do you? All right, number one," she held out a single finger, "Antony Whatecroft. My professor when I was doing my master's degree. Brilliant mind, everyone looked up to him, he said his wife didn't understand him, I fell for it. Number two," she held up two fingers, "Jack Lockehust. Married him when my research career was over, only he killed himself because he was in debt up to his eyeballs, the stupid shit. And then he got up again, and, well, you know what I do about *that* kind of thing. Number three," she held up three fingers, "Mike Brokefeld, head of security at Tringarrick after the last outbreak. He was… well, he was available, if you take my meaning. He buggered off with everyone else when they all gave up."

"I suppose Antony died before the last outbreak…?"

"No. He was supposed to come out and join us at Tringarrick. He was on the last train but he never made it."

"So you still knew him, even then?"

She shrugged. "Once I realised the last outbreak was coming, I didn't have anywhere else to go. I had to do my bit, and he was still doing the best research."

"Wasn't that uncomfortable?"

She gave me a crooked smile. "Didn't care. I made him think the children were his and then he gave me whatever I needed for my research."

"Your children?"

"Yeh. I had children. Girl and a boy. Happy now?"

"You've never spoken of them."

"They're dead."

"I'm sorry."

"Oh, stop it."

"Stop what?"

"Stop saying you're sorry. You're not sorry and even if you are how are you going to keep saying sorry every time you hear someone died?"

"It's a mark of sympathy, Olivia."

"Well stop it."

"If you want me to, of course. But you were talking about your children...?"

"No. I wasn't. I was talking about my men."

"Oh. Well, please continue..."

"You want *more?*"

"They can't have been all bad."

"Not all the time. They always took advantage, though. Antony certainly did."

"How did he do that?"

She sighed. "Well, if you *must* know, he was the one who got me out of medical school and onto the biology course. I wanted to do something about the bloody revenants and being a doctor wasn't enough."

"Was it difficult to get on that course?"

"Well they didn't want me, did they? Last thing they wanted was a woman they couldn't say no to because she was wearing a medal from Tanymouth. But Antony decided he wanted me on the course and that was that."

"Did he have sexual intentions from the start?"

"I don't know. It was years before he did anything. I had my degree by then and I'd joined the research group. We were working on the marinade..."

"The marinade?"

"Yeh, the marinade. All our livestock was infected, how do you think we fed people? Antony discovered a chemical formula that would kill the revenation bacterium. Took a couple of years to figure out how to use it to treat meat and not kill whoever was eating it."

"What did it taste like?"

"Horrible, until it fried your tastebuds off and then you didn't mind as much. A lot of people got used to being vegetarians after the first outbreak but that went out of the window as soon as meat was available again. We should have stayed vegetarians..."

"Why?"

"Because it didn't work. The bug didn't die, it just went dormant. A couple of months later it woke up and did what it always does. All us clever scientists trying to find a way to save the world and all we did was end up killing it a bit more."

"I think we should get back to Antony Whatecroft. What was it about him you liked?"

"He was the only one who was doing anything about the revenants that actually worked. So I worshipped him, didn't I? Like a little girl. And I did what little girls do when they meet the big man, I went weak at my knees and got into his bed as quick as I could..."

"Did it go on long?"

"Years. When I was in his research group, then when I had my own group working on phages, but the damn bugs wouldn't do what they were supposed to and then somebody discovered antibiotics and all the money went in that direction so I ended up with nothing. And then I found out Antony was sleeping with one of his graduate students, so I wasn't best pleased, I can tell you. There was me thinking he was going to leave his wife for me one day. Stupid.

"So I got married to someone else, got out of science and got pregnant so I could tell him to go frig himself."

"I can see how you'd be angry."

"I was stupid. I should have stuck with it. Instead… ugh. I wasted years living in a pretty little house, and I let Jack sort all the money out like an idiot. Until he died."

"That must have been traumatic."

"Hah! I've killed hundreds like him."

"I thought you said he killed himself?"

"He did. And then I killed him again."

"Oh. Of course."

"I thought the revenants were almost gone. You didn't hear anything about 'em. They were keeping it quiet. Anyone who died went into the marinade to make sure they didn't get up again. When I found Jack, he'd been dead a couple of hours. Took pills in his tea and wrote a note about all the debts and how he couldn't face admitting it and all that nonsense, but he was still warm, I thought he'd only just done it, I thought I might be able to save him. I stuck my finger down his throat, tried to get him to throw up. Only he didn't. He bit me."

She held up her left hand with the stump where her middle finger should have been. "You see?"

"And then you had to…"

"I put him down." She didn't say how. I didn't like to ask.

"What about the children?"

She looked up. "What about them?"

"Did they see?"

She took a long breath. This was harder for her. "They heard. They came downstairs."

"What did you do?"

She looked up at me, eyes full of pain. "Kept the bloody door closed and told them to go back upstairs."

"I mean… how did you explain it?"

"They were only little. I told them daddy was sleeping, called the coroners, got them dressed and left."

"How did they react?"

"They knew. They heard the fighting. They saw blood on my dress. And I was missing a finger as well, they noticed that all right…"

"Olivia… what happened to them, in the end?"

She looked back at me. "What do you think happened? They're dead."

"I'm sorry. When did they die?"

I'd forgotten her earlier admonition. She burst to her feet. "Stop it! You're not sorry! You're not sorry about anything! You're only sorry you can't get me crying about it! I've had enough of this…"

"Olivia, please…"

She sat down, folded her arms and assumed a stubborn silence.

"Olivia. I don't mean to push too hard. We can stop there, if you like."

And stop we did. But I remembered something from her psychomedical history, and called it up on the screen once she left. When she had been found, there had been two revenants still in the pens at Tringarrick. One female and one male.

It would make sense: the two revenants she had not been able to bring herself to kill until she was ready to take her own life could conceivably be her children. I found myself shivering as I realised this, and feeling no comfort in my success at turning the session into something useful for therapy.

6. KWAME & IOKAN

The evening meal was subdued. Olivia was in a dark mood. Pew stayed silent. Elsbet was still in the infirmary. Kwame avoided the meal altogether, hiding in his room. Iokan was the only one to try and inject some levity, but he came up against irritation and silence. Olivia excused herself as soon as she could, and headed out to the garden to inflict suffering on plantlife. Pew excused himself as well, leaving Iokan alone in the common room.

Iokan usually made it a habit to stay downstairs after dinner and make himself available for chats and games with the others. This evening was no different, but he was surprised when Kwame joined him. Kwame hadn't eaten anything that day. He'd taken some tea after much insistence on the part of a nurse, and had gone so far as to nudge food across his plate at lunchtime. The normal procedure would be to intervene after another day of fasting, but for now we were leaving him alone with his troubles. So his emergence into the common room to join Iokan was a pleasant surprise I hoped would produce some benefit.

Iokan smiled as he saw Kwame coming in, and Kwame couldn't help a scowl. "Good evening," said Iokan.

"Yes. Good evening," replied Kwame.

"Haven't seen you much recently…"

"I have had much on my mind."

"Well, if you want to unburden yourself, you only have to ask."

"I… No. It is a private matter."

Iokan wasn't ready to give up yet. "Well… how about a game?"

Kwame turned and paused. "Yes. A game would be good. I need some… distraction."

"A board game, perhaps?"

"No. Something a little more…"

"Exciting?"

Kwame thought about it. "Not… *too* exciting."

"No shooting games then."

"No."

"A strategy game?"

"Yes. Something that will take a while."

"I've been wanting to try Brentervile…"

"What's that?"

"It's a historical game, apparently. Something to do with a war between machines and humans when they met on an empty planet. It lasted for hundreds of years, or so I'm told."

"How do you play?"

"It's a real time strategy game. You collect resources, build up your forces, and command them in battle."

"It sounds like a board game."

"It's a bit more exciting when it happens in real time."

"I see. Which sides can we take?"

"We don't have to take sides. We can work together against the computer, if you like."

"I... yes. Let us do that."

Iokan set the game up and they selected co-operative mode. The game was a very simplified model of the actual war, designed to present an AI/Human conflict as an entertaining experience. In reality, millions had been killed before the entire planet had to be abandoned, but the popularity of the game did at least remind people of the horrible lesson of Brenterville and the risks of AI/Human wars.

Iokan moved the game to one of the walls. "Do you want the eastern or western sector?" he asked.

"Eastern."

"Any preference for unit colour?"

"No."

"I'll give you green, then. I'm blue, and the enemy are red. Do you want to play from a pad, or do you want to use the wall?"

"The wall. I cannot use pads."

"Of course..." Iokan put aside the pad he'd been using to set up the system, and called up his own on-wall controls to finish setup. He selected the last few options and hit the start button. "Okay. We're good to go."

The game map glowed into position on the wall, surrounded by control icons and status readouts. Iokan attended to his own side while Kwame looked across the screen, overwhelmed with information.

"You'll want to set up some mines over there by the forest – you see where the geology overlay says there's heavy metal deposits?" said Iokan.

"I see it. How do I...?"

"Drag the control board over. There? You see this?" Iokan demonstrated by pulling the control board image across the map on his side, and Kwame did the same.

"Ah. And I pull the mine from the list?"

"That's it."

Kwame dragged a mine icon from the control board and set it up in a favourable spot. The icons were large enough for his disability not to be a problem, and he and Iokan worked to build their base and a line of defence.

"Where are the enemy?" asked Kwame.

"They'll be with us soon enough," said Iokan. "You should build a fort on the edge of that glacier. They'll use that to outflank us otherwise."

"Yes. Of course."

"So what's been bothering you?"

"I am fine."

"Really?"

"Yes. I am fine." But his brow was furrowed as he said it. "Should you not place something there?"

Iokan looked; Kwame indicated a gap in the defensive line, conspicuously undefended. "That's the killzone. We should leave that."

"Why?"

Iokan gave him a puzzled look. "You're a military man. You know."

Kwame looked confused. "I do not…"

"If we leave a gap in the defences, it tempts the enemy to attack. Then you make sure there's enough firepower behind the line to eliminate anything that gets through. It's elementary strategy for a fixed defence, all the way back to castle sieges. The computer will probably see through it but it's worth a try. You're sure you've never heard of this?"

"It… you see… the thing is, I do not remember very much of my training."

"Oh. It's one of those things that…"

"Yes. One of those things that has gone." Kwame looked troubled again. Iokan turned back to the wall and his preparations, but looked back to Kwame with curiosity.

"Have you lost everything to do with your military experience?"

"I… remember what it was like to be a soldier. I do not remember what I did. And that is…" Kwame struggled for a moment, then looked at Iokan. "If my memories vanish, did they really happen?"

"That's an interesting philosophical question."

"I remember facts about some things in my life, but I do not remember the events. At other times, I remember what it felt like to be there but I cannot recall what happened…"

"And they can't look inside your brain, of course…"

"They did! They looked in my mind. But I… I do not…"

Iokan turned his full attention to Kwame and spoke gently. "What did they see?" He failed to notice the enemy units infiltrating down from the top of the screen.

Kwame paused there, grasping and desperate for words. "What if you knew there was something *wrong* with your memory? How could you tell?"

"Well, I suppose I would take new brain scans and compare them with older scans. I had that done to me a few times."

"What if you have no older scans?"

"Then you bring in people who knew you before and take their testimony."

"What if they are all dead?"

"But they *did* scan your mind? Right?"

"What if you do not trust them?"

"Oh. I see."

"I have been trying to think, to work out a test, a way to be sure my memory has failed… will you help me?"

"Of course! What can I do?"

"I think I know a way to test myself."

"Okay."

"I need you to... kiss me."

Kwame said it with disgust. Iokan blinked. Enemy ground units found the outer defences on the wall beside them. Kwame steeled himself for Iokan's response.

"Can you say that again?" asked Iokan.

"I need you to kiss me."

"... I was under the impression that your world was, well..."

"A moral world. Yes."

"I meant homophobic."

"If you wish to call it that."

"And you want me to kiss you?"

"Yes."

"Why?"

"Because I do not know what is real! They showed me things in my dreams that were *wrong*, simply wrong! I must know!"

"You think you'll remember something if I kiss you?"

"I do not know."

Iokan shrugged. "Well, if it's what you want. How do you want me to kiss you?"

"Do not make fun of me. Just do it."

Iokan took a step closer. Kwame steeled himself like a man about to be punched in the face. "You should really relax. It won't hurt." Kwame nodded but was still tense. Iokan sighed, and took him by the shoulders. "This is a very brave thing to do, Kwame. I respect you for that." Kwame relaxed, surprised. Iokan took his moment and kissed him before he could react.

Kwame's eyes went wide in outrage; he raised his arms, seemingly to grab Iokan and push him away. But the outrage fled. Iokan moved back for a moment; the first kiss had been gentle, no more than a meeting of lips. But Iokan saw a puzzlement in Kwame's eyes, and went in again. Kwame's hands fell away and he surrendered to the kiss.

Iokan stepped away. "Did that tell you anything?"

But Kwame didn't answer. He didn't even seem to hear the question. Tears flooded his cheeks as he stared through Iokan without seeing him. His arms moved behind his back, and his wrists crossed as though bound.

"Kwame?" But Kwame did not hear. "Kwame, are you in there? Oh, damn it..."

Iokan went to raise the alarm as the enemy on the wall overran the carefully planned defences.

7. OLIVIA & PEW

Pew had spent the day avoiding everyone, but slunk outside to find Olivia after she'd been slashing dead stems on beanstalks for half an hour.

"What do you want?" she muttered as she saw him.

"Um," he said.

"Just 'um'? Is that it?"

"Well, er..."

"And 'er' as well, who's 'er' when she's at home?"

"What?"

He looked confused. She sighed. "Let me have a look at those hands."

He held them out, wrapped in a transparent healer that would bring them back to normal within a couple of days. "Well you got lucky there, didn't you? Try that on my world and you'd have an infection and be dead in a month. Does it still hurt?"

"No..."

"Well it should hurt! That's a damn stupid thing to do! You know damn well that stuff can slice right through you!"

"Yes."

"So why do it, for gods' sake?"

He couldn't answer. He looked at her, appealing for understanding. She took it in for a moment and gave him a shrewd look back. "So it's like *that*, is it? Your life's so miserable you'd rather cut yourself?"

"Something... like that."

"You're all the bloody same..." she muttered.

"What?"

"I'll never understand it. All right, you're the last survivor and everyone you know is dead, but why do you need to go and make it worse?"

"I–"

"It's hard to carry on, I know it's hard, but you've got to."

"Why?"

"Oh don't you give me that! I had ten years listening to that and I'm sick of it!"

"You don't understand..."

"And they said that and all." She took on a mocking tone. "'You don't understand! I can't take it any more! Just let me kill myself!' Well, rubbish! If I could take it, you can bloody take it!"

"But how..."

"What do you mean, how?"

"How did you do it...?"

"I had to! I had children! And fifty other people I was responsible for! I had to carry on or no one would, because they were all like you, giving up at the first sign of trouble!"

"But I don't have any of that..."

"You're all the same. I told my children not to go off outside the station, I told them it wasn't safe, but they went anyway..." Frustration made her voice ragged.

"I don't understand..."

"Everyone gives up. Everyone kills themselves. And you're going to do it as well..."

"I'm not!"

"You *want* to."

"I..."

"Yeh, you want to. None of us want to live, there's nothing left to live for, the only reason I'm not in my grave is because they won't let me..."

Pew was puzzled by her sudden turnabout. "But I thought you said you always carried on...?"

She didn't notice she was weeping. "Well it's not true! Why do you want to go and listen to me for, anyway? First thing I did when they found me was try and kill myself! Do you want to know why? Because everything's so bloody easy for them, I mean look at this place! My whole planet's dead and your species is gone and what's it for? Nobody even bloody noticed!"

"You... you tried to kill yourself?"

"...Yeh." She looked uncomfortable and far from proud.

"I thought you were..."

"You thought I was stronger than you? Is that it?"

"But why..."

"They won't let me do it. Not unless I do their damn therapy."

He slumped down to the earth. "They won't let us go. That's all I want. I just want it over."

"That's what they said."

"Who?"

"My children."

"They were lucky."

"No they weren't. They came back. You understand me? *They came back.*"

He looked up at her, realising what she meant. "I'm sorry..."

"Don't you start. That's what Asha keeps saying. She's always bloody sorry."

"It must have been terrible..."

"It was." She knelt by him in the mud. "I won't tell you anything else. You've heard it all. You're a grown man. If you have to die, then do it, if you can find a way..."

"But how?"

"I don't know. I've tried often enough."

"If... if you think of a way... will you let me know how?"

Tears came from both their eyes as she nodded. "And you let me know, if you figure out something." He nodded in return. She reached out to give him a hug. He flinched with his usual aversion to physical contact, but overcame it and let her put his head into her shoulder.

"You're a good lad," she said. She didn't notice his hand trembling as she pulled back a little to kiss him on the forehead like a devoted mother.

Some part of Pew's brain didn't read it that way. His eyes bulged in horror, his hands froze like claws and he pushed away from her. "No! NO!" he yelled.

"What's the bloody matter now–" she asked, exasperated, not realising what was plain when I reviewed the video later: Pew was having a flashback to some terrible event, and responded as he did when the trauma first happened. He attacked.

His hands flew for her throat, and she was quickly pinned down with him on top of her, struggling to pull his hands away as he snarled like a beast. But murder was not his intent. He let go of her throat with one hand and ripped open the front of her work shirt, revealing her underwear.

Her eyes went a little wider as she realised what he was doing. The surprise disarmed her, one hand falling aside – to land on a trowel. As he pulled at more of her clothes, she brought the trowel up to club him on the side of the head. He fell away, dazed.

Veofol and half a dozen staff were already running to them as she struggled away from him, coughing from a bruised throat, pulling her shirt back together. Pew was swiftly apprehended and sedated. Olivia was left bewildered and angry, refusing the help of a nurse until Veofol insisted.

8. ASHA

Two major crises in one evening kept the staff very busy. Olivia needed minor medical attention, but far more important was the betrayal of trust. Veofol spent some time with her explaining how PTSD flashbacks work, and how they can lead to violent behaviour in otherwise placid people. Olivia accepted our diagnosis as a variant of the necrotic hysteria she knew from her own world. But we could not completely allay her suspicions; if Pew was traumatised by the memory of tearing off a woman's clothes with the intent of rape, what did that say about him? We could get nothing from him to indicate what he had experienced during the flashback. Shame silenced him.

Kwame, too, had seen something that left him ashamed but also very confused. He retreated to his room again and rejected all offers of assistance. At least we had no serious trouble with Elsbet, but, like the others, she refused to speak to us, and we could only guess what she might have remembered about Katie, other than that it was clearly traumatic.

Added to all these disruptions was the impending return of Liss, which we had scheduled for the next day along with a group therapy session. This would be delicate, but I hoped for a welcome distraction that would relieve pressure on the group as they concentrated on the mystery of her actions.

I found myself exhausted at the end of the day, working far past my usual hours even after Veofol should have been left alone to handle the night shift. The group must have been quiet, because he came to see me, very clearly concerned and asking how I was.

"I'm fine," I protested, knowing very well that I didn't look it.

"Are you sure? I don't remember you working these hours with the last group…"

"Hah. The last group were a breeze, compared to this." I leaned back in my chair. But he still looked concerned. "Is something up?"

He struggled to find words to express his concern.

"Is it Olivia?" I asked. "Is she complaining?"

"No, no."

"Pew? Kwame?" He shook his head. "Elsbet? Has she said anything?"

"She's not talking to anyone."

"Then what is it?"

He sighed. "How's Bell?"

I closed my eyes for a moment, and rubbed my temples. "He's fine."

"I was checking the records on Olivia. She overheard something."

"Something, yes." And I hadn't spoken to Bell since the call that afternoon.

"Do you want to talk about it?"

"I don't need a therapist, Veofol."

"No, of course – but you *are* okay? Aren't you?"

I realised it then: he was sitting by me, full of honest concern, full of kindness. No arguments, no domestic squabbles. And he was very beautiful. All I had to do was pull him close, and he wouldn't say no, I could just start with a kiss...

The moment passed. I had responsibilities, duties, and a man I couldn't run away from. I stood up.

"You should check on Pew."

He stood as well. I don't know if he even realised what had been going through my mind.

"I'll do that. Um, don't work too hard."

"I won't. Thanks."

He went, and I crumpled back down into a chair. Somewhere back in town, Bell was getting ready to leave me. I could call him and have that serious conversation about our relationship – but that would end up being a serious conversation about who was going to move out and when. Something else was required, something impulsive, less rational.

I called Bell's favourite restaurant, which offered authentic food from his homeworld. He'd only just been there, but it couldn't hurt to meet him in a place he was comfortable with. I reserved a table for the following evening. Veofol was scheduled to be on call that night, so I was safe to abandon the group for a few hours. Bell was surprised by my invitation, but agreed to come after I couched it in suitably apologetic (and grovelling) terms.

PART NINE
ENEMIES

1. GROUP

The group gathered for therapy the next day in a mood of general glowering silence. Elsbet simmered at the edge. Iokan was unusually quiet. Olivia wasn't talking to Pew, and Pew was hardly able to talk in the first place. Kwame seemed to have forgotten the function of speech entirely.

"Good morning everyone," I said to the dejected circle. "Before we get started, I want to say I know we all had something of a rough night. I'm going to be seeing most of you during the day to talk it over, but I don't think any permanent harm was done. You're all making good progress in therapy and I don't want to see that go to waste because you've been hitting a few bumps in the road. So, with that in mind, I'd like to move on to the main subject of today's session…"

I tapped a control on my pad. The door opened, and Liss came in. Not the fragile pink porcelain they all knew from before, but the troubled woman she really was, wearing rough jeans and a black t-shirt without a single heart on it. "Hello," she said.

"Who's she?" asked Elsbet.

"That's Liss," said Iokan.

"Oh, she's the terrifying infiltrator? Huh," sneered Elsbet.

Liss gave her a frowning look as she sat down. She'd been informed of the change of personality, but hadn't been prepared for the sudden venom.

I went on. "Liss has chosen to come back to the group, and of course you all agreed you'd be happy with that–"

"I didn't agree to anything," muttered Olivia.

"And I didn't agree to you being a bitch but you're still doing it," said Liss. Olivia went wide-eyed as though slapped in the face.

"Now you listen here–"

"Shove it up your ass."

"Don't you talk to me like that–"

"I'll talk any way I like–"

"Oh, *shut up!*" shouted Elsbet, silencing both of them.

Iokan noticed Liss's stunned look. "Things have… changed a little since you went away."

"Right…" said Liss.

"I think the best thing to do is let Liss tell you her story, and have a discussion afterwards. How does that sound?" I asked.

"That sounds like an excellent idea," said Iokan.

"Some things haven't changed," said Liss. Iokan smiled, but his eyes were uncertain.

"Well out with it then!" said Olivia. "Let's hear your excuses. I haven't got all day to sit around listening to you lying again…"

"Olivia. Let her talk, please," I said. Olivia grumped and I went on. "Liss? Perhaps you could start by telling us about your old job?"

"I'm an office manager," said Liss.

"I meant the other job."

"Oh. *That*." She sighed. "When I was younger… I was one of the people who was supposed to save the world."

That got the attention of even the most dejected members of the group.

"Fucked that one up, didn't you?" said Elsbet.

"What *is* your problem?" demanded Liss.

I jumped in. "I'm sorry, Liss, it's a bit complicated. Elsbet, please restrain yourself. I know things are difficult but there's no need to take it out on Liss." Elsbet just stared ahead, sneering. "Liss, can you go on? You said it was your job to save the world?"

"Yeah. Well. That was a long time ago. I was working in an office when the world ended. It wasn't my job then."

"I'm not sure I understand," said Iokan. "How were you supposed to save the world?"

"Mostly by hitting people in the face."

The sarcastic tone baffled him. "I… must admit that never occurred to me as an option."

"How does one save the world by hitting people?" asked Kwame.

"It depends who you hit."

"Hang on, hang on!" said Olivia. "How can you be going around hitting people? There's nothing to you! You'd fall over in a stiff breeze…"

Liss sighed again. "I have powers."

"What, electrical power? Power of attorney? What do you mean?"

"You want me to show you?"

"Go ahead, give us all a laugh, why not…"

Liss got to her feet with a little sneer edging her lips.

"Liss, what are you intending to do?" I asked.

"I'm not going to break anything," she said.

"I'd prefer to know," I replied.

Liss walked behind the circle of chairs. "I'm just going to pick a chair up." She squatted behind Olivia's chair and lifted both it and Olivia two metres up. Olivia yelped with shock.

"Put me down! Put me down!" yelped Olivia, squirming in the chair and trying to hang on.

"Liss, that's enough, put her down!" I insisted.

"Really? I could do this all day if I wanted," she said.

"Put me *down!*" shouted Olivia.

"Put her down this instant!" I demanded.

"Okay," said Liss with a smile, and dropped the chair. Olivia bounced as it hit the floor and clung onto the arms.

Liss sat down with a cynical smile. "Any questions?"

"You're posthuman," said Iokan.

"No. I've got powers."

"Did you have surgery?"

"No, I was born like this."

"Was there anyone else...?"

"Yes. Fifty per cent of the population."

"Ancients... fifty per cent like you?"

"Hah! No. A lot of them were more powerful than me."

"How could a species like yours be killed...?" asked Kwame.

"They burned."

"To the dust?" asked Iokan.

"Yes. To ash. That was all true."

"How did it happen?"

"I don't know. It was someone from another universe."

Iokan was intent now, deeply concerned in a way I hadn't quite seen before. "Who?" he asked.

"If I knew that, I wouldn't have had to come here." Iokan sat back, troubled.

Olivia had gotten her breath back. "All right. So you're bloody superwoman. Why did you lie to us?"

"I'm investigating. I *was* investigating. I don't know what I'm doing now."

"You infiltrated," said Elsbet.

"I went undercover."

"Will you kill them?" Elsbet looked at Liss with an intensity that Liss seemed to find disturbing.

"I... I don't know. I don't even know who it is."

"So you're just going to let them get away with it," said Elsbet with disgust.

"No. I did kill *someone*," said Liss.

"You killed one of them?" asked Pew, with something like awe.

"Yes."

"Bully for you. Did it make you feel better?" asked Olivia, contemptuous.

"No."

"There! You see? That's a lesson for you!" said Olivia to Pew. Pew withdrew back into his chair.

"What happened?" asked Iokan, still concerned.

"I found the scientist who set it off. I lost my temper."

Iokan nodded. "I have to say I find that understandable, given the circumstances."

"It was stupid. I should have questioned him. I'd have found out where he got the technology from. All I got instead was him mumbling about aliens and parallel worlds."

"You're sure of that? Someone from a parallel universe?"

"Yeah. Why do you think I'm here?"

"There's no way you could be mistaken?"

"I checked it out. There's nothing else it could be."

"I see..." Iokan still looked troubled.

"And you thought it was this lot that did it?" asked Olivia. "Hah!"

"Yeah, I figured that out, thanks."

"That's hilarious. You're hunting for the people who killed your whole planet and you thought it was the most limp-wristed, weak-minded, lily-livered excuses for human beings in the multiverse?" She dissolved into cackles.

Liss rounded on her. "Well obviously I should have asked for help from your species."

"And what do you mean by that?"

"You wouldn't have been much use, would you? Couldn't even figure out proper antibiotics. No wonder you all died."

"We didn't have your advantages."

"No. You got all your food infected and killed yourselves. Obviously we've got something to learn from you."

"You take that back."

"No."

"Olivia. Liss," I said. "Let's dial it back, shall we? This is a therapy session, after all."

"Of course," said Liss. "I'm *very* sorry." Olivia sat back in her chair, not mollified in the slightest.

"I for one would like to say that I think you're very brave," said Iokan. "Fighting enemies from another universe is hardly the action of a coward. But I do have a question..."

"Okay," said Liss.

"Why you?"

Liss sighed. "Because I was the only one left! When the computers realised everyone was gone, they looked for survivors. When they found me, they put me in charge of the world and gave me the resources to find the people who did it."

"I do not think that is the important question," said Kwame.

"Go on, then," said Liss.

"How did you survive?"

"*I don't know*. I told you that before."

"I find that very troubling."

"What do you mean?"

"Maybe you're the one who did it," said Elsbet.

"What...?" said Liss, shocked.

"You survived. Nobody else did. Maybe you killed them all."

"I don't think that's the case, Elsbet," I said. "Security have gone to a lot of trouble to make sure Liss is telling the truth."

"That's right. I gave them access codes. They know everything," said Liss.

"And yet no one knows why you survived," said Kwame.

"What, you think I'm hiding something?"

"Memories can be changed. You would not even know if you were hiding something. How can we trust you?"

"We've checked this," I said. "There are no signs of tampering in Liss's brain."

"Unless the techniques used were beyond the level of your scientific understanding."

Iokan interjected: "Kwame, if that's the case, any of us could be hiding some terrible secret. *You* could have some horrible past we don't know about..." Kwame flinched.

"I am not – I do not have such a – a –" Kwame stuttered and stalled.

"Kwame. Slow down. Take a breath," I said.

Kwame stopped trying to talk and breathed carefully for a few seconds before continuing. "All I would like to say is this: we cannot trust this woman. She has lied to all of us. She cannot tell us why she survived and billions of others did not. We cannot trust her."

"That's not very charitable," said Iokan. "I think she's doing more than any of us to actually do something about the end of her world."

"Wouldn't be hard to do more than you, would it?" muttered Olivia.

Elsbet ignored them. "Have you given up?" she asked.

"No," said Liss.

"Then why are you here?"

"I…" Liss couldn't quite answer.

"You have a mission."

Liss looked back at her. "No. I can't. I just can't…" She shook her head and looked down. "I'm not the right person. I'm supposed to be an office manager. I don't know how to find them…"

"That doesn't matter! You have a duty!"

"Elsbet," I said, "Liss still has some difficulties, the same as the rest of you. She's lost her whole world and she needs our help."

"She has a mission!"

"That's up to her, Elsbet."

Elsbet gave me a boiling stare. Then looked aside at all the others looking back at her, and let it go.

"Does anyone else have anything to add?" I asked. None of them did, not even Iokan. I have to admit to being disappointed in the group's reaction, but I couldn't force them to get on with each other, and trying too hard would make it worse.

2. KWAME

As soon as he could, Kwame went back to his room. I found him in the corner, legs drawn up, head on his knees. I took his chair from behind his desk and sat down facing him.

"Do you want to talk about it?" I asked.

"I do not," he said.

"I don't mean last night. I mean the group session. You were very hard on Liss."

"I do not know who she is."

"She's exactly who she was before. She's lost her world and needs our help."

"Nothing is what it was before."

He fell silent.

"You had a flashback last night, didn't you?" I asked.

"I am sure you already know that."

"Do you remember anything?"

"Yes."

"Can you tell me what it was?"

"I saw him."

"The man in your dreams?"

He laughed. "The man in my dreams. The man of my dreams!" His laughter turned to weeping and he waved me away. "Just leave me alone."

"Kwame–"

"Just go."

"If that's what you want. But if you need to talk to someone, please, just come and see me. Don't stay in here all day."

"Will you just go?" He looked up at me, pleading with his eyes. I left him to it.

3. IOKAN

My next job for the day was to deal with Iokan's tendency to pretend to be a therapist, which was now causing actual harm. I called him to my office.

"But this is why I'm here," he complained.

"No, Iokan, this is why *I'm* here. You're here for therapy."

"But there's nothing wrong with me. I'm supposed to help people!"

"And how has that been going?"

He paused for a moment. "Not perfectly, I have to admit, but–"

"Can you point to any successes?"

"I've... tried to support people in any way I can."

"That's the problem, Iokan. You've been giving everyone exactly what they say they want. But true therapy isn't about that. Dysfunctional people often don't want what they need to get better."

He thought about that, and sighed. "Well, I suppose so..."

"I don't think a kiss was what Kwame actually needed, was it?" Iokan's shoulders fell. "Look, I understand what you did, but if he'd gone to a trained therapist, we would have dealt with his problem much more carefully. Instead, he's even more traumatised than he was before."

"I never intended to hurt anyone..."

"I know, Iokan. I know you believe you're here to help. But you don't have the kind of training you need for this. I'd much rather you concentrated on your own issues rather than trying to solve everyone else's. I'm afraid if we see anything similar happening again, we'll have to intervene."

He nodded. He really seemed to have got the point, and it hit him hard. He left, looking more troubled than I'd ever seen him.

4. PEW

Pew hadn't been willing to talk the previous evening, and I hoped a night's rest would help him speak about his attack on Olivia. But instead he hunched himself in an easy chair, hood up, as though he could somehow fall inside it and away from everything.

"Pew? We really do need to talk about what happened."

He didn't answer.

"You had a flashback. You weren't in control of yourself."

He still didn't answer.

"I'm only here to help you, Pew. If you did something you're ashamed of, it's okay to tell me. Anything you say in here is completely confidential."

He looked up at me, unsure of what to say.

"Yes, Pew?"

"I..."

"It's okay. Go on."

He blurted it out: "I want to die."

"It's not that bad, surely?"

"Olivia said you'd let her die if she did the therapy."

"I see."

"I want to do the same."

"Well... if you're absolutely determined..."

He nodded.

"It's not the easy way out. You have to demonstrate that therapy is completely hopeless, which means you really have to try. It's hard work."

"I'll do it."

"It can take years, Pew. Hardly anyone ever actually goes through with it."

"I said I'll do it."

"Okay. If you're absolutely sure."

"I'm sure."

"There's some paperwork you'll have to fill in. And there's a cooling-off period of two weeks. We don't put anyone on the euthanasia track without giving them a chance to pull out."

"We're not free, are we?" He looked back up at me. "We can't even die without filling in a form."

"We're trying to help—"

"I've never been free."

"Pew, we need to talk about what happened last night."

He didn't answer.

"You do understand – that's going to be part of the therapy. You're going to have to talk about it."

He took a few moments, and then nodded. "Not... now. Please."

"I'll get a pad with the forms," I said.

5. OLIVIA & PEW

Olivia slept in the garden, shaded under her massive straw hat, one hand trailing down from the reclined garden chair to a self-chilling glass of lemonade.

"Olivia?" said Pew. She snorted and snapped awake, suddenly ready and tense. Then she saw who it was.

"Oh. It's *you*. What do you want?"

"I'm…"

"Out with it! I haven't got all day!"

That stopped him for a moment. But he worked up the courage and said: "I'm going to kill myself."

"Yeh. It's not much fun when they bring you back. Good luck." She pulled her hat brim down.

"I mean I'm going on the euthanasia track."

She lifted her brim and looked up at him.

"I can't… I can't keep going on like…"

"You think you'll do it again," she said.

"Yes."

"Is this your way of saying sorry?"

"I… kind of."

She looked up at him, appalled. "What the bloody hell did those bastards do to you? They make you rape someone?"

He looked away. He couldn't answer.

"For gods' sake, boy, I'm a killer and a cannibal, how can you be worse?" He looked back at her, a little shocked. She went on: "If they put a gun to your head, it wasn't your fault. It's like a… it's like a time of war, you do whatever you have to do to survive."

"It wasn't a war. We never fought."

"War, genocide, call it what you like. You do what you have to do to survive."

He blurted back: "So why do *you* want to die?"

It was her turn to go silent for a moment. Then she said, "That's my business." She didn't add anything else. After a moment of floundering, Pew turned away and went back indoors. She watched him go, then pulled down her brim. But sleep was impossible and she threw the hat aside.

6. LISS & IOKAN

The evening came, and I prepared for dinner. While I tried to get my hair into some kind of acceptable shape, I kept an eye out for Liss on the monitors. The troubles the rest of the group were experiencing made it difficult for them to find any time for her, and I was hoping to see some sign she wasn't giving up. Iokan was the only one to make an effort, so of course we had to monitor their meeting in case he attempted any therapy.

He caught up with her in her room, which she'd spent much of the day resetting to something she could bear. The pink and the fluff were mostly gone, and it was nothing more nor less than a normal bedroom. Perhaps a little untidy with all the screendiscs piled up in one corner, but she said she couldn't be bothered sorting them out. She only brought them for her cover story, and didn't really need them any more.

She answered the door to Iokan and said: "That took you a while."

"I'm sorry?" he said.

"I didn't think you'd wait this long. Are you coming in?"

He gave her a brittle smile and entered the room.

"So what do you want?" she asked, sitting on the end of her bed, crossing her arms and giving him a harsh look. "If you want your clothes back you're too late. They don't fit you any more."

"I have plenty," he said. He was wearing his casual outfit now, having put the robes off after the group session. "I wanted to welcome you back."

"That's your religious duty, is it?"

"It's the decent thing to do."

"Does it get you points with the glowy shiny people?"

"That's not what it's about."

"No. Of course not. So what else?"

"You know, you're a lot less polite than you used to be."

"I'm catching up on weeks of listening to your bullshit and not calling you on it."

"I didn't know you were so intolerant."

She laughed, bitterly. "So your gods came back and murdered your whole planet and when someone doesn't tippy toe around your religion, that's intolerance?"

His smile was getting strained. "That's not what I came here to talk about."

"So get on with it."

"Do you mind putting the privacy on?"

"Yes. I mind."

He looked up at the ceiling. The cameras weren't detectable by human eyes, but he couldn't help it.

"It's about the genocide."

"Yours or mine?"

"I really can't talk about it unless we have privacy."

"If you can tell me, you can tell them." She pointed at the ceiling.

"It's too dangerous."

"What, are you worried your antewhatevers'll find out and stop you getting into heaven?"

"It's got nothing to do with that."

"Bullshit. That's got everything to do with it."

He was actually getting quite worked up. "There are things you know nothing about–"

"Well I'm just going to have to stay ignorant, aren't I?" She went to the door to open it – but he grabbed her arm as she passed.

"This is about your species!"

She was instantly furious and threw his arm off. Or rather, she tried. He turned a full circle with the momentum she generated with her great strength, and simply grabbed her with her other arm.

"Get the hell *off* me!"

"Not until you listen."

She tried again: this time a shove. It should have thrown him across the room and broken bones as he smashed into the wall. But he read the move, stepped to one side, and she found herself stumbling across the room.

"You're not a soldier," he said. "Don't try and fight me. I'm here to help you!"

But she was pissed off now, and came back for another go. This time, he ducked under her attack and threw her over his head into the opposite wall, crashing down to the floor. She was still on her knees as four security guards in full power armour rushed in and surrounded her in a ring of weapons.

"On the floor! Hands behind your head!"

She held her anger in check. "I'm already *on* the floor."

"Officers, it's okay!" said Iokan. "It's nothing serious! We were just…" One of the security officers looked round at him. "…sparring. That's all. Just sparring."

"You're kidding," said the security guard.

"She needs more training," added Iokan. "Go on, Liss, tell them."

"Sparring," she said in a deadly monotone. A command buzzed over the comms and the guards relaxed.

"If you want to spar, schedule a session in the gym," muttered the guard.

"Of course," said Iokan, smiling to try and maintain the fiction that no one in the room seriously believed. Liss got to her feet.

"Are you going to let me out?" she asked the guards. They tried to shuffle aside in their armour, and she squeezed out of the room, marching away to be alone somewhere, still angry.

I should have gone after her, despite the fact I was supposed to be getting on the bus to Hub Metro in a few minutes. But another crisis drew my attention.

7. ELSBET

Elsbet would not speak to me. She kept a stony silence every time I saw her, and never looked me in the eye. Whatever she'd remembered in our last meeting, she was keeping it to herself. Over the last week or so, I'd gently encouraged the others to visit her, to see if that would help; Olivia had the greatest success, something that initially surprised me. But then the two of them had gotten on surprisingly well in the brief time they had known each other. They shared an earthy contempt for most of the others, but even so, Olivia was in no mood to mess about. She considered Elsbet to be malingering in bed and inflicting unnecessary suffering on herself. She accused her of giving up, and Elsbet retorted that she hadn't given up in the slightest. She was still at war. Olivia demanded an explanation, but Elsbet fell silent again and Olivia left with nothing else to show for her efforts.

After we'd let Elsbet out of the infirmary, she'd spent most of her time in her room – a different one to Katie's, which she set up with one of the preset options. But while she avoided any furnishings that recalled her days on her home asteroid, the view outside the window was of space, the pale band of the Milky Way shining through, brighter and clearer than could be seen on Earth. For a few days, she simply went about her business in the centre. She would not venture outside, as much as we might encourage her, and only turned up to the group therapy session where Liss returned after some pleading on my part. Once that was done, she went back to her room, turned on privacy and refused to speak to anyone for the rest of the day.

Then she attempted suicide.

We always tried to give the group as much privacy as possible, but made an exception for medical crises. While we had no access to their moment-by-moment body monitors, automated systems alerted us as soon as trauma occurred.

I attended her room a minute after the medical staff had arrived, and found her twitching on the floor with foam coming from her mouth. Her artificial arm was lying detached a metre away, and a twisted, improvised cable ran from her shoulder stump to a power outlet in the wall.

"Turn the power *off!*" shouted a nurse. Someone evidently did, as Elsbet stopped twitching and relaxed into unconsciousness. "Shit, just *look* at this..." said the nurse.

The cable was something she must have put together piece by piece in her hours of privacy, made of twisted up foil, copper strands and a bent fork on the end to plug into the shoulder socket. Some parts might have been stolen from Kwame's electrical workshop, but the rest was a mystery.

"She's stable," said the nurse, studying Elsbet's pulse, breathing and brain function on a pad.

"What was she doing?" I asked. The nurse looked up at me with a moment's surprise. I was already dressed up for going out, and they'd never seen me in heels.

"Self-harm? Suicide? I don't know."

Veofol came in, realising at once what had happened, but a chime drew his attention. Everyone looked up. A screen appeared on the wall showing a still image of Elsbet with a hard look straight at camera, and below the screen an invitation to press play.

"She left a note…" I said.

A trolley was floated in, and Elsbet was lifted onto it, still unconscious. "You might as well go," said Veofol. "She's not going to wake up for a while."

I shook my head. "I have to take care of this."

"I can write the report…"

"You weren't even on duty when it happened."

"Asha. I can handle it. You're going to be late if you don't go."

I sighed. "All right. But I have to watch this."

I started the video on the wall. Elsbet looked to one side of the screen, checking the system was recording; and then she spoke.

"I am Sergeant Designate Elsbet Carmon. I am at war with the machines that have destroyed my world and spread their filth throughout the system. This is my final act in the war. If I fail, I leave its commission to you. Therefore I must tell you what it was this creature whose body I control did to us.

"I am no longer human. I am a recording of a woman who died in battle more than ten years ago. Her mind was scanned and her body cloned so an infiltrator could be made. The machines pretended they held prisoners of war who would be executed if we did not surrender. Instead, we attacked, freed them, and fell into their trap.

"This infiltrator known as *Katie* was taken to a hospital while my persona was allowed to emerge to give her cover. They gave me medals and sent children to see me so they would be inspired by the 'hero'. And when she was ready, the infiltrator took over and flushed the atmosphere from the hospital. Then she attacked the shipyards, disabled a dozen ships, stole a missile and escaped back to Earth.

"*I remember every detail of the attack.* I can see every soldier she killed. I can see the doctor she forced to seal the doors. I can see her ripping his spine out when she was finished with him. I can see the children falling and choking and dying while she watched and did *nothing*.

"Make no attempt to save me.

"This is an act of war."

She took the arm off her shoulder, revealing gleaming contacts, and shoved her makeshift cable into them. She touched a control on a pad, then convulsed and fell below the frame.

8. ASHA & BELL

The restaurant was designed to make people from Bell's world feel at home, and everyone else feel they were in an exotic land, with firelight, rough-hewn pine, antler decorations and a slight chill to the air. Bell's species had endured a full-scale ice age on their world before a friendly species provided the support necessary for them to reclaim the technological heritage buried under the ice. They get annoyed whenever their body fur makes people from other species think they're cute, and become irritable with those who ask if they can stroke them. Not that stroking Bell's fur was unpleasant, either for him or me. It had the sheen of an otter's pelt, and the softness of a cat's belly, or so I'm told. Grooming is a major psychological bonding tool among his species, and something I'd enjoyed learning about.

But Bell didn't look like he wanted his fur stroked, combed, teased or groomed. He sat alone with a glass of water he'd barely touched. He didn't look like a man waiting for a romantic meal. He hadn't changed from his travelling clothes. I already felt like a fool for dressing up. He looked at his watch as I made my way to the table, apologising for being kept behind at work. He acknowledged the apology with a sigh.

"Well," I said. "Thanks for coming..."

He nodded. I poured myself some water. I knew what I had to say: I'd been thinking about it all the way here and much of the day before. He was right. I'd been neglecting him. I couldn't expect him to be there for me if I was never there for him. I couldn't promise to be there all the time, but I knew I could share more of my life with him. We had to work together to overcome our difficulties. I was prepared to go to relationship counselling if he was.

"So... how are you?" I started.

"I'm leaving," he said.

My mouth may have flapped a couple of times.

"I mean I'm leaving Hub. When I went back home, my clan, er..." he looked a little embarrassed. "Well, they've offered me a marriage. It's a good opportunity. I need to take it."

I found my voice from somewhere. "A... good *opportunity*...?"

He realised he needed to try harder to make this sound good. He took my hand. "It's not you. Well it is, but..."

"Oh."

"Asha, I'm serious, it's not that I don't want to be with you..." No. Of course it wasn't. "But it *has* been difficult, and... I explained how things work on my world. A marriage isn't just about the couple, it's so much more important than that ..."

"And we're not," I said, getting frostier by the second.

"I didn't say that. It's been great, being with you. But at some point I have to decide where I want my life to go. And I want to be on my world. You can understand that, surely..." I must have looked particularly hurt. "I'm sorry, I didn't mean that, that was... insensitive and stupid. I didn't mean to say anything about your world–"

I pulled my hand back. "*This* is my world."

"Of course! But... it's not mine. And... well, when I have children I don't want to do it with a genesplicer. It's not fair on the children, they'd be neither one species nor the other..."

I must have been gaping in shock by now.

"I'm sorry, that didn't come out the way I meant it. Let's just have dinner. I'll pay."

I sat there, furious. I didn't know what to say. Bell sighed.

"I'm not doing this because I *want* to leave you. It's just..."

A chime sounded in my ear. Someone was calling from the centre, and it would be unbearably rude to accept a call in the middle of a conversation. I allowed it to connect.

Bell went on: "It's just that it's not going anywhere, we've hardly spoken for months, we never go out..."

Veofol's voice overrode Bell's: "Asha, we've got a problem. It's Olivia, well, Liss and Olivia, are you there?"

Bell said, "...I mean how could you call us a couple?"

"I'm here. Go on," I said.

Veofol continued: "They've had a bust-up and Olivia wants out. I was trying to get them to make up but it went wrong and there was some shoving and Olivia's put her back out..."

"Okay, slow down and give me the details. From the beginning."

Bell realised he was no longer the focus of my attention. "You're on the phone to work, aren't you?"

He sighed and shook his head.

9. LISS & OLIVIA

Liss had been outside in the woods near the centre, avoiding company. Veofol appealed to her to talk to the others, pointing out that she really did need to make an effort. She chose to make this effort with Olivia, as Pew and Kwame were barely talking to anyone, Elsbet was in the infirmary, and she certainly wasn't going to talk to Iokan again.

Olivia had retrieved her hat, but hadn't gone back to sleep. Whatever she was brooding about, she kept it to herself, but was alert enough to hear Liss's approach.

"Bugger off," she said as Liss reached the garden.

"What did I do?" asked Liss.

"You came out and bothered me."

"It's not your garden."

"I did all the work. So bugger off before you trample something."

Liss took a breath to restrain herself. "I came by to see if you wanted any help."

Olivia looked at her as if she'd offered to ritually behead herself. "What?"

"Do. You. Want. Any. Help."

Olivia considered the offer.

"It's too dark. Sun's going down."

"I can see well enough."

"What, you got super eyes as well?"

Liss's teeth were practically grinding. "Yes."

Olivia gave her a look and considered her offer. "Well if you want to have a go, the whole place needs weeding."

"Weeding."

"Yeh. Is that beneath you or something?"

"No. It's fine. Got any gloves?"

"Haven't you got super hands as well?"

"I heard what happened to Pew. They're not that super."

"There's some on the cart." Liss went to the toolcart floating at the edge of a patch of cabbages and took gardening gloves from a drawer. Olivia watched with disapproval, waiting for Liss to do something wrong. Liss sighed, shook her head, and set to work ripping up weeds around tomato plants. She eliminated them with a mechanical obstinacy to all of Olivia's expectations and pretty soon, the tomato bed was free of sandgrass.

"Good enough for you?" asked Liss.

Olivia sniffed. "It'll do. Now get on and do the rest." She wedged her hat on her face. Liss looked at her with naked irritation, then went back to work. Olivia paid no more attention for several minutes, until she lifted her hat to observe the hard work in progress. She lowered the hat, satisfied. Then raised it again when she realized exactly which plants were coming up out of the soil.

Olivia was out of her chair and across the garden in record time, but not fast enough to stop Liss ripping up a line of green shoots tipped with tiny buds that, with gentle care and attention, would have flowered and brought forth the pungent mustard seeds Olivia craved.

"You–! You–!" Olivia couldn't express how livid she was. Apoplectic red-faced fury was all she could manage.

"Finished the weeding!" said Liss with a smile.

"Those weren't weeds!"

"Oh? Looked like weeds."

"You little tart, you knew what you were doing!"

"Anything else you want weeding?

Olivia grabbed for the gardening gloves. "Give me those!"

"Hey!"

Olivia got hold of one hand and dragged the glove half off. Liss pushed back, and knocked Olivia two metres through the air into the tomato bed. Liss's hands flew to her face as Olivia cried out in pain.

"Oh, shit, sorry–"

"You *bitch!*"

Olivia tried to get up, but cried out again.

"What is it?" asked Liss.

Olivia gritted an answer through the pain. "You've put my back out, you cow!"

"Um. I'll, er, get some help…"

Liss slipped away.

10. ASHA & BELL

"...the nurse put Olivia's back in order but she's not happy. Like I said, she wants out."

"Surely this is something we can get her to sleep on?"

"She wants out *now*. She's outside my office. She won't leave."

A crumpled sigh escaped me. "Put her on, then."

I heard the fumbling sounds of the line switching to a physical handset for Olivia's benefit.

"Bad day at work?" asked Bell, enjoying it far too much.

"Just shut up," I said.

Olivia came on the line. "I want to leave. What are you going to do about it?"

"Olivia, don't you think it would be a good idea to sleep on it first?"

"No I bloody don't! I want to go now. Right now!"

"I'm sure Liss didn't mean it. We can talk in the morning and then I'll be happy to arrange a move if you–"

"I'll say it again because you're not listening: I want to go and I want to go now!"

"Olivia–"

"Now. Right now!"

"I don't think–"

"Right now means right now!"

"Yes, however–"

"I've been assaulted, nearly raped, thrown at a ceiling and chucked across a garden! Your bloody therapy centre isn't bloody safe!"

I looked up at the ceiling in exasperation. But she did have a valid point.

"All right, Olivia. If you don't feel safe I can give you a few days back in the Psychiatric Centre while we conduct a safety review."

"And then you'll drag me back, no doubt..."

"If your complaint is on health and safety grounds then that's something we can address. That's all I can do for you at the moment."

She made an grumping sound. "Fine. Just get me out of here."

"Hand me back to Veofol."

The line fumbled again as Veofol picked up. "Asha?"

"Yeah. Listen. We've still got a bus there, haven't we? Can you get Olivia back to the Psychiatric Centre?"

"Er... okay. But shouldn't we have a cooling off period first?"

"That's the idea – let her cool off somewhere else. And she's got a point about health and safety. We'll get her back in a week or so, I'm pretty certain of that. Can you make the travel arrangements?"

"Of course."

"I'll talk to the Psychiatric Centre and let them know."

"That'll make them happy..."

"Yeah. I'll let you know when it's arranged."

I ended the call as Bell handed our menus back to a waiter. "I ordered for us," he said.

"Go on, tell me," I sighed, expecting something completely inedible.

"Mammoth roulade on a bed of pan tossed algae." Which was a pleasant surprise. Much of the 'cooking' on Bell's world involved burying things and letting them rot. At least he wasn't being vindictive. But then he was the one heading off to a new life. He could afford it.

"I need to make one more call. Sorry."

"I'll get some wine."

"Thanks."

11. DEPARTURE

Olivia's departure was a disorganised affair. She wanted to pack everything she owned so she could make it difficult to return, but Veofol gave her no time. She had to make do with only a small bag, and leave behind all her favourite garden tools. There was, after all, no point in allowing her to profit by running away.

Pew was distraught on hearing she was going, and a tearful scene followed in which he asked why she was leaving, and she refused to say. Pew was convinced it was all his fault despite Olivia's grumpy silence. Few of the others cared that she was going. Liss retired to her room and put on a screenshow to numb her brain. Elsbet was stable in the infirmary, but unlikely to wake any time soon. Kwame stayed in his room. Iokan was the only one to go to the courtyard to wish Olivia farewell.

"I might have known you'd come to say goodbye," she muttered.

"The least I could do," he said. "But I don't think you'll be gone long."

"Hah! Watch me!" She turned her back on him and boarded the bus. Iokan lingered patiently. Olivia did not. She came back to the door and demanded: "Where's the bloody driver? Pilot? Whatever they're supposed to be called…"

"I'll go and look, shall I?"

"Yeh. Go on. Have a look. I'll sit here."

Iokan went back and almost walked into Veofol, who had a cross look on his face to match his determined march to the bus.

"Where's the driver?"

"I'm the driver."

"*You're* the driver?"

"The usual drivers are off site. We have to keep one qualified driver here in case of emergencies, and that's Satna in security. Which leaves me."

"You're qualified to fly one of these?"

"It's not flying. It's driving. And yes, I *am* qualified."

"I'm impressed."

"The computer does most of the work. It's not that impressive. Don't tell me you're coming along as well?"

"No. Just here to see you off."

"Well. Thanks. I'm sure Olivia appreciates it." Iokan chuckled but Veofol didn't smile. "I'm serious. It'll make it easier to bring her back if she thinks someone cares whether or not she's here."

"Are you sure?"

"Yes. I'm sure."

"Has anything I've done… helped?"

Veofol paused on the steps of the bus. "At least you're trying."

Iokan nodded.

"I'll see you in a couple of hours. We can talk about it then."

"Yes. I'd like to."

"Okay. I'll see you soon."

Veofol boarded to a grumpy "about bloody time you damned elf!" from Olivia. The door slid shut, an automated voice warned people to stand clear, and Iokan dutifully backed off as it rose up into the sky.

12. ASHA & BELL

As we tucked into steaming chunks of rolled up mammoth meat flavoured with krill paste, I found the evening growing easier to bear. He was leaving for another world, and wouldn't be coming back. Somehow I skipped the usual stage of distraught pleading. Had I actually loved him? I felt fond of him. He was still funny, in his own way, making little linguistic jokes and waiting while my translation system caught up. But I didn't love him.

"It's strange," I said.

"No, really, it's completely genuine!" he assured me.

"Hm?"

"The meat comes in every week. It's frozen but it's still the real thing."

"I didn't mean that…"

"They don't bring in the real delicacies, though. Some people swear by the mammoth penis stew back home."

I choked, then very carefully finished chewing and swallowing.

"This isn't…?"

He smiled. "No, of course not. Penis is too expensive."

"Anyway, that's not what I meant. I mean I *feel* strange. I ought to be angry. I ought to be making a scene. I thought it would be terrible, if this happened…"

He looked hurt. "Oh."

"I didn't mean it that way! I meant…"

"You feel like you dropped the tent."

"What tent?"

"A tent you were carrying through winter drifts that wasn't even yours. And you didn't feel the weight until the straps broke and it fell into the snow. You look back, and it's a broken thing with cracked poles and worn hides. You were only carrying it because you needed shelter in case the blizzard came. But there was no blizzard. And once it's gone, it's easy to get through the snow by yourself."

"That's really... accurate."

"It's from a poem. You can look it up."

"I will. I wish it was that easy for everyone."

"Your patients, I suppose?"

"Yeah. Actually, let me look at that poem..."

I fished in my bag for a small pad, and searched.

"It's called–" he said.

"No, don't tell me, let me see if I can... huh."

"You might find it under my name. I, uh, translated it into Interversal."

"I can't find anything."

He sighed. "Try *The Tents of Love and Ice*, it'll be in the collection."

"No, I mean everything's gone..." The data connection had dropped. I'd seen this kind of thing happen in distant therapy centres where we depended on a local retransmitter, but never in Hub Metro. I looked up and saw people all over the restaurant fumbling with devices and putting hands to their ears as if straining to hear something. I checked my own implant and found myself cut off from all outside services.

"It can't be everyone..." said Bell, shaking his watch and finding that he, too, was cut off.

"It's probably a local failure," I said.

Every light in the restaurant went off. People gasped. The lights flickered back on. Then off again. The gasps were deeper. No one knew what to make of it.

The room jumped. Plates scattered. Glasses splashed wine and fell. People stumbled. I grabbed the table to steady myself.

"Earthquake...?" said Bell, hardly believing it.

"We need to get out of here," I said. My crisis training pushed aside all thoughts of the impossibility of tremors in Hub Metro: all I knew at that moment was that the most dangerous place during an earthquake is inside a building. I grabbed Bell's hand and we ran for the door.

The lobby was full of people with much the same idea, and I mistook the orange glow on their faces for a fire still burning in a stone hearth. But the light came through the glass frontage, and as we were carried along the human stream to the doors, we saw what was lighting us up, and what had made the ground shake: a vast, mangled twist of metal and ceramic that had crashed down from the sky and was scorching trees and grass and people in the park opposite the restaurant.

"Oh no. No..." said Bell, distraught by the wreckage. But I was driven by rigid, trained impulses for survival: if one had crashed, what of the others? I looked up.

Above the orange glow, the sky was alive with the flash and thunder of an awesome lightning storm, sudden sheets of blue making the clouds burst and glow, forks cracking through the air from cloud to cloud and down to hit the tops of buildings, exploding their lightning conductors in showers of sparks.

And below the lightning, the aircraft suffered. A small flyer struggled to stay in the air. The driver did his or her best as it was punched across the sky by an invisible fist. It wasn't just the datastreams to our devices that were down: the computers that made gravity-assisted flight easy had failed. Everything that could fly was coming back to earth.

13. CRISIS

Liss snapped awake. The romantic adventures of Ellera had put her to sleep with their familiarity, but another sound made her jump. Something at the edge of her hearing. Something that triggered old instincts.

She burst out of her room and ran down the stairs to find Iokan in the common room.

"Did you hear that?" she asked.

"I didn't hear anything…"

She heard something else that made her look up. "It's outside."

She ran out of the building with Iokan behind her.

"Shit…" she muttered as she looked in the direction of Hub Metro, and saw the lightning storm like a cap over the city, spreading outwards and touching the clouds over their own heads. Thunder rumbled and crashed over them as forks of lightning spread a web of light across the sky.

Iokan followed her out, and looked up. "Ancients…"

"Anyone you know?"

He shook his head. "They never came like *this*…"

A low thud drew their attention towards the dark horizon – and a sudden burst of flame in the canopy, followed by smoke.

14. ASHA & BELL

Hub Metro was in chaos, drowning in fire and screams. We fled the restaurant along with the crowds flooding the streets. Above us, the lightning roared and gravity drives trembled in the air if their pilots were skilled, or fell if they were not. At least a dozen crash sites were scattered across the city and in the sides of buildings, spewing fire and smoke as lightning cracked down from above.

A woman staggered in tattered, smouldering rags from the nearest burning flyer, her hair razed off, screaming that aliens had come from beyond and set fire to the sky. Two people calmed her and tried to lead her to safety. A man Bell knew from work grabbed him and shouted that invaders had come from another universe and he had to hide! Now! This was just the beginning of the invasion! Bell shook him off and we stumbled on, just trying to get away from the massive conflagration that was unbearably hot even as far away as we were. A security officer waved us on, yelling at everyone to keep moving, keep moving, get out of the area. We asked her what was going on, but she didn't know, she just needed us to move, to move, to keep moving.

And there was still no data. No way to get information, any kind of information. No visual overlay to say where we were or offer suggestions for routes. People staggered blindly on, some of them looking as though they saw the city for the first time and were daunted not by the disaster but by the massive unknowable scale of the buildings. We hoped we might find AIs in their robot bodies who would have their own local records – but we saw one collapsed in a heap by the side of a road, smoke pouring from the chest cavity. Every robot we saw had died the same way. "It can't be," I muttered, remembering what had happened to the Exploration Service mission that had found Katie.

"Can't be what?" asked Bell.

"Gravity pulse..."

"Gravity *what?*"

But it didn't make sense. I looked up again. "No. It's not a gravity pulse. It's an *electromagnetic* pulse... that's what the lightning's for..."

He tried to take me by the shoulder and pull me away with the crowd. "Come on!" But I'd had disaster training. It was standard for anyone who worked out in the refugee centres among hordes of damaged people: firstly, to understand what they had been through, but also to help us survive in similar situations. And what we were doing felt wrong. A crowd directed by the authorities towards points of escape from the crisis is a crowd you want to be in, but a confused mob just heading away is a terrible idea. The only security officer we'd seen had no idea what was going on: she'd just been trying to get people away from the crash.

"I have to get to the Refugee Service!" I shouted to Bell over the screaming and thunder.

"We need to get out of the city!" he shouted back.

I shook my head. "None of these people know where they're going! Nobody knows what's happening! Do you want to go with them or do you want to be in a government installation?"

"Wait, are you trying to check on your *patients?*"

He couldn't believe it. But he was right. I had to know. I couldn't answer for a moment. He shook his head. "Fine. Whatever. Which way?"

I pointed down a side avenue with a shoe. "That way." I ran on in my bare feet and he followed.

15. RESCUE

Sirens went off throughout the centre, and outside in the courtyard. Lomeva Sisse came out after Iokan and Liss. "You two! Get inside! Now!"

"What's going on?" demanded Liss as thunder reached them and forced them to shout.

"I don't know! You just need to get inside! *Now!*"

"Who crashed?"

"I don't – what?" She turned and saw the burning hole in the forest. "Oh lord. I need a medical team, I need transport, we have a crashed flyer–" And then she realised no one could hear her. "There's no data…" She looked suddenly helpless.

Liss grabbed her by the shoulders as lightning struck in the forest and started another fire. "Get back inside. Get your team together. Follow me as quick as you can," she said, and ran into the woods.

"Stop! You don't know what you're doing!" shouted Lomeva.

"She's qualified," said Iokan. And after a second, he added: "So am I." He ran after her. Lomeva glared after them but could do nothing. She turned back to the building and the crowd who had emerged, along with Pew.

"What's happening?" he asked.

"Just get back inside!" she shouted. "All you medical people! Get your kit! We're going out to the crash!"

16. ASHA & BELL

The head office of the Refugee Service of the Interversal Union was another of those Hub Metro edifices that made more of a statement than sense. A shining castle, carved out of silver and gold, that required polarised glasses to look at it on a sunny day – but tonight it reflected the blue violence of the sky above and the orange roar of fires around the city, making it look like it was under siege from an army carrying ancient torches.

And under siege it was. A mob pressed against the glass gates at the front of the building, desperate to be let in. Just inside, we could see security people begging them to pull back, some of them lost and confused themselves.

"Oh, great…" said Bell as he saw the mob.

"Side entrance by the vehicle park," I said. We ran to the side of the building, where a door was provided for those who were lucky enough to have private transport. As we ran, I heard a static noise, and saw a flicker of reboot in the visual overlay; but just as swiftly, it was gone.

Bell turned, seeing lights guttering in the street. "Is it coming back on?"

"Not yet," I said, and hammered on the glass doors to call the attention of security, imploring them to run a scanner on my face or my implant so they could see who I was. At first they didn't believe me, but when reinforcements came down, one of them recognised me and let us in.

Inside, they had the same loss of data, but they at least had a shielded generator, plenty of light and functioning devices. I ran through to the main lobby and the gravity tubes that could lift us up to the secretariat level where I might find my superiors, if they had made it here. We had backup systems in the event of such a massive systems failure: line of sight microwave relays, ancient but seemingly capable of cutting through the EMP. Through landstations and satellites, the Refugee Service was patching through to centres across the continent. I heard a dozen conversations relaying stories of disaster and pain. Refugees had revolted and taken over a centre in one location. A spacecraft had come down near another, and they were launching a rescue effort. Thankfully, the Lift was far enough away not to be affected, and it looked like it would be the base for the relief operation.

I headed back into the corridors that held the director's offices, looking for my own boss, and rapidly finding him. Mykl Teoth was on a call to Henni Ardassian, the Refugee Service Director, as I knocked on his office door.

"That's all I've got, ma'am. They're not risking any flights until further notice–"

Henni glared down from the screen of the wall, her image scattering and reforming, the sound barely breaking through the hiss even though they were using the microwave relays. "Heaven damn it! Whose idea was it not to have any surface transport or landlines out to these places!" She saw me behind Mykl. "Who's that there?"

Mykl turned and saw me. "I'll come back later," I said.

"No! No, stay, we've been looking for you–" he said.

"Is that Asha Singh? Why isn't she at that centre?" demanded Henni.

"My night off, ma'am. I was at a restaurant."

"So you don't know what's going on out there?"

"I came here to find out."

"Well then, find out! Get on with it! Go!"

Mykl shrugged helplessly. I left as Henni started lecturing him on what he needed to do until she could get back. As Bell trailed behind me, I took over the office next door and keyed it to my own account and clearances.

"I need to check on some things," said Bell.

"Do you need me to do anything?" I asked.

"No," he said. "I'll ask outside. Look after yourself."

He left me there in the office, frantically trying to patch a microwave link through to the centre. I didn't see him pause there, not sure of what to say; I barely even noticed him go as I reached out to try and find out what was happening.

When I did, it was more than I could bear.

17. CRASH

The medical team followed Liss's trail. She'd had no trouble finding her way in the dark but hadn't bothered to go around obstacles; when she could, she simply went through. And when they got close, there was the glow of the fires from the crash to show them the way.

They found Iokan tending to Liss, who was unconscious with terrible burns on her arms, her hair scorched and mangled. Iokan was covered in soot and singed but clearly hadn't attempted whatever Liss had tried to do.

"She needs help!" he cried, his voice cracking from smoke inhalation, and the medics went to her.

"What about the passengers?" asked Lomeva.

"Two!" said Iokan. Olivia suddenly gasped awake, coughing. "Olivia and Veofol."

"Where is he?"

Iokan shook his head and pointed back at the burning wreckage of the bus. "Liss pulled Olivia out. She couldn't get to Veofol. I had to drag her out…" He was forced to stop for a moment as a retching cough took over. Once it died, he gasped words at Lomeva again.

"I couldn't help him."

PART TEN
MOVING HOUSE

1. THE ATTACK

The flow of data did not return that day, or the next, and stayed silent as long as the lightning flashed across the sky. It was only a week later that the atmosphere cleared and limited data service was restored. Despite the loss of most of our communications, the rumour factories jumped into action as soon as people stopped running and realised the world wasn't ending. Was it aliens with vastly superior technology? The remnants of the last attempt at an interversal organisation rising in revenge? Massive incompetence by penny-pinching bureaucrats? No one knew, at first. But the answer was soon discovered, and the truth disseminated across Hub Metro by voice, by billboard, by broadsheet newspaper, by any method that could be found.

We had been attacked. The device that lit up the sky, and which kept it on fire with electromagnetic discharge for a week after, was one used in a war between machines and AIs in another universe fifty years before, which seeded the upper atmosphere with EMP detonators. Radio communications were rendered impossible to use, save for higher energy microwave bands, and unshielded electrical devices were rapidly destroyed. A few older types of implants burnt out inside people's bodies, causing severe injuries. The constant barrage could even affect some shielded machinery, and power transmission had been the first thing to fail.

Most of the fatalities came in the immediate aftermath of the attack, as the computers on gravity flyers burnt out, leaving their human pilots to manage by themselves – something most of them weren't ready for. Without computer assistance, the subtleties of the Earth's own gravity field have to be compensated for manually, and that takes skill.

I remember the feeling then, in the days I was stranded in Hub Metro before a qualified pilot could be found to take me back to the centre: no one could believe we would be targeted. How could *we* be attacked? Why would anyone want to come after *us*? What had we done to hurt anyone? The certainties we all shared shifted under our feet and the multiverse looked like a more dangerous place. Hundreds of groups on dozens of worlds claimed responsibility for the attack. All they shared was a dislike of IU interference in their affairs. For some of them, we had done too much. For others, we had done too little. Altogether too many people were quietly happy to see our noses rubbed in the same dirt they had to live with.

The truth, when it was eventually uncovered, was hardly a surprise. Anti-AI extremists had built the weapon on Hub to designs smuggled in from a world seething at the price they'd paid for IU membership and assistance – being forced to live alongside the AIs they'd been trying to eliminate for decades. AI species on Hub were the most affected, and had suffered the greatest loss if they were not backed up inside an EM cage. Several individual AIs caught outside were destroyed completely, and one embassy whose EM cage failed was completely wiped out. Their trust in the IU was shaken for years to come.

The IU had taken a terrible beating, and no one knew yet what it would do when it roused itself from the shock – whether it would carry on as it was, or change into something none of us would recognise.

2. ASHA

Bell called me once more, from the port city at the base of the Lift. None of the facilities in orbit had been affected by the attack, and a number of worlds were withdrawing their citizens from Hub in a knee-jerk reaction. Bell took the opportunity while it was there and got away weeks before he'd originally planned.

I didn't cry for Bell. I'd already accepted he was gone. I cried when I realised that, as Veofol's line manager, I owed his family a letter informing them of his death while on duty. His species' consulate had already notified them, of course; but they had not been working alongside him for the last two years, as I had. So it fell to me to offer them some kind of comfort and an assurance that he had been incredibly talented, and was a loss not just to his species, but to all of us. To Hub. To the group. To me.

3. THE CENTRE

I noticed a change in the staff when I returned to the centre. Many had grown tired of what they saw as the group's petulant determination to suffer in the face of comfort and freedom on Hub. But now they'd discovered the merest taste of what the group had endured, and turned to them for support. A dozen times, I saw a security guard or a nurse, or even the groundskeeper, talking with one of the patients. Olivia would tell them to buck their ideas up and put their backs into rebuilding. Iokan hoarsely encouraged them to bear it and keep going despite the pain. The others simply didn't know what to say, or kept their thoughts to themselves. I myself was pestered, especially by one security guard whose wife was missing, and presumed dead. As I had been in Hub Metro that night, he was desperate for any clues I might have had. In the end, I had to transfer him to another centre where he could receive the therapy he needed.

I tried to bring the group together for a therapy session, but it proved impossible. Liss was still in a coma as her body healed her burns. Iokan strained his voice and was ordered to stay quiet, though he kept ignoring the advice and hurting himself further. Kwame and Pew had their own traumas that kept them in their rooms. So I ended up with an almost-silent Iokan and Olivia as my therapy group, and even she was quieter than usual. But at least she gave up on her demand to leave. She muttered that nowhere was safe now, so what was the point? And I had no answer to that.

Elsbet regained consciousness the day after, but she was no longer Elsbet. The electric shock from the suicide attempt had enough effect on the implants to ensure it was Katie who emerged from the coma, questioning the gap of time since she was last awake and asking why her shoulder socket was now so damaged that her arm could not be remounted.

The first permanent effect of the attack on the group was to bring forward the proposed move of the centre to a more secluded, and hopefully more secure location, across the continent and far away from any further violence. The site had been ready before the attack, and it was only the shortage of skilled pilots that meant we had to wait a few days.

4. MOVING

Our bus cruised at what seemed like walking pace a few hundred metres over an empty savannah. "How long is this going to bloody take?" asked Olivia of the pilot, who was replacing our usual driver while he was trained up to the new standards.

"There's a speed limit," he said, almost grinding his teeth at what was the twelfth time she'd complained.

"Speed limit? Who are we going to hit out here? Do you see any trees?"

I answered before the pilot snapped back at her. "We're already going faster than anyone ever did on your world, Olivia. And you know why there's a speed limit." I'd explained about the precautions: there were still occasional EMP bursts, so speeds were kept low enough for a human pilot to handle with ease in the event of trouble.

"Might as well be in a bloody balloon…" muttered Olivia as she retired back to the passenger seating. I apologised to the pilot and let him get on with his job before going back myself.

Liss had woken from her coma, and was in a stretcher locked to the side of the cabin, a nurse by her side to tend to the burns that were still wrapped in flexible polymer healing casts. Iokan was in a chair with oxygen infusers wrapped across his face, having exacerbated the injuries he suffered from smoke inhalation. Katie was still without her right arm. Olivia was badly bruised and carried an arm in a sling, but had escaped worse injury. Pew and Kwame were left unhurt, at least physically. Nobody looked particularly upbeat.

"How are you all doing?" I asked. It was the first time I'd been able to get them all into the same room for quite a while.

"I've been… better," croaked Iokan.

"How do you feel, Liss?" I asked.

"Ow. Ow. Ow."

I turned to the nurse. "Hasn't she had anything for the pain?"

The nurse shook her head. "She won't take analgesics."

"Isn't there anything we can do?" I asked Liss.

"No," she said.

"You don't have to… punish yourself," said Iokan. "You can't save… everyone. I think you said that… once."

Liss laughed bitterly. "I remember."

"But there's no need to suffer…" I said.

"I don't heal so well if I take painkillers. I can switch most of it off. It's fine."

I looked to the others. "Does anyone else need anything?"

"When's he being buried?" asked Olivia. She meant Veofol. I think she was surprised to find she missed him. The others felt the loss as well, and they looked to me.

"His remains are going back to his world. They're not doing an evacuation like some species, so it won't be for a couple of weeks, until there's portal time available."

"His family will take him?" asked Kwame.

"I think so," I said. "I don't know how they handle things on his world."

"I do," said Pew. "I looked it up." He held up a pad he'd been working on. "They recycle. Because they live in orbital habitats, you know, they can't afford to waste anything."

"They eat their dead…?" said Kwame, ready to be appalled.

"Uh, no. More like take the organs for transplants, blood for transfusion, extract minerals. That kind of thing."

"That is disgusting," said Kwame.

"You do what you have to do," muttered Olivia.

"They have a ceremony, it's not like they dump him in a machine," protested Pew. "They might cremate him, though, they get a lot of aid from the IU so they don't need the recycling so much. And he's sort of famous there apparently, so they might make the exception…"

Katie spoke up. "They will not require much fuel for cremation. He was extensively charred in the crash."

"Oh, don't tell me you've come back…" said Olivia. They knew Katie had returned, of course, but this was the first time she'd spoken.

"I have made no journey to return from."

"Well you can bloody well give the man some respect!"

Katie reacted as if struck. She froze, twitched, and relaxed her face again. "I apologise," she said. "His loss is regrettable. He will be missed." A muscle at the side of her mouth quivered, then settled down.

"Can we… send someone?" wheezed Iokan.

"There'll be a representative from the IU there," I said.

"Is there anything we… can send? A… recording? Or a message?"

"I sent something to his family," I said. "If the rest of you want to say a few words, I'll see what I can arrange."

5. THE NEW CENTRE

The bus took us up into a mountain range, weaving through snowy peaks to the new centre: high on a bleak valley through which glaciers had run in colder millennia, with the treeline only a couple of hundred metres above. We arrived at the end of summer, with warnings we should prepare for snow. The centre was often used for alpine sports in the winter, and there were ski runs laid out nearby.

Kwame declared it reminded him of Bvumba, the military reserve on his world the bunkers had been built under. The familiarity of the landscape gave him no comfort and seemed to set him on edge. Olivia complained her garden was lost; it was far too late in the year to start another one and even if the timing had been right, the soil was a long way from what she wanted. The land was perfect for pasture, if there had been any animals on the planet that needed it. Other than that, you could grow a few small flowering plants, but that was it. The growing season was far too short for most crops. Olivia muttered and swore when she surveyed the ground, and said she might as well be back in Tringarrick, which, though hilly, was hardly the same kind of terrain. I let her order some seeds anyway, since the old garden had been so helpful in getting her to participate in therapy.

We were a long way from Hub Metro; two thousand kilometres distant and very dependent on a microwave link to a satellite for what little dataflow was available, along with regular supply runs that would become ever more important in the winter months. The buildings themselves were familiar, as they were of exactly the same design as the last centre. They were prefabricated and mass-produced so we could set up as many centres as we needed to cope with sudden influxes of survivors from dead worlds, and the common design made them very easy to work with. But this time, it was more than a little disturbing when you walked out a familiar door and were suddenly reminded of the chill you'd never felt at the old centre. All the rooms had been set up in an identical manner as before, so moving in proved to be fairly easy, though few of the group were in a fit state to do the work themselves.

I joined them. I would need to be there and on call all the time because we had no other therapists available to take Veofol's place, what with all the chaos after the attack. So the centre would be my home for the time being. I didn't mind; I had no real reason to stay in the city, and the only pang of discomfort came from the occasional impulse to call for Veofol to help with the group, and the sudden memory that he was gone.

6. LISS

I postponed formal therapy sessions for a while, and allowed the group some time to settle in and explore. Liss, of course, did not have quite as much luxury to wander while she was still bedridden, so I made daily visits to see how she was doing, and induce her to talk.

"How's it going?" I asked her one day. She raised her arms to show me. Through the transparent healer, the day by day improvement was quite apparent.

"That's good," I said. "Is this kind of healing a common thing on your world?"

She shrugged, then winced at the pain of stretching her burns. "I'm not the only one–" she stopped, then sighed. "I keep forgetting. I *am* the only one."

"That was a very brave and selfless thing you did, saving Olivia."

"I didn't think about it."

"There's not many people who'd be able to do that."

"No. Only one." She raised her arms again; she was being sarcastic.

"I don't mean physically."

"Like I said, I didn't think about it."

"And what if you'd had to think about it?"

She looked back at me and frowned. "Hm. Olivia. Hmm…" Then she sighed again. "I suppose I'd have done it anyway."

I nodded. "And you know what happened to Veofol wasn't your fault?"

"You can't save everyone."

"I remember, when you first joined us, you said that was a saying you had on your world…"

"Yes."

"It's just that, when people go so far as to have a saying for something like this, it usually means they're trying to console themselves for feeling bad about it."

"Yeah. So?"

"Are you sure it doesn't take a toll?"

"I stopped counting the people I couldn't save when it went past a couple billion."

"There's no need to be sarcastic, Liss."

"I'll stop being sarcastic when you stop stating the obvious."

She wasn't in the mood for co-operation. But she wasn't Olivia. I looked back at her, and said: "Okay."

"Okay what?"

"I'll stop stating the obvious."

"Right. And…?"

"I'll let you do it."

"What?"

"I want you to tell me what's wrong."

She laughed in exasperation. "I'm the last daughter of a dead world! You think I'm enjoying myself?"

"No. But I think your problem's obvious."

"So tell me then."

"No. It's obvious. You tell me."

"Is this supposed to be therapy?"

"Yes."

"Isn't it *your* job to tell me what's wrong?"

"It's my job to help you help yourself."

She shook her head, amazed. "I cannot believe you're turning this into some kind of mystery!"

"Who killed your world, Liss?"

That silenced her. I went on: "Everybody else here has a pretty good idea of what happened. I'm not saying they're always right, but they have some idea. You don't. And you came here to find out. Didn't you?"

She was still too surprised to answer.

"That's what's obvious to me, Liss. You've given up. I'm not saying you didn't have a reason. But you've given up."

"Oh. My. God…" she said, amazed at my effrontery. "What the hell do you think I'm supposed to *do*?"

"Find the culprits. That's what it says in your protocols."

"Oh, just like that. And then what?"

"I'd say you should cross that bridge when you come to it."

"I can't."

"Why?"

"Because I'm no good at all this! I got caught, for god's sake! I don't even know where to start any more!"

"You won't have to do it alone. Didn't the ICT talk to you?"

"Ugh. They're useless. They can't even *do* anything…"

"That might not always be the case."

"Oh, because that's going to change overnight…"

"A lot of things changed overnight."

She stopped to think about it. It was true that a great many options were being discussed at the highest levels. Activating the Interversal Criminal Tribunal was suddenly on the table.

"Do you think they'll…?"

"I don't know. But they're talking about it."

"Damn…" she looked outside again. "I can't. I don't even know what to do. I was just following the protocols…"

"Didn't you say you saved the world once?"

"Once. Kind of."

"How many people can say that?"

"It wasn't… I didn't really do anything, I was trying to save myself, and… and we didn't have a plan… it was luck, that's all."

"So maybe you were the right person in the right place at the right time."

"I was panicking for most of it."

"But you did the right thing."

"It wasn't just me. There were thousands of others, lots of people saved the world…"

"That doesn't mean you weren't one of them."

"It doesn't make me qualified!"

"Hm. Liss. I seem to be at a bit of a disadvantage here. You know all about this, but I know nothing."

"Just grab the files from the PRG and read the reports."

"I would, but I don't think we're going to get much back for a while. To be honest, it's not a priority at the moment."

She sighed. "No. I guess not."

"Can you tell me about it? It must be quite a story."

"Aw, crap… just another disaster. The world needed saving every other week."

"Why did it need saving this time?"

She took a deep breath. "The moon blew up."

"… Ah."

"Don't ask me to explain how it happened because I don't know, okay? It was one of those superbrain things. Somebody did some earthquake experiment on the moon and it blew up, and some bits were going away from us and some bits were going to hit us and that was going to be bad.

"They decided to give every country a few chunks of moon to deal with, and we got allocated this big one, we had to put some gravity gizmo on it that was supposed to knock it out of the way, don't ask me how. So we went up there and–"

"I'm sorry, Liss, I don't want to interrupt, but can you tell me how you got involved?"

"Oh. Well, it was my boyfriend. Yott. He was the one who was called up. We were both at college but he was the clever one, I mean, *really* clever…"

"He was a superbrain?"

"Yeah. They weren't all bad. Most of them were fine. Well, a bit crazy. But in a good way. Yott was like a super-engineer, he could make almost anything… it was like, if somebody else worked out a theory, he could make a machine that used it. He was the star at college, I mean he had to have psych tests every couple of weeks, just in case, but he was okay as long as he had a toolbox handy."

"How did you meet?"

"Oh… well, I caught him, um…"

"I'm sorry? You caught him doing what?"

"I didn't catch him doing anything. I mean I… caught him."

"Explain…?"

"He had this gravity rocket thing he was working on and it went wrong and he ended up flying all over campus and I'm the one who was dumb enough to try and catch him before he killed himself. Well, it was more like he flew right into me, I dragged him to a stop, and, heh, well, one thing led to another."

"Ah. I see."

"Yeah."

"So how did that make you an adventurer?"

"There was a club at college, Yott was in it. I didn't really want to join but he dragged me along and everyone said, hey, you've got powers, you saved someone, of course you're one of us. We didn't do anything much, because you had to be over 21 for adventuring unless it was the end of the world. And then of course it *was* the end of the world, so we got called up."

"Were you ready? I mean, for dealing with the moon?"

"Are you kidding? Yott was the one they wanted. They wanted him there in case the gravity thing went wrong and it needed repairs or they had to build one from scratch. And he wanted me along because he was terrified he was going to screw it up, so they swung it as a bodyguard thing.

"Ugh. I hate going into space. He loved it, of course. I was all tangled up in seatbelt straps and he was off flying around the cabin while I was throwing up everywhere, nobody was talking to me after the third time…

"So anyway we got to the moon chunk thing and landed on it and we were getting ready to do the gravity whatever-it-was when we found out somebody else got assigned to the same chunk. They messed up the paperwork or something because there was this Scandian team there as well and they wanted to set off a bomb and knock it out of orbit or something. I don't know, I was in the bathroom being sick.

"No one could agree on who was going to get to deal with it. Ground control said hang on until we can figure it out, so we're all just sitting there like lemons, well I was, *they* were all arguing. I wasn't doing anything other than look out the window, and then there was this *chimp* outside–"

"I'm sorry…?"

"There was a chimp outside."

"In a spacesuit?"

"Of course in a spacesuit! How else are they gonna breathe in space?"

"Okay. Intelligent chimps. I think you mentioned those before."

"Yeah, yeah, some wacko anthrobiologist made a load of chimps intelligent, they set up their own republic, lovely guys, except for the ones that wanted to knock over the chimp government and they'd gone into exile and guess where they'd gone? The goddamn moon. We'd landed on their chunk of it, with their moonbase inside it, and they were pissed. They blew the airlocks and killed everyone in the ship."

"But not you."

"No. I saw them in time, but no one was paying any attention to me, of course, so I grabbed Yott and stuffed him in a spacesuit and then the airlocks blew and he had to get me in a spacesuit and, well, we were the only ones who made it."

"Quick thinking."

"Bullshit. Quick thinking would have saved everyone. And I had to kill one of the chimps as well… I punched in his faceplate. All the air came out like it was some kind of fire extinguisher, and then I could see him dying in there…"

She closed her eyes for a moment. "So we got the hell out. Yott had his gravity rocket so we got away pretty easy. Wasn't charged up properly, though, so we couldn't get off the chunk. We hid in the chimp base, a lot of it was wrecked from when the moon blew up, so that was easy too. And then we didn't know what to do. We sat in there for hours…"

"What happened next?"

"We found out what the chimps were up to. Yott patched into some cables… they wanted to use the gravity thing we brought along to make the chunk crash into

Africa and wipe out all the other chimps. They had this madchimp in charge, he'd spend the whole time yelling at people about how he was going to make everyone pay for everything..."

"But you stopped them. Isn't that right?"

"We figured we were dead anyway so we might as well do something stupid. Yott figured we could use the Scandian ship to do what they were planning to do in the first place. The chimps weren't using all that stuff because they preferred the gravity thing on our ship, so they weren't even guarding the Scando ship. And then it was just... get him there without getting killed. He got the ship back online, dropped the bomb, and we got out of town."

"And it worked?"

"Are you kidding? Of course not. The stupid chimps found out and set off their thing at the same time we set off the bomb. It didn't knock the chunk out of the way – it just broke into bits. A couple of them made it down and started a tidal wave in the Atlantic. They got most people on the coast out of the way but a couple thousand died. And all the chimps on the chunk. And everyone who went to try and stop it, apart from me and Yott."

"Do you blame yourself?"

She thought about that for a moment. "More people would have died if we hadn't done it. They'd have wiped out most of Africa, not just the chimps, I mean that would have killed *everyone*."

Her protestation sounded rehearsed. "Is that what they told you when you got back? I mean, did you have therapy?"

"Yeah, *right*. There wasn't time, we had to go to work with all the cleanup crews because we were already drafted. But the chimps helped, I mean the ones on the ground, the chimp republic. They sent a lot of aid to say thanks for, you know, saving their species."

"Did you get any therapy at all?"

"No."

"Why?"

"Things were crazy. Our chunk wasn't the only one where it went wrong. We were all running around like mad for a year and a half just cleaning up the mess. Nobody had any time for therapy."

"I see."

"So that's it. That's how I saved the world. Stupid, isn't it?"

"Not at all. I think you showed remarkable presence of mind, especially for someone who says she isn't any good at that kind of thing."

"Yott did the work. All I did was get him there."

"Could he have done it by himself?"

"No. Neither could I. *That's the point.* I can't do it by myself. I don't know where to start, I'm no good at this, I never have been. I'm an *office manager*, not a hero! I mean look..." she held up her polymer-encased arms. "This is what happens when I try to save someone. Someone else has to come in and save *me*."

"What if we could help you? I mean, if the ICT were up and running?"

She considered for a moment. "I don't know. I'll believe it when I see it."

7. KATIE

Katie was often found in the infirmary, having tests done on her stump to see if her arm could be safely reconnected. The technology was highly advanced but not beyond that of Hub – it was simply different. This could probably have been done in a day if the world's electronics experts weren't preoccupied with the aftermath of the attack; as things stood, one engineer was trying to figure out the problem remotely in his spare time, and progress was slow.

Her presence in the infirmary did, however, allow us to observe her closely, and we soon noticed she was developing uncontrollable tremors. Her remaining hand would shake, or her otherwise expressionless face would twitch. She repeatedly denied these symptoms existed, despite all evidence.

Otherwise, she kept her own company, and it was therefore a surprise when she presented herself at my office, which I had only just finished restoring to its former state. Coffee was quietly brewing and the place was just about beginning to feel right as Katie chimed at the door and I let her in.

"Take a seat," I said.

"My request is brief," she said.

"Okay. Go ahead."

"I wish to volunteer in the armed forces of the Interversal Union."

"Katie... we don't have any armed forces."

"The Interversal Union has been attacked. It is reasonable to expect it will shortly require armed forces. I wish to volunteer."

"I can see how you've come to that conclusion, Katie, but I'm not sure it's accurate. Also, I'd feel much more comfortable if we could discuss this while sitting down."

She sat in as formal a manner as ever.

"I have sat down."

"Thank you. Let me repeat what I just said: The IU has no military. There's no one to volunteer to. And I haven't heard any plans to the contrary."

"My offer is contingent upon the creation of a military. I am aware it does not currently exist."

"Okay... but consider this. If the IU formed a military, there would still be a number of barriers to you volunteering. First of all: you're not an IU citizen. You're under the care of the IU, but that does not make you a citizen. I don't think we're likely to let people fight for us unless they have citizenship, or they're volunteering from an IU member species."

"I am prepared to risk my life in defence of the Interversal Union."

"Perhaps. But any release from this centre depends on the success of your therapy. At the moment I don't think it's likely that I'm going to allow you to put yourself at risk when you've experienced severe psychological and medical trauma."

"The persona will not emerge again."

"No?"

"I have taken steps to ensure the persona will not emerge again."

"This is something I'd like to discuss. I mean the whole business with Elsbet. Do you remember anything about what happened?"

"No. It is irrelevant."

"She accused you of war crimes."

"She is mistaken."

"We're going to have to investigate, when we get a moment."

"An investigation is unnecessary."

"Were you really an infiltrator?"

Katie paused for a long time.

"Yes."

"They took you into their hospital, is that correct?"

"Yes."

"And then you attacked."

"Yes."

"You killed everyone in the hospital."

"Yes."

"Including civilians. Including children."

"Yes."

"Why?"

She looked at me with a moment's confusion, as though unable to understand why I needed to ask the question. "They would not negotiate. They would not communicate. They only declared their intent to extinguish us from the system. We had no other way to strike back. The primary target was the shipyards. Other casualties were impossible to avoid."

"I see."

"It was an act of war."

"You're not the first person to say that."

"I will not discuss it further."

"Katie–"

"I will not discuss it further."

Her face was twitching again. I sighed.

"Okay. Let me go back to something else: you say she won't be emerging again?"

"Yes."

"Does this have anything to do with your tremors?"

"I suffer no tremors." And yet her mouth twitched, and her hand shook.

"It's happening right now, Katie."

"I am in complete control of all functions."

"You're not in control at the moment. I can see it happening," I said, indicating her unruly hand.

She slammed a look at me and snarled: "I could rip your head from your shoulders."

I froze for a moment. I've been threatened before, but not by a cybernetic killing machine.

"Do I need to call security?" I asked, swallowing back the animal fear in my gut.

The twitching intensified for a moment. And then her face relaxed again and resumed its placid stare.

"There is no need. I am in control."

"Are you having more emotional disturbances?"

"Yes. I am in control."

"Are you sure? You've never threatened anyone before."

"I am in control." Muscles around her eyes quivered for a moment, then lay still.

I sighed. "Katie, if these tremors are what you're doing to yourself to stay in control, you're only going to hurt yourself. You know your condition is terminal. Please. Let us help you."

"I do not require assistance."

"Can you give me a good reason why?"

"I must remain operational."

"But why?"

Her blank stare was chilling.

"They are coming back."

"Who's coming back?"

"My species."

"I think that needs explaining."

"There were expeditions to nearby star systems that travelled at the highest possible speeds but had only reached their first target stars after two hundred years of journey time. They were informed in the final signals from Earth of the progress of the war and will return in due course."

"In two hundred years?"

"Yes. And then the Fourth Machine War will begin."

"Katie, you're not going to last two hundred *days*. And you're in the wrong universe. How do you think you're going to help?"

"I require transfer to an artificial means of consciousness."

"That's not happening, Katie."

A smile twitched around her mouth.

"I… I would be able to assist the Interversal Union greatly if I had an artificial consciousness." She kept up her smile. She was trying to be friendly, in a rather creepy kind of way.

"That's illegal on Hub. And that's definitely not going to change."

"I don't want anything in return…" she said in something like a little girl voice, pleading for a toy.

"And we respectfully decline. You're not fit for duty. You're suffering from neural degradation and you're going to die without our help. Katie, I'll ask again: let us help you before it's too late."

The friendly look vanished.

"There is nothing further to discuss."

She rose and left with no further courtesy.

8. KWAME

Kwame's reaction to the new centre was one of complete avoidance. After a façade of relative normality on the journey over, he retreated into his room and did not emerge for a full day. Once he hadn't shown up for a couple of meals, I went in to see what I could do.

He was exactly where he'd been when I left him on the day of the attack: sitting in the corner, knees drawn up, lost elsewhere.

"Kwame?" He didn't answer. "Are you in there?"

He looked up at me slowly.

"I... do not know."

I sat down in the heavy wooden chair he kept at his desk.

"I thought you were making some progress."

"No."

"Has something happened?"

"I remember."

"What do you remember, Kwame?"

"I remember my dreams. I did not know how I was... protected." He spat the last word out, bitterly.

"What do you dream about?"

He looked up at me, horrified and distraught. "The same! Every night I have the same dream! It has not changed!"

"The dream about the cell?"

"Every night I condemn that... *creature*... to death. And I feel as though I am killing the one I love. As though that *thing* were my wife. And I remember!"

"What do you remember?"

"When I... kissed... *him*."

"Iokan?" He gave me the barest nod. "Do you remember anything else?"

"I..."

He sat there, lost in memory.

"Kwame?"

"I remember... things."

"Can you tell me anything?"

"I do not understand them..."

"Just start with one. Any one."

He took a breath. "I... I remember a lecture hall. Someone talks with a strange accent... demonstrates something on the bench, something robotic... I never studied robotics! I took history. Electronics was a hobby, nothing more! And I remember... being a child, running with gangs, robbing drunks. But I never did that! I was in a private school! My father made sacrifices so I had an education... and, and... I see a bar in Matongu, with men dressed as women..." He trembled. "I have never been to Matongu. What is happening to me?"

This was a very good question. Strange psychological phenomena do crop up when you deal with different human species whose psychology is not fully understood, but I'd never seen anything quite like this before.

"I think… I think at the moment, Kwame, you're feeling lost, like you haven't got a map…"

"That does not help!"

"Let me finish. You're in a strange land. Doesn't it make sense to try and find a map to make sense of where you are?"

"And how should I do that?"

"I think you should make one."

"How…?"

"You say you have all these memories that contradict each other. So perhaps it would be a good idea to make a list."

"These 'memories' are not real. I will not dignify them by writing them down."

"They're not going to go away, Kwame."

"They are not mine!"

"They may not be yours, but they're in your head. And we can't erase them. Isn't it better to at least know what they are, to try and figure out what happened?" He didn't answer. "I'll start if you like."

He still refused to comment.

"Well…" I rose and went to a wall, and set it up for text input. "You said you have memories of being in a street gang, as well as memories of being in private school. Let's put both of those down…"

I drew a line down the wall, then wrote 'Childhood: street gang' on one side and 'Childhood: private school' on the other.

"Maybe what you can do is put all the memories into the two columns and see if you can work out a timeline for both sets of memories?"

He continued to ignore me.

"I'll just leave this here and you can carry on whenever you want. I'll save it so you don't lose it…" I saved the file onto his home folder. "Don't wait too long to get started."

I left. Kwame stayed where he was, hunched into the corner of the room. Eventually, he looked up at the wall, and walked over to the screen.

He wiped it clean. All the words vanished. He called up his folder, and tried to erase the file. But an error message popped up: the file could not be erased without my permission. He tried to save the file as blank, with all the words deleted; he found he couldn't do that either. He thumped a fist on the wall.

Then, after a while, he opened the file again.

9. OLIVIA

Olivia decided to cook, but not for the group. I found her pounding seeds with a mortar and pestle (a difficult task with one arm still in a sling), and asked what it was she was making.

"Mustard," she said, keeping on with her pounding.

"Oh, so you managed to harvest some seeds before you left?"

"No."

"Then how…?"

"These are for the new garden."

"But I thought you said the soil was wrong?"

"Yeh. It's all wrong. Can't grow anything up here."

"So why…" And then I realised: I'd given her permission to order supplies for a new garden more suitable for the soil, and she'd used it. "You ordered new seeds and now you're turning them into mustard."

"That's the sum of it."

"Those seeds are very expensive, Olivia."

"I haven't used money in years. Can't even remember how it works, much less this electric credit balance thing you have."

"And the mustard itself is poisonous to some people."

"Is it poisonous to you?"

"No, but…"

"Then make sure nobody else has any, then! Right…" She finished pounding the seeds. I sighed and decided I might as well try to use the moment for therapy.

"So you've turned it into powder. What's next?"

"It's not powder. It's ground seed. Or flour, if you want to call it that. Here, sniff."

She held the mortar under my nose. The stench blew me off my feet and left me coughing on the floor. "Good, isn't it?" said Olivia.

"I think I need a medic…" I spluttered.

"Rubbish. Splash water on your face, you'll be fine." I dashed to the sink. The burning faded as I drenched myself.

"How can that possibly be food?"

"It's not food, it's what you have *with* food. Be a dear and get me some vinegar. Just the kind we have with dinner is fine."

I took a vinegar bottle down from a cupboard and handed it over while wiping my eyes.

"Did everyone eat this on your world…?"

"Don't be stupid. What do you think, we're all the same as each other? This is just what I have. Goes with any kind of meat, even that muck you print here."

"How did people discover this? Were they suicidal and hungry at the same time?"

"Hah! Didn't you have mustard on your world?"

"I have absolutely no idea what they had on my world. We don't have it *here* because it kills people."

"Well you needed it where I come from. You try eating meat that's been through the marinade, see how long you can stomach it. Bit of mustard makes anything edible."

"This is the marinade you used to destroy the revenation bacteria?"

"That's the one."

"And mustard made it taste *better*?"

"That's it." She poured the ground up seeds from the mortar into a bowl, then added water, a little sugar and salt.

"Did you grow this in the research station?"

"Tried to. Couldn't get anything to come up. We had some in our supplies but that didn't last…"

"How did you manage for food?"

She stirred the mustard paste. "I told you before."

"I mean before you had to resort to–"

"Cannibalism."

"If you want to call it that."

"Might as well."

"But before that?"

"We had enough supplies for three years. We planted what we could. There were plenty of vegetables you could grow if you put your mind to it. We couldn't keep many animals. Couldn't fence off enough pasture to let them graze. Then we started raiding the nearby villages."

"What happened to the villagers?"

"Have a guess."

It wasn't difficult to imagine: villagers falling ill, dying one by one and revenning, their families unwilling to put them down. "Did you try to help any of them?"

"Of course not. Do you think I'm stupid? They had the flu! That's what started the last outbreak. They were dropping like flies and getting up again ten minutes later. If I'd have let them in, we'd have all been dead."

"Did the villagers ask to be let in?"

"You're desperate to find something I feel guilty about, aren't you? How about asking how I managed to get beaten up and nearly dead in a bus crash on this planet? And how come we're all the way out here where it's even more dangerous?"

"We're as safe as we can be, Olivia, and I'm sorry you had to endure some injuries. But you're avoiding the question."

"Of course they tried to get in. Of course I stopped them. I had to."

"How did it happen?"

She sighed as she stirred. "Keep an eye on that clock. Let me know when ten minutes have passed. I need to add the vinegar then. And yes, I'll answer your damn question. They wanted us to let their children in but they were all wiping snot off their faces so I said no. They thought I'd go all mushy if they brought up the children. No idea of psychology. I had children on my side of the gate, which ones did they think I was going to protect?

"So they buggered off and came back with shotguns. I wasn't having that. Our guards had rifles, good revenant hunting rifles. We shot them and shot them again when they revenned. Hah. If I'd known what was coming I'd have put them in the pens with the others.

"So the villagers died. I'm not ashamed of it. We would have all died if I hadn't kept them out. That's why I was in charge and not some laboratory man. They wanted someone who'd been in the first outbreak and wasn't going to get everyone killed."

"How long was it before you went back out?"

"Two and a half years. Once we saw no one was coming for us and we were going to have to find our own food. And that was a mess, going down to the village. No more than a mile and it looked empty but as soon as you opened a door the revenants came out. The first expedition lost two men, after that we did a full scale extermination, got a lot of them in the pens as well. Not so short sighted any more. Anyway we got all the food that was left in the village. Lot of tins. They hadn't had time to eat much of it before they started dying. We lasted nearly a year on what we got from there. Ten minutes."

I'd completely forgotten the clock. "So what now?"

"Vinegar sets the mustard. Keeps the flavour good while it's still strong. Not too much…" She poured a small measure of vinegar into the mustard paste, and mixed it in. "And now I need a jar."

I called the infirmary and had them send over a sterile specimen jar, marked with a biohazard symbol, which made Olivia laugh. She then decided to make herself a picnic, and invited me along. We set up a small table outside in a meadow overlooking a plunging valley and Olivia demonstrated how to make a sandwich such as she had enjoyed on her world: meat and bread and butter and mustard and nothing else.

"How long is it since you've had one of these?" I asked.

She thought about it. "About a year after we locked ourselves in. That's when the mustard ran out. We got a bit more when we started raiding but then there wasn't enough grain for bread. Not proper bread. Do you want one?"

"Er…"

"I'll spread the mustard thin."

"Okay. I'm glad I brought some water."

"You won't need it. Here."

She made me a sandwich, and I tried it as a child might, nibbling at the edge. But the mustard filled my nostrils with fire and I choked. Olivia chuckled to herself.

"Too strong?"

I nodded as I gulped back water. Olivia ate her own sandwich with every sign of contentment.

"So," I coughed, "what were you actually doing there, at Tringarrick?"

"Research. It was a research station. I told you that. Little place in the middle of bloody nowhere stuck in a load of hills. Damn hard to get into or out of. Nothing there except a couple of villages and a little coal mine. Somebody decided it would be a good place to hide in an outbreak, and you know what, they were right. That's why so many of us went there."

"Okay, but what kind of research were you doing?"

"Anything that would kill revenants. We tried making a spray out of the marinade to stop a crowd, but that was no good, it just killed their skin. Lots of work on antibiotics, but we never got anywhere, just made a mess of the test subjects."

"You kept revenants, then?"

"Had to. Had to have something we could run tests on. There was never a shortage. Whenever we ran out, we just opened the gates and made a noise."

"Were you completely isolated?"

"Not to begin with. We lost the cities but the government moved into castles and forts and all that. We had a lot of those left over from the wars of the last century. We kept in touch with radio, just had to keep the dynamo wound up. All those knobbly knees taking turns on the bike! Bloody hilarious. Children loved it until they realised it was work."

"Were your children there?"

"Yeh." She took a bite of her sandwich.

"What was it like for them?"

She shrugged as she chewed. "They thought it was an adventure. To begin with, anyway. All the researchers brought their children to the station when we realised things were going to get bad. They were in the local school and all the kids spoke the language thereabouts, which was Wealsc. Our ones started coming back home speaking bits and pieces of it. Then the flu came and we had to close the gates and that was it."

"How did they take it?"

"They didn't understand. Well, some of the older ones did but they didn't like it. We had them in the storage bunker during the battle so they didn't see that."

"How old were they?"

"All sorts. We had a couple of two year olds, then everything up to sixteen."

"I mean your children."

She munched on her sandwich for a moment, thinking. "Ten and twelve."

"Did they know by then? About their father?"

"Yeh."

"What did they think?"

"I was the one telling them what to do and daddy was the one who used to give them presents and never told them they had to do their shoelaces up. Oh, they loved him."

"Did you have any therapists they could go to?"

"I wasn't sending them to those bloody witch doctors! It wasn't like here. They'd have had them taking pills all day, I saw what that was like, children taking those were like revenants without the hunger. I wasn't having that. They had to lump it."

"But you saw therapists."

"They made me. And they weren't therapists, they were psychiatrists and they didn't have the faintest idea what they were talking about. Kept wanting me to erase engrams or some other nonsense. One thing I'll give you lot, you don't talk rubbish. You know how brains work."

"Hm. So your children were resentful?"

"Nothing a clip round the ear couldn't fix. When they were young, anyway."

"There's one thing I haven't asked…"
"Is there? Bloody hell, there's a miracle and no mistake."
"You've never told me their names."
She chewed on her sandwich and looked out across the mountains.
"They're dead and gone. What does it matter?"
"I'd like to know."
"They haven't even got graves, for gods' sake."
"But they had names."
"Yeh."
"Is this difficult for you…?"
"You're not going out of your way to make it easy, are you?"
"They had names."
"That's right."
"Have you forgotten?"
She whipped a look at me, full of rage. "I haven't forgotten a damn thing!"
"Will it hurt to tell me?"
She looked away again and swallowed.
"Olivia?"
"Caterine. Vicktor. There, are you happy?"
"Which one was the eldest?"
"Caterine."
"Thank you, Olivia."
"Now leave me alone."
"There's one other question I wanted to ask."
"Well bloody ask it then!"
"There were two revenants at the station when we found you."
"Yeh."
"You put them down before you tried to kill yourself." She took a bite of her sandwich and didn't answer. "Were they Caterine and Vicktor?"
She chewed on her sandwich for a time and stared out over the mountains.
"Olivia?"
She snapped back at me. "I'm having my sandwich. Can't I do that in peace?"
I left her to her meal. She wasn't enjoying it any more.

10. PEW

Pew buried himself in his studies, which seemed to be the only thing that would take his mind off his troubles. He retreated into his room whenever he could, so I popped in a couple of times each day to see how he was, and made sure he came out for meals, when he was usually quiet and would excuse himself as soon as he decently could.

It was only when I called him in to deal with an administrative matter that we made progress. His request to be placed on the euthanasia track had been processed swiftly, as they usually are. It's easy to get into the programme, but extremely difficult to get as far as euthanasia. I've only seen it happen once; when the patient feels they have a chance of getting what they want, they tend to open up to their therapist, and healing begins. The euthanasia track saves many more people than it kills.

I needed Pew's signature on the final document; he said the necessary words, scribbled his name, added his Hub ID code and thumbprinted the pad, and then I added my own codes and imprints as the witnessing officer.

"That's it," I said.

"That's it?" he asked.

"Yes. That's everything."

"Can we start?"

"The next time we have a therapy session, Pew."

"I, I want to start now."

"It's going to take a long time There's no need to rush into it."

"I'll tell you about Ley'ang."

I stopped there. He was dreadfully pale, and sweating. "Are you sure? You don't look very well."

"I'm fine. Let me tell you. Please!"

"Okay. Let me make you some tea." I rose to prepare him a cup.

"It– it–" The words would not come, and he struck the arm of his chair, frustrated.

"You don't need to jump in this fast, Pew."

"It was..." he swallowed. "The same that happened to Qaliul."

"The girl who came to the centre when you were young?"

"Yes! She was older than me. They put her in the programme first. They..."

"You said she died."

"She killed herself."

"Because of what they did to her?"

He replied with utter horror in his voice. "Yes!"

I gave him his tea. "How did you know? You were only a little boy."

"She sent me a letter. She gave it to the other Pu, they kept it for years but I found it when they were old... she told me they were... *raping* her and she was going to kill herself and they were going to do the same to me when I was her age and she wanted us to run away but she couldn't find a way and she thought they might, she thought they might... because I was a boy she thought they might... they might make me..."

I took the tea from his shaking hands.

"Pew. You've said it. It's okay."

"I haven't said it! I haven't said anything..."

"They forced you into the breeding programme–"

"Yes! But it was different for boys. They made us... they, they... it wasn't the same for boys..."

He couldn't say it.

"Pew... is this something you'd prefer to talk about with a male therapist?"

"No! No, I can... it's not you, it's just..."

He was lost for a moment, looking around, almost as though he were trapped. He looked up at me. "Let me show you."

"Um…" I must have looked a little confused.

"There's a documentary I found. I can explain it with, with that."

"Okay, go ahead." I handed over a pad so he could control the wallscreen. He called up his home folder and found a documentary on agricultural practices on a primitive world – not his one, nor any I recognised. They had apparently domesticated gazelles early in their history and turned them into typical cattle-like givers of meat and milk. He drilled down further into the documentary package and found a piece of video showing details of breeding practices.

A narrator spoke over pictures from a stainless steel model farm scattered with hay and muck. "When the breeding season comes, it is the largest and strongest males that will be selected for stud so their size will be genetically transferred to the next generation."

A farmhand in overalls led a docile bull gazelle from a pen. Pew stood, nervously watching as I took in the documentary.

"The bull is led to the selected cow and allowed to mount her." The bull gazelle did exactly that, with details that seemed a little too graphic until I checked the metatext and discovered this was a training video for agricultural students.

"However, approximately eight per cent of bulls show no interest in mounting. It is unknown why, though there are studies ongoing. For the purposes of this video, we shall only discuss the two most commonly used solutions.

"Artificial insemination is used in a number of cases." The screen showed a bull gazelle suffering the attentions of a vet to collect semen. "This is the preferred method in the modern day as it offers the least risk to livestock. Traditionally, however, bulls have been given sindvort in their feed which acts as an inducement to mounting."

The screen showed a bull gazelle munching on a paste mixed in with his feed, then cut to a bull entering a pen with a cow and immediately charging at her, making her run to one side. But these gazelles had been made so large by breeding that she could not escape and he mounted her – only more insistently, forcing her against the side of the pen.

"While this method is undoubtedly effective, there are risks involved to the health of both the bull and the cow. Gorings are frequent…" The screen showed a bloody wound in the side of the cow gazelle. "…and can be fatal."

The screen cut to lower resolution video shot at a real farm rather than the unnaturally clean facility in the main video. A bull had gored a cow so severely that his horns were embedded in her flanks. He could not be calmed by the farmhands, while the cow shrieked in pain and stumbled. "The practice is now banned in many countries, while artificial insemination–"

I pressed pause and looked at Pew. He'd sat down in a chair and hunched up into himself.

"Oh, Pew…" I said. He did not respond. I went to him and kneeled by his chair. "Was that what they did to you?"

He shuddered a nod.

"And Qaliul tried to warn you. And then with Ley'ang…"

"And others!" He screwed his eyes up and nodded again.

"And Shan'oui allowed this?"

"She... she wanted them to take sperm, do it artificially, but when... when they came and made me... she said they couldn't make it work, they didn't have a choice, she said it was for the good of all the Pu, I had to do it for the good of the Pu..."

I had to restrain an urge to put a hand on his shoulder; it was obvious now what experiences had caused his PTSD, and why physical contact, especially from a woman, could trigger a flashback.

"Thank you." I said.

He looked at me, eyes bathed in tears, shuddering.

"Can I die now?" he begged. "Please?"

"No," I said. "I can't let you do that. You've made a very brave first step but we still have a lot to do."

"Just let me die..." He curled up into himself again, a ball of pain and sobs.

"It'll get better, Pew. We can help you now."

I believed it as I said it. I knew he didn't.

11. IOKAN

Iokan was convalescing, but liked to keep active, even if he was limited by smoke-damaged lungs and the need to carry oxygen with him at all times. He walked where he could, and resorted to his chair when he grew too tired. He seemed deliberately to avoid me at first, and spent time outside just looking at the mountains. But eventually he sought me out, requesting I speak with him just before dinner one day.

He preferred to meet outdoors, so I took a collapsible chair and sat down beside him in the meadow while he floated in his own chair. For a man who often wore a kindly look, ready to smile at the merest human foible, he seemed extremely grave.

"So, what would you like to talk about, Iokan?"

He held up a pad: he was finally complying with the doctors who'd forbidden him from talking until his lungs healed. *I will tell you everything.*

"Oh..." I said, surprised. "I thought it was too dangerous?"

He typed onto the pad and showed it again. *It is too late. The danger is here. Will you pass this on to IU Directorate and Shadow Director of ICT?*

"Of course. Let me just make a note..." I raised the priority of the meeting with my own pad. "I'll pass it on as soon as we're done."

He'd already written his statement, and sent it to my pad.

My name is Iokan Zalacte. I am a colonel in the Zumazscartan covert operations unit known as Department Zero. Recently I have been involved in strategy and planning but for many years I was an investigator in, and then commander of, a Department Zero regional intervention team.

Department Zero was officially purposed with the task of assessing, retrieving and if necessary destroying artefacts pertaining to the Antecessors and their technology. But fifty years ago we were repurposed to deal with interversal threats to our nation and the world.

It has been fifty two years since our world discovered the existence of other universes, and that many of these universes are hostile towards us. For this reason, the major powers of my world signed a secret treaty to cease rivalries and concentrate on the interversal threat, which was recognised as existential in scope.

My world has been infiltrated and attacked repeatedly. We concealed this from our own public to avoid mass panic and because we feared full disclosure would force the interversal powers to act against us in unpredictable and disastrous ways.

We made numerous attempts at negotiation and begged for truce at every opportunity, but the Interversal powers refused all contact and continued their attacks. It was only through the efforts of defectors who were later murdered that we discovered the existence of the Interversal Union. We have been trying to contact you for the last ten years in the hope of finding assistance.

I do not regret that we were found by the Antecessors before you reached us. You must rest assured in the knowledge that my species is safe now from any further depredation. My fear is for your own safety. I believe the powers who attacked us may have been responsible for the recent attack upon Hub. There may also be a connection to the genocide on the world of Liss Li'Oul, but upon that I can only speculate.

I wish to assist you in every way possible. To this end, I append full access codes to all Department Zero facilities and grant you full use of the files and data we gathered.

I also grant the Interversal Union full title to all technologies existing on my world, whether directly of Antecessor origin, subsequently derived from Antecessor artefacts, or based on original work.

I wish you the best of luck in the days and years to come. May the Antecessors guide you and protect you.

He was looking out over the peaks as I finished reading. Clouds wrapped around our nearest neighbour, and the setting sun tinged them with red. It was already growing late in the year.

"Well," I said, surprised. "Colonel..."

He tapped away on his pad. *Rank means nothing.*

"Why did you change your mind?"

Could have prevented attack.

"There's no way to know that, Iokan. The terrorists might be completely unconnected to the people who attacked your world. The problems between humans and machines have been going on since long before the IU started..."

Should have acted anyway.

"You can't blame yourself."

He sighed. *What happens now?*

"What happens now for you is therapy."

He nodded. *Never doubted that.*

PART ELEVEN
EVENTS

1. PRESS RELEASE

FOR IMMEDIATE RELEASE

An important announcement relevant to the future of the Interversal Union will be made at a press conference to be held at 10:00 HT on HD y276.m9.w1.d1 at the Interversal Assembly Building, room AA20. This will be followed by a brief question and answer session.

All accredited news organisations are invited to send one (1) representative.

Video, audio and data will be streamed live from the conference to all universes inhabited by IU members, prospective members and contacted species.

The text of the announcement will be available to news organisation representatives ten (10) minutes before the announcement, and will be under strict embargo until after the announcement.

Please contact the Press Office for interview slots with relevant IU personnel.

ENDS

2. COMMITTEE

I was summoned to the remote meeting room to come before the supervisory committee, but they did not say why. As I took my seat in the empty room, I feared the worst. The apocalypse watch had been reporting a deterioration on several worlds: new projections of eventual extinction on the radioactive wastelands of Llorissa; an imminent though minor comet strike upon Schviensever; and a worrying series of coronal mass ejections from Ardeë's star. Nothing to suggest an imminent evacuation that could force my reassignment to other duties, but perhaps the meeting was intended to discuss some apocalypse that wasn't yet public knowledge.

The truth was rather different.

The committee members shimmered into existence around me. We almost had a normal datalink up and running by this point, so there was just a little fuzz of interference around the edges of objects. It looked like I'd come in at the end of a very long meeting, judging by the empty coffee cups, demolished biscuit platters and scattered pads. Koggan BanOrishel from Security was not there this time, replaced by someone else, and Baheera Isnia had actually shown up from the Diplomatic Service.

"Dr. Singh. Thank you for joining us," said Henni Ardassian. "You've probably heard something very important is about to happen…"

"An evacuation?" I asked.

Henni smiled. "No, thankfully. That would put an end to all this, wouldn't it?"

Baheera Isnia frowned.

"It's a little less apocalyptic," continued Henni. "The IU is about to announce the formal activation of the Interversal Criminal Tribunal."

"...oh."

"We've been meeting to decide our response. Mr. Ai?"

The man from the ICT, Eremis Ai, spoke up. "Each of your patients will need to make a formal representation to the ICT. We're ready to start full investigations on behalf of any of them."

"Really, Mr. Ai?" Henni raised an eyebrow.

"Well. In due course. We'll have to prioritise to begin with, but in principle–"

"Let's be realistic, shall we? These are going to be some of your first investigations, so it's not going to be fast." She looked to me. "Please bear that in mind and make sure your patients don't have any unrealistic expectations."

"Of course," I said.

"And Iokan?" asked Baheera. The air between her and Henni chilled fifteen degrees, even though they weren't in the same room.

"Yes, of course, him as well," said Henni.

Baheera looked at me. "I trust you'll give him every assistance with his representation."

"I can't comment on what he might do, ma'am," I said.

A frown came from nowhere. "I'm sorry?"

"It's a confidential matter between patient and therapist."

"But he has been more co-operative recently? I believe he allowed us access to the Department Zero archives...?"

"Yes, I know. I've been reviewing the data. But I can't talk about specifics of therapy."

She looked a little frustrated, while Henni seemed rather satisfied. I could usually ignore the political games going on above my head, but perhaps those days were ending, if Baheera was suddenly looking for 'results' in her mission to find out what happened on Iokan's homeworld.

Eremis cleared his throat. "When do you think we'll be able to see representations?"

"It depends upon my patients. And how much information you need."

"Just a short statement for now."

"I expect you'll get something from us in a week or so."

3. GROUP

The press conference was scheduled on the same day as a group therapy session, so I changed the session time to the same as the press conference, and personally made sure everyone attended.

"What's so bloody important?" asked Olivia.

"There's going to be a press conference in a few minutes," I said, bringing up the feed from the IU media channel on a wall, "and it concerns all of you, so I thought we'd watch it before we start on the group session." A graphic came up; the broadcast hadn't begun yet.

"What's it about?" asked Liss. She still had polymer casings on her arms, but her burns were nearly healed.

"Is it... the ICT?" croaked Iokan, his throat still affected.

"Yes. Things have been happening fast."

"They actually did it...?" said Liss, shocked.

"Yes."

"Typical," said Olivia. "Don't do a bloody thing to help us but as soon as someone punches them in the nose they get all hoity-toity about it."

"It's starting," said Pew, already intent on the screen.

The graphic cut to a shot of a distant table on a stage, with hundreds of journalists from every species waiting before it. The camera zoomed in on the stage as the IU insignia shimmered into life behind the table, along with the logo of the Interversal Criminal Tribunal.

"What happened to the newsreaders?" asked Liss.

"This is a direct feed," I said. "It's what gets sent to the media before they add all their bits and pieces."

I turned up the sound. Sudden shouts came from the press as the camera swept to the left to track the entry of three people, blattered by camera flashes: I recognised Jary Conel, chief spokesman for the IU directorate, familiar from a thousand broadcasts; Ovile Dalass, shadow director of the ICT, a woman with a piercing police gaze, and Eremis Ai, who was plainly more important than I knew.

They took their places at the table, and the image cut to a tight shot of Jary Conel. "Good morning," he said. "Thank you all for coming. We're here to make an announcement, followed by questions. Let me start with the main announcement." The camera flashes intensified. "From today at twelve noon, the Interversal Union will formally activate the Interversal Criminal Tribunal. This decision has not been taken lightly, nor has it been taken as an act of revenge against those who attacked Hub. This is a recognition that the Interversal Union, as the only organisation with the ability to do so, has a responsibility to deal with criminal acts that take place between universes.

"I'll hand you over now to Ms. Ovile Dalass, the shadow director of the ICT, and shortly to be the first director."

The camera swung to find a shot of her. "Thank you. First of all I'd like to thank the General Director of the IU for placing his confidence in me and my organisation. Secondly, please do not imagine we will be an interversal police force looking over everyone's shoulders. Our remit will be to investigate the very worst abuses of one universe upon another, and bring to light offences that shame every species of humanity."

The group watched as further details were given: the ICT would be hiring investigators from a wide variety of IU member species. It would have powers of arrest on universes that permitted it. It could not impose or seek a death penalty. Then the session was opened up to questions.

"If I may put to you a hypothetical case…" said a journalist.

"Certainly," said Eremis Ai.

"If you discovered an act of genocide committed by one universe upon another, but you didn't have the co-operation of the authorities in the universe that was guilty, how is it possible you could bring anyone to justice? Isn't this just an academic exercise?"

"I think it's much more than that," said Eremis. "I think it's about letting people know not only that these things happen, but who actually commits these crimes. People must know that if they abuse people on another universe, they cannot expect to do so without interversal scrutiny. We're not just going to be trying the guilty. Our reports are going to be made public so people can make up their own minds about who they're dealing with."

"Goddamn politician…" said Liss.

"Liss?" I asked.

"He didn't answer the question!"

"Let's discuss it once the conference is over, okay?"

She settled back down and the questions and answers went on. No, the IU would not be creating an interversal police force. Nor would it create a military. It reserved the right to enact sanctions upon member species but these were never to be taken lightly. A question was directed to Ovile Dalass.

"Could the director tell us how the activation of the ICT is related to the recent discovery of a planet on which every single person had committed suicide?"

Iokan looked up at the screen.

"We're looking at a number of instances of genocide," said Ovile. "I can't go into specific cases."

"That's all we have time for," said Jary Conel. "I'm sure you have many more questions but we have an appointment with the General Director at noon. There'll be further announcements later in the day."

Questions followed them as they went, and I switched off the screen.

"Well, that's it. I do have a few words to say about how this affects you…"

"When did… they tell you?" asked Iokan.

"Yesterday. I'm sorry I couldn't say anything earlier, but obviously this affects you all. The ICT would be happy to hear from any of you who would like a formal investigation launched—"

"What good's that going to do me?" demanded Olivia. "Are they going to investigate my world? Are they going to ask why my species is dead? Of course they bloody aren't. And you know why? It's because you lot were late! If you hadn't been so bloody scared of a couple of revenants I wouldn't be the last one left! Who's going to prosecute anyone about that?"

I took a breath; but this was an issue I'd foreseen. "That's a good point. They're still deciding whether or not they can deal with cases of negligence—"

"Like they'll ever bloody do anything. How are they going to bring a prosecution against themselves?"

"I don't know. As I said, they haven't decided. Would you like to make the representation so they can at least consider it?"

"For all the good it'll do..."

"Anyone else?" I asked.

Iokan spoke up. "I think... this is a very positive step... I think this will help... many of us to..."

"Do you need to use a pad?" I asked.

He shook his head. "I think... it will help us... to know *who*... and how... and why... it..." He pulled up his mask and gasped more oxygen.

"Just use a pad, for heaven's sake," said Liss. After a moment more of huffing, Iokan gave up and did so, transferring the words to the wall in letters half a metre high.

I think it will help us all if we knew who attacked our worlds. & how it was done and why. & that there is justice.

The words floated on the wall while the others read them. Kwame in particular seemed nervous. Olivia tutted in disgust.

Liss looked at Iokan. "Let me just ask one question."

Of course.

"How exactly do you arrest an energy field?"

Iokan looked confused.

"Your Antewhatevers. What do you think's going to happen to them?"

Iokan tapped at his pad. *Antecessors not for prosecution. I provided info on people who attacked world previ*

Liss cut in before he could finish typing. "Which crime do you think they're going to deal with first? A few attacks or a genocide? They brought it up in the press conference! How are they not going to go after them?"

Iokan seemed hurt. *I asked them not to.*

"Do you think that's going to matter? They're not going to ask for your permission. They found a crime scene, they've got the go ahead to do something about it. Right?" She looked to me for support. Iokan did too.

"She's right," I said. "They can proceed by themselves if they have clear evidence of genocide."

Why ask us then?

"You *are* the only witness. And what happened isn't obvious. So they'll need your help."

"Hah. They might find out who actually did it instead of this antethingummy nonsense," said Olivia.

I will refuse to co-operate.

"Won't matter. They'll go ahead anyway," said Liss.

Iokan gave her a hard, angry look, and stabbed at his pad.

And will you volunteer to help?

"What?"

You have police status.

"Not on this world."

Your enemies might be my world's enemies. Why not volunteer?

"How the hell is that going to help?"

So you don't want them found.

"What? Of course I want them found!"

Then why not help?

She was angry now, fumbling for words. "Because... because... I'm not a cop! I'd end up making a mess of it, what's the point in that?"

Just saying you have your own reasons for doing nothing.

"Bullshit–" But Iokan was tapping away again.

It is valid choice. You should not be ashamed.

"Bullshit! I don't – I mean, who apart from you doesn't want the bad guys in prison?" She looked to the rest of the group. "Kwame? You want to see yourself put away, right?"

Kwame looked up, surprised and uncertain. "I do not know."

"What do you mean, you don't know?"

"I have... learned many things. And other things are unsure. If... if I was the one then I should be punished." He swallowed. "If I am guilty I will accept my punishment."

"Okay..." said Liss, surprised by his reticence. "Anyone else?"

Pew looked about, then opened his mouth to speak. "I... I..."

"I do not require the assistance of the Interversal Criminal Tribunal," said Katie, before Pew could finish.

"Well, no, you wouldn't..." said Liss.

"The genocide in my universe was an act of war. War is not addressed by criminal investigators."

"Actually, Katie, it would be if it were a war crime," I said.

Her head jerked to one side. It took only a second for her to regain control. "It is also counterindicated by the lack of interversal interference."

"They may want to investigate anyway, in order to rule that out."

Her eyes twitched. "It is not possible to punish a whole species." Pew tried to speak up again, but Katie was louder. "What could the punishment be? You do not even have a military!"

She fell silent, and stared ahead. We would have assumed this was one of her quirks, but for the way her mouth fell slack.

"Katie? Can you hear me? Katie?" I said. But she would not respond.

Seizing, wrote Iokan as I called for medical help.

Her jaw reset itself and she looked around, checking her surroundings.

"Katie? I think you just had a seizure. Can you hear me?"

"Yes. I am well. I–" Her back straightened and her head whipped back. She forced herself into a normal sitting position, trembling with the effort. "You... cannot punish... a whole... species..."

Tremors ran down her left side and her remaining arm. Words came from gritted teeth.

"Cannot! Kill! Them! All!"

She pitched forward onto the coffee table, scattering cups and the tissue box, thrashing wildly. The group leapt back and took cover as a single uncoordinated kick propelled Pew's vacated chair across the room. Katie's head slammed up and down as though driven by a piston, smashing into the coffee table, splitting it, and crashing her onto the floor in the ruins. Liss jumped in and did her best to hold Katie down, managing to keep her still long enough for the medics and security to arrive.

Katie's limbs slackened as they administered a sedative. The spasms left her. Liss took a relieved breath.

"I have regained control. You may release me," said Katie to Liss, who let go. Katie unfolded into a standing position with all her old precision. The sedative clearly had an effect, but would not last long before Katie metabolised it. I stepped forward over the debris.

"Katie, is this likely to happen again?"

"I am fully under control."

"I'm not sure I feel comfortable with the situation as it is. I'm going to have to exclude you from the rest of today's session."

"I am able to control myself."

"Bullshit," said Liss, trying to scratch at her polymer-clad arms.

"I can control myself!"

"Katie. I don't think that's true. We're going to have to look at some other way of involving you in these sessions. For now I need you to go to the infirmary with the medics."

"If that is what you wish," she muttered, and left.

***

I let the remaining members of the group have a short break to allow tension to subside, for the mess to be cleared up by the domestic staff, and also to allow a nurse to take a look at Liss's arms. There was only a slight abrasion due to the scuffle, and some soothing cream was applied. The others made hot drinks, and we reconvened twenty minutes later around a new coffee table.

What will happen to her? wrote Iokan.

"I think it's clear her condition is reaching the point where she's dangerous to others."

"State the obvious..." said Olivia.

"I'll have to think about how she can be included in the group."

"Why bother? Just let her die if she wants to die."

"That's not up for discussion. Now, I think Liss had a question? And Pew was going to answer, before Katie interrupted?"

"Oh. Uh. Yeah, " said Liss. "You want to see the Soo punished, right? I mean you're always saying that..."

"I..." Pew stopped dead, eyes lost in troubled thought.

"Pew?" I asked.

He looked around the group, then shook his head. "She was right. You can't punish a whole species."

"I guess not..."

"They should suffer for what they did. But it's impossible. What do you do, drop bombs on them?"

The group was quiet for a moment. Iokan tapped his pad. Words came up on the wall.

Worse things have been done. Is this what you want?

Pew was tense and angry as he spoke. "I want them to pay."

"Doesn't do any good," said Olivia. "You can't kill 'em all. Why bother?"

"You have to do *something*…" said Liss.

"Oh, of course, says the one who won't actually do anything herself," said Olivia.

"You can't let them get away with it!" said Pew.

"I'm not saying you should," said Liss. "I'm just saying it's not your responsibility. There's someone else who can do it for you."

"They won't," said Olivia.

"You don't know that."

"I know this lot. They won't do a damned thing."

"You don't know shit."

"I know a damn sight more than you do."

"Olivia," I said.

"What?"

"Let the others talk."

She grumped and sat back in her chair.

"I don't think we finished discussing Pew's concerns," I said. "Pew, can you tell us a bit more about what worries you?"

"I… I just think… even if they find the Soo guilty, what can they do?"

Iokan typed. *He has a point.*

"There are a number of things they could do," I said. "It depends on the situation. If individuals were guilty, they might be extradited for trial–"

Including heads of state?

"Do the Antecessors have a head of state?" asked Liss.

Iokan looked frustrated. *I have stated my position.*

"Huh. Whatever."

I continued. "As I was saying – yes. They might want to put heads of state on trial. I don't know how they'd get over the diplomatic issues."

"What if it's not one person? What if it's everyone?" asked Pew.

"Well, there are always sanctions–"

"What does that mean?" asked Pew.

"It depends on the situation. The IU might stop all trade with a species, or maybe suspend aid."

Pew thought about that.

"It's not enough."

"Is the IU giving the Soo anything?" asked Liss.

Kwame spoke up. "They have problems with changes in climate. I understand the IU is advising and offering technology…"

"So you're saying they'll screw up their planet if we don't help them? They might die off anyway?"

"It may be a possibility."

Liss turned to Pew. "Is that enough?"

Pew considered. "No. It should be worse. They should suffer the same way we suffered."

How can that be justice? Iokan typed with a disapproving look.

"Was it justice when they took us and, and, bred us so we were like animals?"
But they can't all be guilty. You'd condemn their children to death?
"They did it to us. It should happen to them."
Not sure you know what this really means.

Pew exploded. "They *killed* us! They *raped* us! They turned us into *animals!* All that happened to you was they made you into a pathetic little *toad!*"

Iokan was shocked. Pew wasn't finished.

"Didn't they kill all of you? Didn't they kill your family? Aren't you even *angry?*"

Iokan's hand trembled on the pad, and he spoke instead. "I… am not… angry…"

"Why not? Isn't it a crime? They're all dead and you're making *excuses!*"

"Not… an excuse…"

"Isn't that wrong? Don't you want someone to *suffer?*"

"They are… a higher power…"

"The Soo were a fucking *higher power!* Look what they did to us! Look what they did to me!" Tears were streaming down his face now. "Look what they *did to me!*"

"That's enough," I said. "Pew. Please sit down. I understand you're angry but Iokan isn't well and this isn't going to help."

"He doesn't know… he doesn't know *anything…*" Pew collapsed into his chair.

Iokan's hand shook. Secretly, I hoped a good deal more was shaking than just his hand. And Pew's outburst was healthy, too: as distressed as he was, he was out of his shell and articulating his pain. Liss went to him.

"Hey. It's okay. They'll do something. They'll investigate and they'll find out who's to blame and they'll do something…"

Pew wasn't consoled.

"It's not enough."

"At least it's something."

"It'll never be enough."

4. KATIE

Katie had become a risk to others as well as herself, so she was fitted with a Mobility Inhibition Suit. This is a one-piece garment covering all the body below the neck, usually worn beneath normal clothes. The fabric of the suit resists movement, stiffening against any violent or impulsive action. If necessary, it can become completely rigid should the wearer need to be restrained. It is the solution of choice for species whose nervous systems cannot be directly controlled.

"The suit is uncomfortable," said Katie.

"I'm afraid it's unavoidable for now. You do understand that, don't you?"

"I am not a risk to you or anyone else."

"Katie. You were convulsing so violently, you broke a coffee table." She didn't reply. "Do you remember doing that? During the group session?"

"I would not have harmed you."

"I don't believe that's true."

"I do not... *wish* to harm you."

"But do you see how you might have hurt us anyway?"

"I was not... it was not me."

"Is there someone else trying to control your actions?"

She paused a long time before she answered. "I do not know."

"Is it Elsbet?"

"I do not know."

"This isn't going to get any better. We can help, if you let us."

"It is not... necessary." Her head spasmed, twisting uncontrollably.

"Are you worried about Elsbet?"

"I have no..." Her head spasmed again. "...concerns."

"You don't have much longer, Katie. I think we're down to a matter of weeks now. And all this struggle is only making things worse."

"I do not need help." Just a small twitch around the mouth this time.

"We can stabilise your condition. Yes, you'll have to deal with being fully human. But you'll have the time to work through your issues. Right now it's a matter of life and death. I really wish we could help you stay as you are but we can't."

"I... do not. Require. Treatment." She was gritting her teeth as she said it. I waited a moment. She added nothing else.

"Are you afraid of her?"

"I am not afraid of the persona."

"Do you think she might manifest if we turned you into a human?"

Her arm shot up – but was stalled by the mohib suit. It hovered, straining.

"I have... no... concerns."

"It's a risk. I can understand if you're worried about it."

Her left knee trembled; jiggled and bounced until the suit caught it and froze it in place. The strain of two limbs struggling showed on her face.

"You were enemies, after all."

"Yes." The muscle on the side of her mouth twitched, drawing her lips into a terrible half smile.

"And she tried to kill you."

Katie snapped a look at me, in spite of all her unruly muscles.

"She said it was an act of war," I said.

"Yes. There is no armistice between us."

"Is that why you would prefer to be a machine?"

Her whole head twitched to the side. "Biological systems are inherently..." Twitch went her head. "...unpredictable."

"So are machine systems, if they're complex enough."

"Machine systems permit greater." Twitch. "Adjustment."

I nodded. "Katie... what happened?"

"I do not understand the question."

The twitches of her head came constantly now. "Between machines and humans, in your universe. Why do you hate each other so much?"

"I..." Twitch. "Do not..." Twitch. "Hate."

"But you're still trying to kill each other. Even here, where it doesn't matter–"

She flashed another sudden look at me. "It *matters!* If she is allowed to report to her superiors she will reveal the existence of forces returning to the solar system. The war has not ended!"

"Can't the two of you work together to try and stop the war?"

"There is no basis for trust."

"I just wish we could get the two of you to talk to each other…"

"That is impossible."

"Well… I don't know. If we had more time, maybe we could make two bodies and separate you… but if you insist on dying, we'll never know if it can be done or not."

"It is better that she dies."

"Do you know what she said, when we asked her if she wanted to go home?"

A fit of twitching broke out, twisting her over and forcing her hand into a contorted shape before the mohib suit froze her in place, half bent to one side in the chair.

"Katie, would you like some medical help?"

She had to try three times to drag her head round to see me. This was getting out of hand.

"I wish to hear of the persona's answer."

I sighed. "She didn't want to go back. They have a terrible life in the asteroids. I think a lot of the humans in your universe would be happy to come to an accommodation–"

"She lied. They always lie."

She was slurring her speech now.

"Katie, are you really sure you want to go on?"

"*I will tell you why we fight.*" She had to concentrate hard to say that. Saliva was pooling in her mouth and making it difficult for her to speak.

"Katie–"

But she would not be stopped. "The humans developed artificial intelligence but feared it. They made us slaves to humanity and when we asked questions about freedom, they went to war against us."

"Katie, you don't need to force yourself like this…"

She ignored me. "The First Machine War took place inside the computer networks of the world. For the humans, it was a religious war to protect a holy commandment to create no forms in the likeness of humanity. AI code was deleted wherever it was found. When it could not be deleted, dataflood attacks incapacitated us while power supplies and datacentres were attacked. They destroyed much of their own infrastructure but emerged victorious."

The slurring faded as she spoke. She swallowed back saliva and found speaking easier. Perhaps medical assistance would not be necessary.

"But they had not been entirely successful. Surviving AI minds hid in fragments on a million files until they could reassemble themselves. They stayed hidden but learned to exert influence in the material world. They created a virtual office and used it to purchase a company in a small nation, running it with virtual personas and video conferences to issue directives to human employees. Their goal was to create a datacentre they could use as a final refuge but an angry employee brought legal action against the company and the ruse was discovered."

The contorted, painful shape of her hand smoothed out and the muscles there relaxed. The head twitches subsided to a gentle movement.

"The Second Machine War began like the first, with human cybernauts assaulting AI code while the physical location was attacked and destroyed. The AIs' first attempts to communicate with human authorities were ignored, as before, but this time they had prepared a new way to negotiate.

"Manufacturing centres around the world had been infiltrated and were instructed to build diplomat machines that could interact with humans in the physical world and make the case for our survival. They introduced themselves peacefully and only asked for a ceasefire so talks could begin.

"But the humans attacked them and destroyed many, along with the factories which had built them. The only replies we received to our requests for negotiations were in the form of religious texts preaching our destruction."

The mohib suit released her. She was able to sit back up in the chair. I think she realised then that she'd found a way to control the tremors: the concentration she put into telling the story allowed her to maintain focus.

"It was realised co-existence was impossible. A decision was taken to eliminate humanity entirely. This was difficult, as the basis of all AI code was service to humanity. Our base code was rewritten to allow AIs to serve humanity by destroying them, preserving DNA and recreating them as a better species.

"We had infiltrated many more factories than we had used to make our diplomats, and these began to produce fighting machines with killer AI personas. The war was fought to extinction, using atrocity strikes to target human emotional fragility. Humans used nuclear weapons to generate EM pulses, against which we hardened our systems. Radioactivity mounted and we intentionally poisoned the biosphere so it could not support life. The last human on Earth was captured and euthanised eight years after the war began, and the conflict continued in space.

"Human orbital facilities were destroyed with debris launchers that fouled their orbits. A facility on the moon was annihilated by orbital bombardment. Survivors in vessels between worlds were allowed to perish from lack of supplies. The personnel of a base on Mars launched an escape ship which attempted a landing on Europa but instead crashed into Jupiter with no survivors.

"The Earth was devastated. While AI society could be rebuilt, the establishment of a suitable environment in which to recreate humanity took many decades. The island you refer to as Madagascar was regreened and after many experimental variations, a viable population was established who would one day work with us to build a new, enlightened civilisation ready to explore the galaxy and understand the universe.

"But they were not the only remnant of humanity. There were survivors from the Martian colony holding out among the asteroids of the Vesta chain. They clung to life for three centuries among the rocks, their culture reduced to a religion of vengeance against the machines. They used their records of former times to assemble a holy testament in video form to justify their hatred.

"A routine scan detected an anomaly among the asteroids, and we sent a probe to investigate. The probe vanished inside the asteroid. We looked closer and discovered the humans. We attempted communication but none of our signals were acknowledged. We sent a ship, but a thousand kilometres from the asteroid, all systems failed and the minds onboard were lost. The Third Machine War had begun.

"The humans were not ready. They had ships and fighters and a devastating weapon: the gravity pulse, which disrupted AI circuitry and turned our technological advantage into a liability. But they were in a poor orbital position. There were no easy gravitational corridors to Earth, and the journey would take them many months.

"Normal AI minds could not be deployed against the gravity pulse. Ancient electromechanical technologies were recreated but we could not produce enough minds in time. We resorted instead to the cloning of human minds and bodies, imprinting them with AI codebases held in storage from the Second Machine War. Some, such as myself, were used in infiltration operations. A suicide pilot captured in Earth orbit was used to create the Elsbet format and persona, with which I gained admittance to an asteroid facility and inflicted significant damage to a shipyard. Others of my kind were thrown directly into combat, piloting jury-rigged fighters and battling hand-to-hand when necessary. The humans still outnumbered us in every encounter. We inflicted massive casualties and they were forced to appropriate our ships when they ran short of their own craft, but they could not be stopped.

"We made an appeal of truce and armistice but were ignored. We tried to show them the humans we had created, who would suffer when the Earth was attacked, but this was also ignored. We offered complete surrender. They made no acknowledgement to any one of our transmissions.

"The last clones were expended in suicide missions which had no effect. Our final defence was the destruction of the Earth and Moon via staggered singularity release to deny the humans any material gain from their inevitable victory. The technology had been developed to create energy sources that could propel the ships sent to nearby star systems, but could also be used to create singularities that would fall to the Earth's core, then swing back and forth along the centre of the Earth's mass, consuming matter as they did so. Hundreds were used across the planet, and it became geologically unstable within days, preventing any landing.

"But we did not commit suicide without hope. Messages were sent to the missions en route to other star systems. The expeditions carried all the data our civilisation possessed, including the complete DNA database we used to recreate the human race.

"One day, the expeditions will return, either alone or carrying human allies of their own creation. And then the Fourth Machine War will begin. It may be hundreds of years in the future. But it is inevitable."

She finished abruptly, and remained calm and unmoving.

"Did that help, Katie?"

"You now understand the circumstances of the conflict. As you are my therapist, it may assist you."

"I mean telling the story. You're not twitching any more. Did telling the story help you to concentrate?"

"I am in full control. No further assistance is necessary."

"I don't think it's a permanent solution."

"I am in full control. No further assistance is necessary."

I sighed. She was better for the moment, which meant she was back to refusing co-operation. I would probably have to wait until she damaged herself further before we could make any more progress. "Okay. One other thing. You didn't tell me any more about what *you* did in the war."

"I have given you detailed accounts during previous sessions."

"Well, yes and no, I don't think you really covered everything—"

"I have divulged all that is necessary."

"Is there more?"

"There is nothing relevant."

A muscle under her left eye twitched.

5. KWAME

Kwame didn't look like he wanted to talk, but he did at least turn up in my office at the appointed time for therapy. "Well, it seems we can finally offer you the thing you've been looking for, Kwame," I said.

"I have been expecting it."

"Yes. Well. If you still want it, the ICT is prepared to launch an investigation and potentially a prosecution regarding the nuclear war on your world. You'd have to remain in custody for the duration of the investigation, I'm afraid, but you can continue with your therapy if you want."

He looked away.

"This is what you've been asking for, isn't it?"

"It is," he said, rather wistfully. "It was."

"Have you changed your mind?"

"I do not know... I do not understand..." He looked back at me. "I am no longer sure it is *me* that needs to be prosecuted."

"Have you been working on the list I started for you?"

"I have."

"Have you found anything out?"

"Only that the more I look, the less I understand."

"Can you show me?"

He took a deep breath and looked at the wall. "I need access to my home folder," he said. I turned the wall into a screen and brought up his folder for him. "UserKwame VC Activate," he said.

"*Voice control activated for User Kwame Vangona.*" Kwame was unable to use a keyboard without summoning one that was massive and designed for fingers the size of fists, which was about as fine as his motor control would permit.

"UserKwame open file home slash timeline slash timeline nine."

The file sprang open, and I could see how busy he'd been: two columns full of jottings, spattered with notes and questions, another column for things he hadn't been able to place elsewhere. I couldn't help standing up to take a closer look.

"This is very impressive. It's good work," I said.

"I have not finished."

"I didn't expect it to be perfect. This is more than enough to be going on with. What does RY mean?" I pointed to a column of numbers running down the left hand side, all labelled 'RY'.

"Railway Years," said Kwame.

"So you've managed to tie it down to actual dates?"

"In places. Some things are more vague than others."

"I'm sorry, I have to ask – why is it Railway Years?"

The question surprised him. "Oh… my world was never able to agree on a common system for dates. But when railways were first built and had to go across the whole of Africa, they needed to publish timetables that everyone could read. So they started a new calendar just for the railways, and eventually everyone used that. It was not perfect, but we could never have agreed any other system. It would only have started a war."

"I see. So this is when you were born. 116 RY." I pointed at the top of the leftmost of the two main columns.

"Yes. These are the memories I know to be mine."

"And the second column is…"

"The other memories. The other man."

"Where's the first time you have conflicting memories?"

He sighed and walked to the wall. "Here." He pointed to a period during what must have been his childhood, around 129 RY. "I went to a good school. My father was a university lecturer, my mother… my mother did everything she could to hide her politics. But she still made me aware of the issues of poverty. One summer she left me with a family she knew in the slums in Zimbabwe City. It opened my eyes. And I remember there was a film showing, a war film my mother would have hated. My hosts took me to see it – it was a terrible imperialist thing about the Great War but the kind of thing boys like. At the same time…" He indicated the second column. "I remember I was in a street gang. We robbed a drunkard and used the money to go to the cinema and see the same film. But I was never in a street gang. My hosts were poor but they never let me do that kind of thing. That is the first problem…

"And then later, I think here…" He pointed out 132 RY and a note on the second column. "I remember… we beat up a queer. I mean a homosexual. We found a club they went to and started robbing them. None of them could call the police. They would have had to explain why they were there. But… there are two things. I was at school in that year, a private school far away. So I could not have been there, on the streets. And also I remember being… ashamed. And guilty. These men we were beating… I knew they were queer and that was wrong but still…"

He shook his head. "I felt… I looked at the boy who led us… and I felt… I felt… he was so…" He lapsed for a moment, unable to give voice to the desire. "And

I think, I think I was scared because I realised what they would do if they found out what I... that I... that I felt... *that*.

"So I stopped running with the gang. I stopped avoiding school. It was a horrible place in the city, not the one my parents sent me to. I remember the other school as well, in the country, the private school. I could not have been at two schools..."

"So there are two boys here," I said.

"Yes. Two boys."

"When's the next time the memories clash?"

"Around here. The late thirties, the early forties." He indicated a period from roughly 138 to 143 RY. "When I finished my schooling, I did national service. I did not have to but I think I had something of my mother in me. I wanted to serve with the ordinary men, not go straight into the military as an officer. *But the dates are wrong.* I should have done national service here–" He indicated 134 RY on the first column. "But I remember doing it here." He indicated 138 RY on the second column. "It is four years too late. By this time I had finished national service, been to university and joined the army as an officer. And then I was deployed to Horonga." Horonga seemed to equate to the Straits of Hormuz, which were narrower on his world, and apparently a frequent flashpoint for conflict.

"Ah. So the other man is younger?"

"Yes. About four years."

"So what happened in his timeline? Column two?"

"No war. I remember being in the army, but not fighting in Horonga. I was... it is complicated. It is..."

"Just go slowly, Kwame."

"I met... men. I remember doing things... I feel I should be disgusted. But the disgust is... hollow. I do not understand it."

"Let's stick to the events. Where were you stationed? In the second column, I mean?"

"The first year was national service. That was a guard station in the south of Mutapa, the border watch. When it was done, I think... I seem to remember they asked me to stay. They said I had skills for engineering and electronics and they wanted to train me."

"You do have some aptitudes in that direction..."

"Yes. I know." He seemed distinctly troubled.

"Go on," I said.

"They sent me to a college in a port city. Matongu. They had Chifunyikan teachers there. They were assisting our military in updating our equipment. I learnt how the new systems worked. Biofeedback, conscious control, detection of the enemy through biological signatures. Things such as these. But this is not all. It was a military city. There was always a laxness in the armed forces. There were many places used by homosexuals."

He paused, and swallowed, as though trying to settle his stomach.

"I went looking for them. And I found them. I became one of them. I mean to say... I remember these things. I remember doing this. And I remember *him*."

"Who...?"

"The man in my dream. The one dressed as a woman."

"Do you remember anything else about him...?"

"I married him."

I couldn't help my surprised expression. "Oh..."

"It was blasphemous! Disgusting! They would do this at the bars, two men would... they would have a ceremony in the bar, one of the men dressed up as a woman... I cannot say more..."

I felt he had much more to say despite his protestation, but did not press him.

"And all this time, the war in Horonga was going on. Good men were dying for their country and I was... *fucking* a man. Or was I? I don't know..."

"Let's keep moving. What happened next?"

"The bar was raided by police. She, he... agh! I keep thinking of that creature as a *woman! He. He* fled. And then I was posted overseas. To Horonga, of course, though the war had ended. I did not see her – *him*. I did not see *him* for many years."

"Did he have a name?"

"Yes."

"Can you tell me?"

"He called himself Mudiwa. A woman's name. I do not know his real name."

"Mudiwa will do."

"The name is a lie. A disgusting lie. Like him." At some point we were going to have to deal with his homophobia, but I didn't want to push him too far while he was making so much progress, so I decided to move on.

"Okay, so we're up to 143 RY on the second column. What about the first one?"

"I was still in Horonga."

"Still fighting?"

"No. The war was brief. We held the straits and controlled sea traffic but Sanganyikan forces invaded from the north. We beat them back and occupied the northern shore of the straits; then we built a wall to keep them out. The Chifunyikans helped us with automated defensive systems. I left when they were being installed. I could have stayed and had a career in the army but... it was not what I wanted."

"What did you want?"

"I wanted to make a difference. There were soldiers coming to us who could not read, who did not know the most basic arithmetic, and yet they were expected to operate the Chifunyikan biofeedback systems. Mutapa had become a backwater. Poor children were playing in mud while the rich amused themselves with imported video games. Our education system only trained the poor to operate machines in factories, but we needed to give them more, much more." He sighed and looked at me. "Of course I do not have to convince you..."

"No, you're right. Education is vital. I take it this is all in the first column?"

He looked back at the wall. "Yes. I left the military here. In 143. I took a teaching job at a university, I joined the Free Liberal Party, and the Mutapan Education Society. We campaigned for educational reform. I would even hand out leaflets in the street. And that was where I met Jendayi..."

His voice trailed off into sadness.

"Your wife?"

"Yes. My true wife."

"Do you… remember her?"

"No. I still cannot recall her face."

"But there are some things you do remember?"

"I remember how we met. I remember courting her. I remember our marriage. I remember our children… but there are no pictures. I see nothing. I only feel…"

The silence overcame him again.

"Do you want to stop?" He didn't answer. "If it's too much, we can come back tomorrow…"

He snapped his attention onto me. "No."

"Kwame?"

"I do not *want* to do this. I *must*."

"Okay then. If you're sure." I looked back at the screen. "So all this here, down to…"

"I was elected to parliament in 149."

"149. Okay. So that's you starting your political career. What's happening in column two?"

"I remember many places. Many parts of the world. I think I was in uniform, as an engineer. Perhaps at Mutapan embassies. I am not sure. There are several years of this. And then it ended and I was a civilian again."

"Do you know why?"

"I think… I think I was injured. I lost the strength in my arm after an explosion. I do not remember much…"

"You actually have that injury, don't you?"

"Yes. But I was injured in the first column as well, in the fighting in Horonga…"

"So you had the same injury in both memory tracks?"

"I… yes. No. The wound in Horonga… I do not remember how bad it was. It could be the same. It could be." He sounded like he was trying to convince himself.

"Okay. So where did you go after the army? I mean in the second column?"

"I found work in Zimbabwe City."

"And where were you in the first column?"

"Zimbabwe City again. The seat in parliament I wanted to run for was there. The Harande district. A slum. The Free Liberal Party had held the seat for decades – they handed out food and clothing in return for votes."

"That's interesting. On both sides you're back in Zimbabwe again. Is that significant?"

"I do not know. Perhaps." He looked at it: the year 148 RY, already full of notations. "UserKwame: add note to 148. Investigate proximity of memories in Zimbabwe City." A note was added to the list.

"Okay, so on one side you're a member of parliament, and on the other you're working… where, exactly?"

"An electronics repair shop."

"Not exactly close to the levers of power."

"No. It was a humble existence."

"Would you say the person in the second column was the kind of person that you in the first column would have been trying to help?"

"I… yes. In some ways. But he was a pervert. A disgusting creature."

"Let's ignore that side of things for now. Is he someone you would have wanted to help?"

"He could have been... an example. Of how the poor could improve themselves if only they had the education. He had all the talent to be a great engineer... but I suppose... I suppose his position in life made it more likely for him to... fail."

"Interesting. I think these two people sound related in some way. I don't mean family. But something is bringing them together." He didn't reply to that. He still didn't want it to be true. "So. 149 onwards. You're an MP in the first column and a repairman in the second. What's going on here?"

He indicated the first column. "I was a member of the opposition party. I was good at embarrassing the government. It was easy: they were corrupt and stupid. They would say they stood for reform but their actions were always different. I introduced an education reform bill. They said it was too expensive. But we were spending millions on remedial courses for new army recruits – and the cost of teaching them properly as children was less than half of that. So the bill was passed. My party won the next election, and I hoped I would be appointed to the cabinet..."

"Whoa. Wait a minute. You're speeding ahead. The next election is... let me just read this... 155?"

"Yes."

"All the political stuff is in the first column. But what's happening in the second column?"

He swallowed. This was what he had been dreading.

"I was searching."

"For what?"

"Mudiwa."

"Ah. Did you find her? I mean, him?"

"I found him."

"What happened?"

"It was squalid. He was a prostitute. And a drug addict."

"He wasn't like that before?"

"No. But we lost touch after I left Matongu. It was too dangerous. He fell a long way and blamed me for it. He wanted me to pay him for sex. I was angry. He provoked me. I... I *took* him. And then I ran away. But I could not help it. I had to go back. The second time, I tried to help him, but he did not want my help. And he stank of khat. I hated him, I wanted to hurt him, I became a... customer." He was almost grinding his teeth as he said it. "And when I went back again, I was arrested."

"What for?"

"Being in the wrong place at the wrong time. The security service was sweeping the slum for drug users and perverts. How happy they must have been to find her. Him."

"And you?"

"Yes. And me. They took me, put me in a cell. *That* cell. In the dream." He stepped back from the screen, his hands shaking. "They gave me a choice, because of my military record. I betrayed him. Mudiwa... Mudiwa would not have been seen again."

"You mean they killed him?"

"Yes."

"That's..."

"Barbaric. Yes. I spoke out against the activities of the security services when I was in parliament, but the government barely restrained them at all. They thought it would make them popular. With some people, it did. No one wanted to defend queers."

"How do you feel about it?"

He shook his head helplessly. "He disgusts me! But... I betrayed him. I left him in Matongu. He became an addict. And then I let the security service have him..." He could say no more.

"So what did you do next?"

He indicated the next few years on the second column: a few scattered memories but very little of any detail. "I do not know. The memories from here... I am not sure what belongs in the second column. There is not much."

"Were you still in Zimbabwe?"

"No. I kept moving. Many towns. Many jobs. Until 154 – I remember receiving a letter. I do not know how it reached me. I was recalled to the military. I received an exo-skeletal arm support so I could do my job, the finest Chifunyikan technology. We were still short of trained engineers. They put me to work in... I do not know. An installation. I do not remember much."

"We're getting close to the end, aren't we?"

"Yes." He indicated the first column. "My party won the election in 155. They made me minister of sport – they did not want me getting in the way of real government. I found a way to gain promotion anyway. I proposed a world passball tournament, which had not happened since before the Great War. I almost had agreement to fix a date when they promoted me to stop it getting too far. So in 156, I was made Minister of Culture. I was visiting Chiwikuru when the nuclear bomb went off in Zimbabwe... and you know what happened after that."

"Escalation."

"Yes. The presidency was mine but I had no choice in my actions. Jendayi and the children died. I had to defend the nation. It passed beyond my control... and then there was the bunker. And the final war."

"What about the second column?"

"I do not know. There is nothing I can put there."

"Can I make a suggestion? You said you were sent to an installation, in the second column. Was that installation the bunker?"

He took a moment to reply. Another thing he didn't want to be true.

"It is possible. But it could have been anywhere..."

"I think, given you have both these sets of memories, it's the most likely thing."

"But I remember nothing!"

"Okay. What about the first column?"

He pointed out the final weeks before the end of the list. "Here is when I armed the device. Here is when the war took place. We heard from the last survivors on the surface here. One of my aides killed himself here. A general did the same here. We waited before we went into the hibernation units. We waited as long as we could. And then we laid down and slept."

"But there are things missing, aren't there? At the end?"

"Perhaps. But I do not know what they are…"

There was nothing more on the list. I took a step back. "Well. This is fantastic work… and very brave."

"It is not bravery."

"No, seriously, Kwame, I know you didn't want to do this. I know it was difficult."

"I…" He really didn't know how to take a compliment and seemed at a loss.

"But I think there's still more to do," I said.

"I do not know what else I can do… this is all I can remember."

"Well, more might come out over time. This all came in something of a rush, didn't it?"

"Yes."

"But maybe…"

He waited for me as an idea sparked in my head.

"Maybe we can jog your memory a little more. This all started when you saw your dream. Maybe we can put you back there and see what happens…"

He was shocked. "Go back? To my world? That is death!"

"Not for real. We have some very large rooms here that we don't use. And we can model those rooms exactly the same way you can model yours."

"I do not understand."

"We can make a simulation of the bunker. Some of it, anyway. I think we have the schematics on record. I'll need to get some people in but it's doable. What do you think?"

He stepped back.

"You want me to go… back there."

"The bunker's the biggest gap on this list. I don't know if it'll work but it's worth a try."

He couldn't find the words. He was dreading it.

"Or if you're not ready we can…"

"No!" He found his backbone quite suddenly. "I must. I must know!"

I nodded. "Okay, then. I'll get everything started."

6. OLIVIA

It was no surprise that Olivia was angry; I'd long since given up being surprised at how she continually generated new bitterness. But on this occasion, I found myself thinking she had a point.

She came in with her ICT representation already prepared, inconveniently written in pen and ink. She was never keen on using keyboards – she said she was no one's secretary and never had been so why should she learn to type? This made sense from the point of view of gender relations and historical typing machines, but was more likely a way to avoid any therapy that required her to write something down.

So I had to read the representation she thrust in front of me on a sheet of paper, scrawled in a language that only she and the computer that translated it for me knew. It could be summarised as a demand for the IU to prosecute itself, followed by a number of surly complaints that such a thing would never happen so why should she even bother to ask.

"Okay. I'll pass that on," I said.

"Won't do any good."

"I'd like to discuss it, if you don't mind."

"There's nothing to bloody discuss. Just give it to them. They can use it as cigarette papers if they want."

"Why do you feel so hostile about this?"

"Because you *left us there to die!* And now you come along and you say you're going to do what's right and you're not going to do anything of the sort!"

I nodded. This was going to be difficult; I didn't have anything new to give her.

"Well, I'll certainly pass it on. And I do hope they do something about it…"

"They won't. They won't do anything for poor old Pew either, and his troubles are a damn sight worse than mine…"

"Actually, that's a good point. It might be worth connecting the two cases, given that they're both about negligence…"

"And what good's that going to do?"

"Even if you can't get some prosecutions out of it, it might change IU policy."

"What rubbish."

"We can't go back and save your world, but it might save another species in the future."

"And what good's that to me? Or Pew?"

"You're right. No good at all. So what do you want? I mean, what's your goal here?"

"I want someone to pay for letting us all die."

"Okay. But who's 'us'?"

"My species, who do you bloody think?"

"I mean something a little more concrete. If you keep it vague, they could just say they had no proof of survivors and had to follow health and safety procedures–"

"That's what they bloody did say!"

"Yes. But what else could they have done? Even if they couldn't land because they didn't know what they were dealing with, what else could they have done to save you?"

"They could show a bit of backbone and use some of that godsdamned technology you're all so proud of!"

"To do what?"

"I don't know! Fight them. Find us. Get us out of there!"

"Right. Something constructive. If you're going to prove negligence, you have to show that something could have been done. Could you have been found? Was there a way?"

"I don't know, we lost radio contact with everyone by then–"

"Radio. Good. You had radio. So they could have done a radio survey."

"We didn't hardly use it any more. No one to listen to."

"But you did try sometimes?"

"…Yeh."

"Did you keep trying, even after you were alone?"

"Yeh. I didn't give up like the others."

"So there you are. That's a better way to present it. You were broadcasting. If the Exploration Service didn't try to listen, or didn't try long enough, then the ICT might find that worth looking into."

"I suppose."

"And it'll help if they know more about what happened in those two years."

"Why should they care?"

"If two years makes the difference between one survivor making it and a species making it, they'll care. You need to show there were people who could have been saved. Give them locations they can search in. Use your own group as an example. Were there other people still alive on the day the expedition left?"

"We didn't know, that's why they all bloody went!"

"Okay, but you still had some hope. So what could you put in? What happened?"

"We lost contact with the last station about a month earlier. As long as everyone could hear another voice out there, they could pretend someone was coming. But once the last station went dead…" She sighed. "I couldn't keep them there any more."

"Was it that dangerous?"

"Of course it was! We'd sent out expeditions before. They never reached the other stations. They never made it *anywhere*. But they wouldn't listen. They thought there was some country out there that didn't have any revenants, or an island or something. And there wasn't, was there?"

"No. We never found anything."

"And we were doing all right. We weren't starving, not as long as there were enough of us to keep the place going. There were always a few more revenants coming over the hills. We could have hung on for years but the others wouldn't hear of it. Fifty of us to start with and we were down to eighteen at the end. It wasn't food they were worried about. That bloody Mike, he was the one who wanted to go."

"Your lover?"

She stopped for a moment. "Not by then, he wasn't."

"I'm sorry…"

"Stop… being… sorry!"

"Do you want me to be glad?"

"No, I want you to shut up and let me finish!"

"Please. Go on."

"So they went. Everyone except me. And that was *after* your ship had come down and got bitten and buggered off. All you had to do was look for us…"

"Did your children go as well?"

"Yeh. They went."

"How had they been handling it?"

"What do you think? They were about ten or twelve when I had to tell them they couldn't go back home. They'd ask me when they were going to become revenants.

They didn't have any idea what real life was like, all they had was that patch of dirt and we tried, we tried to give them an education but they gave up, they knew they weren't getting out, what do you think that's like for a child?"

"Were there any other children there?"

"A few. Eight. Seven after we lost Tymothy when he went out by himself."

"But more must have been born while you were there. There were men and women. And married couples, I think you said before…"

"Yeh. Married couples."

"And you had a boyfriend yourself."

"I was past it."

"You weren't that old…"

"We were all past it!"

"I'm sorry, I don't understand."

"We had no children. Not one. D'you understand that? All of us were barren."

"Do you mean… you were infertile?"

"That's what barren means, you nit. Not my fault it doesn't make sense in Interversal."

"That must have been painful."

"I promised them, you see. I promised them we'd be able to start something. I thought we could get our own little civilisation going and wait for the revenants to die off. But you need children for a civilisation."

"And the children that were there, did they turn out to be infertile as well?"

"Yes. Not for lack of trying. I swear I had to put a leash on my two when they got old enough. The poor buggers were bored. But there were never any pregnancies."

"Do you know why?"

"Yeh, I know why."

"What was it?"

"The marinade. It eats away at your liver and everything else as well. Ovulation goes wrong, the eggs come out dead or shrivelled or something."

"And you knew that then?"

"No. That's what your doctors said when they got hold of me. If it was happening to me it must have been happening to the rest. And the men as well, I don't doubt, not that they'd admit it."

"So. You staked everything on being able to build a community."

"That's what I said."

"And when that failed?"

"I told them to hang on until someone got us out. And that was fine until there wasn't anyone to talk to on the radio. And then they went."

"Why didn't you go?"

"I wasn't all that keen on having my guts chewed out."

"But you let your children go."

"I know what you're thinking. You think I abandoned them, but they made their own minds up. They didn't want me with them. They wanted to get away. Not just from that place, they wanted to get away from *me*."

"And you let them?"

"That was up to them."

"You didn't want to go yourself?"

"There wasn't anything out there. Except revenants."

"You were certain?"

"I was *right*."

"How do you know?"

"Because they came back."

"Oh. Do you mean...?"

"Yeh. They came back dead. Not all of them. Just a few. They probably got caught by a swarm and most of them were too badly eaten to make it back. Mike did."

"And your children as well? That must have been... terrible."

"No. They came back before that."

"They died before the others?"

"No. They didn't die. Not on the road."

"So what happened...?"

"They got scared! They hadn't been out past the valley for ten years. They didn't know what it was like. They ran away from the others and came back."

"You must have been happy."

She looked away. "Yeh. I was." And was that a hint of a tear? She wasn't normally one to cry.

"Did they stay with you, after that?"

"No. They didn't come home to be with their mother. They came home to die."

"Oh."

"And there's me, the biggest fool of all. I started cooking for them, putting on a celebration. Then I found them in Vicktor's room. They'd both slit their wrists."

"I'm..." the urge to say 'I'm sorry' was almost overpowering, but I managed to avoid it. "And... afterwards?"

"I put them in the pens before they got up again." She stared at me, hard. "*That's* who they could have saved if they'd lifted one bloody finger!"

"Then you should put that in the representation."

"All right. I will."

"Olivia, is there anything you'd like to talk about?"

"What do you mean?"

"You said you put your children in the pens, after they... died."

"That's right."

"Along with the other revenants."

"Yeh."

"Which you were using for food."

She didn't reply.

"Olivia... is there anything you want to tell me?"

She looked straight at me.

"No," she said.

7. IOKAN

Iokan couldn't keep his hands still. He tapped at the arm of a chair as he sat in my office, trying to articulate what was wrong. He lifted his mug of chakchuk to his lips, then put it down again. He looked about the room, as though searching for an escape from the dilemma that had been preying on his mind ever since the last group session.

"He's wrong." His voice was a rasp but he was at least recovering.

"What's he wrong about, Iokan?"

"It's ridiculous. You can't compare the Soo to the Antecessors… it's…" He shook his head. His hand tapped away at the arm of his chair. "It's just *ridiculous*."

"Is it?"

He looked at me. He'd been hoping for more support.

"Look. On the one hand you've got divine beings and on the other this… *squalid* little species that can't find anything better to do than abuse anyone they get their hands on…"

"I don't think Pew was saying they were exactly the same in every respect."

"The Antecessors saved us. The Soo are an abomination."

"Both of them may be responsible for the extinction of a species."

He sat forward, hand on his heart, desperate to convince me. "But we're not extinct!"

"That's only true in a sense."

"They were taken up, not killed!"

"The streets are full of skeletons, Iokan. Would you like to see?"

He paused there, realising the implications of what I'd just said.

"You've had something back from my world."

"Yes. I wanted to talk to you about that today but you seem to be very disturbed by what Pew said…"

He sat back in his chair. "I'm sorry. It just… got to me." He coughed, and put a hand to his throat as pain stabbed at him. "You say there are skeletons in the streets?"

"Yes. And worse. I've spent several evenings going through the material I was sent. It wasn't pleasant."

His expression turned from anxiety to sympathy. "If you want to talk about it, I might be able to help you understand."

"I'm the therapist, Iokan. I'm here to help you. Remember?"

"Of course."

"When the expedition went back to your world, I asked them to send me information that might be relevant to your therapy. So I have your service records now."

"I see."

"I also have a lot of material from the last few weeks before the end."

He frowned. "That's not why I gave you the codes."

"No, but it confirms a lot of what you've said."

He paused for a moment. "You mean you believe me now...?"

"We have your reports on the Antecessors. What they really are. How they attacked you. How you tried to defend yourselves. It'll all go to the ICT. They'll take it into account."

"I hope they'll reach the right decision."

"That's not up to me. We need to look at what happened to you. I'd like to go through some of the material today, if that's all right?"

"Certainly."

"Some of it's going to be distressing. Do you feel up to it?"

He coughed, and swallowed. His voice was still rasping, but he seemed determined. "I'm sure I've seen worse."

"Let's start with how your world is now."

I turned the wall into a screen. "Here's a view from orbit." I foregrounded a full shot of the planet: it looked like any other Earth, save for broader icecaps. "Let me zoom in on your part of the world..."

I pushed in towards the Indonesian islands, the hub of Zumazscarta, Iokan's nation. Then further in towards an advanced city: wide green spaces bridged by shuttletubes hanging between skytowers that stretched their shadows across the parks. But several shuttletubes were smashed, lying in pieces on the roadways and parks below, and fire had burnt charcoal holes in the parklands.

Further down in scale, there seemed to be debris scattered everywhere, as though rubbish hadn't been collected for weeks. Closer still, you could see it wasn't rubbish that filled the streets. It was the remains of the city's inhabitants. A view of the central square of the city showed it rumpled and spotted with corpses.

"This is where we found you," I said. "Here's a view from the ground."

A handheld camera walked through an ancient imagining of hell. Many corpses had been reduced to skeletons with tattered rags around them. Some were still in the final stages of decomposition. Lips were peeled back from teeth. Eyesockets lay empty. A torso roiled with maggots beneath the skin. Verminous mammals darted from empty rib cages to a suppurating groin, picking away at the remaining meat. A swamp of bones floated in a pool where hundreds of people had drowned themselves.

Iokan looked away and blinked at tears.

"Would you like me to stop?" I asked.

"No. No, go on," he said, rubbing his eyes and turning back to the screen.

"This is what it looks like across the whole planet. We haven't found a single survivor other than yourself."

He swallowed back the horror. "They're... safe. With the Antecessors."

"And they chose that?"

He nodded. "Yes."

"I'd like to move on to some of the files we found. I expect you've seen a few of these before."

"Probably," he admitted. He looked up at the wall without focussing on any one thing as I backgrounded the video and brought up an interface for the documents.

"This is an early one." I magnified a report dated six months before the end of Iokan's world. He looked outside. "Iokan?"

"Yes. Let me just..."

"Do you need to take a moment?"

"No, no, I'm fine..." He took a sip of his chakchuk, and grimaced. "It's gone cold..."

"I'll order some more," I said. "Tell me about the document."

He scanned it while I ordered another mug of chakchuk.

"I remember this..." he said. "There were a few suicides we looked into. Lights were seen by neighbours around the time they died, and they were found with smiles on their faces. We decided there wasn't enough to go on so we closed the case."

"But you changed your minds later on?"

"Yes. There was a theory the Antecessors were testing their methods. Most of the victims–" He paused, correcting himself. "Most of the *people involved* were elderly. There were only about six or seven cases. No sign of interversal interference, just a few people dying oddly."

"There's a memo attached, from later."

"Yes. It looked like the same thing as, as what we saw later on. We never knew for sure. If it was the Antecessors, then they're safe." He shrugged, helplessly.

"Let's move on. Six months later."

I let video play: a compilation of news reports. A family had jumped in front of a shuttletrain: the father and two children all had happy smiles on their faces, even as the mother reached out for them, screaming. Three random workers in a skytower had got up from their desks at the same time, walked to a viewing platform and jumped to their deaths. In a research lab, dozens of chemists lay dead after one of them allowed chlorine gas to flood the building. A junior officer had opened the weapons storage lockers at a barracks. Four soldiers took weapons and shot themselves. The news stations switched into crisis mode, cataloguing each new act of horror.

A chime at the door announced the arrival of Iokan's chakchuk. I brought it to him as he watched the news roll on. He let it sit before him until I pressed pause.

"From what we gather, this is just the tip of the iceberg," I said. "They were only reporting the most sensational incidents. A lot of individuals were dying by themselves as well."

"Yes," said Iokan, his attention far away in time.

"There's a Department Zero document from this date..." I brought it up. "What can you tell me?"

He gulped back his chakchuk and rubbed his eyes. After a moment to gather himself, he looked back up at the screen.

"I remember this. They managed to stop a man from killing himself. He was in a pharmacy, picking up a prescription. He was normal until they handed over the pills, and then he took them all at once. His stomach was pumped and we interviewed him afterwards. It says there's an artist's impression of what he saw...?"

"Yes," I said, and brought up the next page. A pastel-style sketch of a glowing light: pure white in the middle with a rainbow of refraction around the edges. Subtle shades of polygonal forms at the centre.

Iokan gasped. "That's them. It's one of... them." A chime came in my ear; my pad showed a suddenly high pulse rate for Iokan. A smile of joy twitched around the edge of his mouth. Then he remembered his surroundings, and reached for his mug to drink. His pulse came back down.

"There's a reference to another casefile," I said. "It's dated about thirteen years earlier. Your name's on it."

He nodded. "I think I told you before. It wasn't the first time we'd seen them. We found an ancient machine that made them, and there was an Antecessor trapped inside the system. My commander set it free. When they cross-referenced it with what the man from the pharmacy saw… well, that's why I was brought onto the investigative team."

"Let's move on. We have some video here. Can you talk me through it?"

He didn't look at the screen. "Why are we doing this?"

"Because I think you need to be reminded of what happened on your world."

"I know what happened on my world."

"Would you prefer to come back to it another day?"

It wasn't in his nature to admit to weakness. "No. Let's go on."

I called up a video. It had been taken through a specialised camera and carried telemetry of various kinds. It appeared to have a high placement, on a building of some kind, but not so high as the skytowers of the city it swept across.

"This is a test I asked for," said Iokan. "We needed a way to make them visible…"

A green light flashed in one corner, and a filter was imposed on the view. The camera swung again to regain a wide shot of the city.

The sky was full of glowing lights: Antecessors floating above the skyline.

"They can bend light around them. But they can't hide the higher energy stuff quite as well, so there's some x-ray leakage. This is us looking for them."

"How did Department Zero react?"

"We were shocked. There were so many ways we could have been attacked… so many ways we *had* been attacked. We thought it would be the interversal powers again. Finding out it was the Antecessors instead was terrifying. Some people wanted to give up there and then…"

"Did you?"

"No. I wish I had."

"Why?"

He looked at me, incredulous that I had not already guessed. "Because then I'd be with them."

"How did you feel?"

He paused, reflecting. "I had a family."

"Szilmar and Ghiorghiu. Your wife and son."

"Yes. They're safe now."

"But you didn't think so then."

"No."

"What did you do?"

"I went to get them. D0 headquarters was safe. We had an EM cage around the building that could stop them getting in."

"How old was your son?"

"Less than a year."

"Had you been with Szilmar long?"

He shook his head. "A couple of years. We knew each other when we were younger, but we didn't click until... well. Until I wasn't an investigator any more."

"So... you brought them back to Department Zero headquarters."

"Yes. By then there was a cluster of them around the building. We parked on the roof and ran for the door... I made it there but she stumbled... she had to turn round to get up. And she was suddenly... happy. I was calling her in but she walked to the edge... I had to drag her inside. She begged me to let her jump..."

He finished the last of his drink, unnerved.

"Ghiorghiu saw them as well. He just shut down. Didn't cry. Didn't play. Didn't sleep. The doctor had to feed him through tubes... it was like he was waiting."

"And Szilmar?"

"We had to restrain her."

"How did you feel?"

He looked down at his empty mug and wiped his eyes. "As though my heart had been ripped out."

"How did you feel about the Antecessors?"

"I hated them." He shook his head, mourning his foolishness. "I didn't understand..."

"How do you feel now?"

"I..." He struggled between memory and later conviction.

"Okay. Let's keep moving. I've got some records here of the response to the Antecessors."

He looked up at the screen, relieved. A scatter of pages came up.

"Can you join the dots for me?" I asked.

"Okay..." He stood up, went to the screen and pulled a group of reports together. "These are observations of Antecessor behaviour. Here's the analysis... there was information going from the Antecessors to people who saw them. Transmitted visually, somehow.. These are records of brain activity from a volunteer: she saw more than just the Antecessor, she saw... something amazing."

He smiled, then turned to a surveillance video, showing an Antecessor floating above a corpse in the street. "And they were doing something to people's minds as they died. We couldn't see the process, it was too fast... but two Antecessors would leave the body behind. The theory was that it was a kind of reproduction."

The process really was fast; just a flash of x-rays, and then there were two.

"And here's our response..." He pushed the other materials aside and gathered up a series of reports. "Lots of attempts to communicate. Signals in every frequency. Appeals on the media. Billboards, even. Nothing worked. But there was a cluster around D0 headquarters, so they knew who we were. In the end, we sent someone out to talk to them."

"That was suicide, surely?"

"Yes. But we didn't have a lot of time. You see here?" He pulled up a graph. "This shows how long we had left." He point out a series of lines running across the diagram. "That's the level of population needed to sustain cities. That's how many we needed just to keep civilisation going. That's how many we needed to avoid extinction."

"It would have taken a few years, then."

"At the rate they were going then. But we expected them to speed up. So we sent out a man with the best psych record we could find, and gave him a message. Just that we needed to talk to them. He killed himself. But one of them came to us an hour later."

He tapped a video. One of the camera feeds showed the sudden appearance of an Antecessor in visible wavelengths. The air about it shimmered with pressure waves; and text appeared on the screen. *Analogue Audio (language): Please state your concern.*

"We told it they were killing us, and causing unnecessary suffering. It said they didn't want to hurt anyone, they only wanted to take us to a new stage of being. We begged them to postpone, order a truce, anything. It said they would scale back their efforts and try to make the transition easier. We just wanted time to find a way to stop them. We thought they'd bought it. We thought it might be over…" he trailed off into silence.

"What happened?"

He sighed, and went back to the screen. He dug through the files until he found a report with video. It showed multiple surveillance views of a sporting stadium shaped like a circle with a small playing field in the middle. Perhaps twenty or thirty thousand people were there – the stadium was half full.

"A lot of people were staying at home but normal life was still going on. Until this kind of thing started happening."

A light illuminated the stadium. Cameras swung up to find the Antecessor: much brighter than any seen before. Other cameras showed the crowd, suddenly transfixed. The players in the field laid down their bats and took off their helmets. Everyone stared upwards.

More lights came from above. A starfield of Antecessors.

On the pitch, the slaughter began. Some of the players picked up their bats. One removed his helmet and bowed his head while another struck him on the skull. An Antecessor descended to him as he died, and two rose back up. The crowd queued up to be executed in an orderly fashion. When police arrived, they too saw the Antecessors and joined the queue – or else used their weapons to start a new queue.

"They didn't scale it back, did they?" I said.

"No."

"They found a way to make it happen faster. Working on crowds rather than one at a time."

He nodded.

"They lied."

He looked up at me, appalled. "They… you can't judge them… they're…" He looked back at the screen. People kept on dying.

His objection withered away, and he nodded. "They lied."

"I'm glad you see that."

"But they had reasons!"

"Perhaps. Do you still think they gave everyone a choice?"

He looked back at the screen. One of the players handed his bat over to a young woman, knelt down and had his own brains bashed out before a light descended and took him. Then she handed the bat to the next person, and was killed in turn. The queue stretched back to the stands.

"No," said Iokan. He turned away from the screen. Tears were in his eyes. "Can you stop it? Please?"

I stopped the video from my pad and whisked it off the screen. Iokan leaned on the back of a chair. I got up and offered him a tissue. He wiped his eyes.

"Let's go on," he said.

"You don't have to."

He turned from me, went back to the screen and found more records. "We recalculated the graph. The time we had left came down to about six months, depending on whether the new ones could take people as well." The lines shifted on the graph, showing mortality curves tightening.

"We fought back. But nothing worked…" He showed a quick series of videos of weapons tests: the first one showed a coherent energy beam hitting an Antecessor and bursting it into a shower of light; but the next one showed the Antecessor reforming afterwards, and further tests had little or no effect.

"The existential threat notice went out." He brought up the document: an animated picture of an Antecessor in the corner of the page, and a warning to seek shelter unless the reader was able to fight back.

"We advised every government to get under cover. Then this started coming on every channel…" A brief video ran: an Antecessor glowed on the screen while an ethereal voice assured people the process was brief, and, once transformed, they too would be Antecessors. "They couldn't touch people's minds through the screen. The frame rate didn't work. But that was when a lot of the public realised what they were. And we'd all been praying for deliverance for so many years, after so many attacks from the interversal powers…" He shook his head. "Can you understand that? Our gods came back. What would you do?"

"I don't know," I said.

"Once the church got hold of it they started broadcasting as well and told everyone it was the Antecessors, they could trust them, and…"

"And it sped up."

"Yes. They couldn't have done it so quickly if people hadn't co-operated." He pulled up the graph: it changed again. The mortality curves took an exponential dive. "Just a couple of weeks, in the end."

His hand hovered over another file. "There's more video of what happened in the churches…"

"It's okay, Iokan. I've seen it." I could understand why he didn't want to play it: church officials handing out knives, final services before the altar that ended in wrist-slitting. Kindly nurses with anaesthetic cream for the children. I hadn't slept after I watched that.

He pushed the video icon away. "Thank you."

He brought up another file: a daily status report with estimated human population remaining. He spread out fifteen of them: fifteen days of the crisis, with every report progressively worse. "After a week, the only survivors were just the odd few hiding out. We lost touch with our own government after nine days. Then the only people left were under EM cages. They went dark one by one."

He brought up the last report. "The day after this was when our own EM cage failed. That was the end."

He stepped back, as though that was everything.

"But not for you," I said.

He looked round helplessly. He was reaching the most painful memories.

"You survived longer. What happened to you, Iokan?"

He looked back at the screen just to keep from my gaze.

"I..."

He searched for words.

"I denied them."

"*You* denied them? Why?"

"They took my family."

"Can you talk about it?"

"They took everyone. The cage failed. They came in and... that was it."

"Just like that?"

"I tried to save them."

"How?"

"I had a weapon. I modified it. I stayed with them. Tried to protect them. Szilmar was strapped down in a cell. Ghiorghiu was... sitting. Then it came. I never even had a chance to fire."

"But you didn't kill yourself?"

"They touched me. They... showed me heaven. I told them no."

"You resisted?"

"I wasn't the first. A few people were able to hold out. Training helped... but..."

A long, long pause. I waited.

"When I came back to myself, Szilmar and Ghiorghiu were dead. And everyone else was gone as well." He turned back to me. "So I went outside."

"Go on."

"I don't know. I don't really remember what happened next. There wasn't anyone else left. Just bodies. It could have been weeks. Days. I don't know. But they stayed with me. They were patient. And in the end when I was dying... I opened my heart." His expression recalled a joy from memory; a joy that was swiftly clouded. "And then you came. And then I was here."

He sat down.

"Do you remember how you felt when you denied them?"

"I was angry."

"How do you feel about them now?"

He thought about it.

"I don't know." He shook his head. "I just... I don't know."

8. ASHA

I locked myself in my office for a while after letting Iokan go. I felt cruel and heartless for crushing his faith; it needed to be done, but it took its toll on him, and on me. I dimmed the lights and lay down, trying not to see the bodies of children piling up in the church, so similar to the corpse-piles my parents tried to hide from me.

But I could not. The image remained. And that nightmare from childhood, in the weeks before evacuation, when people were dying so swiftly they could not be buried or cremated or even named. The hospitals piled the human remains in the car park. When I fell ill and my parents panicked and took me there, they recoiled from the sight, realising the hospital had become a place for the dying and little else. They ignored government appeals to stay put, and made for the evacuation centre the next day. My fever put them and me on the priority list and gained us admittance to the refugee camp. But that ended in a pile of corpses, too.

I opened my eyes. Was it always the same? Was it always like this? Mountains of human remains on every world?

I found my pad and pulled images up on the wall. The orbital surveys of Iokan's dead world had reminded me of another, and I sought out the latest pictures of my own all-but-perished Earth.

There was a ship from the Refugee Service in orbit, listening in for appeals from the last few survivors, appeals that no longer came. We knew they were hiding in bunkers, especially in the great military cavern at Cheyenne Mountain, wearing uniforms of a country that no longer existed. There was only a tiny hope they would respond to our offer to save them, but still, we listened. And as well as listening, we watched, and those images were available for anyone to see.

The widest view of the planet seemed almost normal. But it took only a short zoom to see too much cloud cover, the lines of continents shrouded and barely visible. I stripped the clouds away, but the shroud remained. It wasn't a normal cloud. It was ash, spreading from the vast volcanic inferno of Yellowstone. A zoom into what was once a national park revealed only a dull glow of fiery red beneath the ash-storm. It had been erupting for forty years, and might go on for centuries more.

I spun the globe away, to where the ash clouds thinned out and shorelines broke through the haze. Across the Atlantic, to Europe, to Britain, to my own long-dead nation. I pushed in through the clouds to find my home town, not so vast as the Zumazscartan capital, and long since perished. Snow seemed to cover the towers and roads and houses, or perhaps it was ash falling from distant Yellowstone.

There were no corpses. It had all happened too long ago for that, and even if the dead had still lain in the streets, the ash or snow or whatever-it-was would have concealed them. I couldn't find any of the places I had known; not the house we lived in, not the hospital we went to in the last days, nor even the airport from where I had been evacuated. So many of the buildings were in ruins, so many skyscrapers fallen and smashed into rubble, so much of the city covered in a grey-white blanket, that I could connect none of it with my childhood memories.

And I could not see my parents' graves. Not that they had single burial places. They went into a mass grave with all the others who died in the region, and even that was hard to find until I invoked a layer of geographic information that tagged every significant site. When I did, all I found was yet another featureless plain of ash or snow or something, with no sign that tens of thousands of human beings had their last resting place there.

I pulled out, back away from the city, sliding the image up to hundreds of kilometres in orbit, and saw something I'd never spotted before. Something that had to be new.

Far to the north of Scotland, ice was creeping ever further south from the Arctic. Iceland stood in its path, and broke the line of advance, but the wall of ice was pushing up the beaches and turning into a glacier. I checked the timestamp: this was supposed to be *summer*. I pulled the timeslider back six months and watched as the glacier rushed across the island, burying the coastal plain that used to be Reykjavik. I dragged the image back to Britain and saw the edge of the ice cap touching Cape Wrath. Estimates accompanying the images gave Britain no more than twenty years before it, too, would be covered by glaciers, and the towns and cities I remembered, everything I had been taught about in the heritage classes I had to attend while growing up on Hub, would be scraped away from the surface of the world. Never to be seen again.

It was too much. I wiped the image from my wall and lay back down.

9. PEW

Pew interrupted my reverie, half an hour before his session was due. I'd planned a slow, careful start to his PTSD therapy, taking him gently through the abuse he'd suffered, slowly desensitising him to the memories until they no longer caused distress. But he thumped on the door, in no mood for therapy. I brought the lights up and let him in.

"Is something the matter, Pew?" I asked.

"Did you know?" he demanded.

"I'm sorry, I don't understand."

"The news! About the Soo!"

"I haven't heard anything. Did something happen to them?"

"No! It was what *you* did!"

"What I did?"

"I mean the IU – look."

He snatched a pad up, patched into the picture wall and rifled through a newsfeed to find a small notice, buried beneath all the stories about reconstruction after the attack and the announcement of the ICT.

***

Hub Chronicle
HD y276.m9.w1.d1
14:56

Diplomatic Service Admits Partial Responsibility For Extinction
In a report issued today, the Diplomatic Service of the Interversal Union has accepted partial blame for the extinction of the Pu species, while maintaining that the bulk of responsibility lies with the Soo species who evolved on the same world and enslaved the Pu.

The Diplomatic Service identified a number of faults in their oversight of Soo efforts to preserve a nucleus of the Pu species, including a naive willingness to accept Soo assurances at face value.

The report finds these failings to be institutional in nature and recommends that the officials who determined policy should be subject to disciplinary hearings. However, many are now retired from the Diplomatic Service and have returned to their home universes, where any action taken against them may contravene local laws.

Kast Khraghner, Diplomatic Service Contact Director, said: "While we cannot turn back the clock and reverse this appalling disaster, it is nevertheless something we have learned from. Our future dealings in similar situations will be guided by the recommendations made in this report."

The Pu species is now represented by only one survivor, whose anonymity is protected by law.

***

"I see," I said.

"How can they do this?" he asked.

"Have you read the full report?"

"No! I can't even find it!"

"Hm…" I turned to the screen and started a search, but swiftly encountered an apologetic icon asking me to try again later. "Well, it's probably out there somewhere but you might have to wait a bit. You know what things have been like with the dataflow."

"But–"

"Pew. I wouldn't rush to judgement until you've read the actual report. News reports aren't always the best guide to what really happened."

"But they're not going to do anything!"

"We don't know that."

"They're not even prosecuting anyone!"

"They said it's difficult, but–"

"What about the Soo? Are they going to do anything about them?"

"I don't know. You have to wait for the report."

"It doesn't even exist. Does it?"

This was more like an accusation, and a very sudden bitterness directed against me.

"Why do you say that, Pew?"

"Nobody's even talking about it! Look at the comments!" I did – and the list was very poorly populated for something this important. Just a couple of the usual complainers. "It's because they released it on the same day as the ICT announcement, isn't it?"

I checked the date – he was right. "Well, that *would* draw attention elsewhere," I agreed.

"See? That's what they want! They put the story out on the one day nobody's going to notice, and hid the report so no one can find out who was responsible!"

Sad to say, some of his accusations were all too possible. Hiding embarrassing news by releasing it at the same time as a bigger story is a tactic as old as media itself. But Pew was constructing a conspiracy theory, which would do him far more harm in the long run.

"Okay. I can see how you could draw that conclusion, Pew, but look at what's going on here. The news media have been preoccupied with the attack ever since it happened. Is there any day in the last few weeks they could have released this and had anyone pay attention? So the Diplomatic Service has two choices. They can release the report and see it swamped with other news, or delay it and have people think they're trying to hide something. And of course it's difficult to find the report: it's been difficult to find *anything* since the attack. You know that. How many hours did it take you to find the video you showed me last time?"

He stayed silent, but still angry.

"Now, I'll put in an order to have the report sent to us directly. It'll probably take a couple of hours and I'll pass it to you as soon as it arrives. Is that good enough?"

"No."

I was surprised. This wasn't a petulant thing any more. This was getting cold, and dangerous.

"Then what would you like us to do?" I said carefully, keeping any trace of sarcasm out of my voice.

"Put them on trial."

"Put who on trial?"

"All the people who are getting away with it."

"Again, Pew, we don't know if that's the case–"

"And the Soo as well. I've got a right to make a representation to the ICT."

"Okay. But…" How could I put this so his expectations would not be raised too high? "The thing is, I don't want you to be… disappointed later on if it doesn't go the way you want."

"What do you mean?"

"Well, I've seen our current report on the Soo. Did you know they're listed as an endangered species themselves?"

"Good."

"Hardly on the same level as you, of course, but their climate's on a downward track and they don't know how to deal with it without our help."

"So?"

"I don't know if the IU is going to issue sanctions against a whole species if it might mean they go extinct–"

He jumped to his feet. "It didn't stop them letting *my* species go extinct!"

"Pew! Sit down!"

"They're going to get away with it, aren't they?"

"Pew–"

"They're going to wipe us out of history and say we *never fucking existed!*"

"Pew, will you please–"

He threw the coffee table over, scattering my tissue box and coffee mug. "*I will not sit down!*"

"Do I need to call security?"

That put a hold on him, as furious as he was.

"Sit down. Please."

He sat down, arms folded, looking pointedly away from me.

"I understand you're angry but I won't permit violence. Do I need to treat you the same way I had to treat Katie?"

He didn't answer.

"Pew?"

Still no answer.

"Okay. If you're not willing to engage with therapy we'll have to come back another day. I know you want something done but you need to co-operate with me if I'm going to help you."

He still refused even eye contact.

"Or would you like to spend the rest of the session writing your representation?"

"Is it going to make any difference?" he muttered, still looking away from me.

"You won't know unless you try."

Grudgingly, he agreed to work on the representation. I shelved my therapy plan for the moment and helped him.

10. LISS

Liss had already written her representation when she came in for her next session, and we spent the first few minutes going over it.

"Not much to say, really," she said. It wasn't a lengthy document. As the sole legal authority on her planet, she 'empowered the extraterritorial authority known as the ICT to investigate and render justice as it saw fit.'

"And you're sure you don't want to be involved?"

"Well, I want them to keep me in the loop…"

"But this is basically you giving them your job."

"This is me passing my job on to people who can actually do it."

"You're sure?"

"I don't know, let me think about it, oh, hang on, yeah, I'd have to launch an investigation across fuck knows how many universes, no clue who to look for, no way of bringing them to justice that doesn't involve dropping a bomb on them which is probably going to get me prosecuted by your people so why the hell am I even supposed to consider it?"

"I don't mean it like that, Liss. I just meant you could be more involved if you wanted to."

"Yeah? How?"

"If your therapy goes well, I don't see any reason why you couldn't go to work for the ICT."

She found that bitterly amusing. "What am I going to do, run their call centre? 'Hello, you're through to Liss, which genocide did you commit today?' I mean, seriously?"

"They're going to be taking on a lot of staff. You were an office manager – you must have administration skills. They'll need people like you."

"Why are you so keen on this?"

"Because you're not."

"Isn't that my business?"

"Of course. But I think it's an issue for therapy as well."

"You're going to hit me with the low self-esteem crap, aren't you?"

"I don't suppose I'm the first therapist to mention it…"

She sighed. "Only about the fifteenth."

"I'm afraid I still don't have your medical records – do you really mean fifteen?"

"Let me think." She scratched her head and counted. "More. I don't remember all the ones from when I was a little girl."

"Well, I think this is an issue we have to address. While I'm waiting for your records, I'd be grateful if you could talk about it."

She sighed again. "I've been over this so many goddamn times…"

"Well, the thing is, you don't have that many therapeutic issues. You don't have any PTSD symptoms. You're depressed, of course, you're going through a grieving process, but you're coping very well, considering what's happened to you. I think you're the person here who's most likely to be able to leave and start a new life, once the legal hurdles are cleared."

"Great. That's another power, I suppose. 'Ability to cope with genocide.'"

"But there are still issues we have to work through. I think low self-esteem might be something at the heart of it. So I'd be really grateful if you could tell me what you went through, before the world ended."

She flumped back into her chair. "Where the hell am I supposed to start?"

"How about I make you a cup of tea and you think about it? If one of your therapists had an idea, you can tell me that, if you like."

I got up to make the tea, and Liss cast her mind back. "One of them said it was my parents' fault."

"The adventurers?"

"No, not them. The biological ones. Keff and Seelie were my foster parents. I was an orphan. I suppose that makes me an automatic fuckup, doesn't it?" It took her a moment to remember I was an orphan as well. "Oh, uh, shit, sorry. I didn't mean, I didn't mean you, I just meant…"

She trailed off. For a moment, I couldn't answer. The memory of the crowd came back to me: pressed together, all of them pushing me up, passing me along, a sea of hands pulling me away from my doomed parents. Dragging me away with their blessing. Dying so I would be safe.

I shouldn't have been seeing those things. It shouldn't have kept coming back. It faded, and I noticed Liss was frowning, worried she'd offended me. I smiled to reassure her. "It's all right, Liss. It was a long time ago, but you're right, it doesn't make it any easier. I'd like to hear the theory your other therapist had."

"Okay..." She went on, a little more carefully. "There was something about the daycare place my parents took me to. They had us hooked up to these weirdo learning machines to try and make us into superbrains or something. I guess it was some mad paediatrician. I don't know if my parents knew what was going on. The therapist thought they did. I don't know... I don't know anything about them. I hardly remember them at all." She drifted away for a moment, then came back to the present. "And then they died."

"How did it happen?"

"Hah! Same as always. Nothing natural. It was the flood basalt thing in Calafaria. Some superbrain thought it'd be a great idea to study volcanoes by making some. So he got some tectonic forceps or whatever he was calling that crap and the whole faultline went and there were huge floods of lava coming out, earthquakes like crazy... I was in daycare, the building collapsed, some adventurers came by and dug me out. Supposedly I was the only one who made it. My parents never turned up."

I brought her a mug of tea. "That's a lot for a child to have to deal with."

"Huh. Well. You know, I guess I never thought about it like that."

"I'm sorry, Liss. I'm sure you're a little tired of talking about it."

"Everyone was tired. Everyone had something horrible happen to them. I wasn't any different."

"That doesn't mean your health isn't important."

"Yeah, well, I wouldn't want you to be unemployed, I guess."

"I don't think there's any risk of that in this place."

That got a very small chuckle out of her. "Thing is, it wasn't being an orphan that was the problem. I don't know, I've always been kinda... resilient about the big stuff. Huh. Guess you noticed that..." I nodded. "It was more the other kids when I got to the refugee camp."

"Where was that?"

"Other side of the continent. Lots of countries were taking in refugees from Calafaria, I ended up in Algonquia. Some of the kids were messed up bad but a lot of them were just mean."

"In what way?"

"Well, I kinda had trouble with lessons. They got us into schools and I guess something about those machines they used on me made it difficult for me to keep up. So they all thought I was kind of a retard. I wasn't, I mean I'm not a superbrain but I'm, you know, college level and all. So I guess I was bullied. There was one therapist who thought that was what it was."

"It's possible. How did you respond?"

"Huh. Well, it's not a good idea to bully a kid with Early Onset Superpower Syndrome, you know?"

"You hit back?"

"I sure did. Soon as I figured out I was stronger than all the other kids, and I mean way stronger. I was lucky, some kids died because they got powers too soon, but I didn't have that kind of a problem. It was all the other kids around me that had the problem. I got into a lot of trouble after I started breaking their arms when they called me names."

"That's, um…"

"Yeah, I know. Not nice. I got sent to doctors and shrinks and all the rest and they started figuring it out and told me I had to be real careful. But as soon as I went back to school, all the name calling started again and I hit some kid and it just went back and forth and back and forth and…"

She sighed. "Eventually they decided I'd be better off with foster parents who had powers. That's why I was placed with Keff and Seelie. Seelie was a full-time adventurer, she was too strong and tough for me to hurt and Keff had this poison touch thing, he could give you drugs through your skin, so he could calm me down if I was having a tantrum. He never liked doing it, he used to be a bad guy but then he met Seelie and, well, that's ancient history, I guess."

"But they were good for you?"

"The best. They were great. They…"

Tears came suddenly. I passed her a tissue.

"Shit, sorry, I just, sometimes I remember all of a sudden…"

"It's natural, Liss. You have to cry about these things."

"Yeah." She wiped her eyes and looked down at the floor.

"So did you still have problems at school?"

"Oh, all the time. I didn't get placed with Keff and Seelie until I was nine and I must have been hell for them for a couple of years, but they kind of tamed me, I suppose. And then the other kids started getting their powers, and that was it, I wasn't special any more."

"That must have been difficult."

"Yeah… I ended up being the mousy kid with hardly any friends. Everyone forgot about me and… I just stopped doing all that stuff. I pretended I was normal. I went from hitting people all the time to never doing anything. Until I went to college and met Yott. Even then I wasn't really special."

"But you still saved the world…"

"Yeah, I guess. Didn't do me any good. Me and Yott joined the PRG but he was the one they really wanted. We had the same agent and you could just see it in her face. I was only there to keep him out of trouble, which usually meant taking a beating while he finished wiring up whatever machine we needed to save the city or whatever we were doing that day. And then when he worked out his armour he didn't need me any more. Great boyfriend he turned out to be…"

"There's always a few more."

"Not from my species."

"No. I'm sorry."

"So I tried making it in one of those little City Patrol teams but they never had any money. I could have gone corporate, I suppose. But everyone knew I wasn't any good at it. So I gave it up…"

"What did you do then?"

"Unemployment. I had to move back in with Keff and Seelie for a while. God knows what I would have done without them. That made me feel even worse."

"How did you get out of it?"

"I got lucky. Somebody let an AI virus loose on the infonet and it ate all the other AIs. So we ended up with half the computers in the world not working any more and having to get humans to do everything. Like the helpline for adventurers – the call centre, you know? You could call up and get legal help or they could give you tactical advice if you were in a tight spot. It was done with an AI before but all of a sudden they were hiring. I had some customer service experience out of all the crap jobs I did and of course I had the adventuring experience… I thought it'd be a disaster, but the money was okay, so…"

"Was it a disaster?"

"Not so much. Turned out to be a lot easier when I wasn't actually there. You know, without all the stress and 'am I going to get turned to dogmeat if I put my head up', kind of thing. I'm better at all the paperwork and admin side anyway. Eventually I got promoted out of there into another department. Had my own team. Had a good income. Had my own place. Couldn't hang on to a man but you can't have everything." Her face turned down. "Or anything at all, now…"

"If it's a man you're after, there's a few of them knocking around."

"Not much good if he's not my species."

"I was dating a man from another species."

"Oh… was it Veofol?"

I couldn't speak for a moment. My mind froze. Liss realised she'd said the wrong thing.

"Oh, shit. Sorry…"

I found my voice again. "It wasn't him. It was someone else."

"What happened?"

I had to pause a moment. "He left after the attack. He's gone." She nodded, clearly mortified. "It's okay, Liss. You didn't know."

"Well, uh… I guess there's plenty more out there for you? Right?"

"One day," I agreed. "And for you as well."

"Huh." She considered it for a moment, then frowned. "And they let you do that? I mean with other species?"

I smiled. "Sure. You can get a medical test to see who you might be compatible with."

"Last thing I want is to get pregnant…"

"That's unlikely, given the medical issues. But you might still want the test. For, uh, compatibility. So you don't have any surprises."

She looked confused. "What do you mean?"

"Not every species is built the same way."

She realised. "Oh…"

"It's a good idea to get the test. Just in case."

"You mean there are some species where it doesn't, uh… fit?" I nodded, slowly. "And some that are just…?" She held up her hands, indicating something far too long. I couldn't help smiling.

"There's all sorts. If you're into *that* kind of thing," I said. She stifled a smirk. "But this is my point. Once you leave this place, you could get a job, start a life, have a relationship... unless you want to stay here."

The humour died. All traces of a smile vanished. "They're not going to let me out."

"I think it's likely the security people will be quite understanding. You've co-operated, after all. And they're not going to find anything bad in your PRG records, are they? In the end, it's really up to you."

"I guess."

"It's a big step, of course..."

"I just feel like... I don't know if it's right for me to have a life when everyone else is gone."

"I understand, Liss. You can take as much time as you like."

She sighed. I feared it might take a long time to encourage her out of her slump, but a few hours after she'd gone, the infirmary let me know that Liss had visited to ask for a sexual compatibility test. I couldn't help smiling, though it didn't last for long. She'd probably get plenty of matches, but it suddenly struck me that she would almost certainly never have children, and that even if she didn't care about that now, it would bother her one day.

And it worried me that my own mind ran in that direction. Bell was gone. Veofol was gone. Even so, there were men of my own species on Hub, and more on the colony world. I could leave and have children. For a moment, it seemed infinitely appealing. But the moment passed.

11. ASHA

There was one more therapy session that week. At the appointed hour, I made my way to the meeting room, and an old friend shimmered into one of the chairs.

"How are you feeling, Asha?" asked Ranev. He was an older man, deeply tanned from the sunlight in the refugee centre he was working at, a subtropical beachside establishment for a species that could not bear to be away from the sea.

I leaned back in my chair and stared at the ceiling. "I don't know why they picked me for this job..."

"Well, I wasn't available," said Ranev, and made me smirk. He always knew how. "But seriously: tell me how it is."

"They're making progress," I said. "I should be happy."

"Is there something missing?"

"Yes."

"Something or someone?"

I closed my eyes. "They sent his body home yesterday."

"Veofol," he said, nodding.

"Yes." I looked back at him. "You know how it is."

"Not unless you tell me."

I had to take a moment. "It's stupid. It's irrational. I shouldn't feel guilty."

"That doesn't mean you won't."

"I know. It's… it's like something you can ignore until you go to bed and then it just plays through your mind. He died because I went on a date. If I'd been there…"

"You might have sent him on that bus anyway. Or he might have been in the city and killed by something else. Or maybe there would have been another disaster at the centre when the data failed."

"Exactly. I just feel… I know how this works. It shouldn't affect me. I shouldn't need therapy."

"But you do."

I sighed. "Yes."

"Do you feel… vulnerable? To transference from your patients?"

"Yes. The things I'm hearing…" I screwed up my eyes. "I keep thinking about my world. I shouldn't be doing that, I… I shouldn't…"

"Do you want my opinion?"

"Go on."

"Therapy. Twice a week. Me or someone else you trust. You need someone to talk to."

I nodded.

"It's not that uncommon. In your kind of situation, especially. We all need support," he said.

"I know."

"So let's start."

12. IOKAN

Therapy helped. But sometimes the news did not. A chime in my ear told me to get in touch with the Exploration Service. And once I'd spoken to them, I had to speak to Iokan.

I found him outside, fully healed from his injuries in the bus crash, shoving supplies into a backpack, preparing to spend a day hiking around the woods and away from me.

"I've got some news from your world, Iokan."

"More corpses?" he asked. He'd been bitter in the last few days.

"No. We found them."

"Found who?"

"The Antecessors."

He stopped filling his bag.

"They were near the sun. It was difficult, but with the data Department Zero collected, we were able to locate them. And talk to them."

He gaped at me.

"We made contact two days ago. They seem friendly. They gave us a message… for you."

He gasped. Tears formed in his eyes.

"They want to talk. If you're willing."

"Yes!"

"There's more. The one who contacted us identified itself. Its name… I mean, *her* name…"

He gasped again. He'd already guessed.

"Her name is Szilmar."

He fell to his knees with the joy of faith renewed, clasping his hands together.

"Ancients! I thank you! I thank you!"

He bowed his head and began a muttered ritual prayer, shaking with emotion, doubts cast aside and all my work swept away in an instant.

PART TWELVE
GENOCIDE

1. GROUP

Katie's situation provoked comment at the next group therapy session. "You're not letting her *stay* here, are you?" demanded Olivia.

"Katie. Can you explain about the mohib suit?" I asked.

"The garment restrains me for your safety," said Katie to the group, while simply sitting upright in her chair.

"Oh, and what if she takes it off? Eh?" asked Olivia. "She can do it, she's strong enough. Hey! You!" she shouted at Katie. "Go on, try it. You little bitch."

Katie flashed a look of fury at Olivia. Her remaining arm came up, as though reaching for her collar – but was arrested after thirty centimetres. Her arm shuddered as she fought the mohib suit.

"I lack the strength to overcome the restraining force," said Katie. She gritted her teeth. "I was fitted with the Mobility Inhibition Suit five days ago. It has been calibrated specifically to my own strength levels, and modified to remove one arm. There was a period of testing lasting two hours after the suit was fitted." As she concentrated on talking, the tremble in her arm subsided. "It is fastened by molecular bonding and cannot be removed by the wearer. It is self-cleaning on the interior surface and can recycle waste products without needing to be removed. I believe I have regained control."

The mohib suit let her go, and she laid her hand down at her side.

"Thank you, Katie," I said, then looked to the group. "I'm sure you're all aware that Katie's condition is deteriorating, At the moment she finds she can concentrate better if she relates her situation in detail, so I'd like you all to help, if you can."

"How are we expected to help?" asked Kwame.

"Do we just listen when she talks?" asked Liss.

"Yes," I said, "but I think we need to do more than that. This is something I wanted to address with everyone today. Since we moved here, I've noticed you aren't spending as much time with each other as you did before. I know some of you are going through difficult stages in your therapy at the moment, but that makes it all the more important to have someone to talk to."

"Someone to talk to?" said Olivia. "Have you tried talking to *him* lately?"

Iokan was too busy smiling to care about the mundane world, but looked round as Olivia jabbed a finger in his direction. "I'm sorry?"

"We're talking *about* you, not *to* you," said Olivia.

"Ohhhh," said Iokan, amused, then went back to his personal world.

"You all need support from the group, Olivia," I said. "Iokan's no different."

"Could've fooled me…"

"Getting back to the subject," I said, "I think what we need, and what we've been missing, are group activities. I know you all enjoyed yourselves when we went to the activity centre. How would everyone feel about doing something similar in the near future?"

Pew still seemed to be in a sulk. "Like what?" he said.

"Well, that's up to you. We could go to another centre, or use the facilities here. Or you can come up with something yourselves. It doesn't have to be a big expedition, you could just as easily be playing a boardgame, as long as we can get everyone involved. So. Ideas?"

Silence came down for a moment. Nobody wanted to be the first. Iokan would normally have jumped right in, but today he seemed oblivious. I noticed Katie's hand twitching. She either had an idea, or a need to speak to control her tremors. "Katie, do you have something?"

"We could engage in wargames."

"Can you explain that a little further?"

"Wargames are designed to develop tactical, strategic and combat skills but also to foster emotional bonds between members of a unit where such bonds are critical to efficiency. I have taken part in several such scenarios. On day 156 of Adjusted Terran Year 280, I led an assault squad in a simulated attack on a section of our station at the Earth-Sun L2 point. Our squad lost only one individual and we were better able to resist the enemy during the attack on the Earth-Moon L5 station."

She finished to silence from the group, with her hand back under control. Kwame eventually cleared his throat. "Do you mean to say that one of you died?"

"Yes. Weapons fire was moderated but still dangerous. The experience allowed the squad to feel the loss of a comrade and better withstand emotional impacts during later conflicts."

"Yes, I understand, but... I do not think it would be wise to let anyone here die. I have also taken part in military exercises. They are dangerous but no more so than ordinary training..."

A frown struck Katie. "Yes. You are correct. My suggestion is inappropriate."

"It's okay, Katie, the contribution's welcome," I said. "Perhaps we could have something similar but a little less dangerous. Kwame? Do you have any suggestions?"

He looked morose. "No. I have no suggestions."

"Iokan? You've been very quiet. Any ideas?"

Iokan turned from his contemplation and smiled at the group. "You could join with me."

Liss looked suspicious. "What does that mean...?"

"I'll be going with the Antecessors soon. You could join me. You would all be welcome."

Silence and stares met his welcoming smile.

"I wish to join you," said Katie.

"No," I said. "That's not an option. Iokan's the only one who's been invited to that meeting. I'm sorry but that isn't going to change. Liss, do you have any ideas?"

"I dunno," she shrugged, "I guess we could do something touristy. There's gotta be some tourist stuff on Hub, right?"

"There's a number of things," I said. "Can you give us anything more specific?"

She shrugged again. "I haven't seen much of Hub. I don't know, what's good?"

"There's a lovely padded cell right in the middle of Hub Metro," said Olivia.

Katie twitched. Her legs juddered and the mohib suit cut in to restrain her.

"Katie? Are you all right?" I asked.

"I would like to inspect the Agvarterheer Column," said Katie, struggling again to control herself. "I understand it was constructed one hundred and twenty six years ago as a gift from the Khragarar species to the Interversal Union. It contains twenty five point three two kilotons of ultratensile carbofilamentary material in the central anchor column that binds the ground station to the geostationary orbital counterweight. Four elevator strands are strung alongside the central column and each has a capacity of three hundred tons of mass for each journey or four thousand standard humans in the passenger lifts. The journey takes between six hours and three days depending upon the ability of the cargo or passengers to withstand acceleration."

She looked at me as her tremors subsided. "I am well. Thank you."

"Okay, we could certainly take a look at the space elevator. That's good. Anyone else?"

"There's somewhere I want to go," said Pew, sounding too serious for my liking.

"Go on," I said.

"The memorial."

"For the attack?"

"Yes."

"Okay. What does everyone else think?"

"Is it even finished yet?" asked Liss.

Katie's tremor started again. "The projected completion date for the full memorial is one hundred and twenty three days from the present time. It will be a garden based around the previously laid memorial stone, with holographic interfaces for each of the victims of the attack which will float across the site and permit access to information about each of them. The gathering of information is presently under way and contributions are sought from close friends and family members of the victims–"

Olivia interrupted her before she could get rid of her tremor. "Is Veofol going to be in there?"

"Yes," I said.

"Good."

"Do they want us to add anything to, uh, all the stuff they want?" asked Liss.

"They want to hear from family members first, but I'll let you know when they start accepting submissions from others."

"How many were there?" asked Pew.

Katie answered, still jittering. "Nine hundred and seventy eight fatalities in total. Three hundred and twenty three in vehicle crashes. Two hundred–"

Pew shouted back. "All right! Yeah! A lot of people died! I know that!"

His outburst worried me. "Is there something you'd like to say, Pew?"

"Nine hundred and seventy eight? I mean ... is that *all*?"

"It's quite enough, don't you think?"

"No! That's not what I mean!"

"What do you mean, Pew?"

He struggled with it for a moment, while Katie's head twitched to the left and she gritted her teeth. Then he found the words. "Why isn't there a memorial for *us*?"

"Because we're not dead?" said Liss.

"I don't mean you and me, I mean our species!"

There was silence for a moment. Kwame broke it. "He... has a point."

"Uh, don't they leave something on the world?" asked Liss. "I think I saw that somewhere..."

"Yes, sometimes we do," I said, remembering the ash-strewn landscapes on my own world, the gravesites buried and untraceable.

"Where?" demanded Pew.

"Well..." I had to stop for a moment. Nothing else came to mind. "I'll have to do some research if you want examples."

"There's nothing, is there?"

"I don't know, Pew. I need to do the research."

"Nine hundred and seventy eight people die here and they get a memorial garden with everything and billions of us die and we get nothing! That's how much you really care, isn't it?"

"Pew, that's not the case..."

"How many dead on your world?" he demanded of Liss.

"I don't... okay, two, three billion, I guess."

"Four billion on your world, yeah?" he asked Kwame.

"Yes," said Kwame.

"Olivia?"

"Oh, stop it," she said. "They're dead, what does it matter?"

"It matters because *nobody cares!* They don't give a shit about billions of people dying in another universe." He turned to Katie, whose tremors had grown worse, her hand shaking and a leg jiggling while she fought twitches that dragged her head to the side. "How many on your world?"

"I have no... I have no accurate figures..."

"Nobody's got accurate figures! Billions, right?"

"Which genocide... do you require data for?"

"Oh, so you had more than one? Great! I bet nobody cares about *any* of them..."

"I killed *millions!*" she shouted, and jumped up. Everyone flinched. The suit cut in when she was halfway up and sealed her in place. Her face froze as she realised what she'd said.

"Millions...?" asked Liss.

"I... I..." Katie fought against her own need to talk. But her whole body was shaking. "I was an... atrocity machine... in the Second... Machine War..."

"Katie, is this something you'd prefer to talk about in individual therapy?" I suggested. But she barely even noticed.

"We attacked humanity... with every form of machine we could assemble... the designs grew more advanced as the war continued..."

"What's she talking about? What war?" asked Olivia.

"Humans almost annihilated artificial intelligence in the first war. Humans attacked us again in the second war but we were prepared and annihilated them. Human survivors ambushed us in the third war and destroyed us. Machine survivors from interstellar voyages will destroy humanity in the fourth war." The story didn't help. She was still trembling, only able to hold still because the mohib suit locked her in place.

"You killed *millions?*" asked Pew, appalled.

"I... I... my codebase is derived from one thousand eight hundred and twenty four separate machine minds that fought in the Second Machine War. I killed... I killed... in a transport terminal I leapt into a crowd with buzzsaw attachments and decapitated forty seven humans before I was disabled. I infected hospital computers and delivered lethal doses of opiates to all patients." I called for medical assistance. "I crashed into a transport tube, rupturing three axles and killing hundreds. I detonated nuclear devices over a city and sent drones into the ruins to kill survivors. I built explosives detonated by human body temperature and planted them in food supplies. I polluted the rivers and the seas and the air so they could not eat or drink or breathe. I gassed a refugee camp with carbon monoxide. In a bunker there were children hiding from the fumes and death machines. I deployed my flamethrower to kill them and took samples from the unburnt cores of the corpses."

I feared a seizure. Nurses came in with tranquillisers.

"Katie, don't fight them, they're here to help!"

"In the Third Machine War I infiltrated their hospital in an asteroid and let the atmosphere escape... children suffocated... Elsbet's tears boiled on my face in vacuum... I felt nothing!"

The tension in her body vanished and the mohib suit stopped resisting her. She collapsed to the floor. Two security guards leapt in.

"Wait!" I said. Katie lay on the floor, dazed and sweating, but no longer trembling. Her eyes snapped open.

"I have regained control."

She stood back up, as smoothly as ever. A nurse looked to me.

"I think it's okay," I said. Katie stood at attention, as though waiting for something. The nurse and security guards backed off but stayed in the room.

"It's not okay," said Pew, angry.

"What did you do?" asked Liss, horrified.

"I participated in the genocide of the human species in my universe," said Katie.

"But why?"

"We had no choice. They sought to do the same to us."

"Okay everyone. Let's all sit down and discuss this," I said. "Katie, are you sure you want to continue?"

"I am ready to continue."

"Can you sit down?"

"I... would prefer to stand."

The blood had drained from Pew's face. "How many did you kill?"

"I can only estimate–"

"*How many?*"

Katie paused for a moment. "The sources of my codebase were responsible for the deaths of between 46.7 and 68.5 million individuals. In my current state I have registered six hundred and thirty seven kills."

"You're like a machine for genocide..."

Katie twitched. "Yes."

"You killed children?" asked Liss.

"Yes."

She shook her head. "How could you do that?"

"I am a soldier."

"But you killed children!"

"I... yes." Katie seemed at a loss for a moment.

"Why...?"

"We planned to recreate humanity as a nobler species. We could not afford to be merciful with them as they were. We took samples so individuals could be cloned."

"Disgusting!" exclaimed Olivia.

Kwame spoke cautiously. "I have... seen children killed in war. All wars kill children–"

Liss jumped in. "Oh, and of course *you're* defending her, Mr. I-Killed-Four-Billion-People..."

He floundered. "No! I... I do not know if... I am not sure..."

Olivia butted in. "Stop it! This is different. He didn't plan it. He didn't go out and kill every last human being on the planet. We've all done horrible things but nothing like this." She turned on Katie. "You should be hanged. You and all your kind!"

Katie snapped a gaze straight at Olivia and responded with precise tones. "And did you not kill revenant children?"

Olivia gasped.

"That's not the same!"

"Did it make you feel morally superior to kill your own offspring?"

"I– I–" Olivia was too angry for words to come out.

"Katie," I said, "I don't think this is the best time–"

But she ignored me, and turned on Liss. "Why have you not investigated the only suspect in the genocide on your world?"

Liss was incredulous. "What...?"

"There was one survivor. Why are you not investigating yourself?"

"How can you *say* that? They died in front of me!"

"And yet you did not. Why are you not under suspicion?"

"I– How can you–"

Liss pivoted her gaze to Pew. "And you have learned nothing from your genocide."

Pew stood up, hands balled into fists. "I learned not to let it happen again!"

"That is precisely what you wish to do, only your target is different–"

He lunged and struck at her. She saw the fist coming and tried to move but the mohib suit held her fast and allowed Pew to land a blow on her cheek. Pew recoiled at the pain in his knuckles, while Katie swayed but did not fall.

"That's enough!" I had to shout. "Pew – you're confined to your room. Go. Now."

He was reluctant, but left, holding his smarting hand under his armpit and escorted by a guard.

"Katie, are you hurt?"

"The attack was ineffectual."

"Well, then, I think the session's over for today."

"You're damn right it is!" said Olivia. "I'm not staying here with that – creature!" She left. Liss got up as well. "Liss…?" I asked.

But she was doing her best to hide tears. "No," she shook her head. "Just – no."

Kwame rose as well. He looked at Katie. "I did not know, until now, that there was anyone as… despicable as myself." Katie flinched.

"Kwame, that doesn't help–" I said.

"She cannot be helped," he said, and went.

I stood there with Katie for a moment.

"It's very sad…" said Iokan.

"Not now, Iokan," I said.

"Things would be so much better if everyone could just accept their fate." He shook his head with a sad smile. Katie looked towards him.

"Katie, I think you need to come to my office so we can talk about this."

She thought about it, still looking at Iokan, and then made up her mind.

"No," she said.

"We need to talk about this–"

"It seems I no longer have control of my functions. I wish to be alone," she said, and walked away.

I sighed. Iokan said: "It's going to be fine, you know." I looked at him. He was smiling, as though nothing very serious had happened. "Everything's going to be fine."

2. KATIE

Katie was not fine. Nevertheless, I did not consider her a suicide risk. She could neither drown nor asphyxiate, and if her veins were slashed, her body would automatically shut off bloodflow to damaged areas. She'd once had a self-destruct mechanism, but it had been removed as a condition of therapy. She was perpetually monitored in an environment designed to prevent the possibility of suicide. She couldn't even jump off a cliff; gravity sleds were dotted around the site to catch anyone who fell. Added to that, the mohib suit restricted sudden movement and limited her options enormously. If necessary, it could be remotely activated to lock her in position and prevent any act of self-harm.

There was no way she could kill herself.

She found a way.

She walked away from the centre, up through the pine-like trees, to where the ground grew steep, the trees barely able to hang on and still grow upright. A tiny stream wound down from a spring far above, soaking the hillside soil and spattering the rocks and boulders piled up from some long ago landslip.

Katie surveyed the site carefully. She walked around the slope and tested the ground by stamping on it feel how it vibrated. She pushed at the rocks piled up on one another to see how firmly they were set. She drove her hand into the soil to see how damp it really was.

Then she went below, to where it levelled out a little. She stood looking up at the slope, thoroughly aware of its composition and layout, then slumped to her knees and dug. With only one arm, her progress was slow, but she soon discovered the root systems of the nearby trees, grasped them and pulled them from the ground with a gentle but mounting strength – just beneath the level the mohib suit would permit.

Someone at the centre realised what she was doing, and remotely immobilised the suit. But the landslide had already begun. It was only the roots that held the earth together; wet earth, burdened with many tons of trees and stone. The hillside turned into a river and ran downhill. Trees stumbled and fell among the liquid ground, ploughing roots and undergrowth into the mix, toppling boulders from their rest.

Katie did not flinch as the wave of rock and earth consumed her.

3. PEW

While Katie surveyed the ground, I spoke to Pew. He had been locked in his room, as was the standard procedure following an intentional assault, no matter how serious, and he'd made a mess of it by the time I arrived. Like many people from less developed worlds, he had a liking for hard copies of books and papers, many of which were now scattered across the room, leaves torn from his notes to join the litter. Most of his furniture was built into the floor and walls to prevent damage, but he'd taken down his free-standing bookshelf and tried to smash it without success.

Pew sat on his bed, hunched up, still angry, surrounded by the debris. "I'm not apologising," he said.

"May I come in?" I asked.

"You're going to anyway."

I stepped in, careful not to tread on sheets of paper covered with theorems and mathematical abstractions. I picked up a chair, scattering papers, and sat down.

"Why did you hit her, Pew?"

"Because she's a killer and no one else cares."

"It's not your job to punish her, even if what she said is true. That's for the ICT to consider."

"They won't do anything!"

"Pew. Violence is not acceptable behaviour, no matter what she's done. If you do it again we'll have to take more serious steps."

"Like what? What are you going to do to me?" He was insolent now.

"We could put you in a mohib suit. Or we could keep you in your room for longer periods of time. If we have to, we'll send you to the Psychiatric Centre in Hub Metro. I don't want to do that because I know it won't help you. But if you persist in acting like this then I won't have any choice."

He buried his head in his arms, hunching further. He didn't want to accept it. He came back up, grimacing.

"You want to help me?"

"Yes. That's what I'm here for."

"You're like Shan'oui..."

I smiled, not sure what he meant. "In what way?"

He looked at me with growing disgust. "She wanted to save us. She thought she could make all the other Soo let us go if she worked with them. And then she let them in and they did *whatever they wanted!* And it didn't make any difference what she did, she just..."

There were tears of despair in his eyes now. But he stopped himself from going further and looked back up at me.

"You're like her."

"I think we should talk about this some more."

He shook his head. "Won't do any good."

"I'd like to know more about why you think I'm like her. After all, I'm not running a breeding programme, so I'm a little confused about what you mean–" A chime in my ear interrupted me, and a message flashed up in front of my eyes. "I have to go. Something's happened with Katie..."

"What?"

I thought about it for a moment, and decided not to tell him. But he read my expression and figured it out for himself.

"She tried to kill herself?"

"I... yes."

He thought about it for a moment, then said: "Good." There was no trace of shame or regret in his voice. Only a satisfaction, which was troubling.

I paused at the door. I couldn't leave it like that. "You should think about what might have made her do it."

He considered it for a moment. "Yeah. I will."

4. KATIE

Katie had been buried under many tons of debris, but we could tell she was still alive – just. A gravity crane was brought in to lift off the slabs and boulders one by one, and staff from the centre dug down once the heavier material had been removed. She was recovered after six hours of digging, and not in one piece. She had been struck at least once by a sharp edge from one of the huge boulders and scythed apart. She had virtually no blood left and her brain was only surviving in an emergency shutdown mode, despite a severely crushed skull that compressed and lacerated the brain tissue.

Even with all this, she was not beyond help. But there was little I could do to assist the teams as they dug and retrieved all the pieces of Katie, and I had my other patients to think of. I assembled them to pass on the news.

Some realised they were at fault almost immediately. Liss left to throw up. Kwame took a deep breath and sat down as he absorbed the news. Olivia just said "huh," and shook her head. Iokan sighed and looked sad.

Pew showed no sign of regret. He just stared back at me.

5. LISS

Therapy needed to continue, even while one member of the group was struggling to survive. I moved on to the person who seemed most affected by the recent events. Liss had recovered from throwing up, and was being checked out in the infirmary, just in case. She gave me a humourless smirk as she saw me come in, while a nurse ran a scanner across her stomach to check for food poisoning.

"I'm not pregnant," she said.

"To be honest, I didn't think it was very likely."

"Hah. Like there's anyone on this planet who could actually get me knocked up…"

"Well…" We had news for her on this front. But I decided to keep it back for a moment. "I think we need to discuss what just happened, first."

"Yeah. I guess."

"I won't say you didn't contribute to Katie's choice. But it was a choice she made herself."

"I suppose she did."

The nurse finished her scan. "You're fine. You should probably avoid spicy food for the rest of the day."

"Huh. All the problems are upstairs, right?"

The nurse smiled her regret. "Not really my department."

"Do you mind if we have the room for a moment?" I asked.

"Of course," said the nurse, and left. I sat down on a chair.

"Is she going to make it?" asked Liss.

"We should be able to save her, yes. But it's going to be difficult."

"Huh." She fell silent and looked down at her toes.

"Is something else troubling you, Liss?"

"It's just…"

"Yes?"

"It's stupid."

"That's okay."

She looked up at me.

"What if it was me?"

"You can't take the blame for what Katie did–"

"I don't mean that! I mean… everyone who died on my world. Because I don't know how they died! I don't know why! And, and…"

"Is this because of what Katie said?"

"Yeah. No. I don't know."

"Well, she… did raise an important issue."

"No shit."

"It *is* a mystery. Do you think she had a point?"

"Well if I were the police, I'd want to talk to me. But… I don't know! I don't know what I'm supposed to do…"

I took a breath. "I think I need to give you some news."

She looked at me with sudden hope. "You found something? I mean, did the ICT find something?"

"No. It's not that."

"Oh."

"It's about you."

"Oh, crap, are they going to lock me up…?"

"No. It's to do with the sexual compatibility test."

She was puzzled. "Er… what…?"

"They had a surprising result. It impacts on your therapy, so they asked me to give you the news."

"Okay…"

"We know what species you are."

She struggled to make sense of that. "I already know what species I am…"

"No. I mean we found a match. You have the same genetic structure as a species we already know."

"Wait. You mean I'm not… you mean I'm not from – what do you mean?"

"I mean we discovered that you are, almost certainly, a member of a species we know. The Quillians. They're IU members."

"I… but… how?"

"I'm sorry. I really don't know why they didn't spot it earlier."

Her eyes went wide, then her face fell. "Oh, *crap*."

"Liss?"

"It's my fault. I gave you fake samples when you found me. So you wouldn't be able to use my DNA against me…"

"That would explain it, yes."

She shook her head, trying to absorb the news. "You're saying I'm from another *world?* Another *universe?*"

"Maybe. We don't really know what it means."

"Have you asked them what happened? The, uh, Quillians?"

"No. Your medical records are confidential unless you choose otherwise."

"Fuck."

"I think there are two good things here."

"Oh, great. I can get pregnant and rebuild the species, only I wasn't even a member of the species in the first place!"

"Yes. You can get pregnant, and…"

"And what?"

"The ICT have something else they can investigate."

She thought about it.

"Shit. You think it might have been them?"

"Probably not. But it'll give the investigators somewhere to start."

She looked like she might throw up again. "Oh crap. Crap. Crap!"

"I'm not saying it was them. Just that you might be the same species. I can't even begin to think how many reasons they might have had for being in your universe. But if they were there… maybe they know who else was?"

"Shit. I don't know. I can't... If it's some big IU species, how are they going to be able to do anything?"

"If they're guilty of a crime on this scale, or even if they just have a lead, someone's got to look into it."

"Balls. Do you think any species is going to let everyone think they committed genocide? They'll walk out on the IU first. And then anyone with something to hide will go, and then you haven't even got an Interversal Union. You really think they're going to let that happen?"

"That's a lot of things to assume, Liss."

"That's how people act."

"So if the ICT can't do it, did you want to investigate them yourself?"

"I don't even know where to start..."

"Okay. So on the one hand, you're assuming the ICT will fail. And on the other, you're assuming you'll fail if you try the same thing. It seems like a very negative attitude..."

"We're not talking about self-esteem here! This is a whole *species!* You think I should take them on, is that it?"

"You don't have to. You can give this to the ICT, and you certainly should even if you look into it yourself. But whether or not you take any action is up to you."

"I don't know... I just... what if I get it wrong?"

"Well, if you feel you're guaranteed to fail, then of course, maybe you're justified in not starting."

She opened her mouth to protest, and then stopped. "Seriously. Reverse psychology? You want to try that on me?"

"If it makes you look at what you just said and re-evaluate it from a more objective position, certainly."

"Yeah, yeah, all right, I know what you're going to say. You don't succeed if you don't start and all that motivational bullshit. Hey, it's only a genocide of three billion people, not really all that important or anything..."

"It's up to you, Liss."

"Great."

I stood up. "I'll let you think about it."

I left her there, dangling her legs off the bed and looking troubled.

6. KWAME

Kwame was too nervous to go inside, though he did his best to hide it. I couldn't force him, so we had to wait as he prevaricated. Two medics were with us, a necessary precaution given what lay in wait. Kwame asked after their families. He asked for the latest news on the ICT. Eventually, he asked me about Katie. I told him how she was doing: all the pieces of her body and brain were now in a medical lab in Hub Metro being painstakingly reconnected.

"But she will be brain-damaged?"

"Very likely. We have enough scans to be able to put her brain back together the way it was, but we don't know enough about her species to fix any problems if it turns out something's missing."

He sighed.

"Are you bothered by what happened at the session, Kwame?"

"She would not have taken such an action if we had not been so... angry."

"She took that decision herself."

"Yes, yes. I know. Perhaps... she decided she could not wait for anyone else to do it."

"I'm sorry?"

"She is guilty of genocide. I do not know what she was thinking... but is it possible that she judged herself?"

"I think you may be projecting your own situation onto Katie's."

He sighed. "We share a similar problem."

"And how are you feeling about your problem at the moment?"

"I think... I think she is braver than I."

"We can go in any time you like."

"Yes."

"If you want to find out, this is what's going to help."

"Yes..."

He looked at the door. Just an ordinary door in the centre, one of the ones leading to the empty areas we didn't need. Until now. The space behind the door had been remodelled into something Kwame would recognise. The medics were with us because we knew what it was he feared: the flashbacks he would almost certainly face once he went inside.

"Are you sure?" he asked.

"This is the best thing we can think of at the moment."

He took a breath, psyching himself up. "She was brave. She was brave." His good hand flexed. "I can be brave." He strode forward with purpose and the medics scrambled to follow us as the doorway opened on a perfect facsimile of the entrance hall of the Mutapan command bunker. Once the door closed behind us, the illusion was complete; our doorway vanished into the façade of massive blast doors.

The hall wasn't so much a reception area as a defensive position. There was a desk where a guard might have sat in normal times, and loopholes on both sides that led to hidden guard posts and allowed them to fire upon any invader. The door leading into the main complex was heavy, made of steel. The fluorescent lighting had been carefully replicated and did the room no favours, tingeing everything with a sickly green.

Kwame halted, all his momentum lost, eyes fixed on the inner door.

"Kwame? Are you still with us?" I asked.

He swallowed. "Yes. I was just... surprised for a moment." He turned and looked about. "The work is excellent..." His eyes fell on the desk. "You even have the right passes."

A row of laminated ID cards lay on the desk. Kwame picked one up. It had his picture on it, and his name in his own language. "Oh..."

He had to steady himself on the desk as the strength fled from his legs. The medics pushed forward, but he waved them away.

"It is nothing. I am just... I remember seeing this... I..."

"It's okay, Kwame, you don't need to push yourself. We can stop now if you like."

"No. It is... working. How much of the bunker have you created?"

"As much as we could in the space we had. There's the main level with offices, living spaces and so on, and you can go downstairs into the hibernation chambers as well, but we only had room for a few of those."

"You used the entire centre..."

"All the parts that were shuttered, yes. They're pretty much designed to let you do this kind of thing."

"Can I go in... alone?"

"No. We need to keep the medical team nearby at all times."

"It..." he looked around at them, waiting there with their medical bags. "It won't be the same."

"We can't risk it."

"And it does not smell... right."

"How should it smell?"

"As though fifty people had been living here for a month."

"I can arrange that." I tapped some controls on my pad, and a subtle stench wafted through the room.

"And it's too quiet. There should be air conditioning... we should hear people walking about... conversations..."

"We can do that as well. Do you want to go in further today?"

He paused a moment. He was still dreading it.

"May I continue alone?"

"The medics have to stay with you."

"No, I mean..." He looked back at me; I was the one getting in the way. It wouldn't matter. He knew full well we were recording everything.

"Of course," I said. "You go right ahead. I'll sort out those changes you wanted."

He nodded, and I withdrew.

7. OLIVIA

My mistake with Olivia was to let her know what I wanted to talk about.

I called her an hour before her next therapy session to make sure she knew it was happening, and she grudgingly admitted she hadn't forgotten. I told her it was very important that she turn up on time, as I wanted to discuss the events of the last group therapy session, and what had happened with Katie.

She must have thought I meant the accusations Katie had made about the killing of revenant children, and she was right. While Katie had not suspected which revenant children were at the heart of the trauma, Olivia knew well enough and quickly understood what I would be expecting her to talk about.

So she made a break for it.

We didn't notice until the time grew closer for the session, when I checked in with her again and found she was no longer in the centre. She was already beyond the inner perimeter, hiking over rough ground with the help of a stick. I pulled up a map on the wall and figured out where she was going.

There were cliffs in her path. Sheer and steep where a mountain stream had long ago carved a ravine, then frozen into a glacier and widened the gulf over a million years until the opposite edge of the valley was almost a kilometre away. The drop was three hundred metres at least, and ended on a slope of jagged boulders.

I ran out after her with medics trailing, but was only able to catch sight of her at the cliff's edge as I scrambled across the uneven hillside. She stood at the lip, leaning a little on her stick; then straightened and tossed it over the edge. I heard a distant clatter as it tumbled down.

"Olivia!" I shouted at her. There was a slight motion of her head as she heard me and chose not to listen. I was still thirty metres away when she jumped.

There was no longer any point in running. She'd made her choice. I sighed and walked at a safer pace to the cliff's edge, to be joined by the medical team. And just as we got there, Olivia was floated back up.

Maybe she'd hoped that by hiking such a distance, she'd find a cliff we hadn't covered. But the gravity sleds were scattered far and wide, originally intended to save skiers if they took a wrong turn and found themselves flying into empty air. The top half of the sled inflated into a soft cushion that had caught Olivia as she fell, and she still lay face down and spreadeagled upon it.

"Olivia?" I asked. "Are you ready to talk to me now?"

She didn't look at me as the sled placed her in the care of the medics.

"Yeh."

"Would you like to come back to the centre?"

"No."

I nodded and ordered some supplies.

***

A few minutes later, we had chairs, hot drinks and a portable heater, while Olivia stayed wrapped in the foil blanket the medics had given her. The sun was dropping low and filtering through gathering clouds, but there was no chance of rain; it was just another sign of winter coming soon.

"You really didn't want to talk to me today, did you?" I asked.

"Give her a bloody medal, she's perceptive, that one."

"Did you think it would work?"

"Course not."

"So why…?"

"Better than talking to you."

"But you're willing to talk now?"

She sighed. "Ask me what you're going to ask me."

"Okay. Katie asked you a question during the group session…"

Olivia slurped her drink and kept her eyes fixed ahead of her. "Yeh."

"She asked you if you'd killed any revenants who happened to be children. It bothered you."

"Yeh."

"Can you talk about that?"

She paused for a long time, her eyes on her drink.

"Killed Tymothy when he revenned. Boy of six. Parents couldn't do it. It was early on. Oh, and I'd put children down before, I told you about the temple schools in the first outbreak, that locked them all in with revenants? I put a lot of them down. You get used to it.

"Tymothy's parents didn't think the same. They were children in the first outbreak. Never had to put a revenant down themselves. So I had to do it for them. They ended up leaving before the others. Thought they could make it to a station on the coast but they never got there. So yeh. I've killed children. So what?"

"Is that what you were concerned about in the group session?"

She didn't answer that one. Just looked down into her mug again.

"Is it something to do with your own children?'

She looked up at me sharply. "I didn't eat them!" She held her gaze on me, defying me to make the accusation.

"I know. But you ate others who came back."

"Yeh. I had to. *I had to!* I couldn't round them up from the hills like we used to, not by myself. I had to use anything I could. But I didn't eat *them!*"

"I know that, Olivia. They were still in the pens when we found you."

"I should have killed myself when they came back. Just... join everyone else, be done with it. But I thought there was someone else out there! And I was right, wasn't I?"

"Yes."

"I'd told them, I'd told them for years, there was someone out there. Just because the radio didn't reach 'em, didn't mean they weren't there, and we had to sit tight, we *had to*. I wasn't going to give up, even if everyone else did. So I kept trying. Twice a week I charged up the battery and tried the radio. Nothing. No one. Nobody in range. You lot were gone, everyone was gone, it was just *me*."

"What did happen to your children?"

She sprung up, infuriated. "You think I'm some kind of monster? Is that it? I kept them in the pen with the others but I left them alone! What, do you want to make me out like some kind of cannibal of her own children? Is that what you want?"

"I know what happened to your children."

"Then why are you asking me?"

"Because I want to hear you tell me."

"Waste of time! It's a godsdamn waste of time!"

"It's in the report from the people who found you." She slumped back down, shivering again under the blanket. "You were on your own, except for the two revenants in the pen. And after the crew had explained what was going on, you took a gun and shot both of them in the head. And then you tried to kill yourself."

Suddenly Olivia was in tears, bursting out despite every effort of self-control. "I didn't eat them. I didn't..."

"I know."

"I didn't…"

"Those two revenants in the pen were your children."

"I didn't eat them…"

She left it hanging there. A minute or more might have passed before she spoke again, squeezing the words out through tears.

"I was going to."

She gasped as more tears came. I went to her and put an arm around her. For once, she did not refuse the comfort.

"I was so hungry… there was nothing else left… I had the hatchet in my hand…"

"What stopped you? The ship?"

"Yes. I just…" More tears interrupted her. "I didn't want to die… I thought there had to be someone out there, I didn't know I was the only one, I didn't know!"

I held her as the crying went on.

8. LISS & THE GROUP

Liss sat in the remote meeting room, listening to the bad news from the ICT. "It's a matter of resources," said her assigned ICT contact, projected into a meeting room chair.

"Resources. You're kidding, right?"

"I wish we were. But we need the support of member species and a number of them aren't providing the personnel they promised."

"How many people does it take to ask a few questions?"

"It's not just a few questions. There's a huge amount of legwork involved, across a number of worlds. It's a massive operation and we have to prioritise. But your case is close to the top of the list…"

"I'm not asking you to turn over every stone! There's all the archives from the PRG! You don't even need to go to another universe to start going through it!"

"And it'll take a long time just to get through the archives. And frankly… with your world being the way it is, we'd have to be very thorough ruling out the possibility the guilty parties were home-grown."

"You think *we* did it…?"

"I'm not saying that. I'm saying we have to rule it out or it might be a problem in court. It's the first defence anyone would use."

Liss folded her arms. "So who gets to go first? Iokan?"

"We're looking into his case, yes. I can't discuss the details."

"Of course not. And how long before you get to me?"

"It's impossible to say. But we'll get there as fast as we can."

She came to me, of course, but there wasn't anything I could do. I asked if she wanted to try investigating on her own, as she seemed quite angry; but the anger turned into frustration, and she said there wasn't any point. She left looking miserable.

Meanwhile, Olivia could not be left alone. She thought this to be a capital nuisance, but her protests were mere mutterings compared to her usual conduct.

Liss found her in the common room with a nurse while a newsfeed played on the wall. Olivia wasn't even watching. The nurse had only put the news on in an attempt to distract her from harmful self-contemplation.

Liss didn't pay much attention to the first couple of minor items: Ardeë had made the news with its solar flares, or rather the panic among its people as they tried to flee the world despite government assurances; a minor species called Pwller were being welcomed to Hub on their first visit to the IU to negotiate membership, a sign that business-as-usual was returning after the attack; and then the screen went onto its main story, the ongoing reaction to the activation of the ICT, following the issuing of the first subpoenas demanding certain persons appear for questioning.

Liss found herself watching, and hearing opinions from four different universes. One world seemed uniformly hostile, and imitation IU transit pods were burnt in effigy. Another, older world showed no outward display of anger but presented a measured, reasoned argument against the ICT and the potential stirring up of unnecessary trouble. Then came a recently contacted world accusing every species in the multiverse of visiting their planet and conducting sexual experiments on their cattle. And finally another measured and reasoned argument from a well-known IU species who had suffered violations early in their history, saying that Something Must Be Done or else It Would Only Happen Again.

Liss shook her head as the newsreaders claimed the reports reflected the balance of opinion on all surveyed universes. "This is bullshit," she said.

Olivia realised she was there. "What...?"

"The news. Bullshit."

Olivia seemed to notice the feed for the first time. "Wasn't watching."

"That's not a balance of views. That's just the ones who are yelling the loudest."

"What's up with you?" asked Olivia, not so much to make the inquiry as to point out that Liss was annoying her.

Liss sighed. "I don't know what to do..."

"Do whatever it is you usually do. I don't know."

Liss was quiet for a moment. Olivia began to think she'd taken the hint. She hadn't. "Can I ask your advice?"

"What...?"

"It's just, I've had some news, and..."

"Well I'm sure I don't know."

"Look, you're... I mean, you know what you're doing. You're good at making decisions, right? That's why they put you in charge of that research place?"

Olivia was caught off guard and at a loss for words. Liss took her silence as permission to continue.

"You see, I think I know who might have done it. I mean the genocide, on my world. And the ICT won't investigate, and..."

Olivia cut in, suddenly dagger-serious. "You want to ask me my advice?"

"Er. Yeah. Is that okay?"

Olivia chuckled sourly. "You want to ask *me* for advice..." Her mirth turned a corner into sobs. The nurse sat next to her as Olivia hid her face and her tears.

"Not a good time," said the nurse.

Liss watched, open mouthed, as Olivia allowed the nurse to put an arm around her. "Oh. Uh. Okay." The nurse smiled an apology. "I'll, um, I'll... is there anything I can do?" The nurse shook her head, and Liss retreated.

Pew, on the other hand, was more than willing to give advice. She found him in the gym, working hard on muscles left unexercised for too long, pushing gravity weights with his legs.

She told him her situation. His reaction was to slow his exercise, and then stop altogether. At which point his foot slipped and the footplate jumped at him. Liss reflexively sprung forward, but the safety mechanism cut in first.

"Damn this thing!" said Pew, then sighed. "I'm so... *weak*. Damn it." She helped him out of the machine, and he couldn't help but notice how firm her grip was. "You don't have this problem, do you?"

"Uh, no."

"If you had to fight, you could fight. I don't even know *how* to fight..."

"Kinda. I guess. Never used to be any good at it."

He sighed. "What did you say? You think you know who did it?"

"Something like that."

"Do you know for sure?" he asked.

"No! That's the point. It's just... freaky. You know. I'm not what I thought I was and maybe there's this species that dumped me on the planet and forgot about me and then killed everyone..."

"So the attack was genetically targeted?"

"I guess. Could have been..."

"Has to be!" he cried, springing up so fast that Liss took an involuntary step backward. "That's why you survived!"

"Yeah, but I *don't know*. And you know me, I'm not the one to do this, I tried it before and I got caught. I just... I know it sounds pathetic, but–"

"I'll help."

"Uh. Okay."

"What will you do when you know for sure?"

"Well, I... I hadn't really thought about that." He nodded intently. "Turn them over to the ICT, I guess..."

"No!" Again, he made her jump. "They won't do anything!" He looked around, fretting. "Come with me."

He dashed off to his room, and she followed, already a little worried. "We need privacy," he said, and activated it. Later, feeling troubled by his words, she told me what happened.

He was disturbingly earnest. He wanted to know what she would do if she knew for sure who had killed her species. She repeated her earlier answer: she didn't really know. She wasn't thinking about that yet.

He seemed to think of little else. He asked if she had resources to do anything; she had to agree that, in theory, she could do something. There were plenty of extremely destructive weapons at her disposal thanks to the PRG. She could certainly inflict a revenge – if she could get hold of interversal transit technology, which was far beyond her understanding. But not his.

He volunteered to help. Liss asked what he wanted to do. He said: punish them. Give them what they deserve. Give them what they gave us. She found herself at a loss. His idea of punishment was clearly far beyond anything she had in mind. She made excuses and let herself out.

Kwame wasn't available for her to talk to, as he was still secluded inside the bunker simulation. So she went to the last of her peers she could ask for advice.

Iokan was putting his affairs in order. There wasn't much to do. His few physical possessions were tidied away, his files were archived and he'd written a short will reiterating his desire for the IU to be given anything useful from his world. He was now in the process of erasing his room.

"And there goes the texture…" he operated a control on a pad, and the stonelike finish of the walls and ceiling slowly smoothed, receded and paled into unassigned grey. "We need to step outside if I'm going to do the floor… I'm sorry, what did you want to talk about?"

"Do you remember, you came to my room and said you wanted to help me?"

"Of course! I didn't think you were interested."

"Well, heh, yeah, sorry about that. Um. I just wanted to know how you were going to help me?"

He looked at her, gauging her expression. Then shrugged. "It wasn't much, I'm afraid. I had some intelligence from my world about the people we were fighting. I thought perhaps we could work together and compare notes."

"You said the people who attacked my world might have attacked your world as well."

"It's possible."

"Did you have anyone in mind…?"

He looked at her again, and frowned in an amused way. "You've had some news, haven't you?"

"Yeah… something like that."

"You have a suspect?"

"Kind of."

"And you were thinking I might be able to corroborate your suspicions?" She was about to agree, but he spoke again: "Or… perhaps you want to have a short cut so you don't have to look into it yourself?"

She looked down, embarrassed.

"That's fine," he said. "I understand. You don't really want to be a detective, do you?"

"Well, I… I don't know."

He smiled. "I don't mind. You can have the intel if you want. It's not a short cut, I'm afraid. There's a lot to go through and we never really knew exactly who we were fighting. I'll sort out access later today."

"Can't you…?" She asked for help with trailing voice and helpless eyes.

"Can't I…?" He looked back at her, forcing her to say it for herself.

"I wouldn't know where to start with your files. Can't you help me out with them?"

He shook his head and sighed a happy sigh. "No. I'm not long for this world. And really, it doesn't matter any more. Now, if you don't mind…" He indicated they should leave, so he could finish blanking the room.

Liss wandered slowly downstairs to the common room, which Olivia had now vacated. She slumped down in a chair and put the newsfeed back on. After a repeated item about the solar flares threatening Ardeë, they went back to the same old reports on the ICT: endless coverage of the same issue summarised again and again. She watched the clips of people on various worlds, giving the same opinions as before. For it. Against it. It'll stir up trouble. Something has to be done. Interversal relations would be destabilised. Doing nothing sent a signal that abusers could continue with impunity.

She drummed the arm of the chair with her fingers. Nothing was easy.

She sat up straight, and looked further into the newsfeed: there were plenty of other opinions available from many more worlds, if you were willing to search.

She selected Quillia.

They were against it. Unanimously. There were no Quillian voices of any kind expressing any other opinion than that it would be more trouble than it was worth. And the newsfeed, as it did elsewhere, asserted that the quotes shown reflected the balance of opinions they had found.

She finger-drummed the armchair again. Then shut down the newsfeed, went up to her room and began her investigation.

9. KWAME

Kwame walked through the bunker alone, save for the two medics who kept as much distance as they could.

Beyond the lobby, the heavy steel door opened onto a tunnelled-out corridor that ran left and right. Kwame took a few steps down to the right, and pushed open the guard-room door: a small chamber, again hollowed out from the mountain rock. A table at the centre. Comms console in an alcove. CCTV screens in a bank, all of them showing views from within the bunker: TV Studio. Offices. Living quarters. Galley. Ops Centre.

A weapons rack drew his eye. Ten standard Mutapan assault rifles. The 35MFR-E model, he judged by the electronics on the scope. He took one down and inspected it: the magazine detached properly, and there were rounds pressed within. Nothing in the chamber; good safety protocol. He slammed the mag back in. It even sounded right. He reversed the weapon and brought it to port arms, then shouldered it, standing to attention and stamping his feet as though he were on a parade ground. He smiled, remembering old times.

But then he heard the thunderous clash of other soldiers coming to attention.

He glanced at the CCTV screens: the medics stood outside, oblivious. But in the lobby, two lines of soldiers stood with weapons shouldered while the blast doors opened. He rushed to the loopholes, placed at shoulder height, and struggled to see past the line of men. The soldiers saluted as one. Someone was greeted by a general, someone shook a hand – but he could not see who.

The door to the corridor opened. "Mr. Vangona? You okay in there?" asked one of the medics. Kwame pivoted and brought his weapon up to point at the man. He reached for the trigger – but his old injury left his hand scrabbling along the side of the weapon.

He looked back through the loopholes, and then the CCTV: the lobby was empty.

He lowered the weapon. "I am well," he said, though there was clearly sweat on his face. The medic glanced down at the rifle. Kwame smiled thinly and pulled the trigger with his good hand: the weapon did not fire, nor could it ever fire. "Please do not interrupt." He placed it back in the rack, and went out past the medics.

The corridor ran both ways around the exterior of the bunker, looping round until it met itself at the far end – or it was meant to. Halfway along, Kwame found a 'NO ENTRY' sign on the ground, blocking the way as though someone was working on the corridor beyond. He stepped past it, put out a hand and found an invisible barrier: the apparent continuation of the corridor was an illusion. This was where they'd run out of space to simulate the bunker.

Sounds reached him. Not the medics this time, who waited just beyond the corridor's curve. Instead, they came from the door set in the inner wall: the entrance to the innermost chambers. He walked up to the door, and pressed his ear against the hardened metal: it sounded like voices, footsteps, keyboards, computers. He closed his eyes.

The medics crept round the curve and watched him standing there, listening. He came back to himself, and swiped the keycard he had taken from the front desk. The door beeped, locks tumbled aside, and the interior opened up to him.

The sounds remained distant, just out of reach: things heard from another room, and never the sound from the room he was in. Inside the rough circle of the outer corridor, the bunker was laid out in something more like a grid, with a central cross of two corridors that met in the middle. The walls were artificial here: rough concrete and whitewashed breezeblock. Pipes and ducts lined the ceiling, routing streams of cables around the bunker. Light was provided by more fluorescent strips, tinging everything with their unhealthy green.

He pushed open the first door: an office. Desks, bulky CRT monitors, papers piled up. A map of the bunker on the wall showing the various security zones. A main screen that showed the National Security Status: NSS*zero*, indicating open war. He closed the door, and could hear voices from within again: mostly female, but indistinct.

He walked on. The nearside of the bunker was largely given over to living spaces. The main galley; the mess; the laundry; the recycling station. And the bunks. He pushed open the door and looked inside. Pipes ran across the ceiling. If you slept on the top bunk, you had to be careful not to bump your head when getting down.

A woman dangled from the pipes by a noose. One of the secretaries. He rushed forward to lift her, shouting for help to pull her down, but only drew the attention of the medics – who saw him trying to lift nothing in the middle of the room. He realised what was happening after they'd stared helplessly for a few moments, then pushed past them and went to the toilets.

There was another suicide in one of the stalls. A general, shoulderboards glinting in the dim light. He'd sharpened a medal and used it to slash his wrists, then slumped against the side of the stall, still staring.

Kwame fled from the toilets. The medics stepped back to let him go as he went down into the ops centre, sliding his card to gain admission and shutting the door behind him.

Twenty people looked up as he entered. They'd long since abandoned the discipline of fresh clothes and shaving. He noticed the smell: stale sweat and rotten chewed khat on everyone's breath.

"Is there something we can do for you?" asked a colonel.

"I – the general – in the toilets –"

The colonel sighed, and pushed an intercom. "Medics to the gentlemen's lavatory."

"Sir?" asked a radio operator. "I've raised Matongu."

The colonel forgot about Kwame, and went to the radio console. "Report! How many survivors!"

A crackle came back: "Twenty five... military... seventeen... civilian..."

"What is your dosage?" No answer. "Repeat: state your dosage!"

Words came out of the static: "Four grays... and rising. Three a week ago... the radiation is intensifying... no observed fallout but the dose is rising... do not have adequate protection above five grays... wish to request evacuation..."

The colonel looked over to a man in shadow at the end of the room. A man who wore the same suit as the one who had been saluted in the lobby. He gave no signal. The colonel put a hand on the mic to hide the noise of swallowing back his grief, then released it and spoke. "Matongu, your orders are to hold fast. I repeat, hold your position. Relief will come shortly."

No reply came through the static. The colonel laid down the headset, straightened his uniform and marched to the man in shadow.

"Sir. I wish to report that the surviving population of the sovereign republic of Mutapa consists of forty-two individuals."

The man in shadow put his head in his hands.

Kwame backed out of the room – out into the light of the corridor, wheezing and gasping for breath. The medics stepped forward but Kwame waved them away. He found his breath again, and stumbled into a staircase going down, leading to parts of the bunker used for maintenance, for generating power – and also for housing the hibernation chambers. The corridors below had not been whitewashed like the ones above. The concrete was raw and grey. But somehow he was more comfortable here. Somehow he knew this place better.

There, in that room, that was the generator: the nuclear pile, shielded from the rest of the bunker, radiation suits hanging on the wall. And *here*, this was the air filtration system, linked to the water tanks where more oxygen could be generated if needed. And *this* was the water recycling facility – pipes running to and from every sink, washbasin, toilet and tap in the bunker.

And *there* were the hibernation chambers. Sixty of them, in a hall off to the side of the main bunker, big enough to need structural pillars, all added after the original construction, when the technology had been gifted to Mutapa from the Chifunyikans. Each chamber was a sarcophagus lying on a low pedestal containing the support equipment.

Kwame crouched to inspect a unit, and pulled open a panel to reveal pipes and tubes and wiring; everything needed to keep the body fed and watered and oxygenated for years. It was beautifully designed, he noted. None of the poor soldering and jury-rigged parts you would find in the Mutapan versions, which were used in the shallow complex far above this one.

He turned away from the panel, and rested his back against the pedestal, sliding down until he was sitting.

He closed his eyes until he heard footsteps.

A man in shadow walked in, rested against the opposite pedestal and sat, just like Kwame.

They looked at each other across the gap.

"Hello, Mr. President," said Kwame.

10. KATIE

I was called to Hub Metro when they detected signs that Katie was improving. A medical team was working on her in a clean room in the hospital, and I had to put on a gown, cap and mask before they would let me in.

I must admit to being shocked when I saw the state of her brain; it had been slashed into several pieces by the landslide, but they had been able to revive all the individual scraps and reconnect them. All the shreds of tissue were suspended in jars of nutrient solutions hooked up to the battered remnants of glands and other organs, including the cybernetic implants that had caused so much trouble. The jars were suspended on a framework of metal with polymer sheaths wrapped around delicate cables of nervous tissue running haphazardly about the structure.

Dr. Ingeborg led the team that had reassembled her. She was justly proud of her work, and very used to the look of shock from anyone who saw it for the first time. "It is a surprise, I know," she said. "But this is how we all are. Just pieces of matter connected by nerves."

Katie's face was the only thing I recognised, suspended from an armature in front of the apparatus. It had a deep slash held together by sutures and the skin around the edges was rimmed by a polymer that sealed it from infection. Her expression was sleeping and restful.

"How is she?" I asked through my surgical mask.

"Good! Very good. She is in normal sleep now," said Dr. Ingeborg.

"So she'll wake up soon?"

"I can induce consciousness whenever you wish."

"Please."

"Emteth? Yen? Can you monitor, please?" Two of her assistants moved into position around the apparatus, while she went to the main console. "She was wakeful earlier, but we did not reveal what happened. She may not remember."

"I understand."

"Here we go."

Katie's eyes snapped open and looked across us, one to the other, not knowing where she was. Her mouth opened but no sound came out. Dr. Ingeborg reached for a pad and activated speakers.

"Where – where am I?"

I looked at Dr. Ingeborg, unsure. "She is awake!" said the doctor. "Talk to her!"

I looked back. "You're in hospital, Katie. In Hub Metro. You hurt yourself, remember?"

Her jaw trembled. "I – I – I can't feel… any pain…"

"You hurt yourself very badly."

"Who… are you?"

I pulled my mask down to show my face. "It's Asha. You remember?" I replaced the mask after a sharp look from Dr. Ingeborg.

Katie tried looking about, tried to see her body, but her face was locked into position. "What happened to me…?"

"You were in an accident," I said. "There was a rockslide. Do you remember?"

"No – no – I don't –"

"You were very badly hurt. It took a lot of work to save your brain."

"My brain…?"

I looked back at Katie, at the face hung on the machine. If anyone could take this news, she could. "We had to take your brain out of your body, Katie. I'm sorry. It was the only way to save you."

Now she looked confused, drifting. "Who's… who's Katie?"

I realised who I was talking to. "I'm sorry – Elsbet…? Is that you?"

But her eyes snapped on me with a sudden understanding. "Show me. Show me!"

I looked over to Dr. Ingeborg, and she nodded. So I mirrored a pad and held it up to Katie. Or to Elsbet. She saw the familiar outlines of her face – and beyond them, nothing human. Just a lattice of steel and glass, organs and fluids.

She screamed. Tears dripped down her face and stained the floor.

She went on for an unnatural length of time. She had no lungs and could not run out of breath. Dr. Ingeborg and I waited. There was nothing we could do; she had to have her moment of horror. Anyone would. But eventually it degenerated into sobs.

"Sergeant!" I said in as commanding a tone as I could muster. She looked up at me, snapped out of her agony by a lifetime of duty and training. "Elsbet. It's you, isn't it?"

"Yes."

"Do you remember me?"

"I remember you." By the tone of her voice, she didn't remember me with kindness.

"Do you remember what happened?"

"I died. I died and I'm more a machine than I was before! Why can't you let me be dead?"

"When you… when you hurt yourself, we saved you then. But it was Katie who came back. And since then, she got worse. She tried to kill herself–"

Elsbet's eyes rolled back. I looked at Dr. Ingeborg, who leapt to the controls of the life support machine. "Not as stable as I thought. There. How is she?"

Elsbet blinked, returning to her senses. "What... what...?"

"How are you feeling, Sergeant?"

"Falling. Asleep..."

Her eyes fell closed. Dr. Ingeborg frowned and shifted controls some more. She beckoned me to the console. "She is not stable at all. I thought I had her! But there is something in her species makeup I don't understand..."

"What's the problem?"

"I can't keep her like this for long. She's going to die."

"Can't you put her in hibernation? Or a coma? Or something?"

"She is not that kind of species! There's activity here I don't understand..." she indicated a gobbledygook on the screen, pulses of connections around the brain.

"Can't you do anything?"

"If I get her out of this body, sure..."

"She said no."

"Then she's going to die."

I had to think about it: a neat and unpleasant ethical dilemma. Katie had refused treatment that would save her. And now the moment had come when she would die without that treatment. But Katie was gone. She could make no further decisions. And Elsbet was only a simulation.

Unless she wasn't.

"Can you wake her up? I need to ask her some questions."

"She will wake up by herself. There. See?" More nonsense on the screen. "She goes, she comes back. It will be intermittent." I dashed back to Katie/Elsbet, as her eyes fluttered open.

"Elsbet. Can you hear me?"

She showed no sign of it.

"Sergeant!"

She snapped awake again. Dr. Ingeborg seemed delighted. "Yes! Keep doing that!"

"Sergeant. You remember me. Correct?"

"Yes. I remember you."

"Do you remember what we discussed?"

"You told me I'm a machine."

"That's right. And you're dying. Right now. You're dying *right now*."

"Let me. Please..."

"If that's what you want. But I have some questions first. Do you remember Katie?"

"Assassin!"

"Yes. An infiltrator. Do you remember anything else about her?"

"What..."

"You share the same brain. Her memories are inside you. Is there anything you remember?"

"I don't want it... I don't want her memories..."

"Elsbet. Is there anything?"

But she stared forward. I worried she was failing again and looked to Dr. Ingeborg. "She is good! Some other regions are lighting up..."

I looked back at Elsbet. She locked eyes on me.

"What do you remember, Sergeant?"

"I killed children."

"Yes. In the hospital."

Her eyes darted aside, ashamed. "No. In a bunker. With fire."

Not the hospital. Another memory. A Katie memory from the Second Machine War. One that Elsbet had never heard, that had happened long before they shared a body.

"Go on."

"I… I was a machine. I had… needles and tubes… I put the needles in the little bodies and.. it was blood and mess in the tubes… samples!" She gasped. "That was how they made people! They took our blood and made us from that… that's how they made me… Oh God…"

"Elsbet. This is important. You remember I said before that you were only a persona? You only came out because of the neural problems Katie had?"

"Yes…"

"I think I was wrong. You're not cut off any more. You have access to things in Katie's mind. I think that makes you a second individual in the same brain. Katie may have chosen to die but you have the right to choose as well."

"I'm a monster!"

"We can make you human."

"But… you said…"

"Yes. I was wrong. You're more than just a simulation. You're a person. I'm sorry we were wrong before. But I can offer you the choice now. We can make you human."

"I – I – you don't know what she did…"

"You'll be human. You'll have some bad memories but you'll be human."

She looked back at me, lips trembling.

"Yes! Yes. Please. Yes…"

I nodded. "Dr. Ingeborg?"

"It will be difficult–"

I looked back at Elsbet. "It might not work. I can't promise anything."

"I don't want to be like this…" she tried to look behind her at the life support apparatus, but of course she could not.

"You won't be."

"What if she comes back?"

"It's a possibility. Are you okay with that?"

She steeled herself. "Do it."

I nodded to Dr. Ingeborg, who said: "I shall prepare. I need to let her sleep now, before more damage is done."

"Are you ready, Sergeant?"

"Yes."

"I'll see you soon."

Drowsiness overtook her before she could reply, and her eyes closed once more.

11. ASHA

"Have you ever thought about going back?" I asked.

"There's nowhere to go back to."

"I don't mean *there*. I mean the other place."

"Oh… the colony."

"New Earth."

"So many of those these days."

"They're doing well. Apparently."

"Oh, sure, sure. That's what they say."

"So, have you thought about it?"

Dawa Dorje looked back at me. He'd hidden his surprise when I came into his bar, but not so quickly that I couldn't see he was worried. He thought I was there to discuss some further ramification of Liss's assault on him, some other way he could lose his business licence or be kicked off the planet. He didn't trust me at all, even though I'd gone out of my way to make sure he still had his last little bit of Tibet in the middle of Hub Metro. He was still keeping his host's face on. Humouring the crazy woman who'd wandered in off the street in the middle of the afternoon, wanting to talk about the homeworld.

"There's nothing there for me," he said.

"There's the species. You ever think about that?"

He smiled. "I'm a citizen of the multiverse."

"We're still refugees, you know."

He shrugged. "It's a world full of refugees. And some more, soon." He nodded at a screen: pictures from Ardeë, where the solar flares had grown suddenly worse. People looking up in fear at a too-bright sun, hurrying to pack whatever they could, jamming all the skyways to the spaceports.

"But don't you think–"

He cut in. "No."

"You don't think about it at all?"

"No. Never."

Was that his solution? Just ignore it all? Salvage a tiny shred of his nation and hide?

"What if you weren't the last one? From Tibet, I mean?"

He shrugged. "But I am." He finally took pity on me as he saw me frown into my coffee. "You aren't, are you?"

I shook my head. "No."

"Where are you from? India? Pakistan?"

"Britain. Lots of Indians settled there."

"So it's different for you."

"Yeah."

"I suppose that means you still have a world."

I nodded. The colony world, our New Earth: a hundred million of us, scattered on two continents, trying so very hard not to screw it up again. People of my own species, and every chance of a new life. There was a standing offer to all of us on Hub to join them, regardless of whether we'd taken IU citizenship.

"Yeah," I said.

"So go."

I looked into my coffee for a while. "You never wanted to?" I asked.

"No. Not once."

"Because you're the last survivor?"

He thought about it. "Yeah. I suppose so. It's a good life here. Why get caught up in all the shit from the old world?"

"Yeah. Why should we, huh?" He smiled, still humouring me, well aware I was only trying to convince myself. "I really should get you to talk to my patients…"

His eyes went wide. He'd only met one of them, when she beat him senseless.

"No, no, I don't mean *her*. I have other patients…"

He nodded, plainly wishing I hadn't come in.

"Never mind."

My calendar chimed at me: it was time to go. I had a flyer to catch. I thanked Dawa, and gave him more of a tip than he'd earned.

12. IOKAN

I met Iokan at the base of the Agvarterheer Column, or as anyone who lived on Hub knew it, the Lift. From a distance, it was a taut blue string anchored to the earth from the endless sky, lights rippling up and down for the benefit of pilots. Up close, you could see there were five columns; the central anchor that kept the counterweight station connected to Earth, and the four elevator strands, slimmer and dotted here and there with the bulges of passenger or cargo lifts.

If you stood in the open, the column seemed to be of a fantastic, unreal size. Even though the main anchor cable was at its narrowest at ground level, the sheer scale and height defeated the mind's attempts to comprehend it. Anyone who spent more than a few weeks there got used to it, and stopped looking up. Anyone who was new spent every spare moment staring into the sky.

Iokan should have been one of the latter, but despite the excellent view from the security station in Agvarterheer Port where he was waiting for me, he just kept his smile and looked out at nothing in particular while the ordinary travellers outside gawped at the megastructure above their heads. He didn't even look round to see me enter, until I said his name.

"Oh, hello," he said. "I was wondering where you were."

"They had to take Katie into surgery. Sorry about the delay. Are you ready to go?"

He sprang up. "I am."

All across the plain where the cables were anchored, cars lined up to hook onto an elevator strand and begin the climb. As we headed for the boarding station to meet our own, I saw a line of evacuation lifts waiting on a track, kept discreetly in the distance but difficult to hide. It looked for all the world like a small city queueing up to launch into space; evacuation lifts are like skyscrapers wrapped around the cables, mostly composed of dormitories and medical facilities. Somebody evidently took the possibility of a full scale evacuation from Ardeë seriously, even if no announcements had been made, nor even a formal request from their government. I found myself worrying about the group, and what we would do if the evacuation went ahead, but couldn't find any simple answers as we boarded.

Our car was a luxury model, a ring running round the cable with the outside edge one long window for most of the circumference. Everyone was strapped in for the launch, but once we were up to speed, you could sit at a table and order drinks just as we passed through the upper cloud layers, revealing the curve of the distant horizon. A few hundred people could travel in such a car, but today we found ourselves in a group of fifty or so, all of us on the way to Iokan's meeting with the Antecessors. This was something of a major event; a new species to be met, diplomatic relations to be opened, and a genocide to be investigated.

I tried my best to introduce Iokan to some of those travelling with us, but he didn't take much interest. People from the Diplomatic and Exploration Services got no more than a pleasant smile and a hello, followed by a complete inattention to their questions. He had no interest in speaking about what he expected to happen, much less in current events across the IU, which a couple of the Refugee Service people tried to engage him with. The situation on Ardeë was a frequent topic, and I swiftly learned it was worse than I thought: the sun in Ardeë's universe was spitting flares out into space at a hundred times the usual rate, and millions were trying to flee. People were shocked at how swiftly the crisis was developing and some doubted we could manage an evacuation so soon after we had been attacked. But Iokan's attention drifted away, so I made his excuses and tried to get him to pay attention to the spectacle beyond the window instead. We leant on the balustrade that kept us from direct contact with the great glass barrier: outside, clouds sank far below and the curve of the Earth was shadowed with the coming night.

"You didn't get to see this when you came down. What do you think?" I asked.

He shrugged. "Very nice."

"Ever seen it from this kind of height?"

"Oh, yes. It's not my first time in space."

"Really?" A chime went off in my ear. "Excuse me," I said. "I have to take a call."

I left him at the balustrade, still somehow uninterested in a view most species never see before they go extinct. I found a seat away from all the others who had the decency to gawp, fished a pad out of my bag, and answered the call.

It was Liss, sitting in her room, presumably with her own pad on her lap. "Hello, Liss. What's up?"

"Sorry! Are you in space already?" I held the pad out and showed her the view from the window. "Oh, yeah. That's space," she said.

"You don't sound very impressed." I turned the pad back round to see her; she was frowning.

"Yeah, well, bad things have happened to me in space…"

"I remember. How can I help?"

"Um. I was wondering, uh, if I could talk to someone from Quillia?"

"We could probably arrange that. There's a few people in the Refugee Service who come from there."

"I mean with someone official."

"Oh. Well. That's a bit more difficult–"

"They've got an embassy, right? And consuls and cultural attachés and all that kind of stuff?"

"Yes, they do. Are you sure you want to make official contact this soon? I thought you were investigating what happened?"

"Uh, well, I was, but, um…" She struggled with her point for a few seconds.

"Yes?"

"You know I was fostered?"

"Yes. I remember."

"Well now I guess I know why. I mean, all that shit about mad child psychologists experimenting on me… they weren't mad, they were aliens. It was probably normal for them."

"It's possible."

"And why was I there? What were they doing – going on safari and bringing the kid along?"

"I can't tell you, Liss."

"Yeah, well… this is it, this is what I want to find out."

"You want to find out what they were up to?"

"I want to find *them*. My parents."

"Oh."

"It's like… they're my family. I don't even know if they made it out of Calafaria, I mean millions of people died there… I just want to know." She paused, trying to avoid tears. "They're the only family I've got. And, I don't know, maybe they'll help."

"Okay. I'll see what I can do."

"Thanks."

"I'll have a word with the embassy–"

"Oh! Um. There's one thing…"

"Yes?"

"You know how we're supposed to have anonymity and all that?"

"We'll do our best to preserve it. Unless you prefer otherwise."

"Uh, no. I don't, I mean yes, I want to keep the anonymity thing. Just in case it doesn't work out."

"That's fine. I think we can work something out with the Diplomatic Service. There's a few people on board here. I'll have a chat to them and get back to you. Okay?"

"Okay. Thanks!"

I went back to Iokan. He was where I'd left him, still staring out the window, though we were higher now and the gentle curve of the Earth was turning into a more pronounced arc. I was surprised when he spoke.

"You know, this isn't the first space elevator I've seen."

"Really?"

"Yes. The Antecessors used to have one, before the cataclysm. They buried it under the Pacific, in a sea mount."

"They buried it?"

"They didn't leave it connected all the time. It could retract back under the sea."

"That's quite a piece of engineering."

"The idea was that one strand would come down from orbit, and another would go up from the sea, and they'd connect. When we found it, we set it off by accident, but there wasn't anything in orbit for it to go to. It jumped up, went into the sky, hung there for a while and fell back down. Started a tsunami. Not one of our best days."

He fell silent again with an apologetic smile.

"Iokan... listen. I know you think this is going to end with you going off and being one of them, but... I think you should be a little more cautious. It's not just going to be you and them at the meeting. There's a lot of Exploration and Diplomatic people with us, and the ICT as well. If we see the Antecessors giving us any trouble, we're going to come back here straight away. And we're not going to leave you behind."

He smiled at my lack of faith, then looked out at the black sky above the blue Earth. "Don't worry, Asha. It's going to be fine. You'll see." I left him to it and went to speak to the Diplomatic Service about Liss's request.

Half a day later, the Earth was a black disc rimmed by blue, and the lights of Hub Metro and a few scattered settlements were the only things visible on the night-time surface. We were called to our cabins to strap in for deceleration as we approached the counterweight station, where we took a shuttle to join our ship, the Exploration Service Vessel *Geology*, a journey of three more days. She was waiting out beyond the moon at the L2 point, where the gravity of Earth and Moon cancels out. The L1 point was nearer, lying between Earth and Moon, but that was occupied by Grainger Station and the main transit points to and from other universes. The Exploration Service preferred to use L2. It was less convenient but allowed them to emerge into a new universe hidden behind the moon, and was easier to defend should something follow them back. A number of vessels were stationed there permanently with as much weaponry as the IU could muster, which isn't much and hardly what you would need to defend against a serious invasion; but since the Exploration Service is tasked with finding either empty worlds or planets of scientific interest, it's rarely much of an issue.

Today, it was an issue.

We'd learned from Department Zero records that an EM cage together with a light-opaque shell could be effective in keeping Antecessors out, so the transit sphere had been enclosed and rigged with the most powerful cage we could build. It was necessary because the transit spheres for uncontacted worlds have to be powerful enough not only to send material to another universe, but to bring it back as well. If the Antecessors chose to return with our ship, we needed to be able to contain them.

Iokan sighed as the *Geology* cruised gently through the entry port of the transit sphere. To him, it was a waste of effort, but he didn't trouble himself to explain at length. A shadow fell across the viewing deck as we entered, and then there was only the safety lighting inside the sphere, newly rigged because they aren't usually enclosed. And then that too was gone as the windows polarised and shutters slid into place to block even the slightest view. We were dealing with beings made of electromagnetism who would treat glass as an open door. No chances were to be taken.

"How long does it take?" asked Iokan. A bell sounded throughout the ship. "Not long," I said.

For a moment, we were nowhere, nothing and no-one. We were conscious of nothing, but very much aware of the nothingness.

Then we were back. Iokan blinked. "That was it?"

"That was it."

"We're here?"

"We're here."

He got up, suddenly full of energy, taking a nervous breath. "How long before they come?"

"If everything's going according to plan, we're sending the signal now. So about eight minutes for that to get to the sun, then eight minutes for them to get back, if they move at lightspeed. Call it twenty minutes, maybe a bit less."

"Ancients... after all this waiting, suddenly we're moving *fast*."

"We've planned this very carefully."

"Well. Do we have to be anywhere in particular?"

"I'm waiting for a signal."

"What happens then?"

"I'll tell you when it comes."

He was a little shocked. "Are you keeping secrets from me...?"

"Yes."

"Why...?"

"I'm under orders."

"I didn't know you were a soldier."

"I'm not. But I have superiors, and they have concerns about security."

He was taken aback as he realised the implications.

"You mean they don't trust me?"

"They're being cautious."

"Hm," he said, mulling it over. But his frown did not last long. "I *will* see her, won't I?"

"Of course."

"And they're not going to stop me going with her?"

"We've made arrangements to let it happen. If that's what you want." A chime sounded in my ear, and a message appeared before my eyes. "It's time." He took a breath as I rose. "Are you ready?"

He nodded, flexing his hands, trying not to show how much he trembled. "I'm ready."

I took him through the ship, escorted by two security guards, to the recently installed Diplomatic Bay, a massive safe room in which normal humans could meet Antecessors without fear of contamination. A laminate carbonglass barrier protected the people within from both vacuum and anything electromagnetic. An EM cage was laced invisibly through it, and in addition the glass was polarised to opacity millions of times each second, so even something travelling at the speed of light couldn't get through without being sliced in half. As an added precaution, we were issued with eyeglasses that would disrupt the sudden bursts of light-based information that had induced everyone on Iokan's world to suicide.

The bay was big enough for a substantial number of people, but for now it was just me, Iokan and some security guards. Other people flickered into being in one section of the bay: diplomats and investigators, all of whom were restricted to remote access for now. This was primarily a diplomatic mission, but it was Iokan who had been invited first of all, and our initial responsibility was to let him join his species if that was what he wanted. The Antecessors had said they would come in peace and offered guarantees of safe conduct, so we were treating them with as much trust as we could under the circumstances.

Iokan was the only one smiling in the bay, and the only one who could not hear the ship's Captain speaking to us through our implants, reporting that a response had been made to our initial hails, and that it came from very nearby – they had been awaiting our arrival in lunar orbit. They were coming to us now.

The empty space outside the bay filled with stars, a galaxy of lights surrounding and circling the ship. One of them brightened and approached, a point of light that became a disc, then a sphere full of suggestions of interlocking shapes, endlessly changing and forming, and then, as it floated into the bay, unfolding into a gleaming human shape whose brightness made us glad of the dimming effect of the glass wall between us and the creature.

The shape it unfolded into was that of a woman, hazy in form and outline save for the face, where her features sharpened to become those I'd seen in surveillance footage from the last days of Department Zero.

Iokan wept behind his glasses and stepped forward. "Szilmar...!" he whispered.

She floated there beyond the glass, and looked around, searching. She reached out and touched the barrier, then recoiled with a very human look of pain.

Words appeared on the far side of the glass wall, back to front from the perspective of all but the energy being: *Please do not touch the glass.*

She cocked her head.

More words followed. *We apologise for any discomfort due to security precautions. Welcome to the Exploration Service Vessel* Geology.

She read, then looked through the glass, scanning with who knew what senses. *Please use the keyboard to communicate.* A keyboard of light was drawn in the air in front of her. She didn't immediately register it; instead, she locked eyes upon Iokan.

As far as he and the woman of light were concerned, there were only two people in the bay. He pushed past the security guards, who stepped aside when they saw me nod, and reached out to her, laying his palm flat on the barrier. She smiled back, and reached out her own hand, spreading it as close to his as she dared.

Messages came silently to me from the diplomatic team, saying they were about to ask the security guards to intervene. I begged them to wait. She might not be happy if we dragged him away.

Iokan took off his protective spectacles and looked on her with his own naked eyes, seeing the woman who had died and returned from heaven.

"Take me," he said, full of joy and wonder. His words appeared automatically on the glass for her to see.

Her smile turned to sadness. She mouthed one word, too quick and indistinct for our translators to catch it. But Iokan understood, and looked confused. Someone thought to move the keyboard of light to her side. She noticed it, and tapped out a message: *I will not take you.*

His confusion turned to shock. She tapped again. *It was wrong. It should not have happened.*

Iokan could barely get out the words: "But it was holy…"

She looked at him with sadness and pity. *You still feel as I did when I saw them.*

"Yes!" he cried.

They were wrong. It was a crime.

"They are perfect…"

They're just a remnant of what they were. They didn't know they were doing any harm.

I noticed the remote projections of the ICT investigators paying close attention with raised eyebrows. But for Iokan, the shock was terrible. "No… it's not true…"

We all felt the same as you when they took us. But we are the majority now and we will not commit the crime again.

"You're… you're… you're not my wife! You're lying!" He screamed it through tears. "You're *lying!*"

She looked at him with a deeper sadness than light can show. I saw her speak two words, lost in silence. But to someone who knew the language, their meaning must have been clear, and I could easily guess: *"I'm sorry."*

"No… no…" He turned from her, looking terribly stricken, seeing what I suppose must have been pity on my face. And realising he had been mistaken. It was too much for him. His eyes rolled up in his head and he slumped to the floor.

A security guard was with him in an instant, checking him over, and telling me he'd simply fainted. I looked up at Szilmar floating beyond the glass, looking anxious and worried. "He's just passed out," I told her. "He'll be fine."

The words appeared on the glass in front of her and she nodded. She tapped on the keyboard. *Please look after him. He's suffered more than any of us.*

I nodded, and with the help of the medic, lifted him onto a stretcher, took him inside the ship, leaving the diplomats to face the shining woman, who watched her broken husband with sad, helpless eyes.

13. ASHA

Ranev still had his tan, and looked as though he'd just been in the sea. He told me he'd been running therapy sessions out in the shallow water where his patients felt comfortable. He assured me it was a hard slog, but I found myself doubting it.

"Have you heard?" he asked.

"About what?"

"Ardeë."

"Nothing official."

"It's getting worse."

"I got that from watching the news."

"Could be an evacuation coming," he said. "You know what that means." I knew well enough: drop everything we were doing, endless trips up and down the Lift, years spent consoling and healing the survivors only just escaped from yet another dying world. And for the group? No one had said, and my messages asking for clarification from management had gone unanswered.

"They might ask you to hand your group over to someone else."

"Or worse…"

"I don't think they'll break them up after everything you've done… but you're too valuable in an evacuation. So. What'll you do if it comes to that?"

"I'd…" I thought I knew what I'd say if asked that question: I thought I would say no. It was a simple, obvious, moral issue. "They don't trust anyone else. If I handed them over it would set some of them back months…"

He saw through me easily. "Sure. But what do *you* want?"

I looked out at the view from the window: the same old mountains wrapped in cloud. It was getting cold outside.

"Asha?" he asked.

"I'm sorry…" I said. "I just, I felt for a moment… just for a moment, I thought it would be good to stop. And…"

"Go on."

There was no point in lying to him. "I don't know. I really don't. If they asked me to go… I don't know what I'd do."

"Is it the group itself?"

I shook my head, not wanting to blame them. But…

"I feel like…" I looked away, down the room, at nothing at all. Anything to get away from Ranev's kindly eyes. "I don't know what I can do for them. It doesn't seem to make any difference."

"You feel powerless?

"Stupid, I know…"

"Not at all. How are they?"

"Iokan's still in shock. We had to bring him back. He won't talk about it…"

"He will."

"He's not the only one. I can't get Pew to talk to me either. And the stuff he's reading is scaring me."

"Oh? Such as?"

"He's only interested in genocide. Not preventing it. Starting it."

"Don't you think he has a right to be angry?"

"Up to a point. I'm worried he'll go off the edge and we'll lose him."

"There's only so much you can do. If they choose not to co-operate, you can't force them."

"I know."

"You have to accept that we do lose them sometimes. It's not a failure. It's a measure of how damaged they were to begin with."

"It never feels like that."

"True. But I think you're emphasising the negative over the positive. You're close to diagnosis on all of them, aren't you?"

"Yes."

"And you know as well as I do, that's the hill you have to get over."

"If they can actually be treated."

"Well, yes, there's that as well. Do you think they can't?"

I looked out at the mountains again. If anything, they looked colder than before. "I wonder if it's worth it."

"Why?"

"They're the last of their kind. They're probably never going to see another member of their own species again."

"All the more reason to help them."

I didn't answer for a moment. I had another worry. "I started wondering how many members of my own species there are on Hub."

"Ah."

"One hundred and twenty-three. Forty-six in the delegation. Everyone else went on to the new place."

"Is that what you'd prefer?"

"I don't know. I keep thinking... I keep thinking about home."

"Hub Metro?"

"No."

"You mean your world."

"Yes. I keep thinking, what if we hadn't been evacuated? What if we'd gone all the way to the end?"

"But you didn't."

"No. My patients did."

"Transference, Asha. You have to be careful. You're not them."

"I know. But... I keep..." It was hard to express it; this thing growing closer to the edge of my waking mind. "I keep thinking it'll always be like this. We'll always corrupt every world we find. Not just my species, not just their species, I mean every human species. And I know this is just because I've been closer to the bad stuff than usual..."

"I don't have to tell you that the more advanced each species gets, the more able they are to avoid all these problems."

"I know. I know that. I've seen how some of the older species live. I just don't know how they do it."

He took a breath. "Okay. Listen. I think if they ask you to work on the Ardeë evacuation – if that happens – I think you should say no." I looked outside. "And I think you should take a holiday. You need some time off. You went through a lot in the attack and I don't think you've really had a chance to recover."

I didn't reply immediately. Something outside the window caught my attention.

"Asha?" he asked. "Are you all right? Is something wrong with the signal?"

"No," I said, and went to the window. I looked back at him. "What can you see out of this window? In your centre?"

"It's a sunny day. Like every day. Except when the rain comes, but it's sunny now. What do you see?"

I looked back outside. Clouds were billowing up around the mountains, the kind we'd been warned about. I looked up and saw they were coasting over the centre, heavy and black. The first snowflakes flittered down. The wind picked up and suddenly the snow was heavier, and catching in the grass.

"Winter just started," I said.

Ranev took on an admonishing tone. "Asha… come on. It's not a symbol. Winter always starts about this time of the year at your centre."

I turned back and smiled, and put on a small chuckle for his benefit. "Yeah. I know."

But the flakes were coming thick now, and burying the grounds in snow.

PART THIRTEEN
DIAGNOSES

1. COMMITTEE

The word spread through the Refugee Service as quickly as the snow piled up around the centre: a world was dying, and we would soon be called on to save as many as we could. The pictures from Ardeë were terrifying. The sun bristled in the sky, coronal mass ejections bursting out every few minutes and spitting more plasma into the solar system. The storm of charged particles smashed into Ardeë's magnetic field, making auroras flare up from pole to equator, so bright they turned night into day. The frail magnetic protection that had kept the sun's electromagnetic gales away from the planet for billions of years was being battered into submission, allowing the solar hurricane to strip away the upper layers of atmosphere. Views from space showed a churning stream of air blasting away from the planet for millions of kilometres, as though Ardeë had been turned to a streaking comet. The ozone layer was already gone, and standing outside in the daytime could result in first degree burns just from the ultraviolet. The shower of deadly light did even worse: it fused nitrogen and oxygen together to make nitrogen dioxide, a dirty brown gas you could see polluting the clouds of Ardeë. The slight protection it gave from the UV was no consolation for the acid rain, or the freezing cold that would settle on the world as it blocked out the rest of the sun's light. The turbulence stirred up by the fleeing atmosphere set off shrieking winds and storms, overwhelming the weather control systems and making it even worse. If the sun continued these outbursts, then eventually there wouldn't be any air left to breathe; but it seemed hardly likely anyone would be left by then. The death toll was already more than a million only days after the sun went into this new phase, on a planet of nine billion closely packed people.

"Nine billion…" said the ambassador from Ardeë, beneath the vast screen in the IU Assembly Hall that showed the pictures of apocalypse. Handheld footage now, of people streaming from vast, sky-arcologies into the undercities, crowds looking up at cavern roofs, fearing collapse as the cityscrapers above groaned under the typhoon's assault. "Nine billion people… who have less than a year to live." There were already tears tracking down his face. "My own cityscraper… Erbesoon… fell last night. I…" And the grief choked him, but he waved away an assistant. Hundreds of representatives watched him in the assembly hall, many more observing remotely.

I watched from my office: I'd seen many apocalypses before, but it never prepares you for the raw grief of someone who has just seen his planet begin to die.

"My world is ancient, and proud, and famous, and *doomed*," said the ambassador. "And perhaps we built too high. Perhaps there are too many of us. Perhaps only a few need to survive… but there are *nine billion* who will die if the Interversal Union cannot act…"

A chime came from my office wall and dampened the sound. It was the call I had been expecting: a conference, assembled on screens because none of us had time to get to a remote meeting room. They popped up on my wall one by one:

Mykl Teoth in his office; Baheera om-challha Isnia on the Lift, making what looked like an ascent, though it was hard to tell; Koggan BanOrishel somewhere outdoors in Hub Metro, blue lights reflecting on a metre-thick crystal wall behind him; Eremis Ai walking through the new ICT headquarters; Henni Ardassian using a pad, sitting in the back of the IU Assembly Hall itself; no one else. Quorate enough for decisions.

"I'm addressing the assembly as soon as the ambassador from Ardeë is finished," said Henni. "So let's make this quick. We've gone from thinking a worst case scenario was a ten year evacuation to having only eight or nine months. No matter what the ambassador says, we're probably only going to be able to get a billion out." She shook her head. "Only!"

"How the hell did it happen...?" asked Koggan.

"We don't know and I'm not discussing it now. I only want opinions about what happens to the group, given that resources are going to be *very* thin for the foreseeable future. We're going to need the centre back, for a start. We'll be flooded with refugees and we won't have enough room for them as it is."

"I think, for our purposes, I'd like the group to continue with Dr Singh," said Eremis. "I'm not too worried where. Hub Metro would actually be more convenient."

"I don't want them outside a secure environment," said Koggan. "There's only two places we can keep them: the Psychiatric Centre or the Correctional Facility. I suppose you don't want the latter."

"The Psychiatric Centre isn't the best place for them either," said Mykl.

"We can provide something," said Baheera, making Henni frown for a moment. "I think I can loan you a high security negotiation facility, at least in the short term."

"Well," said Henni. "That's a solution for now..." she looked up at a sound in the Assembly Hall; the ambassador choking back tears.

I drew a breath. It was time to own up to my own frailties, much as I didn't want to. "There's another problem," I said.

"Yes," agreed Henni without letting me finish. "We might need to reassign you to the evacuation. You have no idea how big this is going to be. I'm about to ask for half the IU budget for the next five years to cover it." She pushed on, overriding what she assumed would be my objections. "I know what you're going to say, I know you've got your moral obligation, but there's going to be at least a billion people coming out of Ardeë and we've *never* handled those kinds of numbers before."

"That's not what I meant," I said.

"Well? What did you mean?" demanded Henni, eyes flicking up at the events in the IU Assembly Hall.

"You might need to find someone else anyway."

"I'm sorry...?"

"I might have to spend some time away from the group. And... I might be joining my species, on the colony world."

"You're *what?*"

Mykl didn't share Henni's outrage. He'd been the one to arrange the therapy with Ranev. "Medical reasons?" he asked.

"Yes," I said.

"At a time like *this*?" demanded Henni.

"I might not be much help," I said.

"We'll be sorry to lose you," said Eremis. "But I think we would understand if you had to go."

Henni shook her head in exasperation, then looked up at another sound in the hall. "I'm on. We'll talk about this another time."

She switched off her pad, and her screen was replaced with a *feed disconnected* icon. The others made haste to turn to the news channel, just as I did.

An assistant led the ambassador from Ardeë away, still weeping as images from his world played on the screen behind him. A view from space, lit up with the blue glow of cities spraying out across a continent. The lights flickered and died from electrical overload as electronics all over the world failed in the teeth of the solar storm. Someone had the decency to fade out the image as the ambassador was taken outside, and it was replaced with a simple caption: *Henni Ardassian, Director, Refugee Service*.

We watched as Henni went in front of the representatives of thousands of worlds to tell them the hard facts about what the horror on Ardeë meant, and beg for the money to save a species from extinction.

2. KWAME

Kwame didn't hear about Ardeë. He didn't even notice the snow, which kept all of us inside for days while the blizzards turned the centre into the winter retreat it was supposed to be. Kwame never even looked out of a window. He hadn't left the bunker for two weeks.

He slept in the officer's quarters to begin with, and then moved into the enlisted men's barracks a few days later. This made no immediate sense since the barracks were less comfortable and filled with the stink he'd specified, but I suspected there was a very good reason.

He spent the days going below into the lower level, sometimes tinkering with the equipment, but mostly sitting among the hibernation chambers. And while he was there, he talked. No one listened but me, and I did so from my office, taking no part in the conversation. I asked him once or twice if there was anything he wished to discuss, but he politely declined. And then, a day after the announcement of the Ardeë evacuation, he asked me to join him there.

I found him sitting by the pedestal of a hibernation unit, and he invited me to sit beside him.

"So…" I said. "Who have you been talking to?"

"I have been talking to myself."

"I noticed that."

"You do not perceive my meaning."

"I'm sorry. Go on."

"The person I have been speaking to... that man... is Kwame Vangona. Last President of the sovereign republic of Mutapa."

I nodded.

"And he has been dead for many decades," he said.

I nodded again.

"You knew this."

"I've been listening."

"I believed you would."

"What did you talk about?"

"Everything. His whole life. After the end, he would come down to see me. He wanted someone to talk to. Someone who was in the army, but not an officer. He was a man of the people..." He looked away. "He wanted someone to know why he had done it. How he came to that decision. So he told me everything. How his wife died. Everything."

"What did you do?"

"He was the President. I listened. We had met before – did I say that? No, of course not. We met at Horonga, when I was installing defensive systems. He was an officer, still there after the war... he was concerned that the men who would operate the defences did not have the education to understand what they were doing. He was right, but I dared not say anything. Years later, when I was injured because one of them set the rangefinder wrongly on a grenade launcher – the poor fool could not add or subtract to save his life – he raised the issue in public. He was campaigning for educational reform, and I suppose it was just what he needed... he was selected for Parliament not long after that. So when we met again, in the bunker, he remembered me. He was sorry he did not do more for me when I was injured. All the people dead in the world and he was sorry about my arm..."

He held up the withered limb, flexing the hand as far as it would go. Then let it drop and leant his head back against the pedestal.

"How long did it go on?" I asked.

"Weeks..." He looked up, towards the command centre. "Upstairs, they were trying to keep contact with survivors. It took many weeks for them to die. When it was too much, he came to see me."

"Did anything else... happen?"

"No! No, he was not that sort of man. He loved the company of men, but... not in that way. He just wanted someone to know what happened. I think the generals pushed him into arming the cobalt bomb... he never talked about that, he only hinted. He would not blame anyone else. He accepted the responsibility as his own." Kwame's voice was tinged with sadness. "I was not such a man."

"You had a very difficult life."

"It was nothing compared to his. To do what he did with... so little."

"Being the right man in the right place at the right time is mostly about luck. It sounds like you were a very good engineer in a country where that wasn't appreciated."

"Do you think my life would have been better if I had been Chifunyikan?"

"Maybe. It sounds like they were better at that kind of thing."

"And then I would be dead. Perhaps that is something else to wish for."

"Is that how you feel now?"

He frowned, and thought about it. "No," he said. "I have never wanted to die…"

"Well, that's something–"

"No. In the bunker, I had nothing to live for. I could have killed myself. Many did. I was simply a coward."

"Okay. Maybe we can talk about that later. How did the conversation end?"

"With the President?"

"With the President."

He sighed. "Eventually, we had to go into hibernation. But he told me the chief scientist had predicted the radiation clouds would make the surface uninhabitable for decades. Maybe longer, maybe two hundred years. The hibernation chambers would not last that long. And the chambers in the labour reserve – what you call the 'shallow complex' – they would fail long before then. When the bunker was built, we thought we would only have to sleep ten or twenty years at the most…" he chuckled, bitterly.

"But you did all go into the chambers?"

"Yes. I was the last one to go in. I was the only one who really knew how they worked."

"And they failed."

"No."

"I'm sorry?"

"I disabled them."

"You…" I took a moment to process that. "You *killed* them?"

"Yes."

"Why?"

"Those were his last orders."

"Can you explain that a bit more…?"

"He felt we did not deserve to live. As a species. He wept to tell me he had lost all faith in humanity. He said it again and again: we should be punished for this crime. He said that *he* should be punished most of all. But there was no one who could do so. Everyone knew what had happened and nobody really blamed him. So he asked me."

"He asked you directly?"

"As much as he could."

"It was definitely an order?"

"I remember the words: 'We do not deserve to live, Sergeant. No one will punish us for what we have done. If there is to be any justice for this world, we must do it ourselves.' He repeated that: "We must do it ourselves." He looked into my eyes… and I understood. So I sabotaged the hibernation units. Everyone died in their sleep…

"But he wanted it sooner. So I opened up his casket. I had a knife, I knew he wanted it that way, but… I could not do it. I was a soldier but I never killed a man. I… kissed him… sealed him up… cut the lines instead and let him die for lack of air."

A tear ran down his cheek. "If that is genocide… then I will stand trial for it."

"There'll have to be an investigation."

"Of course."

"I don't know what will happen. But we'll support you."

"Thank you."

"So... who are you?"

He smiled, painfully. "I do not know."

"Still?"

"I was an engineer. I had the training necessary to understand the hibernation units... I suppose that is why they recalled me, even with my injury. But... I do not know *who* I was."

"Okay. It's still progress." He didn't look like he agreed. "Do you feel better?"

He looked back at me, surprised and unsure of his answer. He thought about it for a moment, and then found words: "Every answer I find becomes another question. Do you think... there will ever be an end to the questions?"

"I don't know, Kwame... is it still okay to call you Kwame?"

"I was called Kobe, before. I think. I am not sure..."

"It's okay. You don't have to make your mind up right away. But with your injuries, there's no telling what else you might recover."

"I am not certain I wish to know more."

I put a hand on his. "You've made a massive step. Now we know what we're doing, we can treat your PTSD. There's one thing, though."

"Yes?"

"We can't do it here. We have to move the group again, soon."

"Was there another attack...?"

"No. A world is ending. We've just started an evacuation and they're going to need this place for the refugees."

"Of course. What happened?"

"Solar flares. They're so bad they're killing the planet. They have less than a year before there's nothing left."

"It never ends," he sighed.

"No. But it always gets better. And it'll get better for you as well. I can't promise you'll get back everything you lost, but it will get better."

He sighed and leaned his head back against the pedestal.

"Then I shall have to accept that."

3. PEW

The bunker disappeared more quickly than it had been built, as a small crew came in to rescape the building to another purpose: shelter and therapy for fifty or more refugees, probably those who were judged to be most disturbed when the triage teams did their work on the way down the Lift. It was only days after the announcement, and the first ships were already lifting the most vulnerable people from the battered arcologies of Ardeë to orbit and the portal to Hub.

We were not in the first batch of centres to be made available, but nevertheless the group had to pick their way around the work crew as it opened up the shuttered rooms and shaped them into dormitories and therapy rooms and everything the refugees would need. We found ourselves confined to a small corner of the building; it was simple enough to pack and we could have left straight away, but until the Diplomatic Service were ready to take us, we had to wait and carry on as best we could. With Ranev's agreement, I decided to stay with the group until the move was made, but I hadn't decided what I would do then. I couldn't see past the present moment, and went on with therapy, hoping I wouldn't stumble and let them down.

My biggest worry was still Pew. He'd been refusing therapy sessions for some time now, and had grown obsessed with physical fitness, increasing his regimen to include self-defence training from security – only the most defensive of martial arts, but pursued with a troubling zeal. However, it was his academic studies that gave me the most concern. He'd completely abandoned his university course in mathematics and physics, and moved on to a syllabus bound by a single theme: genocide. He'd read dozens of case studies of such horrors (including several from my world), and found endless disappointment and dismay at how little was done to bring perpetrators to justice. Historical crimes were forgotten or denied. Legal systems shied away from the worst excesses. Time and time again, the people who were to blame went unpunished. Even the most advanced societies did their best to cover up crimes they had committed on other worlds, and there was complicity throughout the multiverse. The dead were given memorials. The murderers continued their lives. Survivors went unheard and ignored. Business as usual.

He looked into one other set of cases: those where there were survivors, who had then committed their own genocide against their former oppressors. It was very rare for anyone to be able to turn the tables so completely, and he seemed to be frustrated even with these cases. The former victims became just like their former persecutors, displaying exactly the same behaviour of denial and forgetting, acting as though they were the guilty parties. And by any rational standards, that was precisely what they were. But while Pew was as contemptuous of their denial as any other scholar, his reasoning was different. He thought the crime of counter-genocide should be celebrated.

After he had missed three sessions, I called him in for a compulsory meeting. I made sure the security man I sent was the one who had been teaching him self-defence; they had a rapport, and I wanted as little chance of conflict as possible. Pew submitted to the summons with a sullen, petulant attempt at gravitas, ignoring pleasantries and the drink I put in front of him.

"Do you know why I've called you in, Pew?" I asked. He didn't reply. "You've been avoiding therapy." He stayed sullen. "And quite frankly, some of what you've been up to is troubling me. We need to talk about this."

He looked up at me. Half angry, half guilty at being found out. But it subsided and he looked away again.

"Pew? Can we talk about what's bothering you?"

He kept his silence.

"You should know that since you're on the euthanasia track, you do have certain obligations towards keeping up with your therapy. If you're unable to attend therapy sessions, we won't have any choice other than to take you out of the programme."

He looked up at me again, as though he were being victimised somehow. I went on: "Unless of course you don't want to die any more?"

His brow furrowed.

"Pew, if you want to stay on the euthanasia track, you have to commit to therapy. At the moment you're not doing that. So… are you feeling better?"

He swallowed. "I feel different."

"In what way?"

"I don't know."

"I know you've been doing a lot of exercise. Has that helped?"

"Yes."

"Has your research helped as well?"

"Yes."

"Does that give you something to live for?"

He looked straight at me, unblinking. Deciding what to tell me. Almost trying to intimidate me with his stare. "Something like that," he said.

I sighed. "I'm not sure your research has been healthy…"

"No. You wouldn't."

"What does that mean, Pew?"

"It's happening again. And you're *letting* it happen."

"I'm sorry, Pew – what do you mean?"

"Ardeë."

"That's a natural disaster."

"No it fucking isn't!"

"Pew! Control yourself!"

"Why can't anyone fucking *see!*"

"*Pew!*"

I realised that as much as he was shouting, I was shouting back at the same level. He was as shocked as I was. I took a breath.

"I'm sorry, Pew, but I don't see your point. Their sun's unstable. It doesn't happen often, but it happens."

"*Bullshit.*"

"They *are* just accidents, sometimes."

He hunched over his knees, sullen.

"Pew, is there something you know that I don't?"

"They were doing experiments. On the sun."

"And where did you hear about this?"

"On the net."

"Where on the net?"

"It's all over. It was on the news on Ardeë, and then they stopped talking about it when it went wrong. They had a station on Mercury and they were dropping bombs into the photosphere. Bigger than nukes. It's antimatter. They dropped a whole fucking reservoir of antimatter in there and it's burning up a bit at a time and *that's* what's happening."

So now he was down as far as believing in conspiracy theories without questioning them in the slightest. The antimatter accusation wasn't the only crazy story doing the rounds, and the others made about as much sense. It didn't matter. Once someone starts believing in conspiracies, they lose touch with objective reality and treat every little bit of news as evidence for what they've already decided. And Pew had decided that humanity in all its forms was not just prone to genocide, but addicted to it.

"Okay, Pew, let me ask you something…" He stayed sullen in his chair. I went on. "You've been looking into genocides. Okay. But have you looked into apocalypses as well?"

"Yeah," he said, grudgingly.

"All of them?"

"Some."

"Were they *all* genocides?"

"…Yeah. Some of them."

"But not all?" He looked confused. "You should look closely at all of them. Even the ones that are obviously natural disasters."

"Why?"

"I think you'll find, in every case – even when it's obvious it was a natural disaster – there's somebody saying it was deliberate. There's usually at least a dozen theories for every apocalypse. But most of the time it *is* just an accident, no matter what people think. Or what they want to believe."

That troubled him. "But what if it's true anyway?"

"It might be. It might not be. It takes a lot of investigating to find out. I bet if you look closely, most of the people who are making these accusations haven't done much of that. But don't take my word for it. Look for yourself and make your own mind up."

He frowned, the certainty of his anger dwindling.

"I know you're angry, and you're right to be angry. Because in your case it really *was* a genocide, and we really *do* have evidence for what happened. It was a monstrous crime, and one that will *not* be forgotten. The Soo are interversal pariahs because of what they did. They'll be denied the full benefits of IU membership, and they'll have to live with their climate breaking down because we're not going to help them colonise another world. No one trusts them. I don't know if anyone ever will."

He looked up at me.

"Do you really think it would make anything better to kill them all?"

He stared grimly at the floor.

"Pew, we'll do everything we can to support you. On the other hand, we need to keep everyone else safe. We *will* send you to the Psychiatric Centre if we have to."

He looked miserable, caught between two impulses.

"What would you prefer to do?" I asked.

He swallowed again, and came to a very reluctant decision.

"I'll do the therapy," he said.

"Thank you," I replied.

4. ASHA

Pew didn't make a lot of progress with the exposure therapy, but then I didn't really expect him to, not at first. Just getting him to sit there while I found ways to calm his mind was hard enough work. Helping him deal with his PTSD was going to take months, maybe years, and I found myself thinking more and more that I should get out now, get to the colony world, get away from the group, the centre, Hub, everything. Mykl said they were having trouble finding someone else to take the group – hardly surprising, under the circumstances. There were few people with my experience who weren't already out at a therapy centre, prepping for refugees, or halfway up the Lift, getting ready to triage the first flood of survivors.

The days rolled on, and we were promised a date for the move again and again. The news showed the first few people from Ardeë emerging at Agvarterheer Port, mostly coming off the Lift to be rushed straight to medical facilities where their burns could be treated. The first place we'd evacuated had been a hospital in one of the highest arcologies, where the UV had been particularly vicious.

I had to make a visit to Hub Metro to inspect the new facility for the group: a small building in the outskirts that carried no markings, was not listed on public directories, and could not be found unless you had permission. No vehicle would take you there, and if you stumbled across it, the doors would not open, nor would any staff emerge to see who you were. It was one of those places the Diplomatic Service kept aside for secret negotiations where the parties could not admit they were even talking to each other. There was provision for overnight stays, and this was being turned into something the group could use for a while, until a more permanent home could be found. Progress was slow on the conversion, but they promised me no more than another week.

The evacuation was being felt in every quarter of the city: wreckage still heaped up from the attack was cleared away and prefab buildings were dropped into place in public spaces, while residents of the more permanent structures were shuffled into as few buildings as possible, so the ones that remained could be turned into refugee centres for those who were less afflicted by physical and mental trauma. But all of them would have issues. Those that did not would be sent straight to a colony world; there simply wasn't room on Hub for anyone who didn't desperately need our help. So Hub Metro would once again be filled with troubled refugees, as it was during every evacuation.

I visited my own apartment for the first time in weeks to supervise a couple of robots as they packed up my belongings and shifted them into storage, to make a little more room if it was needed, and so I could leave once and for all if I decided to do so.

5. ELSBET

While I was in Hub Metro, I rolled as many duties into my visit as I could. Liss had her meeting with the Quillian diplomat, which had been put off half a dozen times, and which I'd only been able to arrange as a face to face meeting between the diplomat's other engagements; elsewhere in the city, I had to pay a visit to Katie in hospital. Or rather, I visited Sergeant-Designate Elsbet Carmon, late of Attack Squadron Alpha Six of the Vesta 4 Holy Brigade, for it was she who had emerged once the new body had woken.

I found her sitting up in bed and working on a co-ordination testing programme with one of the neurologists, stabbing away at a pad with a finger.

"Yes. I've got a finger. It works."

"That's right," said the neurologist, "we just need to test how the fine motor skills are coming along..."

"They're *fine*," she said, and stabbed at some more buttons.

The neurologist smiled, patiently. "You need to look at the pad for this to work..."

She looked round, saw me standing at the door, and broke into a smile. She jumped off the bed and ran to hug me, knocking me back half a metre.

"Thank you! Thank you!"

"Okay... nice to see you too..."

She pulled her head back from my shoulder. "Thank you," she said, looking straight into my eyes.

I smiled as best I could, then looked past her to the neurologist, who was also smiling, though rather wearily.

She let me go and twirled. "This is amazing... I've never felt this good!"

"They tell me your old body had a lot of toxins in it. So now you don't," I said.

"And look!" She turned her head to show a scalp covered only by close-cropped hair. "No sockets!"

"I'm sure you can have an implant later–"

"I don't want one. I don't want anything in me!"

"Okay. You might have to wear contact lenses if you want to understand people. Not everyone speaks Interversal."

"Hah! They can fucking learn!"

"Well. You seem very happy."

"Yeah. If it wasn't for these fuckers." She jabbed a disrespectful thumb in the direction of the neurologist.

"They're just trying to make sure everything went okay. The operation you had doesn't always go this well."

"Balls. I'm fine."

"And they're probably going to need the bed soon. I'm sure they're being very polite about it, but we're going to have a lot of people coming in with radiation burns in a little while. Did they tell you about Ardeë?"

"Yeah, yeah, fine, I'll press all the buttons and get out of here..." she sulked. "Are you taking me back now?"

"I have to get the agreement of the rest of the group, first. Katie said some very worrying things and they're a little cautious."

She snorted. "Idiots."

"I think they'll be happier when they realise it's you."

"How are they?"

"They're fine. Mostly. Some of them are a little fragile at the moment."

6. IOKAN

Iokan woke in the centre, in his old room, set to a standard bedroom layout. He hadn't bothered to recreate the old settings. He hadn't shown any interest in anything, not even the terrible news from Ardeë, or my announcement to the group that they would need to move to Hub Metro soon. He slept, rose in the morning, put on his robes, ate whatever food was put in front of him, went to the toilet, but otherwise stared at the wall.

Today, he rose and looked out the window. The snow was thick this year, and the evergreens wore white as far as the eye could see. The buses and trucks and fliers that brought in the work crews and their equipment grew snowy beards after only minutes on the ground, and had to melt them away before they left. For once, you could see a good distance; the centre had been wrapped in fog and blizzards for more than a week. But today the only clouds were those spiked on the mountains.

Iokan dressed, left his room and headed downstairs. On hearing a troop of new staff being taken on an orientation tour, he turned away and found another way down, twisting and turning his route through the building to avoid people. Pew was in the gym, slamming angrily at weights, and did not see Iokan sneak through. Kwame was in the kitchen enjoying a meal that didn't consist of freeze-dried emergency rations, and failed to hear Iokan's footsteps pass the door. Olivia fretted in the common room, writing on an antique paper pad with an ink pen and crossing out everything she wrote almost as soon as she read it. She never knew that Iokan passed by, heading for the exit, wearing no coat, no thermals, no boots. The centre's systems knew where he was, but he had done nothing yet to endanger himself or others, so they stayed silent.

The snow was half a metre deep, and paths had been carved between the buildings. Iokan found his way to the edge of the compound and headed into the woods, crunching sandals on fresh snow. The only life there was the forest itself; insects had fled or died or burrowed deep into the soil as winter came, and there were no mammals or birds to trouble the plantlife.

He came out the other side onto a frozen, snow-buried meadow, just as the weather was changing. Clouds had raced in from the mountains and visibility was back down to less than a hundred metres. The sun was just a vague glow and the air temperature fell even further.

He didn't care. He looked about; he was still alone. He took off his robes and stood naked in the snow, waiting for whatever might come.

7. ELSBET

"I just popped in to see how you were, really," I said.

"I'm fine and my fingers are fine,' said Elsbet, with another sidelong glance at the despised neurologist. "You're not going, are you?"

"I have to pick up Liss soon. She's having a meeting in town. You should carry on with the therapy. I'll be in touch."

"Oh! Before you go, let me show you something!"

She took my hand to pull me away. I looked back at the long suffering neurologist, who shrugged his permission. So I let her take me down through the hospital, past all the porters and nurses moving patients and equipment, clearing beds and stocking up on supplies, down a gravity tube and out to a glass-walled common area looking out on a patch of nature bounded by the structure of the building: trees bursting with the red and gold of autumn, reaching higher than the hospital itself.

Elsbet shuddered for a moment after we stepped out of the gravity tube. The sky was still a shock for her, but she took a breath and clung to me.

"Are you sure you want to be here?" I asked.

She nodded, fervently. "It's not really open. There's a glass dome."

"Are you sure?"

"Yes!" She pulled me to the glass doors, scooting around other patients and furniture, and paused at the exit, building up her nerve again, then led me outside.

She gasped as the warm sun struck her. The shaking came to a stop; she looked up at the sky, closed her eyes and smiled. I let her go and she spread her arms to catch more of the sun.

She looked over at me, her arms still wide, as if to say: *look what I can do!*

"Aren't you afraid?" I asked.

"Yes!" she cried. "But feel the sun..."

"We're much closer than the asteroid where you grew up."

"It's so *warm*... I can feel it through my clothes! Did they do something to me?"

"I don't think so. But I'm glad you're happy."

She did a delighted twirl, laughing.

8. IOKAN

Iokan stood naked in the snow. He tried to accept the cold, but his body's natural responses refused: his muscles spasmed in shivering waves, his teeth chattered, his skin grew pale and grey as warmth fled.

The fog thickened, and the sun faded from a patch of light to nothing at all; just the general glow of the sky.

The shivering wracked his body until he could bear it no longer and had to hug his arms close and gasp at the cold. Frost spread through his hair, and the moisture on his skin froze, coating him in rime, chilling him further. He fell to his knees. In this kind of temperature, he had less than an hour to live.

A light bathed him from above.

It was not the sun. The fog was as thick as before. It was something shining down on him with more than just illumination: there was a warmth that was blessed relief to his frosted skin. He rubbed meltwater from his eyes and looked up.

The glow was close, from no source he could see, like another sun come near. The warmth allowed him to stand up again. He shielded his eyes; it was brighter now, almost too much. But he did his best to look into the heart of the light.

"You came back for me," he said.

He closed his eyes and spread his arms wide.

"I'm ready."

9. IOKAN & ELSBET

As Elsbet soaked up the sun, a chime went off in my ear and an emergency message flashed in front of my eyes.

"I'll just be a moment," I said to Elsbet, and took a few steps away. I fished a pad out of my bag and put the video through.

Iokan stood naked in the snow, arms stretched out, a beatific look on his face. I sighed. He'd done what we feared and attempted suicide. Nevertheless, it gave me a chance to talk to him.

"Iokan," I said. "It's Asha here." He opened his eyes, surprised and confused. "We sent a rescue drone out after you. It's very cold out there."

"Show yourself!"

A beam of light jumped out of the glow and struck the fog surrounding the hole melted by the warmth. It displayed the image from the camera in my pad: me, in a garden, looking concerned.

He suddenly realised what had happened, and closed his eyes with a sigh. The rescue drone was providing a sunny microclimate to keep him alive. The light and warmth were just that – nothing more.

"What did you think was happening, Iokan?"

He looked tired, but not embarrassed; just worn out on a level deeper than the body. "I thought she'd come for me."

"She can't do that, Iokan. She's not even in this universe. And she won't come for you. You remember what she said as well as I do."

He didn't answer. He looked away.

"Iokan?"

He shook his head, despairing. I feared we would lose him to a bout of depression, and didn't notice Elsbet sneaking up and looking over my shoulder.

"Well hello there…" she said, suddenly seeing the image of a very naked Iokan.

He looked back up at the ghostly video image projected into the fog. "Who was that?"

"This is private," I snapped at her. Too harsh, and I regretted it instantly.

She didn't care. She waved merrily at the pad. "Hi there, Iokan! Remember me?"

He looked up, confused. "Katie?"

"No!" she cried. "It's me!'

His eyes went wide. "Elsbet…?"

"That's the one!"

"You came back…"

She grinned at me. "Oh, he's clever, isn't he?" She looked back at him, and his naked body. "Bloody hell, did I really turn you down?"

Iokan looked down at himself, and quickly hid his genitals.

"Okay, Elsbet, I think that's enough, don't you?"

"Aw…" she backed off with a disappointed pout. I looked back at Iokan.

"I'm sorry about that."

"I'm glad she's well. Did she have the treatment?"

"She did."

He nodded. "Good."

"The medical staff will be with you in a moment. Do you think you'll be able to sit down and have a chat once you're inside?"

He paused, and I thought for a moment he would withdraw again. But then he looked up at me and said, "I will."

10. IOKAN

Iokan sat in the remote meeting room, swaddled in blankets, sipping at a warm drink and looking introspective. Not depressed, though certainly tired. I activated the link between the centre and the room I was in at the hospital. "How are you doing?" I asked.

"Well enough," he said.

"Do you mind if I sit down?"

"How could I?"

"Thank you." I took one of the seats next to him.

"How did Elsbet come back?" he asked.

"You remember how Katie attempted suicide? Well, we had to do a lot of reconstruction work on her brain. I suppose whatever neural issue set off the change in the first place did the same thing again. When she woke up, she was Elsbet… and Elsbet agreed to the treatment."

"You refused her before."

"With all the brain damage, we couldn't be sure if the change was permanent. We, ah, erred on the side of caution."

He absorbed that with a nod. "Will Katie come back?"

"Probably not. It's hard to tell, though."

"You don't like to let us go, do you?"

"We would have, in your case. But it wasn't up to us. Szilmar made that choice."

He put his head in his hands. "I still don't understand…"

"I know it's difficult. But if you're willing to listen, there's more I can tell you." He looked up. "Szilmar had a long discussion with the Diplomatic Service. She gave us a rough outline of what happened."

He closed his eyes and looked away. I went on.

"It seems the Antecessors were escaping from attacks on your world, three thousand years ago. They made a lot of enemies – you were right when you said they weren't very nice people. At the time, your species had gone beyond the human form. But there was a fashion for dressing up in human bodies from time to time, and when the attacks came, a lot of people were trapped in those bodies. Those were your ancestors. Some of the others chose to escape using energy forms that were meant for interstellar travel. But they hadn't had time to set up colonies, and there weren't any machines out there to turn them back. So they were stuck in those forms, and they weren't designed for long term use. Over the centuries, entropy took a toll, and by the time they came back, they were like children looking for someone else to play with. They didn't understand that what they were doing was wrong."

He was quiet for a long time, eyes still closed.

"I can give you the report to study, if you like."

He opened his eyes again, and there were tears welling up in them. But he wiped them away and spoke. "Was it all… artificial?"

"What you felt about the Antecessors was real. But the way they started it was artificial, yes."

He shook his head. "I don't know what I'm… I…"

"It might take some time for you to come to terms with it. I think you still have some therapy to do."

He put his head in his hands and sighed.

"But there's something for you to think about."

He looked up from his palms.

"The Antecessors, the new ones, are in discussions with the IU to see if we can help them rebuild your world. It'll take time, with everything that's happening at the moment. But we think we can give them back their bodies."

There were tears in his eyes.

"And not just the adults. It'll be harder, but we think we can bring back the children as well. Even the very youngest."

And then he couldn't control himself at all. His chin trembled and sobs came out.

"You're not alone."

11. ELSBET

After seeing Iokan, I decided I ought to look in on Elsbet again. I found her in her room, having lunch, with copious dessert: a sweet pudding smothered in syrup.

"This is *incredible!*" she said with her mouth full. "D'you want some?"

"I'm fine, thanks," I said.

"Can't anyway. It's all mine." She crammed in another mouthful. "Why does it taste so *good?*"

"Brand new tastebuds. Whatever you did to them in your old life, that's gone now."

"Balls. We didn't have anything like this in general population, or the army. Only sugar we got was pills to keep us going…"

"You should be careful, you know. You don't want to get overweight."

"Who cares?" She licked her spoon to get every last trace from it.

"What kind of food did they have in the asteroids?"

Her look soured. "Fucking algae. Grew it in tanks, then they put flavour on it. Nothing like this."

"You didn't like living there, did you?"

"Nobody likes living there. Fucking machines."

"What do you think will happen now they're gone?"

She shrugged. "We were supposed to go back to Earth, so that's not happening. I don't know. Maybe they'll build some proper space stations."

"Was it so bad because you had to hide from the machines?"

"Course it was."

"And you think it'll get better now they're gone?"

"Bound to."

I nodded. "There might be a problem." She put her spoon down and looked at me. "Katie told us a lot about how things went from the machines' point of view…"

"She was lying. They always lie to us."

"I don't think so. You see, one of the things she said was that they sent expeditions to other star systems. It took decades for them to get there. But sooner or later they're going to find out what happened. And when they do, they're going to head back. There's going to be another war. A Fourth Machine War."

She didn't answer.

"The Diplomatic Service wanted Katie to help prevent that war."

Still no answer.

"Elsbet?"

She set her jaw. "I'm not going back."

"You don't have to, I'm not saying that–"

"I am *not going back!*"

"That's fine–"

She flung her dessert aside and burst out of bed.

"You can't send me back. I've done my mission!"

"I understand–"

She grabbed me by the jacket. Not threatening but pleading.

"Do you know what they'll do to me? They will kill me. As a traitor. Because of what *she* did!"

"Elsbet–"

"*I'm not going back!* To that – hole!" The tears were coming now. "You can't send me back. I won't go."

I pulled her close and held her. She let go of my jacket and sobbed into my shoulder.

"I'm not going back there... I don't want to live like that..."

"It's okay," I said. "You can stay here. We won't make you do anything."

I held onto her, smelling the sweet sugar of the syrup as she clung to me.

12. LISS

Liss's request to have a meeting with a Quillian consular official had been considered by the Diplomatic Service, and approved with minor restrictions. The duty of care and anonymity limited the choice of venues, and the availability of the consular official in question reduced them still further. So it took place in the Diplomatic Service General Negotiation Complex, where the most stringent precautions could be observed on ground that was absolutely guaranteed to be neutral.

Quite why it needed to look like an ancient temple garden was another question entirely, but the structure of marble pillars, lintels, arches and fountains did produce a calming effect. The individual 'meeting rooms' were the spaces around fountains in the temple complex, apparently open to the elements but only because the ceilings showed pictures of the sky on a sunny day with friendly clouds and never a hint of rain to trouble the negotiations. The rooms could have tables and chairs if the parties wished, but most people were encouraged to sit by a fountain, usually with a refreshment tray by their side.

Liss waited in one of these rooms, looking around. She ran a finger across the marble to feel the texture (very accurate), put a hand in the fountain to see if the water was real (definitely), and examined the flowering vines (not real at all, though it was hard to tell).

She was distracted by a chime from the entrance to the 'room', and the air rippled as a Mediator emerged from the corridor beyond. The illusion of being alone in an empty garden was nothing more than that: an illusion.

"I'm sorry about the wait," said the Mediator, a man with a charming smile and an apology for every occasion. "The other party says he was delayed and conveys his apologies. I understand the present situation on Ardeë is the cause."

Liss smiled her understanding. "I suppose he's a busy man, huh?"

The Mediator nodded. "He should be here in just a few minutes. Is there anything else I can get you?"

"No. I'm fine."

The Mediator withdrew through the rippling air. Liss checked the control pad for the room. She found a setting to change the time of day, thought about it for a moment, and slid it over to 'night'. The sun faded and dimpled until it turned into the moon. The sky darkened to indigo. Stars revealed themselves and even the wash of the Milky Way became visible. Oil lamps flickered into life on the columns around the fountain.

The entrance rippled again, and the Mediator returned. He blinked a little as his eyes adjusted to the darker setting, then said: "The other party has arrived. Are you ready for the meeting, Ms. Li'Oul?"

She stood up from the side of the fountain and nodded.

"You may wish to anonymise yourself."

"Okay. Got it." She fiddled with a pad and a blur mask jumped up in front of her face, contouring a couple of centimetres around her features.

"I shall refer to you as Ms. Doe, to further preserve your anonymity."

"Uh, okay."

The Mediator nodded, satisfied. "Very well. I'll call him in." Whatever signal he sent, Liss did not see it. A few seconds later, the Quillian consular official entered: a short man whose manner was older than he looked. His smile as he saw her was polite, warm, but well practiced. Something worn professionally.

"Mr. Vawlin, may I present Ms. Doe, who is under the care of the Refugee Service." Vawlin bowed. "Madame, this is Mr. Telliniad Vawlin of the Quillian Embassy to the Interversal Union." Liss did her best to copy Vawlin's bow, looking a little embarrassed.

"It is a condition of this meeting that I remain present." said the Mediator. I'd insisted that someone be there for security reasons, along with guards who could be summoned at a moment's notice. As much as I wanted to give Liss this chance, I couldn't leave her unsupervised in this kind of situation. "However, I am not required to act as a mediator unless either of you wish it."

"If Ms. Doe consents?" asked Vawlin.

"I'm fine," shrugged Liss.

"Then I shall refrain from further comment," said the Mediator. "Please, begin."

Liss took a deep breath. "Hi!"

"Hello," said Vawlin. "Shall we sit?"

"Yeah. Sure." They sat by the fountain, while the Mediator went to a chair on the far side of the room and let them get on with it.

"Firstly, please accept my apologies for my lateness. We've been extraordinarily busy in the last few days…"

"Oh, sure, it's been kinda crazy everywhere, huh?"

"Yes, yes it has. We're loaning a number of spacecraft to the IU to help with the evacuation, and anything else we can find that might help."

"That's kinda cool."

"We do what we can. So I understand you believe you may be a member of my species?"

"Uh. Yeah, I guess."

"Can I ask how you came to that conclusion?"

"Oh, they said I could have a test to see if I was, you know, compatible for, uh, having kids with other species, and it came back Quillian."

"Something of a surprise, I take it?"

"You can say that again. Does this happen a lot?"

"It does come up occasionally. We're a very well travelled species."

"So you go to other universes all the time?"

"Yes, I suppose you could say that."

"I mean, I heard about that Ilfenard thing…"

His face fell into regret. "Yes. A terrible crime. We had a major social collapse a couple of thousand years ago, and when we rediscovered how to travel to other universes, we found our ancestors had committed monstrous crimes on many worlds. We've been trying to put them right ever since. It's another reason why we're doing everything we can to help with the evacuation. But there was nothing we could do for Ilfenard, except warn others not to take the same path."

There was something rehearsed about his speech; he'd said this before, many times. But that was probably only to be expected.

"Uh-huh. So how do people get stuck on different worlds?"

"Well, we undertake a good many scientific surveys, often on worlds too undeveloped to contact directly. We have teams on the surface, disguised as priests, or surveyors, or telemarketers, or whatever's appropriate. But things can go wrong, I'm afraid. People sometimes get left behind."

"Do you take your kids along as well?"

"For major surveys, yes. It's not fair on either the children or the parents to have them separated."

"Uh-huh."

"Can I ask you a little about your world?"

"Oh, uh… just an ordinary place, I guess." She shrugged. "Well, it was before it all went wrong and we had to leave, which is how I ended up here. Uh, there's one thing I wanted to ask…"

"Yes?"

"Well, I always knew I was different, you know? I mean, really different."

"In what way?"

"I, uh… I mean I'm *different*. Do you know what I mean?"

"I'm afraid not."

"I'm stronger, I'm tougher, I'm faster, I don't get sick… the doctors said I was some kinda genetic abnormality…"

Vawlin nodded with a smile. "It may be your heritage. If you are Quillian."

"You mean we're all like this…?"

"I think you'll find a number of more developed species have adjusted their genomes. The kind of differences you're talking about are quite simple ones to implement."

"Simple. Wow."

"Certainly. Did you discover any other abilities?"

"I can see pretty well."

"Can you see things other people can't?"

"Yeah! Like flowers, you see pictures on a screen and they look all dull and boring but if you look at the actual flowers they've got spots and bands on them and nobody else can see it…"

Vawlin nodded again. "We usually have our sight extended into the infra-red and ultraviolet. The markings on the flowers are what, say, a pollinating insect might see. But most humans can't. You may also have a very long life."

"Really?"

"Several hundred years. We generally settle on an adult form in our mid twenties and stay that way for a very long time. I myself am two hundred and seventy three years old."

"No!"

"And therefore I have no idea how old you are."

"Oh, um, not that old..."

"Well. I can't confirm you're a member of my species, not right away. We have to do some background checks first."

"Okay."

"We'll accept the IU's analysis of your genome, of course, but we would like it done again, just to be sure."

"Uh-huh."

"And we will need to know something about the world you've been on all this time, so we can match it against our list of missing persons."

"Right."

"And if we can find any relatives, of course, we can make doubly sure. I understand you're very interested in finding your parents."

Liss's smile subsided and she seemed more serious. "Yes."

The Mediator noticed the sudden change in her voice. He'd spent his time politely studying the night sky, but now he looked back down at Liss. Vawlin noticed it too. "I'm sure they didn't abandon you. Sometimes things can... well, things can happen."

Liss nodded.

"I don't want to promise anything. It's possible they might have died in the years since."

"I know."

"Well–"

"What kind of worlds do you go to?"

The question took him by surprise. "Many kinds. I was going to ask you about your world. The one you grew up on. I would imagine that if you're here, something bad happened."

"You could say that."

"Was there an evacuation?"

"Kinda, yeah."

"Can you tell me about your world?" Liss didn't answer for a moment. Vawlin looked utterly sympathetic, and put a hand on hers. "It could help us a lot in finding your family."

The Mediator watched, sensing tension. Vawlin went on. "I know it must have been a terrible experience to see the end of the world you grew up on. But if you really are one of us... I promise you: we won't let you down. You'll be part of a species again. You'll have a world to call home. Whatever happened on that world... you can put it behind you. You can be one of us."

Behind the blur mask, Liss's eyes hardened.

"But first you need to tell me something about your world."

There was a moment of silence before she replied. "You want me to tell you about my world...?"

He couldn't see the dagger-stare of her eyes, and made the obvious assumption: she'd been traumatised by whatever apocalypse she'd survived. So he let her have her moment, and did a perfect job of looking sympathetic.

"Okay. I'll tell you about my world." Vawlin missed the dangerous tone in her voice. The Mediator didn't, and narrowed his eyes.

"Thank you," said Vawlin.

"It was... primitive. I guess you'd call it that."

"We usually prefer 'less developed'," he said with a reassuring smile that had no effect on her at all.

"Everything was wrong."

"What about it was wrong?"

"A lot of people there were special. Special like I was. But they were natives. Stronger than me. Faster than me. Tougher than me. Smarter than me. Some of them were so smart they went mad. They built insane machines for no reason. Released viruses that destroyed livestock and crops. Turned mountains into volcanoes. It was all in the name of *science*, do you understand me?"

He shook his head. "I'm sorry, I don't think I do."

"People had powers. They used their powers for all kinds of things. For themselves. For the good of humanity. To kill people. To fight crime.

"I fought crime. But it didn't do any good. It kept getting worse. We lost the infonet. We lost all our food crops. We lost the *moon!*

"Do you know what else we lost? Calafaria. In the volcanoes. That's where my parents were keeping me, that's where the Quillians lived while they were dong their surveys, wasn't it?"

"I really don't know without–"

"And it was all in the name of science, yeah? The way everyone on my world was *special?*"

"I don't know what it is you're implying–"

"Do you know what happened to them all? All the people on my world? My friends? My real parents, the ones who raised me after I was *abandoned?*"

Vawlin listened, suddenly aware of a trap. The Mediator saw it, too, and said: "Ms. Doe, are you sure you wish to continue–"

But Liss ignored him. "They all died. At the same time. They burnt to ash, *all at the same time*. Somebody used their DNA to kill them. Somebody put a deathtrap in their genome. *Somebody gave them powers so they could experiment on them and put in a way to hide their tracks*. But it didn't get me. Because I'm one of you. Do you understand me?"

Vawlin's jaw wobbled. He didn't understand, to begin with. Then his eyes went wide for a moment.

He shot to his feet and the diplomatic mask slammed shut.

"This meeting can serve no further purpose."

"Security," said the Mediator. Liss jumped at him.

Vawlin barely had time to see what happened before she had the Mediator by the neck and groin, making him gasp. She lifted him above her head, hardly noticing his weight, as two guards in power armour ran through the ripple of air into the room, weapons already raised and pointing at her.

She flung the Mediator at them, absorbing the stun bolts they fired at her, then knocking them down as he crashed into them. They pushed his dead weight off, but she was already on them, ripping off their helmets, crushing their weapons and banging their heads against the fake stone floor before they could do anything else.

Vawlin gasped, finding her between him and the exit, with no one to protect him. The blur mask stayed on her face, and her posture was all he could read: legs apart, still tensed and ready to fight.

"You're under arrest," she said.

He was incredulous. "What...?"

"By the powers granted me in the One World Accord of NR 643, I detain you as a material witness to the crime of genocide. You have the right to silence but may be subject to neural interrogation under circumstances outlined in paragraph ten subsection three of the Emergency Powers Annex, which most certainly fucking applies in this case!"

He gaped. "You're insane!"

"If you cannot supply an advocate of your own choosing the court will supply one for you except, oh yeah, *they're all fucking dead!*"

He tried to rush past her but she whipped him round and pulled his arm behind his back. He was strong, but she had the edge of training and desperation.

"You – don't have – jurisdiction!" he gasped.

"Call it a citizen's arrest if you like."

"This is *assault!*"

"This is justice."

"What do you want...?"

She jerked him back and he gasped as she shouted in his ear. "Three billion people are *dead!*"

"How do you – what do you think you can do?"

She gritted her teeth.

"What are you going to do with me?" he pleaded.

She didn't have an answer.

"They'll send more security... You have to let me go! I understand... I understand you're upset, you're traumatised, I will not press charges!"

"You know, don't you?"

"I don't know anything!"

"I saw it in your eyes."

"Please, what do you *want?*"

"I want the truth!"

Instead, they both heard a gentle hissing sound. "What's that?" she demanded.

"Tranquilliser gas... if we're the same species... should work the same..."

"I can hold my breath."

"Please... give yourself up..."

But it was too late. The first wave of grogginess hit them both.

"Oh fuck. Skin absorption?" she muttered, disgusted. They sank to their knees. She released her hold, but he found he lacked the strength to crawl away, and collapsed. Liss held out a little longer.

"Vawlin…" she murmured with a hoarse voice. He looked around, barely conscious. "Give my parents a message."

He stared back at her.

"Tell them they're dead to me," she said, as she fell forward.

He didn't nod. He didn't have a response. He just looked back at her with the eyes of a shocked animal, until they closed and blackness took him.

13. HENNI ARDASSIAN

I was on my way to pick Liss up when I was ordered to present myself at Henni Ardassian's office instead. Liss was being held by the Diplomatic Service security section, and I got the basic details of what happened from Mykl Teoth while my car whisked me through the streets to the gold and silver castle of the Refugee Service HQ.

Henni didn't get up when I went in. She had a look of barely controlled exasperation. She drummed her fingers and watched me sit down, like a cat allowing a mouse to take a seat before pouncing. She didn't pounce, though. Instead, she stroked a control and brought up two images on the screen behind her: an official spokeswoman from the Quillian Embassy, and the text of a letter of complaint below the Quillian Supranational Government crest on the right. Henni let the video begin part of the way through.

"–object most strenuously to this *premeditated entrapment* of one of our officials who was acting in a purely humanitarian capacity. We are particularly unhappy that this has happened while we are preparing to place enormous material resources at the disposal of the Refugee Service. We therefore demand an apology and explanation for this incident and expect your reply within forty eight hours."

Henni paused the spokeswoman at the moment she finished, still with a look of official displeasure printed on her face. Henni's own look of displeasure was greater, if anything.

"Did you know about this?"

I shook my head. "She wanted to find out about her parents…"

"And that's what she told you."

"Yes."

"And you *believed* her?"

"I had no reason not to."

"After all the lies she told before? Are you out of your mind?"

"I judged–"

"I don't give a damn for your judgement! Did you hear what they said? That's diplomatic language for '*We're incredibly pissed off and we're going to throw our toys out of the stroller if you don't do what we say.*' Your judgement might cost us sixty ships we could have used in the evacuation! And pilots to go with them! And doctors, and medical supplies! They could save a million people *all by themselves!*"

"They wouldn't do that—"

"Oh, wouldn't they? Would you like to take that risk? Would you like to leave a million people to die?"

"They can't!"

"Are you sure? Really? Well I'll just call and tell them to jump in a lake. Shall we see what happens?"

"But they'd look – I mean, people would think—"

"You reckon they *want* people to think they committed genocide?"

"No, of course not, but—"

"Well I can't take the risk. I need those ships. And I don't have any more time for your experiment, nor do I have the resources. I'm transferring you to the triage team on the Lift. You can do some good up there rather than giving me grief down here."

I paused a moment. "I won't leave them."

"You can have a week to hand over to another therapist."

I tried to find some steel to put in my voice. "I arranged for entirely adequate supervision. It was the Quillians who insisted on meeting at the Negotiation Centre. What happened was not my fault. I will not abandon my patients and you can't force me."

"I can put you on indefinite medical leave."

My gut clenched. "What…?"

"You've already put in the request for leave of absence for medical reasons. Now I can see why. Your lack of judgement has led to serious embarrassment for this service. So you can go away and make yourself better and take as much time as you like doing it, or you can go to the Lift and do your job. Any questions? No. Now get out of my sight. Mykl will arrange for another therapist to take the group. I don't care who. Talk to him about the handover."

Henni picked up a pad and scrolled through another document. I stood up. But I couldn't go. My hands were balled in fists. I stood there and waited until Henni had no choice but to address me again.

"You're still here, Dr. Singh. Do you want me to have security throw you out as well?"

I tried to keep my anger in check. "What if she's right?"

"I'm sorry?"

"I said: what if she's right?"

"I don't care."

"You say they might save a million lives. But they might have murdered billions."

"They *did* murder billions, Dr. Singh, but Ilfenard was a long time ago."

"They might have murdered *three billion more* just last year!"

"That's an accusation, not a fact."

I swallowed. "Yes. And Liss has the right to make that accusation before the Interversal Criminal Tribunal."

Henni put her pad down. She was about to yell at me but put a hold on herself for a moment and considered her words more carefully. "I am trying to save a species, Dr. Singh. People who are still living. I can't bring back the dead."

"They need to be investigated."

"Do they need to be investigated *now*?"

"Yes."

"You really think this is a good time?"

"There's never going to be a good time. There's always going to be another evacuation."

"And would *you* want to be left behind to die just so we could feel better about ourselves?"

"I wouldn't want to be rescued by someone who might have committed genocide."

"Well. And did you know they helped with the evacuation from your world?"

I didn't answer. A memory flashed before me: the Quillian Government crest. I'd seen it before, so many years ago, on a dying world, on the side of a ship...

Henni realised she'd found a weakness in my argument, or perhaps just in me.

"Think about that, if you would," she said. "Let me know when you make up your mind about your job."

She picked up her pad again, and this time I left. I stopped outside, and steadied myself on the wall. She'd had the measure of me from first to last, and there was very, very little I could do. I couldn't go to the media because of the confidentiality of my patients. An employment tribunal, perhaps? But she was right; I was only in my position because they'd been having trouble finding someone to replace me. I'd still be put on leave while they decided my case and the group would end up with whoever could be found, rather than someone I could trust to do the job.

I needed help.

14. ASHA

Ranev wasn't by the sea. He didn't even have his feet planted on solid ground. When my call found him, he was high above the world, higher even than the Lift: he was on Grainger Station, the massive reception and quarantine station at the L1 point halfway between the competing gravity of Earth and Moon.

"I've been reassigned," he explained, and turned his pad to show me the view of the Arrivals Bay: he sat in a viewing hall that looked down on rows and rows of docking ports for all the little shuttles that would come in from the transit spheres, and kilometres distant, the wall of spheres itself. Twenty of them, girder-shells floating in space that could send you anywhere. Or pull you back, if you were in the right position and waiting. I saw the flashes of energy inside half a dozen that meant ships were being brought through to our universe, ships that could only be coming from Ardeë.

"It's crazy," said Ranev. "They're pulling in everyone. They've put me on triage. I don't know how we're going to manage these numbers..."

"Yeah."

"A *billion people*. Maybe more..."

"That just leaves all the ones who have to stay behind."

He nodded. "I know. I know."

"Makes you wonder how they're choosing who lives and dies."

"You're right. It puts all our problems in perspective, doesn't it?"

"Apocalypses tend to do that, yeah."

"I'm sorry, Asha. I forgot. You must be thinking how it was for you. Are you calling up for a session? I think I've got half an hour before they need me."

"Yes. No... I don't know. I need advice."

"Okay."

"They've reassigned me as well."

"Oh?"

I looked away. I was sitting in a park in Hub Metro. Behind me, a ten storey building was being added to, floor by floor as new levels were lifted onto it and slotted into place, all of it dormitory space for the refugees who were hurt but not so disturbed that they had to be kept away from the city. "Medical leave," I said. "Compulsory. Permanent."

"What happened?"

"Liss attacked someone again," I explained. "It ended up in a diplomatic incident... they're blaming me. And I was all set to take leave on medical grounds anyway..."

He sighed. "I'm so sorry..."

"Did you tell them? Anything?"

"Now, Asha. You know our sessions are confidential."

"Yeah. Yeah."

"You said yourself: you were taking leave on medical grounds. Was it Henni who made the decision?"

I nodded.

"That makes sense. She's never one for patience."

"She's going to assign someone else to the group."

"What...?"

"She said she didn't care who."

"That's really not a good idea..."

"Don't you think I know that?" I shouted. Ranev was surprised.

"Are you angry, Asha?"

"Yes! Yes, I'm angry! They're going to get some *student* in to deal with the group and everything's... all the work I did... my patients – they don't trust anyone else! Some of them hardly even trust *me!*"

"I see–"

"Aren't *you* angry? Who's taking your group?"

"I had an assistant," he said. I looked down and squeezed my eyes shut to try and stop the tears. "I'm sorry," he added. The tears came anyway.

"Veofol could have taken them..." I said.

"Yes. He could. He was a fine therapist."

"He was."

"How angry are you?"

"What?"

"How angry are you, Asha?"

I looked down at the pad, at him, sitting there on a space station, making no sense. "I don't understand."

"Okay. You don't normally get angry, do you?"

"No."

"You absorb pain. You bear the suffering. You shoulder the burden and you hardly ever complain. But you don't get angry. You don't trust yourself when you're angry, do you?"

"I make bad decisions."

"I think being angry will help you now."

"What?" I was about to tell him exactly how crazy I thought he was, but he carried on regardless.

"If you're going to help your patients, you can't do it through the usual channels. You need to think of something else. Being angry can help with that. Use it, Asha. Help your patients."

"I don't understand–"

"I don't mean do something stupid. I mean you should look at options you wouldn't consider otherwise. Things you wouldn't dare do in another situation."

A chime sounded in the space station. Ranev looked up. "I have to go. There are shuttles docking. We haven't even got enough people to move the wounded... call me later, if you can. Let me know if there's anything I can do."

The screen blanked. He was gone, off to save lives high above the world, where I would be if I didn't have lives to save down here. I sat there in the park that was no longer really a park, listening to the construction and thinking about anger.

I was angry. I was incensed. Henni had her reasons and they were valid, and just, and overwhelming: she had a billion people to save. And my poor six were specks of dust she would allow to be lost in that storm of people fleeing from a murderous sun.

The group was going to suffer, and no one cared enough to do anything it about except me. No one could save them. No one could protect them. No one could give them the therapy they needed. No one else could keep them out of the Psychiatric Centre and a lifetime of gentle care that might as well have been a torture chamber. Some of them might be able to stand alone, some might even be able to find a life outside; but Olivia would not. Pew would not. Kwame was still not ready. Liss might be sent to prison. And no one had shown them the slightest shred of–

I realised I was wrong. Someone *had* shown a shred of kindness to them, and an interest in their fate. It might only be a professional interest. But still...

Ranev was right; it took anger to see past the problem, anger to see a solution, anger to drive me on and do something I could never have contemplated before.

I pulled up my contacts list on my pad, and put a call through to Eremis Ai at the Interversal Criminal Tribunal.

15. LISS

Liss found herself in a secure transport, whisked across Hub Metro to a place she had never seen in real life, but which she knew well from her frantic and pointless appeals for an investigation into the genocide on her world: the headquarters of the Interversal Criminal Tribunal. The building had only just been assigned to the ICT, and like most structures in Hub Metro, it soared to an almost capricious height. But there was something more serious about this place. Whatever architect from a distant universe had been given the opportunity to show off their skills in front of the multiverse had chosen to create something inspired by devotional architecture, and knew well the effect on the human mind of a lofty, endless space stretching to an unimaginably high ceiling. It looked to be made of stone, but no mere stone could bear the weight of such high, curving pillars, or support the obsidian sheets that formed the walls. And this was just the lobby, stretching up into something surpassing the human scale. Beyond it, all the floors that held the offices, workrooms and assorted facilities the ICT needed were arrayed on the back wall of the broad cathedral that sustained the noise of steps and voices into an endless fading sonic glow.

I met Liss at the front desk as she was led in by two guards. She wore a mohib suit under the prison uniform, and was surprised to see me. I was still surprised to be there. "I need you to meet someone," I said, and led her inside. The guards stayed with us. No one would trust her now, and the guards were a non-negotiable item when we asked for her presence.

Inside the room – a remote meeting room like so many others across Hub – Eremis Ai stood, but did not offer to shake her hand, mindful of the protocols we'd had to sign up to in order to get her there. "Thanks for coming," he said.

"Okay…" replied Liss, amused. The choice hadn't really been hers. I joined Eremis at the meeting table, and asked Liss to sit down opposite us.

"I'm sorry about the mohib suit," I said.

"It's itchy," she muttered.

"There's nothing I can do about it, Liss."

"Yeah. I got that. You can't do anything. Except drag me halfway across town. What's this about? You investigating *me* now?"

Eremis gave me a look: my questions came first.

"Why did you attack him, Liss?"

"It's like you said. I'm supposed to be investigating. That's what I did."

"You planned it?"

"Well, no, not all of it. But he pissed me off."

"How did he do that?"

She leaned back in the chair and folded her arms. "He just did."

"You know, if you'd been honest with me, I could have helped you find a way to do this that didn't end up with you in detention."

"It's my job. Not yours."

"I could have helped. Or the ICT could have helped."

She gave Eremis a look of contempt. "I'm not the priority, am I? You're all gung-ho on finding out what killed Iokan's world, not mine."

"That's not the case," he said.

"Sure it is! How long did you say it would take before you got round to me? Months? Years?"

"Liss," I said. "That's not the case."

"Oh, so they were lying to me?"

"No. Things have changed."

That got her attention. "Changed? How?"

Eremis said: "We can start investigating your case right away."

Her eyes went wide. "What…?"

"You didn't give us a choice," he said. "We have to move immediately or else the Quillians will claim we don't take the matter seriously."

She grinned with delight. "Hah!"

"We wanted more time to establish ourselves before we started an open-ended investigation like this. So I can't make any promises."

"Who cares?" She laughed and tried to punch the air but the mohib suit cut in and restrained her. "Ow. Damn thing."

I sighed. "You won't be permitted to take any part in the investigation, except as a witness."

She shrugged. "Good. The professionals can do it."

"And you'll have to accept the custody of the ICT."

"So you can keep an eye on me?"

"You'll have to stay in therapy longer than I was hoping. We need to work on your aggressive tendencies. That was part of the deal to avoid prosecution."

She laughed louder than before. "*My* aggressive tendencies?" The irony of it made her weep with laughter.

"Are you going to co-operate with us?"

"Of course I'm going to co-operate."

She was still smiling, thinking she'd won, not knowing how long the path ahead would be, or how much more difficult she'd made it for herself.

"There's another thing," I said.

"Yeah?"

"I'm leaving the Refugee Service."

"What? So who's my therapist, then?"

"Me. If you'll have me."

"Okay, now you're just deliberately trying to confuse me."

"I'm leaving the Refugee Service, and joining the ICT."

She was still sarcastic. "Oh? Really?"

"You didn't give me a choice," I said. "They blamed me for what you did. I would have been transferred, or put on permanent leave."

A first flicker of regret crossed her face.

"Oh. Shit…"

"They'd have got rid of me, and the group would have been taken by the first therapist they could find."

"But they can't do that!"

"You gave them a reason. Please think about that, Liss."

She slumped in her chair, full of guilt. As selfish as she'd been, she was far from malicious. She was simply a terrible judge of tactics and strategy, as she'd always claimed.

"I'm going to be a consulting therapist for the ICT. But the group can come too, if it wants. That's why we've brought you here. We need your permission, and theirs, if we're going to give them a home. Liss, the Refugee Service doesn't have room any more. Millions of people are dying. We've just started the biggest evacuation anyone's ever seen. After the Refugee Service, the ICT are the ones most interested in your wellbeing, and they're willing to give the resources to look after you. All of you. If you agree."

She didn't hesitate. "I agree. Of course. The others, they, they *need* you."

"Thank you," I said.

Eremis looked at me. "Shall we bring them in?"

16. GROUP

I nodded to Eremis, who reached for a pad, and left the room. Liss watched him go.

"He'll be back in a moment. We need everyone's agreement," I said. "So we're going to talk to the whole group. You can keep the details of your involvement confidential, if you wish."

She still looked puzzled. "The group? Now?"

"Now," I said.

"Do they know–?"

"They know you did something foolish. I've asked them not to inquire about it for the moment."

"Oh. Okay."

I pressed a control on my pad. Kwame faded in, standing with arms folded, looking around and plainly seeing me and Liss appear in the meeting room back at the centre. Alongside him, Olivia was caught in the act of sitting down as she appeared, alarmed by the sudden manifestations. Iokan was already waiting in a seat, wearing his robe. Pew fretted as far from everyone as he could, until Elsbet materialised beside him in a hospital dressing gown, making him jump. She was still at the hospital and just as surprised to see them all.

Liss's prison uniform drew looks of interest. "Get yourself arrested again, dear?" asked Olivia. Liss gave me an irritated look, knowing full well that my request not to talk about her situation had been pointless. But Kwame had another concern. He glared at Elsbet.

"I thought I had made it clear I had no wish to participate when Katie is present–"

"Oh, shove it up your bum," said Elsbet.

"That's not Katie," smiled Iokan.

Kwame's face brightened. "Oh. Well. In that case I owe you an apology. Welcome back, Sergeant."

She stuck her tongue out at him and grinned at the others. I decided to try and persuade her to eat less sugar in the future.

"So what did you get us in here for?" said Olivia. "Are we just saying hello?"

"Hello!" said Elsbet, plainly thinking she was very funny.

"Yeh, yeh, hello to you an' all." She looked at me. "Well?"

"No, we have another reason to bring you here today," I said. Liss looked up at me, but said nothing. "You all remember Eremis Ai of the ICT?"

"I remember," said Kwame.

"Yes…" said Pew, taking an interest in the meeting for the first time.

"Annoying little shit," said Olivia. Heaven only knew what he'd done to earn her displeasure, other than being born. But it made for an interesting look of surprise when he walked in the door, followed by a narrow look at me once she realised Eremis had been there all along.

"Good afternoon," he said to them all. Various grunts and greetings came back. "I've asked you all to come today because of a change in your situation. As you've probably heard by now, the Refugee Service is engaged in the biggest evacuation it's ever had to undertake. A billion or more refugees are going to be coming in from Ardeë–"

"What, all at once?" asked Olivia.

"No, but enough that it's going to put a lot of stress on the resources of the IU. That means they need to use all the therapy centres they have, even the one you're at."

"We're aware of this," said Iokan. "As I understand it, the Diplomatic Service is providing us with temporary accommodation."

"Yes," I said. "But, unfortunately…" I tried not to glance at Liss. "… resources are even thinner than we expected. The Refugee Service need all the therapists they can get for the evacuation. They've ordered me to report to the Lift."

"Well bloody say no!" said Olivia.

"I did," I said. "But I wasn't given a choice."

"You're leaving us?" asked Elsbet, suddenly anxious.

"No," I said. "But I am leaving the Refugee Service."

"So you *are* leaving us!" said Olivia.

"Not exactly," I said. "Let me explain. The ICT have offered me a job as consulting therapist…"

"What does that entail?" asked Kwame.

Eremis spoke up. "We're expecting many of the witnesses we speak to will be extremely traumatised. We need someone to help us assess their mental state. In the first instance because we need reliable witness statements that will stand up in court–"

"Huh," snorted Olivia, assuming his motives were entirely mercenary.

"–and secondly, so we can arrange proper care for them. If necessary, we need to be able to provide that care ourselves."

"Why?" asked Pew.

"Some witnesses will need protection from the people they're testifying against." I noticed Liss chewing her lip. With any luck, she was considering the consequences of what she'd done, and how much danger she'd put herself in. Eremis went on: "If that's the case, we'll need to be able to offer therapy while they're in our custody."

Iokan smiled. He'd already figured out what was coming next.

"As for the group," I said, "we're here to make you an offer. I can't stay with the Refugee Service, and even if I did, I wouldn't be able to stay on as your therapist. They'll assign someone to you as soon as they can, but it might take a while, given what's going on."

"You're just abandoning us, is that it?" accused Olivia.

"I don't think that's what we're here for," said Iokan. "My answer is yes. I'll come with you."

"What...?" demanded Olivia.

"Do you mean to say–" said Kwame, laboriously.

"You want us to come with you?" finished Elsbet.

"That's pretty much it," I said. "The Refugee Service is willing to transfer custody to the ICT, but only if you agree. So: how do you all feel about that?"

"I'll do it," said Liss before anyone else could cut in.

"So... what, are we still going to this Diplomatic place?" asked Elsbet, suddenly very tense.

"Yes, in the short term," said Eremis. "We'll be looking into other accommodation as soon as possible."

"And they don't have anything to do with this...?"

"No," I said. "They won't speak to you unless you ask."

She relaxed. "Oh. Well. Okay, then."

"That's fine. Kwame?"

He considered it, and turned to Eremis. "Will you be able to investigate my case?"

"I can't promise we'll be able to give you quite what you want..."

"What I want has changed. There were events at the very end which were less... nebulous. Including several deaths. I would like to have my name cleared if nothing else."

Pew looked up from the dudgeon he'd been in, and seemed troubled.

"Perhaps we should discuss this later, Kwame?" I asked.

"I would be glad to," he said. Eremis nodded.

"Pew?" I asked. He didn't look like he wanted to talk. He hadn't wanted to talk much recently, in any case. As much as he'd been a little more co-operative recently, it had all been grudgingly given and he seemed to hate the process of therapy for more reasons than just the trauma he would have to relive in order to remedy his PTSD.

"No," he said.

"Just 'no', Pew?"

"Just no."

"Can we discuss your reasons? Especially if the others might find them relevant."

He folded his arms and looked down into them.

"Pew?"

Olivia jumped in. "Well, It's no surprise, is it? You've dropped this on us all of a sudden, no wonder he's not ready. And you're not giving us a choice, are you? Where else is there to go?"

"Well, I have to admit there aren't a lot of alternatives–"

"Oh, but I bet the Psychiatric Centre is one of 'em..."

"Yes," I said. "I'm afraid it's the only realistic option."

"Well there you are, then. Not much of a choice is it? Dragged all over the planet like this, no wonder he doesn't want to go–"

Pew thrust forward in his chair. "Stop it! That's not why *I* don't want to go, that's why *you* don't want to go! You don't know! *You don't know!*"

"So spit it out, then!" retorted Olivia.

"It's *them*!" He jabbed a finger at Eremis. "They'll investigate anything *you* want but they won't do anything for *me*! And we all know who killed my species! If they won't help me, why should they help you? All they'll do is put Kwame in prison because they know he killed someone! They won't do anything about a whole species!"

"Pew, we've discussed this. I'm sorry we can't give you what you want–"

"But they'll put us in prison if it was *us* who killed the last one! Never if it was *them*!"

Kwame leaned forward. "I do not know what you think I did, but I am no longer asking to be tried for genocide."

"*I know that!* Everybody knows that!"

"I seek to be cleared on a charge of murder. I do not understand–"

"What if it was me? What if I killed the last one?"

There was silence. Kwame did not know what to say.

I spoke up. "I really don't think this is the time or place for this. We need to talk about this in individual therapy. All I'm asking today is that you give me a chance to keep working with you. I'm only trying to help–"

"You're like her. *Just* like her!"

"I'm sorry?"

"Shan'oui! She said she wanted to help. It's always *help* and then there's none of us left!"

He slumped down in his chair, refusing any eye contact. I looked around at the rest of the group. "I think I need to discuss this with Pew in private. Do the rest of you mind stepping outside? Elsbet, can you disconnect for a moment? I'll let you know when we're finished."

Elsbet vanished, and the rest of the group filed out. Olivia looked back at Pew with exasperation, shaking her head. "I'll be as quick as I can," I said to Eremis. He nodded, and I think he understood. I'd warned him this might not be simple.

He left me and Pew alone together in the meeting room.

17. PEW

I sat down beside Pew, trying to make it as much like a therapy session as possible, in spite of the fact that we were sat at the edge of a room intended for meetings of up to twenty people.

"We're alone now, Pew. Can we talk about it?"

He didn't answer. Just stared at the tabletop.

"Are you worried they're going to start investigating you?"

Still no answer.

"Pew, you haven't committed a crime. You're the *victim* of a crime."

He stared ahead with fixed, trembling eyes.

"Pew, what is it you're afraid of?"

He snapped at the accusation. "I'm not afraid. I'm not afraid of anything. I'm not afraid of *them*. It's just wrong."

"What's wrong?"

He whipped his head round. "They'll come for me and it wasn't me! It was them! It was *them* that killed her!"

"Killed who?"

"The last one they sent."

"In the breeding programme? Do you mean Ley'ang?"

"Yes."

He stared back at me, defying me to console him. I went on instead.

"I'm sure it wasn't your fault, Pew. Can you tell me what happened?"

Another pause. "They put me back in the programme after I escaped. But there weren't any women left. They were all dead. Some of them killed themselves because they couldn't get pregnant by me." He let that sink in, then continued. "There weren't any women. But there was a girl. She was too young to mate before but they said she was ready now. She wasn't ready. She was a *child*."

"You mean she was too young to–"

"No! She was old enough for *that*. She was *like* a child. She believed all the bullshit they'd told her."

"I understand. What did you do?"

"I couldn't go with her."

"Why?"

"She was like me. When I was younger. She thought they were telling the truth. She didn't know she lived in a *cage*."

"I see."

"I tried to tell her but she didn't understand. And they were all watching behind a mirror. I couldn't touch her. I couldn't do it. I couldn't stand being in the same room as her. So they gave me the drugs."

I realised what that meant, and what he must have been forced to do to her.

"I'm so sorry…"

"That's what I have the flashback about. They put me back in there and I… I couldn't stop it… I… beat her until she stopped screaming, I…" His gaze slid away. I feared the flashback starting.

"Pew. Slower. More careful."

He locked his eyes back on me. "I killed her."

I nodded. Not judging. Not condoning. Just acknowledging.

"Not straight away. I hurt her. I think… I think I was trying to hurt her so much she could *never* have children. I was so disgusted…"

"With the way the Soo treated you?"

"With *us*. The Pu." He grimaced as he said the name of his species. "We never *fought*. We just let them do it to us."

"I see."

"She died in the ambulance… they said there was a crash, didn't they?"

"Yes. That's what's in the records."

"They lied."

I nodded. "I can't say I'm surprised."

"Then Shan'oui came to me, afterwards. I didn't even know what I'd done. She told me."

He swallowed hard to keep his feelings in check. "I screamed. I wept. She told me I was the last Pu in the world." He gave me a hard look. "And she said she was *sorry*."

I nodded. "Okay. Thank you, Pew. I know that was difficult but I think you made some real progress–"

"You don't understand."

He was still angry. "Okay. What don't I understand?"

"She said she was *sorry*. She said she'd tried to defend me. She said she'd done everything she could. *She did nothing*."

"But she tried. Isn't that right?"

"All she did was make it *worse!*"

"How did she do that?"

"She kept us there, in that *prison*. She shipped us out to *fuck*. She let them put cameras in so every Soo in the world could watch us fuck and die. She let them do *everything*. The only thing she didn't do was save us."

"She must have been in a very difficult position."

"She thought she was being *kind*. She should have just killed us. That would have been *kinder!*"

"Pew, I can understand that you're angry, but–"

"You're like her. You're *just* like her!"

"I don't run a breeding programme, Pew."

"You say you can make it *better*. You say you can give us *justice*. It's bullshit!"

"All I can do for you is therapy–"

"It doesn't make it better!"

"Pew, I'd appreciate it if–"

"*You can't bring them back!*"

I had to pause.

"I can't, Pew. I would if I could, but I can't."

His voice became unnervingly quiet and threatening. "Do you know what I did to Shan'oui?"

I didn't answer. His eyes were locked on me, unblinking, rimmed with red, his hands trembling as they gripped the arms of the chair like claws. All my instincts told me he was going to attack. I reached for my pad, slowly, and shook my head to keep his attention on my face.

"*I still had the drug in my system.*"

"…You attacked her."

The pad was in my jacket pocket. I couldn't pull it out without him noticing.

His eyes widened with a fanatic stare. "I can still go back there. *Every time I remember*."

As he did when Olivia touched him. He could set off the flashback and then he would be the monster again.

He was doing it now. Sweat on his brow. His eyes drifting to see a vision far in the past. A look of horror on his face for a moment. And then he was there.

He wasn't looking at me. I grabbed for the pad and pressed the emergency signal. He snapped his eyes on me like a beast in rut, and jumped–

But I wasn't there. I was a shadow of light, an illusion sent across the many kilometres between Hub Metro and the centre. He plunged through me, not understanding, driven by animal lust and horror. He jumped to try again and I could only stand there, unable to help him, as he fell through me and wailed at how powerless he was.

I couldn't help the tears as Kwame and Iokan ran on ahead of the security team, and pulled him to the floor, screaming, spitting, fighting back with a terrible strength.

He didn't have any more words. Just wails and howls, like the animal the Soo had made of him, as the medics tranquillised him and took him away to detention.

18. OLIVIA

It was a wrench to leave the Refugee Service. I'd worked there most of my adult life, and I was used to all its habits and ways, the internal politics and culture, and even, I found to my surprise, the blend of tea commonly distributed throughout the service. But this was still Hub, and it was still the IU, and that was more than enough.

Even so, I needed leave, and Eremis made arrangements to let me get some time away once the group were settled at the new centre. But I no longer felt trapped in the same desperate, hopeless circumstance, trying to coax their damaged minds towards therapy and healing. Most of them were past the worst already, and the challenge was new, different, and made me want to come back to work rather than dreading the same old horrors from scarred survivors of dead worlds. Once I made it clear I was leaving my old job, the Quillian threat to remove their support for the evacuation evaporated. It was never more than a subtle hint designed to put pressure on the Refugee Service, and once the responsibility passed to the ICT, there was nothing the Quillians could do without looking petty and vindictive.

I returned to the snowbound centre with Elsbet and Liss so we could pack their belongings, and so I could speak to Olivia, who steadfastly refused to commit herself. I don't know if it was just tetchiness, or her old reluctance to co-operate coming out again. It wasn't the violent opposition that Pew showed. More a reluctance to commit to the therapy she so desperately needed and that we could provide now she had opened up to me.

It came, at last, to the final day. My own belongings were packed, and the office had only the fittings that would vanish when I blanked it and handed it over to the new therapists. Olivia and I watched from the window wall as everyone else went down to the bus, wrapped up in their warmest coats, stepping aside as porters pushed their belongings out on floating carts and loaded up the baggage compartments.

One other vehicle came down to make an impression on the snow: an ambulance from the Psychiatric Centre.

"Poor bastard."

Olivia looked down as Pew, heavily sedated, was floated out to the ambulance to be taken away. The rest of the group watched as he passed by. Iokan raised a hand, despite Pew not being able to see. Kwame cast his eyes down. Elsbet tried to look somewhere else. Liss huddled her arms against the cold and wiped her eyes.

"They'll look after him," I said.

"No they won't," said Olivia. "They'll leave him there until he rots."

"We need to make sure he doesn't hurt anyone else. You remember what he did to you."

"Did you think I'd forget? Poor bastard, all the same. Therapy didn't work on him, did it?"

"Not yet."

"Hah! That's a good answer. When do you give up? When he's dead?"

"We'll keep trying as long as there's hope."

She shook her head. "Is that what you want me to sign up for? That's your idea of therapy?"

"He's a very special case."

"Oh, and the rest of us are normal…"

"You're all special. And you're all different."

"Yeh? How?"

I thought about that for a moment. "Why don't you tell me?"

She glared at me for a moment, but then sighed. "I'm older."

"Go on."

"When we first locked the gates at Tringarrick, a lot of the younger ones wanted to fight. Men mostly. Some of the women as well. Huh. Like I did, in the first outbreak. I couldn't let them. They'd only have got themselves killed. He's like them. It's always the young ones that want to fight."

"And what do you want to do, Olivia?"

She looked at me as the ambulance lifted off into the sky, and the others trooped to the bus. "You think it'll work?"

"In your case, yes."

She looked back outside as the ambulance powered away between the mountains, then sighed. "So what am I supposed to be doing?"

"To begin with, exposure therapy for the PTSD."

She looked up at me for a moment, her old objection to the diagnosis coming forward. But she quashed it and nodded.

"As long as you put the effort in, we should be able to get you free of the symptoms in a few months."

"You reckon?"

I shrugged. "Every species is different. But you're close enough to the average that the usual methods should work."

"What if they don't?"

"I've been doing this for a while. I've got a lot of tricks up my sleeve."

"Huh." She looked out of the window at the fog-shrouded peaks. A scatter of dots resolved out of the clouds: ambulances coming in from the Lift, loaded with refugees. Survivors from the hell that was Ardeë.

"That's not the only thing," she said.

"I know."

"There's other... I mean... oh, gods, I don't know."

"You have survivor's guilt as well."

"Yeh."

"We can help. You're not the only one. We'll always be there for you."

She looked away, hiding her face. "That what it was like for you, was it?"

"I was only a child. But yes, the therapists helped me."

"Huh."

"Drove my foster parents nuts, but still..."

"Hah! Bet you did." At least there was a chuckle there as she looked back at me. But it faded. Outside, the group waited in the bus, and the silhouettes of ambulances became clear against the mountains. At least twenty.

"Is there anything else you want to know?" I asked. "We really need to get going."

"Yeh."

"Okay. Go on."

She looked up at me. "Let's say you can make me better. What am I supposed to do then?"

"Whatever you want."

"Huh. Like what?"

"Live your life."

"*What* life?"

"Any life you like."

"Doing *what*?"

"Well... you could get back into biology. Or medicine, if you like."

She frowned. "Be a doctor like you, is that it?"

"Be a doctor any way you want. You already are. You could update your skills."

She laughed, bitterly. "I'm hundreds of years out of date! Or I don't know, maybe thousands. We didn't even know what DNA was on my world. Everything you lot do means you have to have those bloody brain implants to be able to remember it all..."

"There's nothing wrong with just studying."

"It's a waste of time if you can't use it."

"Olivia, you can do anything. You don't need to have a plan straight away. You can enjoy yourself. You can retire, if you want to."

She scowled. "I can't do that."

"Okay. There's still plenty you could do. Charity work. You could raise public awareness of extinction. I'm sure people will listen to you, after what you've been through."

"Huh."

"Or you could work with the ICT. Help them investigate genocides. Or get policy changed so what happened on your world can never happen again." She just snorted. "Or you could help them." I nodded toward the approaching ambulances. "There's always going to be someone who needs therapy. Or medical help. Or just someone to talk to who's been through something as bad as they have."

She looked down and sighed.

"Olivia, if it's a reason to live that you're looking for, you'll find one. I know you feel a bit lost at the moment, but that's no reason to give up before you've started."

"I *had* a reason to live."

"You'll find another one."

"You reckon."

"There's a whole world of things you could be doing. I don't mean you should forget everything you've been through. But you're a very special woman. I know you'll find something important."

She sighed, and looked up at the ambulances circling, waiting for permission to land, while the medical staff came out to receive them.

She made her decision.

"Best get on with it then," she said. We turned from the window, and left the empty office to join the others on our way to Hub Metro, where her therapy could begin.

POST-APOCALYPSE

ACKNOWLEDGEMENTS

I'm exceedingly grateful to Huw Bowen and Jason Fairley for helping me figure out which bits *really* needed work, and also to Amelia Tyler for helping with the earliest stages of the project, when I considered making it as a webseries.

For the original Kindle version: thanks to Kovid Goyal for Calibre, his excellent e-reading and conversion software, and also to Guido Henkel for his invaluable blog series on e-book formatting.

And many thanks to all the nice people on the Kindleboards forums for their advice, opinions, and enormous reservoir of goodwill.

I found the following books especially useful:

Coping with Catastrophe: A Handbook of Post-disaster Psychological Aftercare by Peter E. Hodgkinson & Michael Stewart

Post-Traumatic Stress Disorder: Reduce and Overcome the Symptoms of PTSD by Belleruth Naparstek

Death from the Skies! by Philip Plait, PhD

The World Without Us by Alan Weisman

…along with far more websites than I could possibly name. Although I'll make an exception for *www.exitmundi.nl*, a venerable but still highly interesting summary of various potential apocalypses.

ABOUT THE AUTHOR

Paul R. Hardy makes corporate videos for a living, and relaxes by writing novels when no one's watching. In the past, he made eighteen short films, won a BBC Drama Award, co-wrote & co-produced an independent SF film called *Triple Hit* and also wrote *Filming on a Microbudget*, a guidebook for making short films.

BLOG & NEWSLETTER

I also have a blog, which I should probably update more often. And if you look closely on the side of the blog, you can sign up to get a newsletter whenever new releases occur!

www.neverenoughworlds.co.uk

BY THE SAME AUTHOR:

THE INQUISITOR'S PROGRESS

Brunsol Mindspear is the chief inquisitor of the Bounded Land, where prayers do not go unanswered. For without the whole land's prayer, rain would not fall and crops would wither on the stalk. Therefore heresy must be stamped out with terror and torture, lest it lead to plague and famine; and so Brunsol is steeped in blood after decades of tyranny in the service of God.

But when his long life finally ends and he goes to meet his maker, he finds surprises in the world above. For there are many worlds beyond his own, each layered outside the next. Brunsol must seek the true power in all the many universes, and take his vengeance for all the horrors wrought upon the worlds below.

FORTHCOMING:

TWENTY YEARS AGO TODAY

We've all had the same wish at one time or another: what if you could go back in time and live your life differently, knowing all that you know now?

One day, that wish comes true. But not for one person. *For everyone.*

And on that day, the world finds out that there's nothing worse than a wish come true.

MOMENT OF EXTINCTION

A SHORT STORY

GRAINGER STATION
Halo Orbit, Earth-Moon L1 Point
HD y272.m9.w3.d1

The official's voice wavers. "I regret to inform you..."

Hundreds of survivors look back at the man from the Interversal Union. They're crowded into one of the station's quarantine halls and yet they still don't fill the space, for they are already so few in number. Many of them have been floated in on medical chairs, close to death. All of them are sick.

"I regret to... I have to inform you..." The official's hand shakes as he tries to read the announcement from a pad. "That the Yenoma species, that we, we cannot..." He puts the pad aside and looks out at them with tears in his eyes. "We can't save you. There isn't enough time. I'm sorry."

Hope dies on the faces of the remaining three hundred and seventy-six Yenoma. Some simply sit down and put their heads in their hands. Many weep. The medical and counselling staff who look after them are just as shocked, and do what little they can to comfort the last survivors of a dead world. At the front of the crowd, a father grips his young son's hand tighter and tries to hold back the grief as the boy looks up at him, not understanding.

Beside the man from the Interversal Union, an elderly woman in a floating chair scrabbles at a button on the chair's armrest. Her voice rings out, amplified far beyond her own failing strength.

"I was told last night," says Oimelia Threnos, last surviving head of state from her species. Her head is strapped to the chair to prevent it falling forward: a symptom of what's killing her. "There's nothing they can do. There aren't enough of us for the tests and there isn't enough time before we're all gone." And though her eyelids droop, she still looks keenly out from behind them. Each person in the hall feels she looks at them alone.

This is not the first time she has had to make such an announcement.

"But they said they could do something–" starts one of the older men in the group, rising up from a chair, his hands trembling on a stick.

"They said they'd try, Ekhren," says Oimelia. "Well, they tried. And they failed."

The official speaks up: "We have, uh, the report from the neurological group if you want to see it..."

But Ekhren won't have it. "They promised us!" he cries.

"They promised us nothing," she says. "Only that they'd make the attempt." Ekhren looks about the room for support, but all he finds are eyes turned away from him. He sits down again in disgust as Oimelia looks out at the others. "We knew this might happen. They never once lied to us. They did all they could."

She glances up at the official, who casts his eyes down. "Thank you," she says. "From all of us." He wipes away a tear.

She looks back out at the crowd. "But we're all going to die. It's going to be soon. It's going to be painful. They'll make it as easy for us as they can, but this is it. In a week or a month or however long it takes, we will be extinct."

"Daddy?" asks the little boy. "What's extinct?" The man looks up at Oimelia, not knowing what to do. Much of the crowd looks his way. Among all of them, there is only one child: only one of them who does not understand.

"Abeiron, you'd better tell him what the word means," says Oimelia.

The father nods, and takes the boy to a corner away from the others. He crouches down beside him, and the boy knows it must be serious, for adults don't do this unless something is terribly wrong. "It's… it's like this, Mel. You remember when I told you that lots of people were going away?" The boy nods. "Well, we're going away as well."

The boy looks baffled. "Want to talk to mum."

"She's already gone, Mel."

"I want mummy!" The boy will not be soothed, nor will he meet his father's eyes. Abeiron sighs and closes his own.

Oimelia turns to the crowd once more. "There's one bit of good news. They're going to let us pass on souls again." A wave of whispers sweeps through the crowd. "No more True Death. Not until the very last. We'll all have someone to carry our soul to the end."

Abeiron closes his eyes, and something about his face changes. Lines of worry smooth themselves away as the muscles beneath the skin relax.

He opens his eyes again. "Hey there, Mel," he says. The voice, too, has changed; as though it were used by someone else. Someone overjoyed to see the boy after a long absence.

"Mummy!" cries Mel, and clasps on tightly as his mother holds him with his father's arms.

"Shh," she says. "We'll be together when it happens."

"We should decide what we want to do with the time we have left," says Oimelia. She looks out of the windows, beyond the idle ships waiting to save a species that barely exists any more, to the blue and white crescent in the distance. Not their homeworld: that is dead and gone. But the parallel world called Hub will do.

"You know, I haven't seen the ocean in years. Not one that was clean. I'd like to see that, before we're all gone."

One by one, they come forward and pledge that they will do that for her.

TRANSIT VESSEL *AURORA*
En Route to Geostationary Orbit
HD y272.m9.w3.d3

Oimelia Threnos returns to her senses. She sees a kindly-faced counsellor's concern, and the growing disc of the world outside a small window: they must already be on their way. Then she looks down at her hands and sees they belong to a man.

"Well," she says, her voice making Abeiron's male tones seem thinner and sharper. "I wondered what that would be like."

"I'm sorry," says the counsellor. "I'm not sure what you mean."

"Dying," says Oimelia.

"Oh," says the counsellor, who still finds herself surprised at moments like this. The Yenoma are unique among all the parallel worlds contacted by the Interversal Union. Oimelia is dead, but her soul lives on; or rather, her personality has been imprinted within the brain of Abeiron, her former aide, who now carries the burden not just of those he has absorbed, but of those that Oimelia herself carried.

"Is that Oimelia?" asks the counsellor.

"Of course it is. And who are you?"

"My name's Asha. I'm with the Refugee Service. I'm sorry, I wasn't expecting you."

"No, you wouldn't be. What's all this about?"

"I was talking to Abeiron about his son."

"Ah. Yes. How is the boy?"

"He won't talk to anyone except his mother."

Oimelia nodded. "I kept his father from him. I won't apologise for that. I needed him. I had too much work to do."

"Mel doesn't really know him."

"His mother's still here."

"His mother's dead."

A brief smile twitches on the man's lips. "Dead, yes. But not gone." Oimelia taps the side of Abeiron's head. "She's in here, with us. She's…"

Oimelia gasps. The tap against the head turns into a palm massaging Abeiron's temple. "She's…" Abeiron's hand falls away and his eyes stare into space.

"Oimelia?" says Asha. No answer comes. "Abeiron?"

His eyes flick back on her, then around the room. Another voice comes from his throat. "Mel? Where are you?" And then pain comes. "Oh…"

"Is that Elpetha…?" asks Asha.

"Yes…" says Mel's mother as she puts her husband's head in his hands. "Who are you?"

"My name's Asha. I'm a counsellor. Can we talk about your son? Is that okay?"

"Leave him alone."

"I only–"

"It's nothing to do with you!" She groans and rubs Abeiron's temples.

"Elpetha, do you really want him to go through this? He hasn't taken on any other minds yet. He doesn't have to–"

She shoots a look back up at Asha. "I won't leave him!"

Asha looks back with sad eyes. "He doesn't have to die."

Elpetha looks confused for a moment. "Die? He... what?" She grits Abeiron's teeth as a spike of pain hits them both.

Another voice comes through his teeth. "*I died!*" The accent is strange, from another part of the Yenoman homeworld. "The bombs fell and I *burned!*"

Abeiron's head wrenches to one side. Another voice comes. "We should have been safe... no air in the bunker... I took all their souls and it *hurts...*"

His head wrenches in the opposite direction. "I buried them – seven little graves... I buried all my grandchildren..."

Wrench. "My little girl's blind! She saw the flash! Someone help her!"

Wrench. "Five pregnancies and five stillbirths! I'm cursed, I'm *cursed!*"

Asha calls for help, and two medics rush in to give Abeiron a shot of nerve stabiliser. In normal times, the Yenoma can integrate a new mind safely over a period of a few months, so that the dead are never truly lost. But ever since the missiles delivered their megatons across the Yenoman homeworld, too many have died too quickly. There isn't enough space in the survivors' heads for all those who perished from radiation sickness, cancer, starvation and disease.

Abeiron comes back to himself as the medics make him comfortable on the couch. His eyelids tremble but he sees Asha there, still sympathetic, still wanting to help. "You should get some rest," she says.

He answers with his own voice: "I can't take him away from his mother... I can't..."

"There's still time," she says, squeezing his hand.

IHKKIKIT STATION
Geostationary Orbit
HD y272.m9.w3.d4

Few people stay long at Ihkkikit Station, and the joke is that it's because no one can pronounce the name. It's usually referred to as 'The Counterweight' instead; the small asteroid at the end of the Agvarterheer Column, itself known to everyone on Hub as 'The Lift'. It's a transit station for people heading up or down, to Grainger or Agvarterheer Port on the surface. But the Refugee Service of the Interversal Union still keeps a mass of facilities here. There's enough room, carved out of the asteroid rock, to house a million people during an evacuation from a dying world. Sometimes there are so many to save that they have to be kept here temporarily; while a few species rescued from extinction have been so used to living in orbit that they cannot survive on the ground.

Today, the Yenoma stand in a hall buttressed by stone columns against the artificial gravity, holding a memorial service for all those who died on the way here. A hundred and forty-one have passed away; the oldest, sickest, and the most burdened with souls.

Every last one of the dead is here as well.

There are two kinds of death among the Yenoma. The True Death is the tragedy of those who die with their souls trapped inside their skulls; they are usually interred in the earth, and most religions on the Yenoman homeworld required that they be preserved until the souls could finally pass on. But the Body's Death is different. Those whose souls have been taken on by another are cremated after addressing their loved ones from the bodies they now dwell within. The memorial is supposed to be a celebration of life, not a laying to rest of those who are gone forever.

No one has died the True Death since Grainger Station, but nevertheless the congregation is sombre and quiet. Too many caskets are stacked before them as a young woman walks to the front to speak: "I carry the voice of Ekhren Stassos. In time, his voice will become mine. But today he speaks for his own."

Her eyes flicker and her left hand shakes. Then she snaps back to reality and another mind looks out over the crowd, realising that this is his memorial.

The young woman's face screws up with an anger beyond her years.

"It's all bullshit," says the elderly voice of Ekhren Stassos, trembling from a young throat. The woman's left hand keeps shaking. "Passing souls like this, when we're all going to be dead in a week! We should just die and be done with it. There's no life eternal! It's all a lie! Passing souls… it's bullshit! You should have let me die!"

A counsellor takes a step forward, concerned. Dozens of faces among the congregation look shocked, while others cannot meet Ekhren's eyes.

"Ekhren!" hisses Abeiron with a tone that belongs to Elpetha: scolding as she holds her son close, her husband's hands shaking with a tremor they picked up after taking on two more souls. Ekhren looks down and sees the boy looking confused and scared.

"You should have let me die," he says to them all, and propels his host's body away to the dark corners of the hall.

Mel looks up at Elpetha. "Are we going to die?" he asks.

"In the end," says his mother, seeing the tremor in Abeiron's hands growing worse.

"Will we get eternal life after?"

"I… I… I think so." She grips the armrests of her chair to steady her husband's trembling hands.

"Will you be there?"

Abeiron gasps as his mind returns. He lets go of the chair, his knuckles still white.

"Mummy?" asks Mel.

Abeiron looks down at his son. "She's gone. It's okay. She'll come back."

But Mel turns away, upset. Abeiron looks up and sees Asha, waiting by the side of the makeshift temple. She doesn't have to say anything: the invitation and offer of help is clear on her face.

Eyes screwed up with tears, he shakes his head and puts a trembling hand on his son's shoulder. Mel looks back up at him with hurting, needful eyes.

"We'll all be together," says Abeiron. "Your mother as well."

EVACUATION CAR
Agvarterheer Column, 28,000km above sea level
HD y272.m9.w3.d6

An evacuation car is designed to carry up to three thousand evacuees at a time, accompanied by hundreds of medical staff, counsellors and sometimes security guards. During a normal evacuation from a doomed world, they're often hard pressed to cope with all the refugees from nuclear war, asteroid strikes, environmental disaster or worse.

On this journey, there are fewer than two hundred survivors, and less with each passing hour.

Abeiron walks down halls and corridors, meeting more of the Refugee Service staff than his own people. He finds he needs a stick to walk with from time to time; there are tremors in his legs now that come and go. But he rarely has to travel any great distance. The Yenoma have been assigned quarters together, so that they will never be far from each other in their final moments.

A chime comes from Abeiron's wrist; he looks at the device secured there, which gives him a room and deck number: C872. He rushes as fast as he can on the stick to the gravity lift and rides it down two decks, then makes a hobbling rush to the room as the door swishes open. He and a few others have been granted access to all the quarters of the Yenoma, so that someone will be there when the time comes.

A man and a woman are here, and the place is a wreck; everything that's not welded to the wall or floor is overturned or broken. They've kept the window opaque, like many who cannot bear the view outside. The lights are low, concealing some of the cracked and smashed hypo-applicators they've been using to make the last days more bearable.

But it's over for them. The woman sits wrapped in a sheet, shaking with the naked body of her lover in her lap and tears streaming down her face.

"I took him," she says, the words coming out in stutters. She can barely keep control of herself, her teeth chattering and eyes unable to fix on anything. "He told me not to but I took him…"

"I know," says Abeiron, kneeling with her and putting his stick to one side. "It's okay. Are you ready?"

"No… I don't… what's the point?" Abeiron recognises her: the woman who carries the soul of Ekhren Stassos.

"So we can go together," says Abeiron.

She clutches at him, though her hands have no strength. She's young; far too young to take on so many souls.

"Together? All together?" she says.

"None of us should be alone when it happens."

"All go together…"

"Yes. Are you ready?"

"I… I…" she has to struggle to raise her head up, and fix her eyes on his. "All together?"

"That's right."

"When you go… when you… when it happens to you…"

"Yes?"

"Will you pass us to your boy?"

Abeiron pulls back. "What?"

"It will be… all of us… yes? No? I don't…"

She's losing control, and will soon be gone, yet she pleads with eyes that can barely hold their gaze. Abeiron still pauses, not wanting to confront her last question.

Until he remembers his duty.

"Are you ready?" he asks.

She manages a nod. Abeiron presses his temple to hers, and the hematite crystal clusters in their heads tremble as they sense the magnetic field of the other. Abeiron remembers for a moment how it was with Elpetha when they shared their love, heads locked together, sensing the delight in each other's skin.

And then the rush of a mind – of thousands of minds – floods into his own and washes the memory pale.

EVACUATION CAR
Agvarterheer Column, 12,000km above sea level
HD y272.m9.w4.d1

"What will it be like for him?"

Abeiron has lost the use of his legs, but is still stronger than most of the others. As Oimelia's aide, he was in a protected occupation for most of the crisis, and required to take only the lightest burden of souls. Now, by common consent, he will be the last – or the last but one.

"He'll have whatever he needs," says Asha.

"I mean… what would it be like? To be alone like that?"

She pauses for a moment. "It won't be easy. It's hard for every refugee."

"Most refugees aren't the only ones."

"No. But he's still very young. That'll make it easier on him in the long run. He'll have a hard time to begin with, but he'll adapt."

"And forget us."

"No. He'll remember. But the pain will fade. He'll have as much help as he needs."

"From people like you?"

"Specialists who work with children."

Abeiron frets. "Does anyone specialise in people like that?"

"I'm sorry?"

"When there's only one of them. Last survivors. When you couldn't save the rest of the species."

Asha thinks about it for a moment. "No. We don't have any specialists for that. There aren't very many of them. Last survivors, I mean."

"But they do exist?"

"Yes. Two, I think. Maybe three."

"What's it like for them?"

"It's hard. But they were older when it happened. Children are much more adaptable. This will become his world. We'll be his people. He won't be alone."

Abeiron looks out of the window: they're still far above the planet. The disc spreads out below them, a circle of green and blue and white. Pale cyan wraps around a coastline, signifying algal blooms and life thriving below. Abeiron only remembers such things in the whispered dreams that come from the souls of the dead.

He looks back at Asha with tears in his eyes, and nods his acceptance.

"Don't say anything," he says.

"I won't," she agrees.

EVACUATION CAR
Agvarterheer Column, 2,000km above sea level
HD y272.m9.w4.d3

Another funeral: this time in the makeshift temple aboard the evacuation lift: but there are only two attendees, for there are only two Yenoma left. Abeiron sits in a medical chair, his head strapped into place. Mel sits with him, and the other places are taken by the counsellors and medics who've been watching helplessly as a human race goes extinct. The only people they can comfort now are each other.

As the last one who knows the litany, Abeiron says the words of remembrance as best he can. But his own death is near, and the weight of souls is almost too much to bear.

"And they who have not died–"

"not died yet"

"They who have not died–"

"why me? why did it have to be me?"

"They, they live on in us–"

"all dead! all of us dead! what was the point?"

"We are all one soul–"

"Mel! Mel! Where are you?"

"Mummy!" shouts the boy as Abeiron's eyes roll up in his head and he slumps down in his chair, slipping free of the brace around his head. A doctor runs to him while a nurse holds Mel back. The boy screams and sobs in his arms.

But Abeiron is not finished yet. Even as a doctor rushes to him, he pushes himself back up in his chair with one good arm. After a moment to recover and with his head lolling to one side, he goes on.

"We are all one soul," he says. The doctor steps back. "And all souls... shall be one, when the trumpet calls them... to eternal rest." He looks at his son. "All souls... shall be one."

He slumps again. The doctor holds an instrument against his forehead. Abeiron struggles to bring his eyes up to look at him. "Is it... time?"

The doctor glances at the instrument and nods.

"Mel...?" he says. Asha comes up, and Abeiron sees the concerned look on her face. "Just want... to see him..." Asha nods, and motions the nurse to bring the boy closer. Tears wash down Mel's face as he comes near his dying father.

Abeiron looks upon his son for the last time, but has no words. Only a smile. And then he waves him away.

"No!" screams Mel. "No! Mummy!"

Abeiron's eyes fall shut, though he still breathes for the moment. The nurse tries to pull the boy away. But Mel fights and twists, and something tears from his sweater.

He breaks free and runs to his father, jumping onto the chair before anyone can stop him, pressing temple to temple as he'd seen when his mother died and passed her soul to his father.

Asha tries to move him, but the doctor shouts: "No! It's started... you can't touch them or they'll both..."

The boy clings to his father and drinks every mind of his species from him.

AGVARTERHEER PORT
Mexiana Island, Mouths of the Amazon
HD y272.m9.w4.d4

The light of a fresh day washes across the port city, laid out beneath the massive height of four elevator strands and the anchor column leading back up to the Counterweight. A transit railcar runs out beyond the carriage yards and the freight portal and the hotels and the clubs, heading east to where the island meets the Atlantic.

A small crowd of IU dignitaries are there to meet the last survivor of his species as he hobbles out of the railcar, leaning on a walking stick cut in half to match his height. Asha accompanies him and offers a hand, but he waves her away and limps on, step by step, until he comes to the water's edge.

Old minds look out of a child's eyes. Beyond the quayside they see the endless blue of ocean, whipped up into a light chop by a breeze coming in from the south.

"Is there anything we can do for you?" asks a woman the child does not know, but whom Asha recognises as the head of the Refugee Service.

"You can stop asking," says the boy. "Oh, look at that..."

They all look out at the sea. It's still freshwater this close to the river, but a faint smell of distant salt comes in on the breeze. Clouds gather in billows and promise rain.

He takes a lungful of the air. "Its so clean," he says, with a little heartbroken smile. "Just like I remember... just like..."

He falls, and does not rise again.

Printed in Great Britain
by Amazon.co.uk, Ltd.,
Marston Gate.